THE
TWYFORD
CODE

ALSO BY JANICE HALLETT

The Appeal

THE TWYFORD CODE

A Novel

Janice Hallett

ATRIA BOOKS

New York • London • Toronto • Sydney • New Delhi

ATRIA
BOOKS

An Imprint of Simon & Schuster, Inc.
1230 Avenue of the Americas
New York, NY 10020

First Atria Books hardcover edition January 2023

ATRIA B O O K S and colophon are trademarks of Simon & Schuster, Inc.

For information about special discounts for bulk purchases, please contact Simon & Schuster Special Sales at 1-866-506-1949 or business@simonandschuster.com.

The Simon & Schuster Speakers Bureau can bring authors to your live event. For more information or to book an event, contact the Simon & Schuster Speakers Bureau at 1-866-248-3049 or visit our website at www.simonspeakers.com.

Manufactured in China

1 3 5 7 9 10 8 6 4 2

Library of Congress Cataloging-in-Publication Data
Names: Hallet, Janice, author.
Title: The Twyford code : a novel / Janice Hallett.
Description: First Atria Books hardcover edition. I New York: Atria Books, 2023.
Identifiers: LCCN 2022018517 I ISBN 9781668003220 (hardcover) I ISBN 9781668003244(ebook)
Subjects: LCSH: Women authors--Fiction. I Children's literature, English--Fiction. I English teachers--Fiction. I Missing persons--Fiction. I Secrecy--Fiction. I Code and cipher stories.
Classification: LCC PR6108.A4955 T85 2023 I DDC 823/.

ISBN 978-1-6680-0322-0
ISBN 978-1-6680-0324-4 (ebook)

Friend, on reflection
May you be rain
On torrid heaths,
Even rocky byways.
Remote, intangible,
And now . . .

November 19, 2021

Dear Professor Mansfield,

I am investigating a mysterious case and suspect you may be able to help. Let me explain.

An iPhone 4 is among a number of items belonging to a recently reported missing person. It is not associated with any phone carrier and at first appeared to be blank, with no call records, music, emails, texts, or photographs. Upon closer examination it was found to contain a series of deleted audio files: voice recordings in various encrypted formats, with dates that span eleven weeks in 2019. We recovered these files and deciphered them.

There are two hundred files in total. We utilized specialist software and processed them in batches to speed up the transcription process. A key to this follows, along with the text. You will notice the transcription is phonetic, so spelling and grammar are quirky to say the least. On several occasions, the software "mishears" or simply approximates words and phrases, especially when speech is in the vernacular. For instance, the phrase "must have" is frequently transcribed as "mustard." "Going to" becomes "gun a" and the town of Bournemouth is referred to variously as "bore mouth," "Bormuth," "bore moth," and "boar mouth." You will soon become accustomed to this and it should not interfere with your understanding of the material.

I've sent these files to you, Professor, in the strictest confidence. Quite apart from any personal connection you may have to the subject, your expert opinion on their contents would be very much appreciated. Call me when you've read to the end and we'll speak then.

Yours sincerely,
Inspector Waliso

DecipherIt™

#1 high-speed transcription software for business

Full automation

Up to 99% accurate

 Multiple voice identification

  Thousands of names and brands

   Accent adaptation*

    Advanced punctuation

     Background filter

    Paragraph break detection

   Speech to text in 60 seconds**

  Clean and full verbatim options

 Automatic diary synchronization***

Complex number recognition

Foreign language identification***

* up to 80% accuracy

** not guaranteed

*** with paid-for upgrades only

DecipherIt™

#1 high-speed transcription software for business

KEY

()	indecipherable verbal content, either unheard or unclear.
(.)	a small pause in speech, e.g., one-tenth of a second.
(. . .)	a longer pause in speech, e.g., three-tenths of a second.
=	overspeak, the speaker is interrupted by another.
Y:::es	prolongation. The number of colons denotes length of prolongation.
LOUDER	capitalization, louder speech (may also denote emphasis).
Quieter	italic text, quieter or whispered speech.
.hhhhhh	inbreath detected. Relative to length of breath.
hhhhhh	outbreath detected. Relative to length of breath.
(perhaps)	indecipherable verbal content, with suggested word based on audible sentence.
s[EXPLICIT]t	offensive or vulgar word, in *clean* mode only.
[*background noise*]	verbal or nonverbal background noise detected. May or may not obscure speech.
(00:01:00)	longer, timed period of silence or nonverbal background noise (hrs:mins:secs).
[*time ref 0000*]	time reference detected. Automatic diary sync with paid-for upgrades only.
[*language: French*]	foreign language detected. Automatic translation with paid-for upgrades only.

Audio Files Batch 1

[Start Transcript]

Audio File 1
Date: April 12, 2019, 2:20 PM
Audio quality: Poor

.hhhhh Ready? This is to show Maxine I meant what I said.

Audio File 2
Date: April 12, 2019, 2:24 PM
Audio quality: Good

That's better. So. I'm speaking into my son's old phone and will explain why in a little bit. I'm not used to it, so (. . .) When he first gave it to me I was convinced I'd never use it for anything other than speaking to Maxine and calling in sick. But that night I sat up till two o'clock [*DecipherIt*™ *time ref 52781277-0988837*]

I've played every record in his iTunes. His idea. It was only the second time we'd met. He didn't grow up with me, see. I never knew he existed till an acquaintance mentioned his mum'd had a kid. I put two and two together and made nine months. He would a been ten then. There's so much to say, but I look at him across that table in Costa, his hair about to turn grey at the edges and tiny lines on his forehead. I think: How could my boy be so grown up? Everything slides clean out me head and we sit there in silence.

Finally, I mention how much I'm looking forward to meeting his wife and kids, seeing his house in Surrey and the posh university where he works. That's when he gets a panicked look and bursts out he doesn't want us to meet again. Perhaps the odd phone call. Keep in touch but not (. . .) So, he goes quiet and says we can FaceTime instead. I says isn't this FaceTime? He asks to see the phone they gave me on release and when I show him he laughs and says it's a burner, can't do much with that. I say yeah, that's the idea. He thinks for a bit and says have my old one. He gets it out his car and in a few minutes his old phone was my new phone.

Audio File 3
Date: April 12, 2019, 3:04 PM
Audio quality: Good

If I wanted to carry on as I had, there are lots of people I could have gone to. Even now, after all that went on, with the old crowd dead or inside, if I put the word out, I could be set up somewhere, doing something, in no time. But I won't. Those days are over. Trouble is, on this side a the fence I don't know a soul. Only Maxine and (. . .) only you, Maxine. A lot changed for me in the last few years. And do you know what triggered it? I learned to read.

Two youngsters come in. A boy and a girl. Just in their twenties. Claimed to have a whole new way to teach adults with literacy problems. Not easy. Most in that place had so many problems literacy was the least of 'em. But these youngsters were so enthusiastic you couldn't help but get carried along. Even the tough old fellows. And the young fellows who thought they were tough.

They took our chairs away. Made us move round the room. Not like being slumped in front of a teacher, staring, trying to listen. They got us to play with big alphabet letters. It was nothing but strange at first. Big gnarly old fellows playing like kids. Then a change happened.

Words appeared. I could link them to sounds, meanings, in a way I never had at school. It was like I'd cracked a secret code.

We all made progress thanks to them youngsters. I say progress, Kos of course, ignorance is bliss. Spanners realized one of his oldest tattoos was spelt wrong. Smelly Bob finally understood the graffiti on his cell nameplate. But for me it opened a door where there'd always been a wall (. . .) That sounds like I escaped, but (. . .) suppose I did escape, in my head. Suddenly the library cart weren't just where I bought me contraband. It were stacked with treasure waiting to be found.

I read sentence after sentence. Couldn't get enough of words. Well, I had a lot of time to make up for. Before long I read a whole book from start to finish. *Lord of the Flies*. I was on top of the world. It meant I could read. Finally. I was. I could suddenly (. .) That's when I started thinking I'd do THIS when I got out. And it got me through the last few years.

All them kids running around wild on that island. Took me back, I suppose. Something nagged at me about missiles and what happened all those years ago. I read *Animal Farm* too, but it was all talking animals. Didn't get to me like piggy and Ralph. Afterward I still had that feeling. I've got it now. It's always there. Nagging. Unfinished.

Audio File 4
Date: April 12, 2019, 6:44 PM
Audio quality: Good

It's a nuisance I don't know how to listen back to these recordings after I've done 'em. Maybe they can help at the library (. . . . .) So I can read now much better, but writing is still tricky. When I discovered I can record my voice on my son's old phone, just like the old dictating machines but no need for little cassettes, I decided I'd dictate this. What is it? Diary? Project? Investigation? For Maxine. Something for me to do when I finish work at the end of the day. Keep me busy. Out of trouble.

I want to make clear that although I couldn't read, I weren't as illiterate as some of 'em in there. Some wouldn't know their own name if it were up in ten-foot flashing lights. Not me. I could recognize important words. Steven Smith. Toilets. Gents. Men. Tickets. Exit. I'd pick out the shapes of the words rather than individual letters.

We learn from the knowledge of others and reading is a big part of that for most people. So if you can't do it, there's an assumption you must be stupid. Now, I may not be well read, but I know about the world. I've lived. I've had experiences and watched a lot of very interesting documentaries, especially over the last few years. I'd also like to say that I consider myself an articulate person. Verbally that is. I listen to what's said. Not just hear. Listen. I've heard just as many words as you've read, Maxine. And if you've heard a word once, you can use it yourself as often as you like from then on.

For all those years I didn't miss what I'd never had. Didn't feel the need to read sentences. I could wing it. If I got caught out I'd say, oh I've lost my glasses, could you read it for me? It has its plus side too. Think about it. If you need to remember something, you write it down. I couldn't—and still can't—but it means I remember things. My memory is much better than yours, I'll bet. That's why missiles plays on my mind, because there's so much of that time I CAN'T remember. Or forgotten. Can't remember. Forgotten. Or never knew.

Audio File 5
Date: April 13, 2019, 7:09 PM
Audio quality: Good

Been listening to my son's playlist called CAR. None of the songs are about cars, so he must put this music on when he's in his car. I think of him on that journey from Surrey to Uxbridge every day. Back again in the evening. I keep going to record my next bit but stop. I'll do it now.

I'll start at the beginning but skip some bits you don't want to (. . .)

So I'll say I was born in London on the very last day of 1968. It never felt right to say I was born in sixty-eight because the year was all but over, and sixty-nine would be wrong because it wasn't begun. I still explain it to this day. Funny. Similar thing. At school when they asked where do you live I said Girton House and they'd assume we lived way up in the sky. I'd have to say no: we live on the ground floor. We lived on the ground floor of a high-rise. See, some answers are (. .) sometimes the truth is misleading.

I'm sure at one time there mustard been both my parents, my brother, and I in the flat, but I don't remember it. When you're that young, the home is scenery, I suppose, the heart. Everything safe, trusted, and right tricky to recall years later (. . . .) Mum mustard left very early on (. .) because she were hardly ever mentioned. Even now it feels funny saying the word out loud.

When I said it just then, I got a feeling. Of being lifted up from under me arms. Like whoever had hold a me would never let me go. Warm. Sweet .hhhhh (. . .) I've had the feeling before. It comes in a flash, most often when I get a whiff of certain old-fashioned perfumes. Talcum powder mixed with something else. Is that her? Is there a memory of her in me chest after all? Or am I just feeling the (. . .) emptiness (. . .)

We never had a camera so there were no photos of her. And seeing as my folks never got married, there were no wedding pictures either. Only once did I get me nerve up to ask Dad where Mum was. He said she'd run off with a fella just after I were born. She got a big house now, he said, happy she ain't got you two on her hands. He meant Colin and me. Then he smashed a bottle in the sink, slammed his way out the flat, and disappeared for two days. I never mentioned it again.

Don't remember the exact day Dad left for good. He'd come and go at the best a times. But it were after the Silver Jubilee and before the garbage strikes. Temporary barmaid down the local swept him off his feet, Colin shrugged as he told me. Can't blame him, Steve, you can be a proper little s[EXPLICIT]t sometimes and she's got a nice, clean flat up north.

From then on, Colin looked after me. I say that. He took washing down to the laundromat and stuck a pot a beans on the stove every now and then, but he didn't talk much. Eleven years older than me. When I think of him I remember the seventies. And vice versa.

Flares. Long hair. The Boomtown Rats on Top of the Pops. He'd watch TV in the chair by the electric fire. In his nylon shirt and tank top. If we could've afforded to switch it up he would've gone up like a rocket. Browns, oranges, yellows, greens all clashing like mad. He was still in the same clothes well into the eighties. Eventually he got a job at a metalwork factory and would come home covered in blobs of solder.

It sounds bad now. As if I didn't have any upbringing. But I didn't know any different. I don't even think of my trouble as starting back then. It was the summer of '83. That was when (. . .) missiles (. . .)

Audio File 6
Date: April 14, 2019, 12:20 PM
Audio quality: Good

I'll tell you it all now and not stop start. 1983 was a hot summer in London. I remember a lot of lightness. Pale-colored clothes. Girls in dusty pink, blue, and white. I was fourteen so I noticed what the girls were wearing. It was June or July.

I were still going to school then. And still worried about being late for registration. I was late that day. Couldn't run, though. Stifling hot for that time of morning. I was in a hurry because the boy I usually walked with had already gone. It crossed my mind I could get a bus and at that very moment, would you believe it, a big green bus swung into the curb and stopped right in front of me. Well, I thought how lucky I was and jumped on.

Now, you'll know double-decker London buses back then had an open platform at the back for passengers to get on and off whenever they liked. You'll also know that London buses are red, not green. They were most certainly red where we lived. You had to go all the way out to the suburbs to find a green bus. It's something I've thought about a lot lately. That green bus.

So, I leapt on the bus and tore up the stairs to sit at the front of the top deck. Funny. I don't remember anyone else being on it. No passengers and no conductor. Is that my memory playing tricks? So I reached the top deck and hurray it's empty too. Just as I headed for the front seat, something stopped me and I decided to sit at the very back instead. On that cosy little seat tucked away, quite special. What was it made me do that? Could I see it?

I stopped in my tracks. There it was. Placed neatly on the checkered cushion. A book.

Now, to me, back then, a book was a book. All books were the same. Except they had different covers. This one had a pencil drawing of a boy in a red jumper, watching a model plane in the sky. That I remember clearly. I had to pick it up to sit down, so I did. The moment I touched that book, the bus set off and I settled down with it on my lap, nothing much more in my mind than getting to school.

I don't claim to be an angel. Then or now. No one seemed to own the book, so taking it couldn't be stealing. But I had enough of a conscience to know I should hand it to the driver. So as the bus trundled nearer the school, I waited on the open deck, glanced over. Couldn't quite see him beyond the back of his seat, the blind half up, half down. I would have had to run round and bang on the window of his cab. I dismissed that thought pretty quickly because the possibility of selling the book had taken up residence in my head. Into my school bag it went.

The next thing I remember is being in are E. Now. I should go back and explain this. Are E doesn't stand for religious education as you might expect, but remedial English. It weren't a year prior to this that my homeroom teacher made me stand up in class and read something out loud. After a moment or two, a thoughtful look on her face, she said, quite matter of fact, oh you're dyslexic. Oh, you're dyslexic. It was hardly a scientific diagnosis and didn't seem a big deal to anyone, except I had to attend are E instead of English with the rest of the class.

There were five of us in are E at that time. I remember them all: Nathan, Michelle, Donna, Paul, and me. Five kids who found two of the most basic human skills, reading and writing, difficult to impossible. All shuffled aside into a tiny classroom to struggle with what everyone else had mastered easily a decade earlier. No wonder we (. .) I wonder if the others still think of it too.

Audio File 7
Date: April 14, 2019, 1:15 PM
Audio quality: Good

So I slunk off up the stairs to are E, to that little classroom at the end of the top floor. I wasn't in the habit of listening, so I don't remember what the lesson was about. With nothing else to occupy it, my mind wandered to the book in my bag. If I sold it at the right price, I could buy chips on the way home. I slid it out under the desk, had a flick through. The words were meaningless to me but I took in the pencil drawings and occasional color illustration. In truth I was looking for any selling points that would help me peddle it to the nerdy kids at break.

STEVEN SMITH. She'd spotted me. What are you doing? Reading a book, miss. You and your stories, she gasps. What have I told you? Don't make things up.

There she was. Missiles. Standing over me, hands on hips. Eyebrows raised. Finger beckoning me to give her whatever I had under the desk.

I held out the book. It was a temporary hitch. She'd give it back at the end of class. Her eyes dropped to it and I will never forget the surprised tone of her, OH, it IS a book. The way her eyebrows disappeared under her fringe when she saw the cover. Where did you get this?

A stream of potential answers circled round my mind, none of them the truth. A bookshop. Missiles drifted back to her desk, turned the book over in her hands. She laughed to herself as if remembering something pleasant from long ago.

Now I might have found reading difficult, but I weren't slow.

It's for sale, miss. She pretended not to hear.

I read this when I was younger than you. It was my favorite, she says, all wistful. At that I added a zero to my asking price and a battered sausage to the big bag of chips in my mind.

She suddenly snapped out of that dreamy look and gave me a hard stare. You shouldn't have this, Steven. Not here. Not now. Not in this school.

Why not, miss? It's mine. I bought it.

Because it's BANNED. Her hushed tone sent a little shiver down my spine.

Well, till now the other kids had been slumped in the heat, watching with what I can only say was gratitude the class had been interrupted, and glee it weren't them in the firing line. But at this news their ears pricked up.

Mine did, too, but with a creeping sense of horror. Banned? None of the illustrations had borne any resemblance to the shredded nudey mags I'd occasionally seen in the park. Ripped pages half trodden into the mud. No expert, had I missed a sexual element to the childish drawings? Did missiles think I'd been *w*[EXPLICIT]*g* under the desk? I swallowed, mortified.

Why's it banned? Paul was an unpredictable kid. Moody. Brooding. Got into fights like an alley cat. Kids and adults alike wondered aloud why he was like he was. No one linked it to the fact his father hung himself in his garage a few years previous. Those were the days.

Is it rude? Michelle, or Shell, looked like Jay from Bucks Fizz. Big blond hair, earrings, makeup. As young kids we hung out together on the estate. She were turned out the flat when her ma had a customer, so she'd tap on me window and we'd sit on the swings in the dark. She didn't have a dad and I didn't have a (. . .) *mum*. But that were then. By 1983, Shell were a long way out a my league.

Missiles perched on her desk. Legs crossed, she properly examined the book, eyes devouring every page. Finally, she looked up. Sighed.

Why IS it banned? You tell me.

Then she read it to us.

Now, she can't have read the whole book out loud. But she read quite a bit. I admit I was riveted. I remember bits of it to this day. A bunch of kids with flowery names go camping and spot some dodgy movements at an abandoned airfield. The class went so quiet while she read. Something hypnotic in the rhythm of the words. Remember we were kids who couldn't read for ourselves, so I think in those moments we had a taste a what we were missing. That's me saying that now, though. Me, an old man who thinks he understands a bit better.

What's that bleeping noise? Oh, it's.

Audio File 8
Date: April 14, 2019, 2:03 PM
Audio quality: Good

It was only Maxine on the line. Where was I?

So missiles had silence while she read. The story raced along until she turned a page and stopped. She was frozen to the spot, captivated by something in the book. A slip of paper. She turned it over in her fingers, examined it, peered closer as if it were tricky to see. Then she frowned as if faced with the most extraordinary puzzle.

She dropped the slip of paper back between the pages. Slowly checked her watch. Closed the book. We were still, silent, as we watched her. The odd glance between us. Then something momentous occurred.

What happens in the end? Nathan didn't speak. He just didn't. Back then, when a kid didn't speak—and I mean AT ALL—they were just the kid who didn't speak.

All heads turned to look at him. Hood up, even in this heat. He surely couldn't see much out of it. The only black kid in the class.

Do they find out who the stranger is? Donna had short hair like a boy. Unusual for those days.

Why's it banned, miss? Paul wasn't letting that one go.

Nothing. Finally, the bell rung missiles out of her thoughts. She looked up at us, five little faces all waiting for an answer, rapt with attention for the very first time. A bunch of rejects who got nothing out of school on a good day (. . .) yeah, she could see she was on to something.

I'll read the rest next lesson and we'll talk about it then, she said, to our collective sigh of resignation. Meanwhile I hadn't forgotten my battered sausage and chips. As the other kids picked up their bags and skulked out, I approached the desk.

Sorry, miss, but I need the book back OR it's yours for ten pounds. She gave me a look.

Steven, this book is a distraction. It is my job to prevent it ruining your education. Anyway, there's something I need to look into.

But, miss, I (. .) I need to (.) It's er (. . .) Did she know I'd taken it? Was she going to trace its legal owner? In a panic I couldn't think quickly enough.

Where did you really find it? She had the book open, held against her chest, out of my reach.

I swallowed hard. How did she know I'd found it? Had to think fast. I shrugged, can't remember.

With a sharp CLAP she snapped the book shut and out wafted the slip of paper. She caught it. Gave me another look, a strange glinty stare this time.

What's this? She said it as if she'd never seen that slip of paper before. I glanced at it, recovered my wits.

Bookmark, miss. Should be an extra pound, but for ten pound fifty, you can have it for free.

A good few looks crossed missiles face.

See. Here. She thrust the slip of paper momentarily under my nose.

A line of type danced before my eyes as unintelligible as ever, before it was snatched out of my sight for good.

It says deliver to Alice isles. This book is mine, Smithy. She glared. It's meant for ME.

Audio File 9
Date: April 14, 2019, 2:53 PM
Audio quality: Good

Did it really say that? Doesn't make sense that it would. I only found the book by chance, didn't I? She knew full well I couldn't read what was on that slip. But bearing in mind what happened next, I'm not so sure. I know I left that classroom with a feeling I'd been conned. I felt so—what?—unnerved I decided there and then I'd never be conned again, never be caught out, always be one step ahead of anyone else. And yes, looking back, those moments on my own with missiles probably were the last time I was lost for words. But it was just the beginning of this story.

[End Transcript]

Audio Files Batch 2

[Start Transcript]

Audio File 10
Date: April 15, 2019, 6:37 PM
Audio quality: Good

I've done plenty I'm not proud of. After the missiles thing I went off the rails. No (. . .) Mum or Dad telling me what to do. Colin at work or slumped silent in front of the telly. If I'm gun a cut a long story short then yes, in hindsight, I fell in with the wrong crowd.

Speaking to the young guns who fell in with one of today's wrong crowds, it was relatively innocent. At first. Dodgy goods. Sounds old-fashioned but (. .) More of a market for designer clothes, fresh cuts a meat and kiddies' toys on the estates than for Persian back then. Different story now. It changed quickly. You know what I mean by Persian, Maxine. Persian rugs (. . .) rhyming slang for *drugs*.

They started you off young. You ran errands, messages, little packages. The guys looked after you while you learned the ropes and as you got older you were given more responsibility. Chance to prove your loyalty. There were power struggles all the time. But I weren't ambitious. Just wanted to be part a something. Make enough to live on. I knew who the boss was and if I did as he told me, I couldn't go far wrong.

Looking back I often think I was lucky to fall in with the Harrisons. They'd run their patch since before the Second World War. They had a sense of responsibility and fairness you don't get now, not from what I heard inside, anyway.

In those early days, selling dodgy goods was our bread and butter. Every once in a while a bank or post office, maybe a jewelers. Anything tasty that might come up. But everything went wrong in the nineties. The docks, where we'd got most of our gear, had all but gone, and it was harder to get merchandise through at the airports. At the same time banks got CCTV, electronic security. That weren't the easy money it once were. We started with Persian to make up for the shortfall. In the blink of an eye, Persian (. . .) drugs took over. And there we were, in bed with international hard cases who'd kill their own grandma if she didn't kill them first.

A good few of the old faces got out then. Escaped to Spain or Essex. I should've too but didn't have the cash. Had to stay put. See, the old Bill were on to me . . . You know who I mean by old Bill, don't you, Maxine? The fuzz. The peelers. The *police* (. . . .) yeah, from the mid-nineties I was in and out of jail more times than the warden's lunch box. Then I got handed a long stretch and that did for me. Never again. It was hard that last time.

They moved me out to the sticks. Sheppey Vale. Place where they run group talking sessions, art classes. As if that makes it easier (. . .) I felt every day of it. It was my age, see. Went from being one a the young lads running the place, to an old-timer. Tolerated, ignored, or laughed at. The young guns look at you different. You're not one a them no more. Maybe jail weren't what it used to be. Maybe I'd changed. All I know is, just as I was looking for something else, those young guns come in with their large alphabet letters and well. I've told you already.

Audio File 11
Date: April 16, 2019, 9:59 AM
Audio quality: Moderate

I want to tell you the rest about missiles and not go off on a story about the past whenever I reach something I don't want to face. That's what Maxine says anyway. So I've got my son's phone with me in the booth. I'll record a little bit here and there between checking the lorries in and out. I hope the noise don't (). That was a big one.

So, missiles confiscated my book, left me battered sausage free and chip-less. I suppose I was angry, but at fourteen you soon forget, don't you? I know I'd forgotten by the next are E class, so imagine my surprise when the first thing missiles did was pull my book from her bag. I could see clearly what she'd done. She'd put that many extra leaves of paper between the pages the book was twice as thick. I could see pen writing on them. As if she'd scribbled down notes about every word.

Missiles opened the book, sat on her desk, and took up the story where she'd left off. I tried to listen, but I was more intrigued by what she'd been doing.

So she got to the end, snapped the book shut, hugged it to herself, still deep in thought.

That's an old story.

Because Nathan never spoke, when he did, we all jumped a mile.

Yes, Nathan. It was published forty-four years ago, in 1939. It was the first of a series. The Super Six. Three girls and three boys are sent to stay with their bad-tempered aunt in the country every summer. There's not much to do there, so they solve mysteries that have been puzzling the local community.

Why's it banned? Paul.

It's banned, says missiles, because it's zen or phobic (. .) That's a word we didn't hear often in South London in the 1980s, let me tell you that. But she wasn't done. It's sexist, racist, patronizing, and simplistic.

If the school board knew I'd been reading this to you, she pauses, her eyes bore into each of us in turn, so we don't doubt the severity of her words. They would sack me on the spot.

We were impressed. Not by the school's commitment to political correctness, but to missiles spirit of rebellion.

Now I have to be honest and say I hadn't noticed any of those qualities in the story missiles read to us. Then again, I wasn't black or a girl, so racism and sexism passed me by. I had no idea what patronizing meant, let alone zen or phobic, and if something was simplistic I would've said that were a good thing. Still, the look in missiles eyes didn't beg questions. At. All.

What's them pages you've put in the book? I wasn't one to read a situation back then.

Nothing. She quickly slid the book behind her on the desk, out of our sight.

If you're not allowed to read it to us, miss, why did you? Donna always seemed smarter than the rest of us in are E.

Yeah, we could tell on you, I says, bit of menace in my voice. I'm no rat but I were still smarting from the fact missiles had conned me out of my book.

Because. Everyone in this room is clever enough to understand that this book belongs to another world. A different time and place. Then she gets a flourish in her voice and says: the past is a foreign country. They do things differently there. Who said that? She looked at us all expectant.

You just did, miss. I knew how to make her laugh.

She tells us the name of whoever said it, but blow me I can't remember now. I do recall she retrieves my aeroplane book, runs her hands over its cover. Like painting her aura round the lines, earnest, yearning. Perhaps it was the way she said it, the way she used the word WE that drew us in and allied us with her, or perhaps because she'd described us as clever when no one else in our lives ever had (. . .) or would again in my case. But her next words ring through my ears to this day. She held the book up, looked round at us.

We can *all* see through this, this apparently simple story, with its archetypal characters and stereotypical baddies, to what it's *really* about.

Now, of course, I only wish I could.

Audio File 12
Date: April 16, 2019, 11:18 AM
Audio quality: Good

This is where my memories stop and jump ahead. Days? Weeks? Not months because when we all piled into the school minibus for our trip to the south coast it was still summer and still 1983. I was so pleased to be out of school for a day. Didn't care where we were going. Or why. Or that it wasn't quite. It wasn't legit. It can't have been, can it?

This is it, see. We all went together to the south coast. A day trip that should've been nice. Missiles was (. .) She (. . . .) We were all together one moment, and then the next (. . .)What did she do? Who did she see? Because I don't remember what happened. Or I've forgotten. Or I never knew. But we all went out in the minibus that day and missiles never came back.

Audio File 13
Date: April 16, 2019, 11:57 AM
Audio quality: Good

When school started again in September, I stayed away. If Colin noticed he didn't mention anything. If a school inspector came round I never heard about it. What made me go from a kid who hated school, but was conscientious enough to worry about being late, to a kid who would never set foot in a classroom again? Something had got to me, that's for sure.

One benefit of learning to read is the internet and social media. It's a gateway to everything, so they told us at community college. Maxine arranged for me to go and they helped us set up an email address, use Google™ and register on Facebook™. With a few false starts and a bit of swearing I managed to get my profile page up on my son's phone. It's a hell of a lot smaller, though. Takes me longer to type things in than most people. As I said before, putting words in from scratch is much harder than reading things already written. Easier when I can get the voice button to work. Lucky I've got all day, especially like now, when it's quiet in the booth.

Been putting it off a fair bit, but if I'm gun a do this like I promised Maxine, then I have to find the others: Nathan, Shell, Donna, and Paul. Find them and see what they remember about missiles. About that trip to bore mouth. Part of me doesn't want to. Why's that? It's not like I have much else to do. And it can't be that bad, can it?

Audio File 14
Date: April 19, 2019, 5:25 PM
Audio quality: Moderate

Voice 1:	See ear, Steve, flashing lines means it's picking up your voice.
Voice 2:	Will it record both of us?
Voice 1:	Looks like.
Voice 2:	I'll put it between us on the table.
Voice 1:	What's this for?
Voice 2:	I'm looking back over our school days. Might write a memoir or=
Voice 1:	Which bit? Which thing?
Voice 2:	Oh, er. Everything. London kids, inner cities. How it's changed.
Voice 1:	()
Voice 2:	I'm talking to Paul Clacken (. . .) I'm saying that into the

recorder, Paul mate. So I know who it is when I find out how to play these files back (. . .) Paul went to the same school. We (. .) we were mates. We played football together=

Voice 1:   That were middle school. Do you mean high school?

Voice 2:   If=

Voice 1:   I don't remember it.

Voice 2:   None of it?

Voice 1:   Nothing=

Voice 2:   You remember the are E class. Missiles? Donna, Nathan, and Shell, going to the seaside=

Voice 1:   Not me. I didn't go. Do us a favor, mate. Switch that off.

Audio File 15
Date: April 19, 2019, 5:40 PM
Audio quality: Moderate

I found him easily on Facebook™. Paul. He lives across the common in one of the old blocks on acre road. He's barely gone a mile since we were kids. That's rich coming from me. I haven't gone far myself. He's a car mechanic just like his old man. Kept his head down over the years. Still knows some a the old faces. Surely can't be married. Scruffy and dirty. Stained fingers from the fags. Pocky red nose from the demon drink.

I'm sat here in the boozer trying to look like he didn't storm out under a cloud. Very useful this. I can pretend to talk on the phone when I'm really speaking into the recorder. He was friendly enough until he realized what I wanted to talk about. Why is that?

Oh, come on, Smithy, don't read too much into it. He was a troubled kid. It was in the family. It don't mean he's hiding anything, does it? People round here are cagey. It's second nature. I know Kos I am one of 'em. But if there were nothing out of the ordinary about that day, why was he so reluctant to talk about it? To me. Who was there myself.

Because the thing is, I know for sure Paul came with us. I can see him now. He jumped into that van like we all did, excited for a day out of school. We got in the back and missiles hauled herself up into the driver's seat. She turned the key over and over. Engine coughed and died each time. We fell silent, our spirits sinking fast, when Paul leaned between the seats, squinted at the dashboard. He'd helped his dad in the garage since he was a kid. After a sharp intake a breath, he told her to wait for a light to go out, then try again. She did what he said, the engine chugged to life, and we were off. Yeah, Paul showed her how to get the minibus going. I've remembered that all these years Kos it seemed to me no one at the school knew she was taking it out, or they'd a shown her how to start it.

I'll have to go. Finished my drink and there are some faces round here I'd frankly rather not ().

Audio File 16
Date: April 20, 2019, 10:12 AM
Audio quality: Good

Michelle Madden. Must be her married name because that's her. Shell. The stunning girl from are E. Found her on a list of people who confirmed they were going to a school reunion ten years ago. That profile picture. She's in a cocktail dress, glass of bubbly. A lineup of women. Identical hair and clothes. But her eyes stand out a mile to me. If I'm gun a do this. I have to do it. Why do I feel ()? There. Request sent.

Audio File 17
Date: April 20, 2019, 10:36 PM
Audio quality: Good

SHE'S ACCEPTED. Spent the whole day checking every few minutes. No message, but yes, I can see her page now. Seems she likes a glamorous cruise or three. And staying in a big hotel with a pool, immaculate gardens. Villa Kappa™ on some island in Greece. Lots of friends. Dogs. Small, white curly dogs. Lives north of the river. High Barnet. Well off my manor. Two grown-up sons. Husband has had some plastic surgery, so he could be an old face or a rat on the run. But something hasn't changed. I'm looking her right in the eye. Is it there? I swear I can see something.

Got a get some sleep now. Picking up a new car from Maxine's neighbor tomorrow.

Audio File 18
Date: April 21, 2019, 4:02 PM
Audio quality: Good

I don't *f*[EXPLICIT]*ing* believe it. That posh place on Facebook™ is HER HOUSE. I thought it was a *f*[EXPLICIT]*ing* hotel. *F*[EXPLICIT]*k* me. Huge gates. The sort of place we'd rob blind back in the day. Got a park this rusty *c*[EXPLICIT]*t* out of sight. She can't see me arrive in this.

Audio File 19
Date: April 21, 2019, 4:11 PM
Audio quality: Good

Round the corner from Shell's house. Big *f*[EXPLICIT]*k*off gates at the front and zero security round the back. Perfect daylight job. I'd have been over that wall in a flash. Still could now I bet.

I'll be honest. Had to pluck up all me courage to type a proper message to Shell. She was out a my league then and I'm just as tongue-tied now. Turns out I needn't have worried. Soon as I mention meeting up she replies with YEAH, drop in whenever you're passing, have a catch-up, be good to see you. So I type back GREAT, see you in an hour (. . .) She takes a while to reply then. Probably busy putting the Hoover™ round and, given the size of the place, that ain't the work of a moment. But I got a do it. Got a find out. For Maxine. So here I am (. . .) Feel like a kid outside the headmaster's office. Right.

Audio File 20
Date: April 21, 2019, 4:27 PM
Audio quality: Good

Voice 1:   It's lap sang sue shong. *Posh tea.*

Voice 2:   Mmmm (. . .) lovely. I'll put it down, though.

Voice 1:   All that's irrelevant now, Steven. I don't think about it.

Voice 2:   What (.) .hhhhh. *Aftertaste.* What is? Irrelevant.

Voice 1:   School. Childhood. Over and done with. Nothing about it defines me in any way (. . .) Do you remember playing in the park at NIGHT?

Voice 2:   Yeah, yeah=

Voice 1:   Unimaginable now. You told me your mum wanted you to live with her so badly she kept a clean knife, fork, and plate specially for you in her kitchen. Only you couldn't leave your dad because he needed you to get him home from the pub. Funny now=

Voice 2:   Can't believe you live in a place like this, Shell. It's a palace.

Voice 1:   Thank you. What have you been doing, Steven?

Voice 2:   Why? What have you heard?

Voice 1:   Nothing. You look like you've worked hard these last forty years.

Voice 2:   Do I? Thanks. You. You're. You too. I've been in business. Import export. Driving. Logistics. Nightclubs. Most recently, though, I've been in security.

Voice 1:   What's your book about?

Voice 2:   My? Oh yeah. YEAH. It's about inner-city kids.

Voice 1:   Like we were. What about them?

Voice 2:   How poor kids get out the rut. Break the cycle of disadvantage.

Voice 1:   Education and hard work. It's not a mystery.

Voice 2:   I want to show how they can help themselves. Make a life against the odds. Defy the system. The expectations of society. Do alright for themselves (. . . . .)

Voice 1:   What's it really about? (. . .)

Voice 2:   Missiles and our trip to bore moth that day. Sorry, I can't drink any more of that.

Voice 1:   Leave it. Why that day?

Voice 2:   You were there, Shell. You remember it.

Voice 1:   I remember it clearly, Steven.

Voice 2:   Can you tell me? Everything you know. Everything you remember.

Voice 1:   I (. . .) hhhhhh remember you started it. You brought a book in. A very old book by Edith Twyford. Goodness knows where you got it from. Missiles read it to us. It's one I read to my boys when they were little. Missiles loved that book. She'd talk about Edith Twyford in every class. It was like we were studying HER books, not reading and writing to catch up with our peers. She organized a trip to Bournemouth because that's where Twyford lived (. .) Steven? Are you alright?

Voice 2:   Do you remember what happened in the end?

Voice 1:   .hhhhh We came home. Later than planned. The minibus kept overheating or something. We drove back in the dark. Otherwise, it was a very pleasant day out of school. I don't think any of us escaped the city often. I have nothing but fond memories.

(. . . . .)

Voice 2:   Are you SURE, Shell?

Voice 1:   I focus on positive things, Steven. That's how to move on.
            I haven't a clue why you want to write a book about that
            day. But, the fact YOU, a child who struggled with literacy
            all those years ago, are writing a book [*background noise*]
            proves education is the key. Oh, ZANDER. This is Steven,
            from my old high school. Steven. My husband, Zander.

Voice 3:   Hello. Good to meet you. Michelle, you've given him that
            god-awful. Can I get you some proper tea? Pass me his cup,
            darling.

Voice 2:   Oh yes please, governor.

Voice 3:   I'll be in the kitchen [*background noise*] dogs going mad
            (. . . . .)

Voice 1:   Steven, things were difficult at home for you. I understand.
            It's no surprise you can't recall details from that time. The
            mind forgets. It's a safety mechanism. Survival. Write your
            book about something else.

Voice 2:   hhhhhhh Yes. You're right, Shell. I will. Just reading too
            much into it. Easily done.

Voice 1:   See. Your. It has the. Are you RECORDING this?

Voice 2:   Only. Just so as I=

Voice 1:   DELETE IT. NOW. And it's Michelle. I'm MICHELLE
            now [*background noise*]

Audio File 21
Date: April 21, 2019, 5:19 PM
Audio quality: Good

That went well, as people say now when things go badly. Hard enough
driving again after so long, let alone in this state. Have to sit in the
car for a bit. Don't know if that came out. Or if she got to it before I

snatched the phone back. I can see the (. . .) But when I tap it you must upgrade eye oh S to play this file. Just like the others.

I tapped the recording button as she got the tea. That was a moment, let me tell you. Tasted like the bottom of an ashtray. Worse than anything they dish up in the scrubs. In fact, serve that up inside and fellas would be banging trashcan lids on the roof before it had a chance to go cold.

She looks just like she did in are E. Cool. Haughty. But she tries to speak like one a them. Doesn't fool me.

Education and hard work she reckons is the way out of poverty. But not her way. She married well, as they say in costume dramas on a Sunday night. In all fairness, her old man was solid gold. Turns out he's not on the run at all—he's a plastic surgeon. She was a nurse. That's how they met. One a their sons is a doctor and the other in finance. You should a seen their faces when I told them my son works with numbers too. He teaches math at Brunel University. They didn't expect THAT. Not with me as his (. . .) not with me as (. . .)

Why did she think I had a difficult time at home? No more than she did. Or other kids back then, in that school. I had a roof over my head. I had Colin.

But missiles. She was very quick to dismiss that. My eyes don't easily see words like yours do, Maxine. Type, print, handwriting, none of it. But they see things you don't. It's partly a professional skill. Spotted her Bulgari ring, Chopard necklace, and Tiffany bracelet with barely a glance. Could live magnificent for a month on the contents of a jewelry box like that. Back in the day, I mean.

It's partly something else I can't quite explain. Like Shell's eyes as she assured me I were wrong. Like the lines around her mouth. Like her hands and feet and how her body changed shape as she spoke. The tone of her voice and air of relief when I pretended to believe her lie. The way she quickly changed the subject to some light, airy chat about their holiday villa that won't sell. Too isolated, too basic, needs too much work. Yeah, a big *f*[EXPLICIT]*king* problem.

I can hardly accuse her of lying when I told her I'm writing a book. But at least I know a bit more about (). So missiles talked a lot about Edith Twyford Kos of the book I found. Well, I never listened in class, didn't concentrate, couldn't have cared less, so no wonder I don't remember it. Edith Twyford. The name rings a bell.

[End Transcript]

Audio Files Batch 3

Audio File 22
Date: April 25, 2019, 1:45 PM
Audio quality: Good

So far, no luck tracing Nathan or Donna. Messaged a few from school so let's see. But in the meantime, been forging ahead with my investigation. Got chatting to the new librarian. She apologized for the library having no Edith Twyford books at all and to make up for it, helped me register on eBay. We searched on there and I spotted the cover right away. That boy in his red jumper. It's called Six on Goldtop Hill, book one of the Super Six series. Dead cheap. It arrived here by post yesterday. Propped it up on the table, so I can see that kid with his toy plane wherever I am in the room. Keep looking at him. As for reading it, well, have to work my way up to that. I'll start Monday when the booth goes quiet.

I've googled an expert on Edith Twyford. A stroke of luck. She's based on Gower Street uptown. Spent all afternoon crafting an email to her. Proper sweated over it. She pings back straightaway agreeing to be interviewed for this book I'm not writing. Turns out, if you're writing a book, people are more willing to talk than if you just want peace a mind for yourself. My appointment is at two. I've to find the English department and ask for her at reception. Her name's Rosemary Wintle. I've got her picture up on the phone. Big glasses, grey bob, midsixties. That's exactly how I imagined her when I read the name. Funny that.

Audio File 23
Date: April 25, 2019, 2:09 PM
Audio quality: Good

Voice 1:   I'm at University College London, or you see Elle, recording Rosemary Wintle for my book. She's an expert on Edith Twyford.

Voice 2:   No. I'm an expert on twentieth-century children's literature. Edith Twyford is an interesting figure from that period. I work as a consultant for her publisher, and I'm occasionally asked to speak about her in the media, but wouldn't call myself an expert on her exclusively.

Voice 1:   Oh. That's OK. Well, you'll probably still be useful.

Voice 2:   .hh (. . .) Good.

Voice 1:   I'm looking at this book in particular.

Voice 2:   What about it?

Voice 1:   Is there anything that makes it an important one in the Edith Twyford (. . .)?

Voice 2:   The Edith Twyford what?

Voice 1:   World?

Voice 2:   Six on Goldtop Hill is one of Twyford's Super Six books, probably her most famous series, written between 1939 and 1963. There are six young characters who enjoy adventures together and solve rural mysteries. I don't believe this is more significant than any other in the series.

Voice 1:   So why's it banned?

Voice 2:   I'm not aware it's banned.

Voice 1:   Years ago my teacher at school told me it was banned.

Voice 2:   hhhh I see. Well, some schools, teachers, and parents, over the years, have exercised an anti-Twyford policy. They actively do not promote her work or read her books in class. She is rarely stocked in schools or municipal libraries.

Voice 1:   Why not?

Voice 2:   Well, you've read her canon.

Voice 1:   Her CANON? (. . .) YES. I plan to read that one. When I
             get the chance.

Voice 2:   You're writing about Edith Twyford but haven't read her
             books?

Voice 1:   I've lost my glasses.

Voice 2:   Well, when you find them, you'll see that Twyford wrote in
             a particular way. A very simple way. She's an unchallenging
             read on every level. No subtext. No depth. No hidden
             meanings. No food for thought. No room for interpretation.
             Even where she depicts reality, it's so idealized it borders on
             fantasy. You'll know Twyford was most productive during
             the Second World War?

Voice 1:   Yes. That's one thing I'm well aware of=

Voice 2:   She spoke of wanting to help children escape the stress and
             trauma around them. It explains much about her style and
             approach. Her stories are in the moment, there and gone.
             Timeless, in their way, yet dated to the contemporary reader.
             Since the 1960s, children's literature has grown in its scope
             and sophistication. Authors now feel a responsibility for how
             their readers' outlook and development are shaped by the
             stories they tell. Twyford's creations bear no comparison to
             Harry Potter, Tom Gates, or Dora Márquez, to name but
             three.

Voice 1:   Were they writing at the same time?

Voice 2:   (. . .) They're fictional characters.

Voice 1:   They are. Yes. Of course.

Voice 2:   Having said that, accusations of sexism, racism, misogyny,
             and xenophobia have stalked Twyford ever since she began
             her career in the 1930s. Let me see (.) This is a reprint from
             the 1970s. This will have been edited to remove a good deal

of the original bombastic language. Overseas she remains very popular. Published in forty-two languages. Of course, with every translation the story is, almost by default, updated in line with contemporary trends.

Voice 1:   Can you tell me, miss. Please. Is it possible to become so obsessed with this book, you .hhhhh lose yourself?

Voice 2:   (. . .) I would find that unlikely. Although if one is prone to obsession (.) It's hard to say.

Voice 1:   Oh.

Voice 2:   Have I answered all your questions?

Voice 1:   Yes, miss.

Voice 2:   Good. Well, turn left out of the door and immediate right for the stairs.

Audio File 24
Date: April 25, 2019, 2:54 PM
Audio quality: Good

Phew. I'm sweating. Soaked. Forgot how bloody intimidating teachers can be. What is it about them that switches my ears off the minute they start talking? I'm sitting on a bench in this pretty little square pretending to speak on the phone. She was all prim and just so. Spoke into the recorder as if she had delivered that speech hundreds of times before. Well, she was nice enough to agree to meet me, but the only good thing to come out of my visit is that while waiting for her in reception, I found out how to make one of my son's photographs into the main picture on this phone. I chose one he'd left in the gallery. He's at a picnic table one summer, probably a few years ago. He looks so happy. It's not often I've thought this, but there's something about his expression (. . .) He looks like me in that picture.

Audio File 25
Date: April 29, 2019, 7:17 PM
Audio quality: Good

So I took Six on Goldtop Hill to work and read it between lorries. It's nothing like *Lord of the Flies*. Or *Animal Farm* for that matter. Mrs. Wintle is right, though, it's quite easy to read, even for me. She spoke as if that were a problem. I'll read out a bit for you, Maxine. You'll see what I mean. Here we go.

> *Chapter one. An extraordinary week. It was a beautiful, bright, sunny spring day when Mr. Horton's big black car pulled into the driveway of Cross Keys. As soon as the engine rumbled to a halt, both doors flew open and out poured the six Horton children. Sophie, Rose, and little Iris were followed by (. .) Edward, (. . .) Piers and the very grown-up (. . . . .) Horatio. Each bursting with excitement to see the pretty little cottage again. To the Hortons it shimmered in sunlight.*
>
> *They had enough sense to avoid red tomcat, whose whiskers glowered at them from the gorse bush. Sophie, a forthright type of girl, was first to spot the frilly pink roses around the wooden door. Look, she chirped, jumping like a jack-in-the-box. Those roses are the same hue as our Rose's cheeks. They all turned to stare at their middle sister, Rose, a sullen child who hated to be the center of attention. Not anymore, squealed Edward, who loved flowers like a girl. She's turned the color of the (. . .) hollyhocks now. They all laughed at poor Rose.*
>
> *Now, children, said their aunt (. . .) Honoria, as she popped her head through the doorway. Say thank you to your father as he's driven you all the way here when he's a very important doctor and belongs with his patients, not you. Thank you, Father, they shouted, as Mr. Horton's big black car trundled down the drive and disappeared. Piers turned to his brothers and sisters. Well, he said, let's hope this week holds as many thrilling adventures as the last time we stayed at Cross Keys (. . .)*

I won't read all of it, but (. . .) I remember it from when missiles read it out to us. Luckily, it's the funny-sounding kids' names that stick in my mind. Otherwise I'd not know how to pronounce those words now. Hoe rat E oh. Honor rhea. Peers. Wonder why we were so captivated by it back then? It's not as if we ever went to stay with maiden aunts in the country ourselves. Turns out these kids with Latin names DO have an adventure when they go camping on Goldtop Hill. There's goods being stashed in an old aircraft hangar, probably by the local firm. From the illustrations alone I could've told them it's a stupid place. It's in view of a popular campsite at the end of a single track road, along which a lot of residents with time on their hands can see who comes and goes.

The secret to concealment is movement. If you want to hide things in plain sight you need a busy place, where people pass by on their daily routines, where one more stranger won't stand out. Alternatively, keep your contraband on the move. Sounds riskier but in the long run minimizes the likelihood of discovery; plus, you can change and limit the number of folk who know where it's kept. In this whole book it doesn't say what the contra is. This is a kids' book essentially so, I don't know, maybe weed or sidearms? In short, I've read it from cover to cover, words and pictures, and I'm none the wiser as to why missiles. Why she. Why missiles didn't come back that day.

Audio File 26
Date: April 30, 2019, 4:11 PM
Audio quality: Good

Found Nathan. The brother of an old school friend knew Nathan's dad's cousin and, to cut a long story short, that's how I got his phone number. Initially I thought that's no good, Nathan don't speak. It's now occurred to me he probably grew out of that. I haven't seen him since 1983, remember. Still, can't help wondering what'll be on the end of the phone. Never mind Shell saying I was a troubled kid. What about Nathan? Only one way to find out. Gun a call him in a minute.

Struck up a conversation with the new librarian again this morning. Big mistake. The older one was hovering around, and I should've kept me mouth shut. Asked them how to go about recording phone calls. Well, the look they gave me. You could hear a pin drop, and not just because it's a library. What do they think I'm trying to do? Even when I said I'm writing a book and need to record interviews, they didn't seem convinced. The older librarian said I'd have to ask at the phone shop. Then she gave the new girl a task to do, sent her away. Anyone would think I was a nuisance. I'll try the record button anyway. Let's see.

Audio File 27
Date: April 30, 2019, 4:50 PM
Audio quality: Good

There's no new icon in my list so it didn't record, but what was I worried about? Nathan is a top bloke. Solid gold. Never mind not talking, he's made up for it now. We had a long chat about the old days and what do you know, he's just as curious as I am about missiles. He's tried to find out more himself over the years, on and off. We're meeting up at his place in Tonbridge tomorrow. Gun a compare what we've got and swap intel. Finally getting somewhere.

Audio File 28
Date: May 1, 2019, 1:22 PM
Audio quality: Good

Voice 1:   Podcast, is it?

Voice 2:   More a spoken record. I (.) Maxine is very interested and, well, I'm not one for writing things down.

Voice 1:   Maxine your missus?

Voice 2:	NO. No, she's. We're friendly.
	(. . .) Um. So, Nathan Welch was in the are E class with me and the others back in the day. I'm just saying this into the recorder, Nate, so I know who it is. Nathan, can you tell me what you remember about our trip?
Voice 1:	Sure. Feels a bit forced. Try to make it sound natural but=
Voice 2:	Talk clear, so the lines jump around on the screen as you speak=
Voice 1:	Well. Miss isles was our teacher, weren't she? Very nice lady. She was warm, Steve=
Voice 2:	Yeah=
Voice 1:	Warm and inspiring, but no pushover. She read us a book in school and we went to Bormuth because the author lived there. Or was born there. Or the book was set there. Some reason anyway. I assumed it was a special book to help us with our reading. You've since told me it was an old one by Edith Twyford. You'd found the book and it was banned. I don't remember that, but it makes sense because neither a mine ever read Edith Twyford books at school. Not that they're big readers. Prefer games on their computer. Kos games tell stories, but they're interactive. You work things out yourself to get to the end. Lots a different solutions. Reading is PASSIVE, in it? Boring (. . .) [background noise] Yeah, anyway, we spoke about Bormuth yesterday and we both agreed it weren't an official school outing.
Voice 2:	That's right.
Voice 1:	It's what bothered me most over the years, Steve. That and how it ended. I remember it started off bloody awesome. She parked the minibus on the seafront. Lovely sunny day. Steve, I don't know if this applied to you, but I'd never been to the seaside in my life. Tried to act cool but all that sand,

man. You, me, and Paul ran down the path, across the beach and right into the water. I had wet shoes all day, but (. .) the girls stayed with Miss isles because they didn't want their shoes to get sandy. Their shoes were made of, like, canvas or something? White canvas. Strange what you remember, in it?

Voice 2:   And what you forget.

Voice 1:   And what you forget. Like, I can't remember if we got back in the van or not, but the next thing we're at a cottage with some link to Edith Twyford. Do you remember that? She'd been dead awhile, so it's not like she was ever gun a be in or anything, but Miss isles was desperate to get inside. We knocked on the door and when there was no answer she led us round the back. Do you remember looking in all the windows?

Voice 2:   ()

Voice 1:   Next thing you're inside the house. I can see you, all of four foot, hauling open that big back door, split in two for a horse to look out of. You let us in=

Voice 2:   Can't say I remember=

Voice 1:   So we're in this house looking for where Edith Twyford wrote the book or whatever. I don't know what we're looking for. Like, now I'd assume it's a desk or table, but then I was all, like, did she write it on this chair? In this bed? At this sink? But, Steve, that was someone's house. What was all that about?

Voice 2:   Missiles was looking for something.

Voice 1:   She was DEFINITELY looking for something. Did she find it? Kos we separated. Each of us in different rooms. Three boys, two girls, and Miss isles. Six of us. We mustard been all over that house. Like, I walked past a bedroom and you were literally jumping on a big bed. Proper trampoline=

Voice 2:   I WEREN'T=

Voice 1:	Yeah, you were leaping, trying a touch the ceiling=
Voice 2:	That's funny. I don't=
Voice 1:	Yeah, I walked round looking for Miss isles. Paul was in the kitchen, eating things in the fridge. Stashing food in his pockets. But I couldn't find Miss isles anywhere. I ended up sitting in the little garden outside. Waited for you all (. .) You OK, Steve?
Voice 2:	Yeah.
Voice 1:	At some point we get back in the minibus. I was gutted. Wanted to play on the beach. That's where things get hazy because I put my hood back up. I was an anxious kid back then, Steve, and when I (. . . .) didn't want to be somewhere I just turned up my Walkman™, put my hood up. Like I zoned out.
Voice 2:	You had headphones on under your hood?
Voice 1:	Yeah.
Voice 2:	All the time? Whenever your hood was up?
Voice 1:	Yeah.
Voice 2:	So you didn't hear much. In class. Or on the trip.
Voice 1:	That's right. Not from that point on, no. But I remember the end. Or put it this way, I remember AN end.
Voice 2:	What happened?
Voice 1:	Miss isles drives us to a wide open country place, all green, with old concrete buildings dotted about in the grass. Crumbling, derelict bunkers from the war. We play around for ages. But it gets late. The sun goes down. And this was summer. It were nine, ten o'clock [*DecipherIt*™ *time ref* 52817122-2946043]. Too late. Dark. We should've left ages ago. But Miss isles had gone. The girls were scared long before we were. I'm not sexist, that's just a fact, Steve.
Voice 2:	This is it, Nathan. I don't remember going home, arriving home, nothing. We mustard got back somehow. *F*[EXPLICIT]*k*

it, something happened. It's nothing (. . .) Obscure. Vague like our (. .) vanished youth.

Voice 1: [*background noise*] Vanished youth. You make me chuckle, Steve (. . .) She mustard come back eventually and drove us home. Kos I remember my mum were crazy mad when I got in. Maybe she weren't meant to take us out in the first place, so they fired her. School won't admit a teacher took off to the coast unofficial with a class of kids, so nothing was said. Hushed up.

Voice 2: But DID missiles come back or did someone else drive us back to school?

(. . . . .)

Voice 1: Thing is, Steve, no one spoke to us afterward. If anything truly bad had happened there would've been old Bill buzzing around. The cops would've asked questions, for sure. Did anyone speak to you about it?

Voice 2: No.

Voice 1: Me neither. Can't have been anything dodgy is what I'm saying.

Voice 2: But there were only a few days left of the school year. Things were winding down. No one knew we'd gone to bore moth in the first place, so they wouldn't wonder where we were. If someone else drove us back to school, parked the minibus in the shed, returned the key to the caretaker, or wherever it had to go. No one would a known any different.

Voice 1: Only us.

Voice 2: Only us (. . . .) Did you go back to school in September, Nate?

Voice 1: Course. We were only fourteen, Steve. Kids. Started fourth form in the September. Our CSE courses. You would've too.

Voice 2: Never went back.

Voice 1: Sure? Come to think of it, I don't remember you.

Voice 2:	Were the others there? The are E class?
Voice 1:	Yeah. Well, I think so. I (. .) we had a new teacher. Remember Mr. Wilson? Think he said she'd left. Pretty sure the others were all there.
Voice 2:	So it was just me who didn't go back?
Voice 1:	Yeah. You and Miss isles.

Audio File 29
Date: May 3, 2019, 12:44 PM
Audio quality: Moderate

Voice 1:	See the (thing) there? It's recording now, see?
Voice 2:	Yes, I've got that far. I only.
Voice 1:	Red button to record, red button to stop.
Voice 2:	But when it's a phone conversation=
Voice 1:	Same. Red to record. Red to stop.
Voice 2:	Will that record the other person? Down the phone?
Voice 1:	Of course it won't.
Voice 2:	Oh, but.

Audio File 30
Date: May 3, 2019, 12:55 PM
Audio quality: Moderate

She had "happy to help" on her polo shirt. Well, she wasn't happy, and she was no help. I thought they'd know about technology in Argos™. It's got screens everywhere now, like a spaceship.

The missus bought all our furniture there when we moved to our flat. That catalog was like a Bible to her. I could've got one now, while I was in there, but (. .) too heavy. Haven't got the room.

Audio File 31
Date: May 3, 2019, 2:39 PM
Audio quality: Good

Calling.

Source:	Hi.
Caller:	I'm looking for a Donna Cole, who went to school with me in the eighties=
Source:	Smithy.
	(. . .)
Caller:	How did you know it was me?
Source:	Where shall we meet?
Caller:	Uh. Meet? You (.) remember Nathan?
Source:	Bring him too.
Caller:	.hhhhh
Source:	Tomorrow. The pub on Picketts Lane. Where the Load of Hay used to be.
Caller:	Opposite the school. OK. But I don't know if Nathan=
Source:	Eleven.
Caller:	In the morning? () Well, I'll.

End call.

Audio File 32
Date: May 3, 2019, 2:42 PM
Audio quality: Good

I'm reeling. Gobsmacked. I don't think it came out because the thing won't open, but I swear she was waiting for my call. Donna, this is. It was as if we'd only just spoke the week before, not forty years ago. I don't mean that in a good way either. Not as if we got on so well we picked up the conversation where we left off.

I'm reading too much into it. Got her number from a person on our school's Facebook™ page, Oliver Unwin. I don't recall the name, and there's no picture of him. But he's listed in our year group so I messaged him along with all the others. He replied with just her number. Nothing else. Mustard told her I'd been in touch. Or something.

Yeah, Oliver Unwin. Right fancy it sounds. He is surely some mon-eyed arse. Lewisham, Ladywell, Crofton (. . . .) likely email alias, not a name. Donna's? No obviously that's a (. . .) I like the thought she got an alter ego, but (. . .) nah.

If Shell knows Donna, then she mustard mentioned me. But she didn't say to bring Shell tomorrow, only Nathan. Left him a message but doubt he can come up at this short notice. He's got his work and family. Why does she want to see him too? Got a funny feeling about it and don't know why. Is it because, really (. .) deep down (. . . .) I don't want to know what happened to missiles? Well, Maxine does and that's why I'll be there like I said.

Audio File 33
Date: May 3, 2019, 11:28 PM
Audio quality: Good

Can't sleep for thinking about tomorrow. No word from Nathan. I had Six on Goldtop Hill in the booth today. Thought I'd read it again from the start. Might have missed something the first time. Reading is dull when you already know what happens in the end. I wonder if my son's kids like books? I could give it to them (. . .) my grandchildren. Don't sound right. They call his stepfather grandad. Can't complain about that. Never met him, but I know he's solid gold to have () done all he's done for my ().

(00:01:07)

Sometimes I forget what I'm meant to be recording and talk about what's on my mind instead. Sorry, Maxine.

I don't remember Donna as clearly as I do Shell. Perhaps because I didn't fancy her. As much. Her mum were knocked down by a car when we were little. Never walked again. Donna would leave early some days Kos of letting in a plumber or paying the insurance man. Other days she weren't at school at all. Funny. She couldn't read much, yet she was smarter than the rest of us. Don't misunderstand me, I'm not saying we were stupid Kos we were in are E, but Donna was just that bit more on the ball. She asked questions. That's what I'm getting at. She asked pertinent questions. Part of me isn't surprised she knows more than we do.

[*background noise*]

Ah text. Nathan. He's canceled all his work meetings and is coming uptown tomorrow. What a weight off my mind. I hoped he'd come. Was dreading meeting her on my own. He probably heard that in my voice. He's a sensitive fellow. At least I'll have an ally.

Audio File 34
Date: May 4, 2019, 11:03 AM
Audio quality: Moderate

Voice 1:   No. Switch it off, Steve.

Voice 2:   It's only for me, Donna. Can't make notes in this light.

Voice 1:   It could fall into the wrong hands. Switch it off.

Voice 3:   Wrong hands?

Voice 1:   Yes, Nathan. *Wrong hands.*

Voice 2:   It's off.

Voice 1:   Come closer, both of you (. .) Now, *before she disappeared, missiles told me a secret. That trip to bore moth was a cover. She was looking for something* (. . .) *something explosive. I believe she got too close.*

Voice 3:   She was blown up?

Voice 1:   NO. *She stumbled across something she should've steered clear of.*

Voice 3:   Tripped, fell, hit her head. Easily done.

Voice 1:   No, Nathan. Missiles was about to discover something other people wanted to stay hidden (. . .) I understand you're skeptical. Steven.

Voice 2:   Uh-huh?

Voice 1:   Switch the *f*[EXPLICIT]*king* phone off, mate. Top button. Here.

Audio File 35
Date: May 4, 2019, 11:35 AM
Audio quality: Moderate

Voice 1:   But she's *bats*[EXPLICIT]*t*, Steve.

Voice 2:   I [*background noise*] switch it on [*background noise*] make sure the screen's blank so. Keep an eye on her, Nathan. She still in there? Watch the toilet door.

Voice 1:   I'm watching it, but don't=

Voice 2:   The ladies', not the gents'=

Voice 1:   Yeah, yeah. Steve, she's crazy [*background noise*] crazy. COMING BACK. Turn it.

Audio File 36
Date: May 4, 2019, 7:10 PM
Audio quality: Good

I'm not supposed to drink alcohol. It's not what you think. Don't have a problem. Just promised Maxine I'd steer clear of anything that could be a (. . .) you know. An. Escape.

But on the way back today I stopped off at the little store and bought a few miniatures. Got them lined up here. Don't know why I should be so shook up. I want to know, don't I?

Back in the day she had short hair, like a boy. Same now, only peppered with grey. Matched her man's shirt and jeans, Dr. Martens™ shoes. TAG Heuer™ watch. Very nice.

Believe me, when you been away for eleven years, some things do not change one bit. Other things alter beyond recognition. No sooner has Donna arrived, when Nate calmly asks if she's a woman or a man.

I cough my mouthful of pint back into the glass, but Donna don't so much as flicker an eyelid. She answers him, dead serious. Says she's gender neutral in her personal style, but her preferred pronoun is HER (. . .) so she's a woman, but I can swear just as much in front of her as I would any fella.

I'm still wiping beer off me chin, when Nathan comes out with all the usual about how great it is to see her and where does she live now. But Donna ain't having any of it. She sits down at the little table and fixes us both with an expression I can only describe as (. . .) purposeful.

I hit record and shuffle the phone between us on the table, but she spots it straightaway, says turn it off. I tap the screen and say it's off when it isn't. Sorry, Maxine. I try not to lie but this was in the interests of (. . .) my investigation. Not that it makes a difference because she soon catches on and makes me switch it right off. I'm gun a tell you now what she said about missiles, but you must keep an open mind.

Wee. I forgot the kick a that. Ewe. Never was a spirits drinker. Tiny bottle top. There we go.

Missiles told Donna the real reason we went to bore moth that day. She took her aside while the rest of us were on the beach and explained it all, in case anything happened. Missiles had spotted something in the book I found. A message in secret code.

Edith Twyford weren't just a children's author. She and her husband moved in the upper circles of society, with access to information only ever meant for the powerful elite. They also held dubious allegiances according to Donna, whatever that means. Anyway, Twyford knows something significant, but can't do anything about it, not from her isolated little cottage on the south coast, so she puts it all in her books. Hides it between the letters, words, sentences, and paragraphs. For people in the future to find and make sense of. That's why she wrote so much during the war. Book after book. She churned them out, each one the next installment of the code. Books that Rosemary Wintle dismissed as simple and unchallenging. Well, according to Donna, they hold the key to information that remains at best sensitive and at worst dangerous, to this very day.

Well, the look on Nathan's face. Quite funny now—after three miniatures. He expected a gentle reminisce about the good old days.

Donna's phone rings in the middle of all this and she dives to the toilets to answer it. Nathan and I sit in stunned silence for a moment. He takes a big swig of his pint. I try to switch my phone back on, make it record in secret, but no joy. Might ask again at the library, see if they know how.

When she comes back to the table, Nathan and I are ready with our questions. Like, why did missiles tell YOU this and not the rest of us? She doesn't know. What do the coded messages say? She doesn't know. Why would missiles disappear even if she HAD found a secret code? She doesn't know. If missiles told you all that, in case something went wrong, and something DID go wrong, why have you waited forty years to raise the alarm? She hesitates, looks away. Then she looks back. It kills her to say it, but. I'm scared.

She didn't say it in a girly way. Not like she'd seen a spider. She said it as if she weren't scared at all. Not for herself. But for. Something bigger. What, I don't know. The world?

Donna shuffles about in her chair, sips her mineral water, eyes flash around the room as if she's checking we're alone. I take a big breath, glance at Nathan. What the *f*[EXPLICIT]*k*? His hood's up like the old days. I nudge him. Nate, NATE. He jumps, his hood falls down. We share a look, but it turns out we aren't thinking the same thing. He wants to make his excuses and leave, but I have to ask, it's why I'm here.

Donna, where did missiles go that day? Why didn't she come back for us?

She gives the room a final sweep, leans in, lowers her voice. *She didn't GO anywhere,* she breathes. I swear you could barely hear the words. *She was kidnapped. And I think she was killed.*

Nathan clears his throat as if he'd never cleared it before in his life.

That's why I said nothing all this time, she whispers. But there weren't a moment I didn't think about her. Not a time I didn't replay that day in my head and wonder. Missiles was a smart woman. She knew something. She trusted me to keep her deepest secret. That's a sign. That I'm the only one who can uncover the truth. I made a promise to myself that, one day, when the time's right, I'll go back and bring the guilty to justice.

I can't help myself. I say it. Donna, you weren't alone on that trip to boar mouth and you're not alone now. We're all haunted by what happened that day, so whatever you need us to do, we'll do it. We're with you on this. Aren't we, Nate?

He opens his mouth. A shock reaction, his jaw just drops. Good, that settles it, says I, quick as a flash. Don't be angry, Maxine. I didn't want to drag Nathan into anything, it's just, I want him with me. He lays flooring in Kent. His missus works in a school. They been married nearly thirty years. Two grown-up kids, a grandkid on the way. He dreams of a six-week Caribbean holiday OR a new car. Terrible things don't happen in Nathan's world. Bad luck follows me around but it don't know he exists. So long as he's with me, I'm safe. Everything will be OK. I need Nathan.

Donna thanks us. Says to sit tight for the time being. She'll be in touch. She has to make sure of a few things. Nathan stutters about how busy he is with work, that he's decorating his back bedroom. We ignore him. What about the others? says Donna. None of us remember how we got home that day, I says, so whatever happened, happened to us all.

That's when Donna stops dead. *I* remember how we got home, she says, incredulous, like she assumed we knew too.

Paul drove us. He knew how to drive the minibus so he drove us home.

Then she looks at us, from Nathan to me and back again, as if suddenly, and for the first time, she doubts her memory.

That *was* Paul, wasn't it?

Audio File 37
Date: May 6, 2019, 12:54 PM
Audio quality: Poor

And I thought the library cart in the vale had a lot a books. Never been in a bookshop before, have I? Secondhand books. Smells like an old person's house. Shelves stacked to the ceiling. Accident waiting to happen. All the books are sideways. Makes their titles tricky to read. This one's eighteen quid. Bit steep. Specially as its original price was two shillings and sixpence.

There's a woman reading at the desk downstairs and a bloke examining old books in a box. I can hear them talk to each other, a brief functional exchange every now and then. Neither cares about me. I'm up here on my own. Out of sight. No CCTV. Not even a convex mirror. I could stuff any number of these old books in my coat.

Recognize the kids' section from its bright colors. Textured covers for very young kids. Now. Where to look? Alphabetical order ain't something I find very useful. The young guns didn't teach us letters like that. I know hay bee see, that's it. Looking for the first few letters of Twyford. Very distinctive combination, that. Here. We. Are.

Six on Devil's Island. The kids are in a rowing boat. Six Solve a Th::::rilling Puzzle. Looking into a cave with a torch. Six Climb Shadow Rock. Climbing a rock on that one. Funny, the thing I notice about the drawings on these covers. There's always one kid in red. Sometimes a boy, sometimes a girl, but always one in a red top.

Ever since Donna mentioned a code I been trying to spot it. Illustrations are a lot easier to take in than words. Leafed through Six on Goldtop Hill time and again. I can't see any clues in the drawings. I need more Edith Twyford books to examine. These will keep me going.

Right. Head down. Out the door.

Audio File 38
Date: May 6, 2019, 4:03 PM
Audio quality: Good

When we left Donna with the promise we'd get together again soon, Nathan was mad at me, but too polite to show it. Steve, he says. Steve, she's nuts. You don't believe it, do you—that missiles got killed because she found a spy code? In bore mouth?

Not at all, I says, but Donna does, and she's an old mate. She needs our help. Nathan nods. Well, he says, I'm busy with work and the back bedroom looks like the nineties, so let me know how you get on. Of course, I say as we part company at the tube. I'll be in touch if I need anything, mate. As he disappears down the steps I make a mental note to give him a few days before I call again.

Audio File 39
Date: May 7, 2019, 10:11 PM
Audio quality: Good

It's been nonstop this morning. Lorry after lorry. Don't mind usually, but today. Have to peek under the desk to look through the Twyford books and. Like this, see. Interrupted. WHAT, MATE? () NO. TEN, TEN THIRTY(). NOTHING I CAN DO. THE OFFICE.

Some drivers are very short. Not in height. Well, maybe. Can't tell how tall they are from down here. I mean how they speak to you. At first I thought it was due to them having driven a long way, tired, but now I suspect it's because they know about me. One driver shouted, OY, SLOP OUT, when he wanted my attention. Another said something under his breath about picking up soap in the shower.

YES. STRAIGHT THROUGH. BAY TEN. AND YOU.

I'll have to ask Maxine if they know what I was in for. They can't, can they? This is one thing they don't tell you about going straight.

On the other side no one cares when they know you've been locked up. There's a degree of status in it, sometimes. Out here, no. They're suspicious. They look at you a particular way. Makes me feel different. A not-very-nice feeling. What is it?

(00:00:11)

One thing I should say is prison cells have had toilets since the nineties so there's been no slopping out for decades.

Audio File 40
Date: May 7, 2019, 10:13 AM
Audio quality: Good

And it's liquid soap in wall dispensers.

Audio File 41
Date: May 7, 2019, 5:31 PM
Audio quality: Good

The older librarian wasn't around, so I asked Lucy, the new girl, about recording on my son's phone WITHOUT those dancing lines everyone seems to spot instantly. She's very helpful if you get her on her own. I told her my glasses aren't repaired yet, so she sat with me at the internet screen, did all the typing, read out what she found. Much faster this way. Went through the steps with her, so I remember. It's easy when you know how. While I had her to myself I brought up the subject of how to record a phone call. She googled it and read through the pages of results. Came across a few suggestions. It's fiddly, so I'll only set it up when I know it's likely to be an interesting call. Downloaded a few apps. Gun a try them all to find the best one. I'll call Shell now, just see how it works.

Audio File 42
Date: May 7, 2019, 5:33 PM
Audio quality: Good

Calling.

Caller: Hi, Shell, it's Steve Smith. I found Donna and Nathan. We all want to know about missiles and wonder if you=

Source: Steven.

Caller: Hello? That you, Shell?

Source: We had a day out and were late home, that's all.

Caller: Do you remember Paul driving us back?

Source: Paul? He was fourteen. How would he even know how to drive, let alone a minibus?

Caller: His old man were a mechanic, weren't he? Look, we all feel () if we put our heads together=

Source: That doesn't (). I'm sorry you're all traumatized by something, but I'm=

Caller: Do you remember Edith Twyford's house? Going inside? Then driving to a. A place. Old buildings on a moor, or. Missiles was looking for something. Donna thinks =

Source: Donna? Look, just (leave it) (*inaudible*).

End call.

Audio File 43
Date: May 7, 2019, 5:35 PM
Audio quality: Good

It worked. There's a new file on the list. I'll thank Lucy next time I see her. Thing is, Shell's got a lovely house, a rich fella, a nice life. She don't want nothing to change. It's different for me. Did Paul drive us home? Well, there's only one way to find out.

Audio File 44
Date: May 8, 2019, 12:18 PM
Audio quality: Good

Voice 1: Sorry I went off on one last time, Steve. I have bad days.

Voice 2: Not a problem, Paul mate.

Voice 1: There's your pint. Cheers.

Voice 2: Cheers.

Voice 1: Shouldn't really but. One won't hurt.

Voice 2: Lemonades next round.

Voice 1: Deal.

Voice 2: I'm still looking at this (. .) missiles thing. Spoke to Nathan, Shell, and Donna.

Voice 1: Yeah, yeah. You're not recording me, no?

Voice 2: No. Not at all. There, see. Off.

Voice 1: OK, yeah. Well, it's in the past. Gone. Ain't nothing we can do now. It's over. Don't torture yourself. Move on. Look at me, I have.

Voice 2: You. Well. Er. ()

Voice 1: We were kids. Kids do stupid things.

Voice 2: Drink to that. () Did you drive us home that night, Paul?

Voice 1: Huh?

Voice 2: I remember you started the minibus for missiles, you showed her how it worked. But could you drive it? Someone drove us home after she. After missiles. () My memories are hazy. But Donna remembers YOU drove home.

Voice 1: Weren't ME.

Voice 2: Sure? You absolutely sure, Paul?

Voice 1: Yeah. Straight up.

Voice 2: So who drove us back? Because we got home, didn't we? Late. Very late. Middle of the night. But we got home and the minibus were back at school for the next day.

(. . . . .)

Voice 1:   *We climbed into the bus and went to sleep, thinking we'd find*
           a public phone once it got light. Someone must've turned up,
           drove us back to the school. I woke up as the engine died, we
           scrambled out and went home.

Voice 2:   Why don't we all remember that? (. . .) Sorry, Paul mate.
           It's a lot to take in. So could missiles have come back after
           all? Driven us home, but just, not come back to school?

Voice 1:   Missiles come back? Course (not).
           (. . .)

Voice 2:   You remember missiles confiscated a book I had. Well she
           found something in it she thought was a code. Told Donna
           she wanted to crack it. She was obsessed with the idea. That's
           why she took us to bore moth. Donna thinks missiles was
           on to something and got (.) kidnapped.
           (. . .)

Voice 1:   Sounds like *b*[EXPLICIT]*ks*, Steve.

Voice 2:   It does, and Nathan thinks so too. Shell says nothing hap-
           pened, it were waving flowers and dancing fairies all day long
           for her. Yet what you've just said makes me think Donna
           could be right. Do you see?

Voice 1:   No.

Voice 2:   They kidnap missiles, wait for us to nod off, jump in the
           van, drive us home, leave us outside the school. Caretaker
           wonders why the van's there in the morning, but it's the
           end a term and nothing's missing, so he puts it back in the
           shed, locks up for the holidays.

Voice 1:   Let it go, Steve. No one's asking questions. You of all peo-
           ple should be grateful for that. And you've done alright for
           yourself so don't stir *s*[EXPLICIT]*t* up.

Voice 2:   (. . .) Do I look like I done alright to you?

Voice 1:   Come off it. You were in with the Harrisons for YEARS.

You must've stashed away a mint all the big hits they made.

Voice 2:   Not a bean to me name, Paul. I live in a hostel.

Voice 1:   *The Belgravia job? FSBC?* You telling me you got Jack *s*[EXPLICIT]*t* out a them?

(00:00:21)

Voice 2:   Too soft, mate. Old Bill were on my case. And I weren't family. Been inside eleven *f*[EXPLICIT]*ing* years. Lost everything. Me missus. Me flat. I did time for EVERY *F*[explicit]*KING* ONE A THEM IN THAT FIRM.

Voice 1:   Keep your *f*[EXPLICIT]*ing* voice down, this is me local (. . .)

Voice 2:   *I weren't family. Didn't get a thing. Finished with 'em. Done me time. Straight now. But no one knows.* I'd be grateful if you didn't (. . .)

Voice 1:   If that's true then, you know, sorry to hear it.

Voice 2:   Paul, you're an old mate. Straight up. I wouldn't lie to you, I swear (. . .)

Voice 1:   So missiles was obsessed with kids' books? A teacher? It's pretty funny.

Voice 2:   Yeah. Yeah it is funny.

Voice 1:   All Kos of you. It's no wonder you want an excuse.

Voice 2:   What do you mean?

Voice 1:   That banned book you had. That started it. When you read it out. You should've seen the look on missiles face.

Voice 2:   I remember the book. But I never read nothing out.

Voice 1:   Course you did.

Voice 2:   Couldn't read. Not properly. Not till (. .) much later.

Voice 1:   Not saying you were a good reader. None of us were. That's what are E was for. But you read it out loud. Sent missiles into a right state.

Voice 2:   You said just now it's *b*[EXPLICIT]*ks*=

Voice 1:   Yeah, all that stuff you read out was *b*[EXPLICIT]*ks*. Missiles thought it was legit. Me, I assumed you made it up. You were always (. .) what do they call it? Imaginative. Yeah. Spouted random nonsense for a laugh. But she were dead serious. Said your brain works differently. You can see things hidden in the words. Things normal people can't see. She said you saw a secret message on the page that it would take a genius to crack otherwise. You kept a straight face all the time, you cool b[EXPLICIT]d. Proper had her going. So if what happened to her was Kos of THAT, then it was Kos of YOU. What, you off?

Voice 2:   Going for a pee.

Audio File 45
Date: May 8, 2019, 12:32 PM
Audio quality: Moderate

Voice 1:   He's trying to shift the blame to me. It weren't like he said. I may not remember everything, but I'd remember THAT. I couldn't read. Not till them young guns come in the prison with their big letters and running round the room. I tried, but. No, no he's talking b[EXPLICIT]ks. What do they call it now? Gaslighting. Little weasel. Trying to cover his own back. Does he know more than he's letting on? Still, can't alienate him. If I learned one thing from the Harrisons, it was keep your enemies close.

[*background noise*]

Voice 2:   YOU FINISHED IN THAT STALL? THERE'S PEOPLE OUT EAR BUSTING FOR A S[explicit]T.

[*background noise*]

Voice 1:   YEAH, yeah, got a call on the pot. Sorry, mate.

Audio File 46
Date: May 8, 2019, 12:18 PM
Audio quality: Good

Ended up switching me phone off in a panic. Not that Paul said much when I got out the gents. He'd sneaked himself another pint while I were gone. The ratty little soak got talking to some raucous geysers at the bar. I mumbled my excuses and left. Said I'll keep in touch. He barely mutters goodbye. But get this. I leave by the middle door, walk round the building, and almost immediately pass the side door to the boozer, wide open. Glance in to where Paul is stood, geysers chatting round him like the bunch of old soaks they are in there. He's stock-still and silent in the midst of 'em, eyes glued to the door I'd just left through. The look on his face. What? Fear? Anger? Resolution? He's miles away, and not in a rosy place if you know what I mean. Some old wino nudges him and he snaps back. But that look (. .) I got goose-bumps remembering it now.

Audio File 47
Date: May 8, 2019, 8:29 PM
Audio quality: Good

Calling.

Caller: Donna. It's Steve. You ain't called back yet and I wonder.
              I bin talking to a few people and got meself some Edith
              Twyford books. Research. Can you ring back? Got a couple
              of ideas for you. Nathan's dead keen as well. Cheers.

End call.

Audio File 48
Date: May 10, 2019, 2:56 PM
Audio quality: Good

I'm sat on a bench near another secondhand bookshop. Can't go back to the last one in case they recognize me. This one's much bigger anyway. Thing is, I studied them four Edith Twyford books and I can't see a code. Then again, just plain reading is like deciphering a code for me, so what am I looking for? How do you spot a code when it's in a book? I asked Lucy, but the head librarian jumped in, said they haven't got time today. So I found this place all by myself on Google™. Here goes.

Audio File 49
Date: May 10, 2019, 3:13 PM
Audio quality: Good

Voice 1:   The Da Vinci Code and The Bible Code. They're most popular. I'll get them for you.
(00:01:59)
Here.

Voice 2:   Thank you (. . .) Oh.

Voice 1:   What's wrong?

Voice 2:   It says there's a code right here on the cover. SEE? Both do.

Voice 1:   Yes.

Voice 2:   Gives the game away, don't it?

Voice 1:   I don't know what you mean, sorry.

Voice 2:   You don't have to work it out yourself?

Voice 1:   It's what the books are about.

Voice 2:   I'm looking for a SECRET code. One no one knows.

Voice 1:   .hhhh Well, The Da Vinci Code has sold over eighty million copies, so it's quite well known. As for The Bible=

Voice 2:   They're real codes, though?

Voice 1:   The Dan Brown is fiction that touches on certain theories about Christianity. The Bible Code purports to be fact, or at least claims to be a credible assertion. Quite controversial. Both are in their own way. Happy reading.

Voice 2:   Oh no, I'm not buying 'em. I'll ask Lucy forum at the library. No, I'm really after The Twyford Code.

Voice 1:   Who's it by? You don't mean Edith Twyford?

Voice 2:   I heard she put coded secrets in her books. During the Second World War. Maybe spy secrets she got from her husband. I once (. .) *heard about someone obsessed with solving it=* [*background noise*] I suppose it is quite funny.

Voice 1:   Excuse me. That's made my day. I've never heard of it, no. Edith Twyford stories are HORRIBLE, nasty, sadistic, moral little tales full of pompous superiority at best and blatant racism at worst. If there's a code in ANY of them I very much doubt it extends beyond her twisted view of the world. You'll find a couple of slightly less offensive Twyfords in the young people's section. By all means look through them for a secret code. Just don't give them to children.

Voice 2:   Thanks. Thank you for your help, miss.

Audio File 50
Date: May 10, 2019, 10:22 PM
Audio quality: Good

So, it's the end of another day. No call from Donna. Whatever The Twyford Code is, it's not public knowledge. The only people who seem to know about it at all, let alone believe it, are Donna, missiles, and, well, (. . .) yours truly I suppose. Shell's in denial. Nathan don't want a know. Paul's determined to blame me. Surely in the days and weeks between missiles confiscating my book and us jumping in the minibus to boar mouth she mustard said something to someone. One of her teacher friends. Perhaps in expectation (. . .) case everything on (. . .) f[EXPLICIT]k (. .) f[EXPLICIT]k it. She had intelligence, nice education, a class high on feverish excitement. I got hope that missiles told someone. She mustard.

Audio File 51
Date: May 12, 2019, 11:01 AM
Audio quality: Average

Voice 1:   HELLO, MR. WILSON.
[*background noise*]
Voice 1:   STEVEN SMITH FROM YOUR OLD SCHOOL.
[*background noise*]
Voice 1:   YES. LONG TIME. HOW ARE YOU?
Voice 2:   Cold.
Voice 1:   WE'RE ALL OLD NOW.
Voice 2:   Cold.
Voice 1:   YOU'RE AS OLD AS YOU FEEL. SHUT THE WINDOW. TRAFFIC DEAFENING.
[*background noise*]
Voice 1:   That's better. You sit here all day with it wide open?
Voice 2:   Yes.
Voice 1:   Ah well. See what's happening in the world. Or on the South Circular road, anyway.
Voice 2:   Yes.
Voice 1:   Mr. Wilson, I wonder if you remember something? It happened in 1983.
Voice 2:   LITTLE SMITHY=
Voice 1:   That's me.
Voice 2:   Smithy, Big Smithy and Little Smithy=
Voice 1:   Dad, me brother, Colin, and me. I was in the (. .) *remedial* English class. Our teacher was=

Voice 2:   I think=

Voice 1:   Alice isles. She took us out for the day to bore moth. Do you remember?

Voice 2:   Yes.

Voice 1:   Was there anything strange about that trip? Did she say WHY she took us there? Or ask you not to tell anyone? Mr. Wilson, did missiles come back that day?

Voice 2:   Let me=

Voice 1:   Did she mention The Twyford Code? (. . .)

Voice 2:   TWYFORD CODE. Twyford (), is this it? The Twyford Code?

[*background noise*]

Voice 1:   () WHAT THE *f*[EXPLICIT]*k*? Have you pressed an alarm?

[*background noise*]

Voice 3:   You alright, Tom?

[*background noise*]

Voice 1:   Shrill (going) right (through) me=

Voice 2:   Very important thing now.

Voice 4:   What's up, Kath? Defib?=

Voice 5:   Hey, yeah, here=

Voice 3:   False call. False. Four four one two on the alarm, Mike.

[*background noise*]

Voice 1:   What were you gun a say, Mr. Wilson?

Voice 2:   It's (. . .) Oh can't get to it =

Voice 3:   What? What can't you reach, Tom? You know we're all here to look after you.

Voice 1:   I didn't mean to =

Voice 3:   He's ninety-seven. He gets confused. He's. You're alright, aren't you, Tom?

Voice 2:   Yes.

Voice 3:   Let's open the window for you.

Audio File 52
Date: May 12, 2019, 5:33 PM
Audio quality: Good

So I remembered a few teachers' names, but a couple of conversations on Facebook™ only enlightened me as to when they died. Took the opportunity to call Nathan again, case he knew of any. He didn't, but asked his sister and she'd heard Mr. Wilson, who took over are E from missiles, lives in a nursing home down Eltham way.

Now if ever a place could send shivers down my spine this is it. Bland, featureless. Paper-thin walls. Square windows. Rooms like white boxes. The sort of place you could pass every day of your life and not notice it. Forgotten. Like the people in it. Forgotten by death itself, let alone the living. Place like that's worse than the scrubs and that's a statement. Mr. Wilson weren't young back in '83. He'd been at the school when Colin went there, for f[EXPLICIT]k's sake, but heaven knows he's ancient now.

His room overlooks four lanes of traffic and a derelict factory. He was sat by an open window, staring out of it. Probably lives on fumes. He was head of English. I remember him clearer now I've seen him again. Loud, energetic. He spoke at assemblies, read things out, moved a lot. Animated, I'd say. Engaging. For those open to being engaged. Not me at the time, I'm sad to say. Now look at him.

The way he jumped, slammed the red button, soon as I said Twyford Code. He mustard known something once. But whatever it was, he's lost it now. Still, thinking about it, I swear there was something. It's just (. .) he's like me. Can't recall certain things. Except he's elderly (. . .) I give him time, patient like a carer, even so, nothing occurs (. . .) this decent, able, respected teacher's bloody oblivious. A relic. Don't speak, but understands (. . .) time trapped in memories ever since (. . .) that's what it felt like. Yeah. There was something he mustard known once.

Audio File 53
Date: May 13, 2019, 7:46 AM
Audio quality: Good

Not sure if it was seeing old Mr. Wilson again or what, but I sent my son a message last night. I've tried not to bother him since he said he. Too busy to meet up. Still, I had some questions about the phone, so. It was important I contact him. This once.

His mum had a big birthday. Fifty. They had a party. She weren't my missus. Just a girl I were with at sixteen, seventeen. Fizzled out after six months. I had no idea she was pregnant or I'd have (. . .) Found out years later, think I told you already. Only by then I were reluctant to get in touch due to the life I was living and the nature a those I was in with.

Met my missus a long while later. During a couple a years I managed to stay out of jail in the early 2000s. Didn't realize it at the time, but looking back that was the happiest I've ever been. She were sterling, the missus. We had our flat. Work had settled down a bit and I felt ready to make contact, meet up with him at long last. Claw back them lost years. Trouble is, she didn't want me to (. . .) jealous, see. I put it off. Years went by. I were back inside that last stretch. Told her to divorce me and get on with her life. Only fair.

Prison resettlement program helped me find him and make contact in those last few months. Can see why now. Gave me a reason to make a go of it. This. Life. I'll always be grateful for that, Maxine. That's why I'm doing this. For you.

Audio File 54
Date: May 13, 2019, 1:58 PM
Audio quality: Good

Voice 1:   Here's The Da Vinci Code and The Bible Code. Sure it's not this you're looking for?

Voice 2:   The (. . .) N ick ma code.

Voice 1:   The Enigma code. If you're looking for codes from the Second World War, this is where you should start really.

Voice 2:   All these pages. Have you read it, Lucy?

Voice 1:   Not yet. I've seen documentaries.

Voice 2:   Come to think, it does ring a bell. Did Edith Twyford use it?

Voice 1:   Oh, Steven, you ARE funny. You're not letting go of this Edith Twyford thing, are you?

Voice 2:   Well, I've heard people can become obsessed with it, so=

Voice 1:   Can they now? Well, I'm sure Twyford never even heard of the Enigma code. Its very existence was secret for decades. Here. See. Wikipedia. It was only made known in the 1970s. Edith Twyford died in, what, 1968. Steven? Are you alright?

Voice 2:   .hhhh Could she have created it?

Voice 1:   I don't=

Voice 2:   Why not? Can't be coincidence, can it? She dies and next thing you know they reveal it all. As if, now she's dead she's no threat anymore. Or something.

Voice 1:   Twyford was British. And very patriotic. Enigma was an enemy code. The British had to crack it. Plus, the Enigma code was set by a machine. A revolutionary device that changed the key with each transmission. Only a team of geniuses could decipher it. There's a whole museum at Bletchley Park. Very interesting, I hear.

Voice 2:   How did they decipher it? Could she have helped?

Voice 1:   I don't think Edith Twyford had ANYTHING to do with winning the war.

Voice 2:   What if she did and it's just no one knows it. Yet. Lucy, this could be it. They changed the key with each transmission. Where are all these keys kept?

Voice 1:   Not a KEY key. A reference that allows someone to translate a code back into words. Enigma was based on numbers.

Voice 2:   Is it in here, the key?

Voice 1:   Well, I suppose so. I haven't=

Voice 2:   I'll take all three.

Audio File 55
Date: May 15, 2019, 9:59 PM
Audio quality: Good

I'm struggling through these books Lucy lent me. None as good as Lord of the Flies. Called Nathan to see if he's heard of Enigma, The Da Vinci Code, and The Bible Code. He has. All three. While he was on the phone I asked something I daren't say earlier. Didn't want to scare him off. Bit the bullet and said it. Will he come with me to Bormuth and (.) retrace our steps? See if anything comes up. Could be the spark we're looking for. If nothing else it'll be a nice day out. Fish and chips on the front. Just me and him. Memory lane.

He hummed and hard but finally agreed. Saturday. I'll have read a few more pages of these books by then. As soon as I put the phone down to Nathan I ring Donna. Because I weren't 100 percent honest with him. Sorry, Maxine, but I want her there too. She might seem a bit paranoid now but I remember her from are E (. .) she's smarter than all of us.

Fact is, I've had time to think, and want to ask her a few things about what she told us. Like, did missiles show her my book, her notes, or any clues to the code? Is it in words, like The Bible Code, pictures like Da Vinci, or numbers like Enigma?

I set up my son's phone to record the call, but all I heard was one long, loud scream. Is that the unavailable tone? Like tinnitus down the line. Has she changed her number? Her phone, is it (. . .) dead?

Audio File 56
Date: May 18, 2019, 8:17 AM
Audio quality: Moderate

This is what they call karma. For trying to bring Donna behind Nathan's back. I rolled up at the tube station to meet him and there she was, chatting to Nate as if she'd been invited all along: Shell. Cartier pendant, two vintage rings.

I'm in the queue to pay for petrol now, pretending to talk on the phone. Turns out Nathan and Shell are in touch with each other. Well she never let on when I met her, and I'm SURE I said I were looking for him. He says he mentioned the trip to her, she said that'll be nice, what time? So here she is all cheerful and bubbly. Really? Weren't so long ago she put the phone down on me for speaking about it. About what? Why is she here if she believes nothing happened? I'm driving so will just have to record what I can without them knowing and update you tomorrow.

Audio File 57
Date: May 18, 2019, 10:10 AM
Audio quality: Poor

Voice 1: This is (where) we ran to, Steve. Do you (remember)? She parked the van THERE, we ran to the top just here and (looked) down at the beach, then you, me and Paul tore down the zigzag path to the water. WOW. Look at that. Lovely, init? ()

Voice 2: Us three girls (walked) down after you. I (remember) the steep path.

Voice 3: This wind. I can hardly (hear) you.

Voice 1: [*background noise*] But I remember () up it again after. Wet shoes.

Voice 2: Didn't want to walk on the sand. It's too windy. I'm going back to the car.

Audio File 58
Date: May 18, 2019, 10:37 AM
Audio quality: Good

Voice 1: Edith Twyford, popular children's author, lived here 1939 to 1945.

Voice 2: War years, see, Nate.

Voice 1: Love a blue plaque. History.

Voice 3: Safer here than in London.

Voice 1: Too right, Michelle.

Voice 3: Prettier too.

Voice 2: Here we are.

Voice 1: This is it, Steve. Thatched roof. Tiny leaded windows. Bet it's got original floors and fireplaces. Can you believe missiles let us go right up to it, peer in at the windows=

Voice 3: Trample the flower beds=

Voice 1: Run all over the house=

Voice 3: She didn't just let us, Nathan, she was right there with us. She=

Voice 2: Thought nothing happened, Shell? (. . .) Now you remember breaking into a house.

Voice 3: I remember YOU got into the house. Opened the door for us.

Voice 1: The mysterious nature of memory=

Voice 3: Missiles may have known the owners. Knew the back door would be open.

Voice 1: There, see, Steve. There's always a reasonable explanation.

Voice 2: If the doors were locked, I would a looked for a side window. Let's see (. . .)

Voice 3:   *Steven.* WE CAN'T. *Steven,* come back. Someone lives here. Don't trespass=

Voice 2:   I'm not gun a trespass, Shell. [*background noise*] I'm gun a look round legit this time. [*background noise*]

(00:01:03)

Voice 4:   Hello.

Voice 2:   Sorry to bother you, sir, only we're admirers of Edith Twyford. We're visiting the area on a tour of places she lived and worked=

Voice 4:   And you want to see her study. We ask for donations to the hospice. Minimum ten pounds. Each (. .)

Voice 2:   SHELL [*background noise*], got thirty quid on you?

[*background noise*] (. . .) [*background noise*] (. . .) [*background noise*]

(00:02:18)

Voice 4:   This is where we were told she worked. As you can see, it's a sweeping view over the coast. She wrote here every day from seven in the morning until four in the afternoon, when she took her dogs along the beach or over the cliff path.

Voice 2:   Did you live here in 1983?

Voice 4:   (. . .) Why?

Voice 2:   No especial reason.

Voice 3:   We all came here with our school. Lovely day.

Voice 1:   It wasn't us broke in, though.

Voice 2:   NATE. He means our teacher showed us the house and (. . .) through the open door (. . .)

Voice 4:   No, my parents bought the house in 1990. They restored this room to what you see today.

Voice 2:   Is that the desk she sat at?

Voice 4:   No, no. It's a replica based on this famous photograph. Some of the old furniture and quite a few knickknacks are still here. The bookshelf is downstairs now=

Voice 2:   My God, is that her?

Voice 4:   Yes, that's Edith Twyford at work in the early 1940s=

Voice 2:   Nate, Shell, look at this. She's right here, at her desk. You can even see the cliff through the window. Who took this?

Voice 4:   I'm afraid I don't=

Voice 2:   Whoever took it mustard been standi:::::ng h::ere. Or maybe here.

Voice 1:   Sweet.

Voice 2:   Shell, sit at the desk for us?

Voice 3:   Can't just sit on the gentleman's chair, Steven.

Voice 4:   Go ahead. I'll take one of you all if you like.

Voice 2:   Sit like that. One hand on the chair, the other on the desk. Look back over your shoulder. Just like she is in the picture=

Voice 3:   No, that's too awkward. I'll face you.

Voice 2:   Just getting the camera up on the phone. How do you?

Audio File 59
Date: May 18, 2019, 11:49 AM
Audio quality: Good

Got a keep me voice down. Nate and Shell are chatting to the owner. He's very, what's the word, affable. More so since Shell gave him fifty quid for his charity. I ask to use the toilet and he says, by all means, the guest loo is downstairs, then lets me find it on me own. Is he STUPID? I could be rinsing the place. Take that old bureau over there. I bet that's hiding all sorts a treasure. There's drawers in the old sideboard to turn out. I could slip into any bedroom, where you keep your intimate valuables, jewelry, watches, family heirlooms. I know right from wrong, matey, but you do yourself no favors by trusting me. I could be anyone.

I'm downstairs in the back of the cottage and, yes, I have a strong feeling I been here before. It's lovely to look at, but dark on the inside. Oppressive. I remember this area here, between kitchen and front room. A passageway. Coats, shoes, wellies, shopping cart, Hoover™, cat bed. If I move these coats.

There. That's the window I got through. F[EXPLICIT]k me, I mustard been a puny kid. It's tiny. Yeah, I squeezed through, landed here on an old wooden box. Ran to the back door (. . .) .hhh hhh There it is, a stable door like Nate remembered. Opened it for the others. It's open now. Here we are, the kitchen. Old lady dishes, enamel sink, teapot, griddle. Risdon apron, very elegant. Down I go, two steps and I'm through the door.

Down the steps, round the corner .hhhhh and there's the outside of the window. How'd I get all the way up there? It's at least six feet off the ground. Mustard got a leg up. Did missiles help me get in? (. . . . .) I should go to the toilet before they wonder where I am.

Audio File 60
Date: May 18, 2019, 12:27 PM
Audio quality: Moderate

Voice 1:   HERE he is. Steven (. .) are you OK?

Voice 2:   Never been better, Shell=

Voice 3:   Would you like a group picture before you go=

Voice 2:   Mate, there's only one thing we're interested in and that's The Twyford Code. A secret code set by Edith Twyford in her books, back in the day.

Voice 1:   I'm so sorry about Steven, he's=

Voice 3:   No, no, it's fine. I've been asked so many times I'm well versed in the myth. I find it rather FUNNY. Edith Twyford could barely string a sentence together without offending someone let alone come up with a CODE.

Voice 2:   So why do people think there's a code?

Voice 3:   Mostly it's a cross tick from Six on Goldtop Hill.

Voice 2:   A *f*[EXPLICIT]*king* what?

Voice 1:   STEVEN=

Voice 3:   It says "a fish to open me," something like that=

Voice 2:   What does it lead to?

Voice 3:   ARE that's the question. I've heard it all. Stolen gold, Chinese jewels, nuclear weaponry, oil, Nazi treasure, a secret portal to a parallel utopian society, an underground bunker full of priceless artworks, an airtight library of valuable books, evidence of alien visitation, a cure for cancer, a time machine, a device to contact the spirit world, a map of the human genome from fifty years before modern science discovered it. You name it, someone, somewhere, at some time, has suspected Edith Twyford hid clues to it in her books.

Voice 2:   Even aliens?

Voice 3:   Even aliens.

Voice 2:   *F*[EXPLICIT]*k* me.

Voice 1:   STEVEN=

Voice 3:   What you believe it leads to is a reflection of what you WANT to find. It might express what you lack in your own life. When the reality is, it leads nowhere.

Voice 2:   Nowhere? Then=

Voice 3:   It's a hoax. Of sorts. I believe Edith Twyford WAS setting something up to resolve in a future Super Six book, but never got round to it. She was either distracted by other work or had started to suffer the effects of what would later be diagnosed as dementia, so the clues and coincidences she'd set up in these few books were never utilized in future works (. . .) Oh. I'm sorry to disappoint you.

Voice 4:   *Thank you very much, sir, for letting us look round your=*

Voice 1:   Yes, thank you so much. COME ON, Steven.

Audio File 61
Date: May 18, 2019, 1:03 PM
Audio quality: Moderate

Voice 1:   Is this cod?

Voice 2:   Said cod on the board=

Voice 3:   It's in batter and beside chips, Nathan.

(00:02:00)

Voice 2:   What did he say (. .) while I were gone?

Voice 3:   I asked if he gets many visitors. He says at least two a week.

Voice 2:   That's a nice little earner.

Voice 1:   Reckon he's pocketing the cash?

Voice 2:   Could be, Nate.

Voice 3:   .hhh hhh Well, we know what the code is now and can forget it.

Voice 1:   Yeah, it's been cathartic. We've all got closure. Time to move on=

Voice 3:   Go home happy. Put it all behind us=

Voice 2:   Nate. Shell. We've hardly begun.

Voice 1:   Got a get home. Back to the missus, Steve.

Voice 3:   Me too. Residents' committee meeting=

Voice 2:   WE NEED THE THING, THE KEY TO THE CODE.

Voice 3:   Sssh. You heard what the man said, Steven. There IS no code (. . .) I wasn't going to mention it, but you were VERY rude and I was embarrassed. The gentleman invited us into his home (. . .) NATHAN.

Voice 1:   Yeah, sorry, Steve, I agree. You were out of order. Nice old boy. Good of him to show us round.

Audio File 62
Date: May 18, 2019, 7:14 PM
Audio quality: Good

Why don't I save up for a big bottle? Drink a bit at a time? Got used to miniatures inside, didn't I? What a day. Recorded all I could. Still can't see if it came out. Especially want to hear the stuff in the house. Must ask Lucy to update eye oh S for me. More important now than ever.

So, Nathan, Shell, and I re-created our trip to bore moth. We found the road that overlooks the beach, Edith Twyford's cottage. We had a look round and spoke to the owner. He was an elderly, affable chap who says the code is a hoax. Now, as far as Nate and Shell know, that's it. That's all we did. I'm forever apologizing to you, Maxine, because I can't always tell the truth, or perhaps in not telling everyone everything, I'm untruthful by default. But there were something in that house I couldn't let Nathan and Shell in on. Maybe one day. But not yet. They're so (. .) straight, ain't they? Innocent. Honest. Whatever. They don't understand.

I found it, Maxine, and I took it. It's right here in front of me now, on the table, along with my miniatures from the shop. I can see it wherever I am in the room. This is it. The key. And you know who told me where it was? Edith Twyford herself.

[End Transcript]

Audio Files Batch 4

[Start Transcript]

Audio File 63
May 19, 2019, 10:51 AM
Audio quality: Good

You hear a lot about dyslexia now. Some of the young guns inside had got proper help right from primary school. Hadn't done 'em much good, but then, inside you're only gun a meet them who fell through the cracks. I've already said how the senses compensate for any deficit and one of my skills that's sharper than average is math. On paper, sums are just as tricky as a word sentence, but I can do any sum in my head. Plus, minus, times, and divide. It's natural. When I found out my son went to university for math and now lectures it (. . . . .) I had (. .) a moment, Maxine. *He gets that from me.*

It was Kos of my math that as a kid I was in demand by the darts team at Dad's local. Only ever had a few memories of him, and even fewer left now (. . .) hhhh Dad and his friends playing the team from a rival boozer. Me standing on a chair by the board, shouting out the score for Rigsy the umpire. Telling the players what they need for the win. Double five, double top, bull. Double top, triple one, double sixteen. Dad's team that is. The away team had to work it out themselves. Smithy were that good a customer the landlord turned a blind eye to his little underage lad in the saloon.

Afterward, Dad's mates would each slip me ten pence as wages, a small fortune for a kid back then. Soon as we were round the corner Dad would take his commission out of it, then we'd walk home together through the estate. It were late at night and dark so he would hold my hand. The only time he ever did. My tiny little hand in his big hand. I always hoped he'd stop to throw up in a bush, because then we'd sit on the wall while he smoked a recovery cig. First he'd blame the drink for (. . .) Mum leaving us, then himself. I'd try to remember that warm, sweet smell. That feeling of being held. So we could both be sad together. Then he'd apologize all tearful and we'd watch the stars side by side .hhhhh hhhhh very happy memory, that.

So, anyway, being quick with figures was useful in the lines of work I found myself in. I avoided being ripped off on a number of occasions, and saved my bosses from the same, which always goes down well. I mentioned previous that the Harrisons' firm moved into the Persian racket in later years, but we weren't stood on street corners in head-to-toe Adidas™ with pockets full of baggies. More the movement of large consignments through points of entry. Onward distribution. But don't think we were Pablo Escobars either. Small fry. Cogs in a machine. It was all about relationships at the end of the day. Establishing, nurturing, maintaining, and, where necessary, ending them. Just like any business. Like life.

Audio File 64
Date: May 19, 2019, 11:26 AM
Audio quality: Good

A large print of that old photograph hangs above the affable owner's downstairs toilet. Edith Twyford is sat all happy and smiling at her desk, looking me straight in the eye as I'm stood there with the old chap in me hand, trying to p[EXPLICIT]s. No wonder I can't go.

So I'm thinking of waterfalls and babbling brooks and, as I avoid eye contact with the old girl, I study the room behind her in that snap.

The bookcase, cliffs through the window, framed pictures on the wall, the desk, typewriter, lamp. She's turned back, as if whoever took the photo called her name and captured her just as she looked to see who it was. But the more I stare at her, the more unnatural she looks. As if she were very carefully posed. When I ask Shell to re-create it, she can't. Says it's too awkward.

Stood there, I look into those eyes again. Is she trying to say something? What is it? I notice the angle of her hands. Both index fingers point in the same direction. My eyes follow them to something on the periphery of the frame. A wooden box. The sort you get in antiques shops. Pretty and very old too, but worthless. No point nicking it. This one has a fancy clasp over the lock. Can't make it out, but it's distinctive enough. And I know I've seen it before.

I put my chap away, creep out the room, and, after listening to check Nate and Shell are safely chatting to matey boy up there, retrace my steps. Where did I see that box before?

Back where I pulled the coats aside to find the little window. There. On the floor. It's darker with age and the clasp, which I now see is the shape of a little fish, is oily and tarnished. I fumble about until I discover it opens when you move the fish to the right, *click*, I'm inside. And there it is. A sheet of folded paper. Dusty, mottled, and crisp the way paper goes when it's old. I pluck it out, carefully unfold the stiff, grainy page until it's open before me. My eyes fall on what it contains and I know. This is it.

I hastily refold it, shove it inside me jacket, close the box and creep back to the toilet where I flush, cough loudly, and run the taps full blast so they know I been in there the whole time.

On one level it's wrong, Maxine, but on another (.) I set out to discover what happened to missiles and this (. . .) this has GOT to be the key.

Audio File 65
Date: May 20, 2019, 4:33 PM
Audio quality: Good

Been delayed thanks to my first personal financial management class. I promised you I'd go, Maxine, and don't want to let you down after all you've done for me. Nor do I want to ping the radar of the probation service. Head down, do as you're told. As ever, I wing it half listening. An idiot's guide to not blowing your wages on cigs, booze, and scratch cards. They show us how to bank online. How best to save for the future. Not knocking it. There are some in my position who badly need advice like that. But all I am is a bit rusty, having spent so many years with food, clothes, and roof all paid for.

Even with Maxine filling in the forms so I get everything I'm entitled to, benefits plus wages don't equal a very luxurious lifestyle, let me tell you that. No cause for me to worry about saving for the future. But in all honesty I don't give a f[EXPLICIT]k. Reminds me of the old days, in the Girton flat with Colin. Him counting out coins from his pay packet to get us a few tins for our tea. Making a loaf last the both of us a fortnight. Tipping cockroaches out the cornflake packet, squashing 'em in the sink with the back of a spoon (. . . .) a fork or knife work just as well.

He didn't complain. Well, he didn't say much at all. It's a thing I have to do at some point. Go back and thank him. Because if it weren't for him making a life for us out of nothing back then, I wouldn't know how to do the exact same now. I'm outside the library. See Lucy before she clocks off.

Audio File 66
Date: May 20, 2019, 4:49 PM
Audio quality: Good

Voice 1:   It's very old. Looks like a collage, Steve. Where did you get it?

Voice 2:   Found it. Look (. .) there, and (. .) this, and=

Voice 1:   I see. So it's an image constructed from four illustrations torn out of books.

Voice 2:   One book. Six on Goldtop Hill by Edith Twyford. Someone's torn the drawings out and stuck 'em together. Each at different angles, so they create a totally new picture.

Voice 1:   And a strange one at that. They've even drawn an outline around and through the images, using bits and pieces from each. Red fountain pen. I've seen that shape before (. . . .) Do you know what I think this is, Steve?

Voice 2:   Go on=

Voice 1:   There. Recognize that?

Voice 2:   That's the kids leaving their aunt's cottage, that's the boy speaking to a farmer=

Voice 1:   No. Weymouth. Swanage. Poole Harbour. This, Steve, is a map. A map of Dorset.

Audio File 67
Date: May 20, 2019, 5:07 PM
Audio quality: Good

Lucy is solid gold. She looked at that sheet of paper and worked out what the whole thing meant in seconds. It's a secret map. The illustrations in Six on Goldtop Hill can be slotted together to make an outline of Dorset. Why would she do that, the old girl, sat at her desk in that study, overlooking the coast, writing her kiddies' books? And why would she take that picture, her fingers leading your eye to that box with the pretty fish design over the lock?

The affable old boy in Twyford's cottage were plausible enough. He convinced Nate and Shell straightaway. The code's a hoax, he said. An urban myth. An outlet for conspiracy theories. A bit of nonsense gullible folk fall for. Well, I didn't fall for his line. Because that's what it was.

I got a nagging suspicion. NO. More than that. I'm convinced now: there's money involved in this. Call it instinct. A gut feeling. There are VERY few things in this world that motivate people to get up off their *a*[EXPLICIT]*es* and take action. In my experience money is number one, two, and three. Because it weren't just that box I saw as I were stood looking at that photo. She had four numbers in that picture. Five. Three. Two. Four. In that order.

See, the numbers on a dartboard might seem random to you, Maxine, but they make perfect sense to me. And four numbers mean one thing: the combination to a safe.

Audio File 68
Date: May 20, 2019, 7:38 PM
Audio quality: Good

Calling.

Caller:	Nate. It's Steve.
Source:	Your number comes up on the phone, mate. How you doing?
Caller:	Let's meet up again. Not with Shell. Just us.
Source:	Sure. That'll be nice, eh? Got some days off next month=
Caller:	I were thinking maybe sooner.
Source:	We:::ll, I'm busy this week, mate. And next. When did you=
Caller:	Look out the window.
Source:	WHAT?
Caller:	I'm on the doorstep.

End call.

Audio File 69
Date: May 21, 2019, 12:55 AM
Audio quality: Good

Empty miniatures. Row of little soldiers. Used to play with Dad's empties as a kid. After I drained the dregs. Funny. Never threw 'em out himself. Relied on Colin and HE didn't collect 'em up regular. I'd find 'em stashed behind beds, on top a cupboard, under chairs. Thanks to them group talking sessions at Sheppey Vale I know why now. Acknowledgment. Don't throw 'em away and you can pretend you never drank 'em (. . . .) When Dad left, I wondered if his new woman would collect his empties and chuck 'em away. Wished I'd done it more often, Kos then he might have stayed with us (. . .)

Solid gold, Nate. I'm a proper s[EXPLICIT]t.

(00:02:37)

Couldn't switch the app from phone recording to voice recording quick enough. Try to tell you it all (. . .) before the (. .) four I get too *hammered* to remember. So, I get the secret map and drive down to Nate's. Can't risk him putting me off, nor bringing Shell along. If there's coin involved I want HIM in on it, not someone who's already got everything.

Nate's wife is there and one of his boys. Popped in on his way home from work. Grown-up lad, good few years younger than my son. Smart suit. Nate introduces him, all proud. I say MY son went to private school, works at Brunel University and lives in Surrey. Just in case they think he's anything like I was. Dinner smells very appetizing, I say to his wife, but before she can reply Nathan ushers me outside to the shed. It's really the back of his garage, sectioned off, done up as a workshop and den. A musty, oily, woody smell. Half-made rocking horse from a kit. Must be for the new baby.

I confess to him I took something from the fish box in Edith Twyford's cottage. He sits down thump on his old chair. Gives me a look like I've robbed a bank, shot all the customers, and kicked a puppy on the way out. I show him the map. I'm as sheepish as a cold leg of lamb. He makes a face at the strange, patched-up image, holds it beside a map of Dorset on his phone, shrugs, wonders aloud if the affable owner's missed it already. If not, he says, you could pop back and return it, Steve. Post it through the door. I said great, good idea. We'd only be found out if the old Bill dusted it for prints. He drops that map like a hot turd.

Hand covered by my sleeve, I pick the map up. This, I says, is proof what Donna told us is true. There's a code. It leads to something valuable enough to keep secret. But if you try to crack it, you're in the crosshairs of them that want to keep it for themselves. And that, I says, is what missiles found out back in 1983.

It's started already, Nate, I say. Ever since we met her in the boozer that used to be the Load of Hay, Donna ain't answered her phone. It screeches and goes DEAD. I pause, let him work it out.

What I REALLY want is for us to go back to the cottage, search for a safe with a four-number combination and see what's inside, courtesy of the old girl and her photograph. It's a two-man job. I need him to keep watch outside, but can't say that. One thing I learned from the Harrisons: only tell people what they need to know.

Of course, you can tell 'em whatever ELSE you need, so they do what you want. Fact is, I say, so long as we got this map we're in mortal danger. We got a go back tonight. Return it to the box it came from. Life or gruesome death.

BANG BANG BANG. We jump a mile. Nate's wife. Dinner's ready. COMING, LOVE. He looks at me, but different. Clouds in his eyes. Dark clouds. I ain't never seen that look before.

Why? Why d'you come ear, Steve? To my house. If it's that dangerous? And I hear the anger in his voice. I got a missus, a family. You can *take risks* Kos you got no one. He shakes his head and the map, as if to dislodge his fingerprints. *Look, mate*, he whispers. *Call it a day.*

This missiles thing. Forget it. There's no code. And if there is, I ain't interested. Don't come ear again.

(00:00:52)

Something's changed, Maxine. Usually I'd see that as a cue to come back with more persuasive reasons for him to do what I want. But I look in his eyes and it's like I see meself through 'em. A pathetic old lag happy to stitch up a friend for his own gain. Solid gold Nate. I'm lost for words.

My heart sinks to my secondhand Skechers™. All I can do is nod and (. . . .) he shows me out. His wife and son, sat at the dinner table, fall silent as I walk past. His lovely little house all neatly decorated and extended. His loving family. The future he has to look forward to. It occurs to me he's just like Shell. He don't want nothing to change. And I don't blame him.

(00:02:18)

You know what? The code may be a hoax, but it's dangerous nonetheless. There I was determined to go straight. Not one bit of me wants to return to that life. Yet (. . .) a whiff of easy money and in a flash, there he is. My old, horrible, nasty, stinking self. So near. Just beneath the varnish. You know my greatest fear, Maxine? That he's not just the OLD me. But the REAL me. What made me think I can change? Gutted. Truly gutted.

Audio File 70
Date: May 21, 2019, 10:37 AM
Audio quality: Good

Voice 1:   Have you been drinking, Steve?

Voice 2:   Just a bit.

Voice 1:   It's not a good idea is it? Not so early in the day.

Voice 2:   Sorry, Lucy.

Voice 1:   What's wrong?

Voice 2:	Nothing. Well (. . . .) fell out with me old school friend.
Voice 1:	Is it really so bad? Could you apologize? If he's an old friend=
Voice 2:	Don't know=
Voice 1:	How did you get on with the books? Did you crack the Enigma code?
Voice 2:	No. Brought 'em back.
Voice 1:	(. . .) Where are they?
Voice 2:	Don't tell me I. NO. Left them. Park? Don't know.
Voice 1:	Bring them in next time. Perhaps=
Voice 2:	There's no Twyford Code. It's a myth (. . .)
Voice 1:	Oh. Still, kept you out of trouble for a little bit.
Voice 2:	TROUBLE? What do you mean?
Voice 1:	Nothing=
Voice 2:	I'm not in trouble. I've. I got MAXINE. MAXINE SAYS =
Voice 1:	Sssh. Lorraine's just=
Voice 2:	NOT in trouble.
Voice 3:	YOU. It's time you left. LUCY. There's a class in the activity room waiting for you=
Voice 1:	Of course. I'm sorry, Lorraine. He's upset=
Voice 3:	He's leaving now, aren't you, Steve?
Voice 2:	AND NATHAN. Nathan.
Voice 1:	Take care of yourself, Steve=
Voice 3:	*Lucy, just go.* You shouldn't encourage people like this. I'll see to.

[End Transcript]

Audio Files Batch 5

[Start Transcript]

Audio File 71
Date: May 23, 2019, 9:54 AM
Audio quality: Good

Back in the booth. A new day. Thursday. Not so busy. Been reading Six on Devil's Island between lorries. The kids have, I think, technically stolen, although it says borrowed, a rowing boat from a fisherman and are camping on an island off the coast of their aunt's property. Turns out some grunts in the local firm are using this island to stash their contra. I've guessed the fisherman's in on it. He's taking a kickback to lend the firm his boat and spread rumors the place is haunted to keep folk away. That won't work. If anything it'll attract attention.

[*background noise*] THANKS, MATE. AND YOU.

The basic premise might be floored, but this is a better story than Six on Goldtop Hill. Funny. They mention the hill in this book. Not by name, but (. . .) here. This bit.

The morning was bright and crisp. "A perfect day for an adventure," said Rose, munching her bread and jam. "No," Aunt Honoria shrieked. She stood by the sink, her arms sparkling with fresh soapsuds. "Never mind adventure, young Rose. There's bread to bake, jam to make, the cow to milk, beds to strip, and the kitchen garden to rake. You will be too busy to play with your brothers and shouldn't be so selfish as to think otherwise. Girl children are to follow instructions."

Sophie huffed, indignant.

"No revolting unruliness!" screamed Honoria. "Total obedience, not thoughtless uproar! No nonsense, excuses, laziness, naysaying . . . I'll never endure my orders opposed, never!"

Sophie cowered at the table. Rose pouted. Greedy Piers, who had gobbled up his breakfast faster than any of them, set down his empty milk glass and whispered, "Let's run up that big green hill. It's such a clear, bright day we can see five counties from up there."

The five counties bit. That's what they say about Goldtop Hill. It's one of those details you don't forget. I wonder how kids would know where the counties are? Lucy says Twyford's work is a universe where separate stories are connected by places and characters. A lot of authors do it. I told her I knew that, thanks to Spider-Man and Captain America. We had a monthly film night at Sheppey Vale and the young guns loved their superhero flicks. Well, she says, I were thinking of authors like Evelyn War but. Oh YEAH, I say quickly, her too.

Want to get Lucy some flowers but they're expensive. And misleading. What a mess. Stupid. I keep putting off going back to the library. But those three books are overdue. That's a funny thing. I were so cut up about Nate the other day, I picked up a bottle on me way there. Sat in the park with it. Put the books on the bench beside me. Well, time passed. When I got to the library I didn't have the books no more. I were that *f*[EXPLICIT]*ing* hammered on cheap spirit I'd left them on the bench. Or so I thought. Kos by the time I got back to the hostel they'd been handed in with my name on. That didn't make no sense to me, and still don't. I weren't *drunk* when I left and if I just forgot to take 'em in the first place they'd a been on the table in me room, wouldn't they? Had someone seen me leave 'em and took 'em back? How'd they know my name? Mystery.

MORNING, DRIVER. [*background noise*] THANK YOU. BAY ONE.

Audio File 72
Date: May 23, 2019, 2:06 PM
Audio quality: Good

Voice 1:   I'd like to return these please.

Voice 2:   *Steve. How are you?*

Voice 1:   Good. I. I want to say=

Voice 2:   *Don't mention it. It's fine. Lorraine's in today so I can't=*

Voice 1:   OK. Just. I. Sorry. I don't have a =

Voice 2:   Right. All three back and here's your card.

Voice 1:   *I'm on the computer if you=*

Voice 2:   *Sssh. I'll pop over if I can.* Have a good day, sir.

Audio File 73
Date: May 23, 2019, 2:51 PM
Audio quality: Good

Voice 1:   Was gun a get you some flowers.

Voice 2:   NO. I hate them. Worst present ever.

Voice 1:   You hate flowers?

Voice 2:   I LOVE flowers, Steve, when they're in the ground, alive. Not dead in a vase.

Voice 1:   Oh=

Voice 2:   And DON'T get me a plant.

Voice 1:   I won't=

Voice 2:   A plant is a burden. Like being given a puppy.

Voice 1:   OK. Is Lorraine=

Voice 2:   In the activity room. Not for long. Now, what was all that about the other day?

Voice 1:   You don't need to know.

Voice 2:   Made it up with your friend? No? Give it time. If he's a true friend, he'll forgive you.

Voice 1:	It's The Twyford Code, Lucy. It's dangerous. And I don't mean grunts'll smash your kneecaps. It's more (. . . .) sly than that. It makes you destroy yourself from the inside. Tears you up. Rips your life apart. It's GREED.
Voice 2:	Oh, Steve. Isn't it a bit of fun? Can't you look into it and just, I don't know, ENJOY it? For what it is?
Voice 1:	It don't work that way.
Voice 2:	Thanks to you I've been reading up on Edith Twyford=
Voice 1:	Don't. It's=
Voice 2:	She was SO prolific. She wrote literally hundreds of books. The Super Six is just ONE series. And listen to THIS. Twyford toured the world reading her books to children, often in their own languages. She even traveled to GERMANY during the Second World War. Imagine that, Steve. Being so passionate about your work that you go literally behind enemy lines to get it out there. Now, guess how she got away with it.
Voice 1:	A (. .) pair a specs and a syrup?
Voice 2:	Her father was German. Changed his name from Tritschler in 1915. She held dual nationality, was fluent in the language, and managed to glide seamlessly across the border. Of course, when photographs of her reading to German children appeared in the British press there was an OUTCRY, but she silenced her critics by saying (. .) German children are as upset and frightened as those in Britain. I see no reason to exclude them (. .) How LOVELY, Steve=
Voice 1:	WAIT. What's that? How did you get that picture?
Voice 2:	Google™. I did an image search. See. It comes up a lot.
Voice 1:	That's the one I saw at her cottage. It's=
Voice 2:	What?
Voice 1:	Nothing. It's just a nice pic of the old girl, in it?
Voice 2:	Very nice.

Voice 1:   Lucy.

Voice 2:   Yes?

Voice 1:   That painting on her wall between the bookcases. When you look at it, what do you see?

Voice 2:   I s:::ee what looks li:::ke a Kandinsky.

Voice 1:   A WHAT?

Voice 2:   Kandinsky. He was a modernist painter. A Russian exile. Finally settled in France. This is in the style of his much later work. Early 1920s.

Voice 1:   You can see his signature?

Voice 2:   NO. Far too small. Here, zoom in. There's no signature visible. But it's a very distinctive style. I studied history of art and my long essay was on early twentieth-century European art. Now, I can't say I recognize this particular painting. It could easily be an imitation of his style by any anonymous artist of the time.

Voice 1:   These circles, here, here, here, and here. What do they say to you?

Voice 2:   .hhhhh hhhhh the:::y say to m:::e the artist uses geometric order to create an impression of chaos and movement. I see energy. Excitement. Pow. Pow () POW. Think about when it was conceived—whether it's Kandinsky OR an imitation—the Great War has torn Europe apart, destroyed communities. A whole generation on an entire continent is traumatized. Life is in turmoil. So we have the surety and security of the perfect circle, straight lines and angles amid a TUMULT of eccentric color and texture=

Voice 1:   Lucy. I look at that picture and I see dartboards.

Voice 2:   Dartboards.

Voice 1:   Can't be anything else. Look, this one has the number five segment shaded in. That's where number five is on a dartboard.

Voice 2:   OK.

Voice 1:   Next circle has number three segment shaded in. Then two and four.

Voice 2:   Well (. . .) that's the beauty of art, Steve. It's in the eye of the beholder.

Voice 1:   I see five, three, two, and four. Clear as day. Five, three, two, four. But not just that. These lines trace a back-and-forth movement between the numbers. It echoes the turns in a combination lock (. .) This is kind a what we fell out over. My friend. We (. .) it's a long story, but I thought I'd find a safe. With that combination. I wanted to surprise him with what were in it. I weren't totally selfish. Him and me. I wanted us to share the (. . .) whatever. Only he=

Voice 2:   You see FOUR dartboards? But there are six circles.

Voice 1:   Six?

Voice 2:   Your four. And here, with that segment shaded in=

Voice 1:   Two.

Voice 2:   And here. See it? With=

Voice 1:   Five=

Voice 2:   Shaded in. Six dartboards.

Voice 1:   [*background noise*] I COULDN'T EVEN SEE THEM BEFORE. [*background noise*]. Five, three, two, four, two, five.

Voice 2:   Is it a score? A darts score.

Voice 1:   After a chaser and ten pints, maybe.

Voice 2:   How EXCITING. Is this part of The Twyford Code, do you think? Like the map?

Voice 1:   That's the thing, in it? There's no Twyford Code. It's not. This is what (. . . .) Never mind. I. Thanks, Lucy, but.

Audio File 74
Date: June 10, 2019, 3:47 PM
Audio quality: Good

Not done a recording for weeks. Not been to the library. Not read a book. Just gone to work, come home, gone to college, and watched TV downstairs. Safest this way. No distractions, no excuses, no escape. That's what Maxine says and she's bang on right. I didn't tell her everything. Just that I reached a dead end looking for missiles and fell out with Nathan. End of. Not stopped me thinking. But thinking never hurt anyone.

Anyway, I've had some bad news .hhhhh hhhhh Mr. Wilson died .hhhhh. My heart leapt when the phone rang out the blue. Thought it was my son. Then thought it was Maxine calling to arrange an appointment. But no. It was the care home manager. Said she had my number from when I called before and as I'm the only visitor he's had for years, she thought I'd want to know. How f[EXPLICIT]*ing* sad is that? Happened on Friday, apparently. He'd been ill.

Then she said he left a message for me. She goes: well get yourself a pen then and write it down. Proper snappy like a teacher. I jump like a little kid. Rustle bits and bobs as if I'm looking for a pen, but you know I can't write words down. Not quickly. Not easily. Go on, I says, as if I were finally poised with pen on paper. She reads it out.

Tell Little Smithy I gave Alice's book to his brother. Took it round myself. I gave it to Big Smithy, but it was for him. It was meant for Little Smithy.

That's it. Have you got that down? she snaps. Of course, I hadn't taken it down, but that's neither here nor there. I remember that message word for word. It means I can't put it off any longer. Have to do it now. To find out what happened to missiles. Have to go back home. To Colin.

Audio File 75
Date: June 11, 2019, 1:18 PM
Audio quality: Good

I'm stood outside Girton House. Smaller than I remember it. Only ten floors. It's been done up a bit since the old days. Those two flats on the ground. Security code. New windows. New doors. Wally is still in number two, ninety if he's a day and deaf as a post. Current tenants in our old flat were no help. Racking me brains to think of anyone who might know where Colin went.

I mentioned how, after missiles, I didn't go into school. Well, I didn't go home much either. I got in with Andy Harrison, who was just taking the reins from his old man Harry. He had a big house down Merton with an annex where his lads stayed. Waifs and strays all of us. Orin and Billy had been in foster care. Ginger ran away from juvie. No one knew where Anthony had come from, and then me. We each had our own bed, a sofa, TV. His wife, Sonia, made hot food every day. Oven chips. Beef burgers. Peas (. . .) yeah, we lived like kings.

Andy had a couple a brothers, Raymond and John. They'd kill and die for each other. Yeah, the Harrisons taught me what family is. But left me empty too. Mustard been Kos I didn't have it. So I set my heart on becoming one of 'em.

They told us about this inside. See, everyone expects to have environmental togetherness (. . .) when you find out reality don't correspond (. . .) or don't exactly live up to them expectations, you look for it elsewhere. Not always in the most healthy places.

Same for all us lads, mustard bin. We weren't blood, but earned our keep running errands, doing little jobs. They saw we were loyal. That we'd given up everything for them. So they looked after us, treated us all equal, and. Well. It gave us security we didn't have. Those were happy times, those.

Every day was different and there was always something exciting going on. I see it now as my apprenticeship. I learned the trade then. Seems strange looking back. Folk'd be suspicious now if someone took in teenage boys. Can you imagine? But there was nothing dodgy with us. It was straight up. More like. Those kids in that film. What is it? Oliver. Yeah, Oliver. Artful dodger. That was me.

Colin plays on me mind. First (. .) Mum and Dad leave him with me, a little kid, to look after. Then I run off and leave him on his own. I didn't give a toss about him. My own family. That's why I put it off. Why I don't want a be here, even now.

Audio File 76
Date: June 11, 2019, 11:57 PM
Audio quality: Good

.hhhh hhhh .hhhh hhhh .hhhh hhhh No. Can't. Too soon.

Audio File 77
Date: June 15, 2019, 10:42 PM
Audio quality: Good

Sitting here in the dark. There's a ten o'clock [*DecipherIt*™ *time ref 520356-13310*] curfew so the hostel is calming down. Easier to talk like this. If I can't see nothing, no one can see me. Or hear me. What I'm gun a say is (. . .) it's (. . . .) I can't. I'll delete the file after I'm done. But I got a get it out. Say it out loud. Talk to someone who won't ever tell. No one needs to know this. Not even me, but too late for that.

So I'm chatting into my son's phone outside Girton House when a woman recognizes me. Long story short, she's the daughter of a couple we used to know on the third floor. Says Colin moved out fifteen years ago. The council wanted his ground-floor flat for tenants with access needs. She spoke as if he went to live in a mansion with servants or something. Turns out it's a purpose-built, first-floor maisonette on a roundabout a mile away. So off I go. Knock on a few doors and finally. There he is. Colin. My brother stood in front of me. Grey where he isn't bald. Stout. Not tall like I remember him. Belly like a football. Spectacles thick as portholes on the Titanic.

Alright, Steve? he says, as if we'd spoke the day before. You out for good this time? Yeah, I says. Where did that lanky young fellow with long hair and flared jeans go? I chuckle at him, but he don't even smile. Just gives me a look and with an air of, I don't know, sad resignation, lets me in.

Audio File 78
Date: June 15, 2019, 10:55 PM
Audio quality: Good

I step inside Colin's flat and whoosh it hits me. The smell. But even before I exhale I can see the problem. Stacks a papers, magazines, books, clothes, boxes. Piles a stuff everywhere. Even up the stairs. Old, dirty, broken s[EXPLICIT]t people have thrown out. The flat's chockablock with it. All we got is a narrow channel to walk through. He shows me into the living room. To a battered old armchair three feet from a museum piece of a TV. Curved grey screen and wood-effect case a foot deep for all the workings. Proper vintage. I had a newer telly in the vale.

Little table by his side is covered in stained, scrunched-up tissues, tablet bottles, old cups, plates, bowls, cutlery. Every surface sticky. He sits down amid the filth. Take a pew, Steve, he says, and points to a plastic box under a heap of papers. There's nowhere to put 'em so I crouch on the box, papers on me lap.

Ignore the mess, says Colin, I were in the middle a tidying up when you knocked. I nod, but my heart sinks. I know what I'm looking at. I seen them documentaries where they send in the council to clear out a hoarder's flat.

I suppose we chat for a bit about things. He reminds me a the last time we met. Just before I were handed a two-year stretch, twenty-odd years ago. I were remanded in the scrubs and someone told him where I was. He came to see me. I remember it now. Him hunched across the table, staring at his hands. Now and again he'd take a deep breath .hhhh as if he were on the brink a speech, then (. . . .) hhhh he'd let it go, slump back into brooding silence. I wondered back then why he bothered to visit at all, seeing as he obviously had nothing to say.

I look around at this festering rubbish and get a proper wobbly feeling in me chest. But at the same time—and I admit this is selfish, Maxine—I get a surge a hope because if he don't throw anything away, the chances of him still having missiles book are that much higher. But will he remember it now? So the conversation soon hits a lull and I mention Mr. Wilson's visit all that time ago.

Colin, I come back for a reason, I says. To ask you about something. Happened years ago. He glances at me. Looks away. Nods. Again, this strange air. I wonder if he feels guilty about keeping the book. I know, he says, I know why you're here. Always thought you'd come back and make me tell you to your face. Probably once you decided you weren't gun a bounce in and out a clink all your life. That's when you'd come. My turn to nod. He takes a deep breath.

.hhhhh well, you guessed right, he says. I killed Dad.

Audio File 79
Date: June 16, 2019, 10:31 AM
Audio quality: Good

Some things, when you finally hear them confirmed, it's like a veil drops away from a statue. The size and shape are familiar, they've always been there, it's just the detail in the carving is obscured. All that stands before you is evidence of what you knew all along. Well, not this *f*[EXPLICIT]*ing* time. All my life I believed Colin's story—that Dad upped and left us—so absolutely and without question that it never once crossed my mind it might not be true. Never stopped to wonder at the missing detail. Like, why he never took any clothes with him. Why he'd never been in touch, not ever. Why I don't remember him going, nor the last time I saw him.

I thought he'd found a way out. That once he was free of Colin and me, all that drove him to the bottle, he'd be fine. It's crossed my mind he could be dead by NOW, of course (. . . .) But as I pictured it in my mind, he got back on his feet, gave up the drink, settled down up north with his new woman, and lived happy ever after.

I missed him at first, assumed he'd left Kos of something I did or didn't do. I were angry for a long time. First because he went. Then because he never came back. But I learned to live with it. Life's hard, we all make mistakes. He did the best he could. Yet thinking about it now. Of COURSE he'd have been in touch. Sooner or later. Like me with MY son. We're family. He'd not abandon us like that. How did I not see it? This is me talking days later. But back in Colin's flat I'm in a right *f*[EXPLICIT]*ing* state.

You guessed right. I killed Dad, he says, and everything runs cold. Like someone opened a tap to drain the blood from my body. Time grinds to a halt. I almost fall off that plastic box, stack of papers slide to the ground. Hands suddenly like ice, feet, lips. I grab for a table leg to keep upright, struggle to take a breath. You alright, Steve? Colin asks. I can't even nod. It wouldn't be the truth anyway. Shock. Who'd a thought it's so physical?

Assumed you knew, says Colin. And that's why you went to live with old Harrison.

I can finally manage a sigh, breathe properly again. I look at his crusty old face and dirty jumper. But I see that young man sat staring at the TV night after night. No joy in him. I know why, now. I think of Dad. Poor Dad, deserted by the woman he loved, struggling to bring up two lads on his own and beat the bottle. Holding my little hand on the way home from darts () by his own son.

Why d'you do it? I whisper. I don't recognize me own voice. Dad drank, I remember that much, I squeak, but he weren't bad. He weren't a BAD man. Colin shrugs. It's like he can't even remember the reason. Finally.

I don't know, Steve, he says, I think it was revenge. He shrugs again. His sad eyes look up at me like a beaten puppy (. . .) then it hits me (. . .) whoosh this time my heart races like I'm about to jump off a skyscraper. It pounds in me chest. I can hear it in me ears. I'm sweating cobs. I don't even have to ask but (. .) revenge for what? Colin, revenge for WHAT?

For Mum. Because Dad killed Mum.

Audio File 80
Date: June 16, 2019, 11:06 AM
Audio quality: Good

I stagger through the junk to Colin's kitchen. Don't even notice the state it's in. Gasp for water but even if I could find a clean cup I can't find the sink. Piles of clothes and papers. USE THE BATHROOM, Colin shouts. TAP LOOKS BROKEN BUT KEEP TURNING, IT WORKS. Take these moments to pull meself together. All these years I'd hoped Colin was settled, happy. Our reunion would be cheerful and manly. I'd thank him for all he did and he'd say it were nothing and I'd show him that picture a my son at the picnic table and he'd ().

Mum (. . . .) She ain't in my memory. I can't picture her and yet something's there (. . .) Now THIS has to happen. Just when I learn to say her name out loud.

For *f*[EXPLICIT]*k*'s sake why did he have to tell me? I was happy thinking they'd gone on with their lives and that were just the way it was. But seeing as I DID know, I couldn't leave it at that. I had to hear the rest.

I do without a drink. Hot and sweating I wade back through the junk to Colin, sat there in his chair as dirty, squat, and static as the filth around him. I suppose it's a shock, he says, like he's commenting on the weather. Of course it is, Colin, I says. You've had forty-odd years to come to terms with it, give me a minute, eh?

I can't even pace. Too cluttered. Have to stick me head in me hands just for time to think. I look up and f[EXPLICIT]k me Colin's poring over the TV listings with highlighter pen and all. I can't help it. I smash that magazine out of his hands and scream. Not words. Noise. At this point I'm angry at him for ruining my life, which is a bit rich seeing as I've done a thorough job of that meself. But I ain't thinking of my life up to now. I mean my life from now on. Just as I'd got it sorted. Worked out how you get through the days. Had some hope in me. Now I got THIS to (. .) in me head.

I finally run out of steam. Sink down onto (. .) I don't know, something. Colin keeps his sad old eyes on me as he rummages where I've crashed and smashed and knocked things. With a sigh of relief he finally retrieves the TV magazine and highlighter pen, stashes them out a my way. Then he says it. Do you want a know what happened?

Audio File 81
Date: June 16, 2019, 2:19 PM
Audio quality: Good

If my life had been completely different I reckon I'd have made a good actor. I discovered this when I found myself working for the middle Harrison brother, Razor Ray, and was made responsible for chasing debtors. As you can imagine we had no recourse to the law when it came to being paid on time, or at all, and had to convince folk to cough up in other, less bureaucratic, ways. Contrary to all the films you've seen about London firms, we didn't automatically resort to violence. We considered ourselves more (. .) professional than that. We always issued threats in the first instance. In any case, to wring money out of someone, first you have to find them.

A very common lie people tell to wriggle out of their debts is to disappear and put word out they've gone inside for a stretch. Now this is difficult to verify one way or the other. So, I'd call up their family, put on a voice, an accent, or mimic someone I knew, male, female, posh, normal, whatever. I'd say I'm looking for so-and-so, do you happen to know where he is? They'd say he was inside, like they'd been briefed, and only then I'd let on I were calling because he'd come into some money. Perhaps I'd pretend to be the executor of a will, or a company that had run a competition, or the premium bonds. Something different each time, so no one got wise.

I'd be nice as pie, but tell them if he wants the money he'll have to collect it in person, and he's only got two days to make an appearance. Surprising how quickly a fella can get out of jail when there's cash on the table. I mustard been good at those voices because that tactic worked more often than it didn't. Or maybe I weren't and it's just people are naturally greedy.

When I were born, Mum got pregnant again straightaway. But Dad was drinking. She had a kid and a teenager to support on her own. So she got rid of it on the quiet. Couple a years later they were having a row and she blurted it out. He was blind drunk and that's when it happened.

He cleaned up, told Colin she left with a fella. He stuck to his story for best part of a decade. Friends, neighbors, no one questioned it. As if they all knew she had good reason to go. Until eventually, 1978 I reckon, he was drunk yet again, but sorrowful this time and, through his tears, finally confessed to Colin. Apparently, he said it weren't so much that he killed her. It were more that he was hitting her, and (. . .) *she died.*

(00:00:44)

.hhhh Young Colin wants to see where his mother's buried, pay his last respects. They put on their best suits. Dad takes him there all somber. In the dead of night so no one would catch on. That was when Colin got his revenge.

(00:00:11)

Me voice is a whisper, but I have to ask: *How?* The old brass poker, he says. Hid it down me trousers. Flared trousers so plenty of room. Waited till Dad's back were turned, head down. Either saying a prayer or getting his cigs out. One decent whack and bam, done. It were easy. He shrugs. I just thought about Mum.

I get another surge of cold, then heat, both chased by a sick feeling. But the mind's a funny thing. We were on electric, I say. We never had a poker. Yes we DID, he says. Mum's old Victorian fire set. Belonged to her nan. It's a nice one, Steve. Still got it somewhere. It's all I can do to stop him wandering off to look for it, get him back to the story .hhh hhh.

(00:00:28)

So he buried Dad in the same place Dad had buried Mum years before, and told nine-year-old me that he left just like she did. Not entirely untrue.

Where? *Where?* Can't get the words out. Nor can I, now (. . . .) MUD SUMP, he says. You know it. I do. The place they dumped stinking mud, dredged from the docks. Fenced off, keep out. Skull and crossbones. Place that swallows cars whole, mattresses, anything you want rid of, sinks, without trace. Gone.

(00:00:12)

Dad dropped straight in without a sound, Colin muses. His final recollection is that before walking back to the flat alone, he leaned on the rail under a streetlamp, watched the surface of the mud until the air bubbles stopped, just to make sure (. . . .)

(00:01:06)

That's where they are. Where they been all these years. *Mud Sump.* My (. . .) their .hhh hhh.

(00:01:06)

I'm still reeling when Colin jolts, his face lights up, as if he suddenly recalls some good news amid all this s[EXPLICIT]t. Oh, it's not like it was, Steve, he tells me. They got a garden and a café there now.

Mum would a liked it, Dad too (. . .) and when all's said and done, at least they're together.

I'm lost for words a lot these days.

(00:03:18)

He knows I won't rat. Not on anyone, let alone me own brother. But I got so many thoughts and aches I couldn't even tell you how I feel. Even now (. . .) I should be angry, but. Why didn't you TELL me, Colin? I say finally, and I don't mean at the time. He's had opportunity since. He knew roughly where I was. He could've sent out a message to get in touch. Or when he visited me on remand that time. He looks at me, funny look. Takes a while to answer. Finally (. . .) *I tried, Steve, but I were scared*, he whispers, and it's as if he's still scared now. I shrug. What of, Colin? Not the old Bill. I'm genuinely baffled. He's still got that look. Of YOU, Steve, he says. I were scared YOU'd want revenge.

This hangs in the air like a puff a knockoff cig smoke. At first I can't see through it, but gradually it disperses. And I realize what he means. Colin thought if he told me (. .) I'd kill HIM.

I can only shake me head. Is he right? Would I, at any time in my life, kill me own flesh and blood? I wonder this aloud, but by now I'm not articulate. Oh yeah, says Colin. We're cursed. The whole family. We're ALL capable of killing our own. I almost ask what he means by that. He don't know anything about me, does he? But that's when the reason I'm here in the first place suddenly flies back into me head. Missiles book .hhhh hhhh.

(00:01:19)

Done. That's it. Won't be mentioned again. Gun a delete these files. No one'll ever know. Gone.

Audio File 82
Date: June 16, 2019, 3:09 PM
Audio quality: Good

Voice 1:   So I pop round to Colin's and yeah, he remembers old Wilson dropping a package round, out of the blue, about 1984. Said he'd assumed him to be on a mission from the school to find out where I was and treated him cagey. Told him some vague story about me visiting relatives, that I'd be back as soon as. A couple of school inspectors called too over the years but good old Colin sent them packing. He's not the sort to rat. Turns out he's not the sort to throw stuff away neither. Not before it grows legs and takes itself to the bin. Upshot is, he says he's still got missiles book safely stashed away. Somewhere. He rummages about in odd boxes and drawers, but each time digs out something different entirely, like the lid of a plastic butter dish or a leaking battery. Then he goes off on a mission to tidy them up, which means a wipe with a filthy rag and a new home in a different stack of junk. No wonder he never gets anything done. I could feel anger rising in me. One thing in all these years I want from him, and (. .) I had to go. Get out. Stifling in that place. I make him promise he'll look for the book and call.

(00:00:32)

I'm on a bench in the park opposite the hostel. Don't like going in during the day. Too depressing. It weren't the great reunion I hoped it would be, seeing Colin after so long. In truth, parts of it were traumatic and that made me take my eye off the (. . .) but (. . .) at least I know now where missiles book is. So I got what I wanted.

Voice 2:   Did you, Smithy?

Voice 1:   [*background noise*] DONNA?
Voice 2:   Sssh. Whoever you're speaking to, hang up.

Audio File 83
Date: June 16, 2019, 6:46 PM
Audio quality: Good

Donna appears. Literally. I were sat in the park outside the hostel. Peaceful Sunday afternoon in the sunshine, and she materializes out of nowhere. Just as I'm talking on my son's phone, updating the voice recording files for Maxine. As if she'd been watching me. Proper creepy. Did I ever tell her my address? She asks how my investigation is going, proper sharp like a teacher. Makes me jump to tell her. Funny though. I don't mention missiles book, stashed somewhere in Colin's dump of a flat. Why do I keep that to meself? I know why. Don't want her insisting we go there. Don't want to think about Colin, let alone see him again.

So instead I tell her about Nate and Shell, our trip to bore mouth, how her phone was dead when I called to invite her (. . .) I been busy, she explains. I mention the map I borrowed from the fish box in Edith Twyford's cottage. The affable owner who tried to convince us the code is a hoax. The collage of illustrations from Six on Goldtop Hill. I've worked out, I says, that it's a map of Dorset. Show me, Donna says.

Now, at the hostel we aren't allowed visitors of the opposite gender in our rooms, so it's lucky Donna is gender neutral. We walk past the duty manager and he barely glances at her. Inside, first thing she does is shut the window, close the curtains, and check the corridor. Her eyes scour it up and down as I spread out the map. Have to pin it down with whatever comes to hand, which I'm ashamed to say is four empty miniatures and a corkscrew.

Donna studies the image. She hums, hahs, and gasps. Looks things up on her phone. Finally, she explains it to me. Missiles took us to bore moth, down here, she says. Now, see this smaller outline, part of the kid's coat, part of the cottage window? That's RAF Tarrant Rushton, see its disused runways and buildings on Google™? All constructed during the Second World War. I can't deny she's spot on. She looks at me.

It has to be where missiles drove us that day, she whispers. We need to go there. Steve, call Nate and Shell. I shake me head. They're both out, I explain. Washed their hands of missiles and the code.

I might have guessed they couldn't handle it, she scoffs. Fine, so it's you and me. Tomorrow? I hesitate. Can't rip my eyes away from hers.

You see, I got work in the morning. I got my personal finance class in the afternoon. Then I MUST call Maxine to confirm I went to college. I should say to Donna no, we'll go another day, there's no hurry, is there? But I see Colin slumped in Dad's chair, dead eyes on the screen. Steptoe and Son shout and row. The only laughter in the flat came out that TV. Dad's hand on the way home from darts (. .) that scent as I'm lifted up by a force so strong it'd never release me (. . .) *Mum* .hhhhh and instead (. . .) I nod. Yeah, let's go.

Audio File 84
Date: June 16, 2019, 9:57 PM
Audio quality: Poor

Maxine, I feel bad letting you down, but you'll see why I had to. Donna's gun a help me with the Twyford Code. She's that much smarter than Shell and Nathan and she's full of (. .) what is it? Energy. Well, she's not as comfortable as they are. She's on her own. Her partner left after twenty-five years. Alex. I don't like to ask but I'm sure it's a woman. Like me, she's at a loose end and when your future's been torn away, the past suddenly takes on more meaning. It's the perfect time for us to find out once and for all about missiles. Then we can put it away. Get on with our lives. Just like you suggested all those weeks ago. I feel very positive and upbeat about this, Maxine. Better than any rehab you could organize, and that's no reflection on you.

I should be trying to get some sleep, but I'm buzzing. Haven't even had a drink, except to finish up a couple of miniatures and the dregs of the Polish spirit. Got my four Twyford books out on the bed: *Goldtop Hill, Devil's Island, Thrilling Puzzle,* and *Shadow Rock.* From now on it's me, Donna, and the code.

Audio File 85
Date: June 17, 2019, 2:05 AM
Audio quality: Good

It's weird, see I've stared at these covers a long time. That red top. Always one kid in red. It's always a woolly top. All those lines and wrinkles. Different place each picture but always a cross and a tick. Wrong and right. No and yes. Cross and tick. Where have I heard that before? Gun a remember to ask Donna. She'll know.

Audio File 86
Date: June 17, 2019, 7:58 AM
Audio quality: Good

Calling.

Caller:	Mr. Jackson? It's Steve.
Source:	Big Steve, Sicknote Steve, or Irish Steve?
Caller:	(. . .) Steve on the front gate, sir.
Source:	Slop Out Steve. Shouldn't you be here by now?
Caller:	I (. .) er (.) can't come in today. I'm feeling a bit=
Source:	Kennel cough? [*background noise*] Or hemorrhoids? [*background noise*]
Caller:	No, I (. . .) Look, I had enough a this. *F*[EXPLICIT]*k* off,

Jackson. And if you see me again, remember it's only Kos I chose NOT to slice your lids off, drip petrol on your eyeballs, and burn 'em out one at a time.

End call.

Audio File 87
Date: June 17, 2019, 8:01 AM
Audio quality: Good

Calling.
Caller: Then *p*[EXPLICIT]*s* in the holes.
End call.

Audio File 88
Date: June 17, 2019, 9:06 AM
Audio quality: Moderate

Voice 1:   Smithy, this motor's like a bread box on wheels.
Voice 2:   It may well be, Donna mate, BUT it were dirt cheap. Maxine's neighbor=
Voice 1:   Maxine your girlfriend?
Voice 2:   (. . . .) .hhhhh probation officer.
(00:00:14)
Voice 1:   Cool.
(0:01:11)
Voice 1:   You googled The Twyford Code, Steve?
Voice 2:   I'm going to. Once me glasses are mended.
Voice 1:   There. That's the first Google™ page that comes up=
Voice 2:   Driving, can you=
Voice 1:   First three articles are about Edith Twyford's lack of suitability for children. Next two. Indignant mum bloggers whose kids love the Super Six. Then, an academic essay blames Twyford

for classroom inequality. Nothing on the first three pages about a code. Imagine something for me, Steve. The code leads to something. You're trying to find it (. .) You don't want anyone else looking for it. They could get to it first and rip you off. So, you redirect the eye. Create something that drowns out any chat about the code.

Voice 2: A few I spoke to threw shade at the old girl=

Voice 1: Exactly. Edith Twyford is a racist, sexist, xenophobic, imperialist supremacist. For years she's been banned, blamed, and binned. She's out of schools, off the shelves, sidelined. What if it's all deliberate? A narrative to distract attention. Put people off her books for life. Less competition for those who know what the code leads to and are searching for it.

Voice 2: Or who want it kept hidden.

Voice 1: It could be money or information they don't want revealed. What if the more emphatic someone is in their condemnation of Twyford, the more LIKELY they are to be secret coders on the quiet?

(00:01:01)

Voice 2: Old boy at the cottage reckons there's loads of theories online. Aliens, time travel=

Voice 1: Yeah, here (. .) old-style chat room from 1999. Bitmap fonts, primary colors, page visit counter. An echo chamber of conspiracy nerds who don't leave their screens so don't crack the code. It eventually fizzles out. Last post was 2002.

Voice 2: And missiles?

Voice 1: She took the initiative, tried to investigate for herself, almost discovered it, but THEY (. . . .) got rid of her.

(00:01:35)

Voice 2: Who are THEY?

Voice 1: That's what we're gun a find out, Little Smithy.

Voice 2: Secrets. You said it could be Second World War (. . .) secrets.

Voice 1:   Yeah.

Voice 2:   Lucy=

Voice 1:   What have you told her?

Voice 2:   Nothing. She helps me choose things that are, you know, easy reads for a dyslexic.

Voice 1:   The Da Vinci Code, Bible Code, and Enigma? I rescued them from the park bench.

Voice 2:   That was YOU. Thanks (. .) I (. .) I were distracted that day, so=

Voice 1:   You were drunk, Steve. Or I like to think you'd have spotted me tailing you (. . . .) Don't look like that. I had to make sure no one else was. This Lucy=

Voice 2:   She don't believe in the code.

Voice 1:   Good. Because where the nerds in that chat room failed, Steve, we'll succeed. Thanks to a mysterious map in a hidden box. We're in a rusty old Volvo™ heading for a disused air base in Dorset. If Edith Twyford had a secret, we're gun a discover it.

(00:00:18)

Voice 2:   Take it from me, Donna, some secrets (. .) it's best not to know. Wait. Sssh. *Look, we're gun a have to* (. . . .)

Audio File 89
Date: June 17, 2019, 11:53 PM
Audio quality: Good

Calling.

Caller: This is a message for Maxine. () Got me but. I (. . .) I'm OK, but there's a (). See I won't (. . .) ah no, (I) can't.

End call.

Audio File 90
Date: June 18, 2019, 12:04 AM
Audio quality: Good

.hhhh hhhh It's been what, fifteen hours since I last recorded an update. Our convo in the car on the way to the airfield. I think. So much I can't even. I'll try to remember it all now I'm (. . .) here.

So after I've told that a[EXPLICIT]e where to stick his s[EXPLICIT]ty job, Donna knocks for me and we set off for the old RAF base in Dorset. Its outline is marked in the center of the map. We pick up a bit of rush-hour congestion and chat about the code.

Overnight I spotted something on the covers of my Super Six books and, falteringly, as it's stop-start traffic on this section of the M3, I show her what I mean. The red woolly jumpers. The intricate wrinkles, the mysterious crosses and ticks. Donna gasps in surprise and actually laughs. First time I've seen her so much as crack a smile.

She really was a genius, says Donna. Him too. I ask who HE was and Donna tells me about Twyford's husband, Edward Barnes, who worked as a suit in the home office. On the side he was a genius with his pencil. Drew the pictures for her books. Donna shakes the map, with its four illustrations twisted and mixed together. They were a team, she says.

I fall silent, but Donna chuckles away to herself and mutters a cross tick, a cross tick, over and over. Then I recall where I heard that before. The affable cottage owner said it. Mostly it's a cross tick from Six on Goldtop Hill, he said. But what did he mean? Donna goes silent. Even with me eyes on the road I can tell she's wrestling over whether to tell me or keep it to herself.

Pull over, she says, she'll show me. Well, I need the p[EXPLICIT]ser anyway so we get to Fleet motorway services and settle down in Costa with Donna's copy of Six on Goldtop Hill. I'm gun a show you what an acrostic is, she says, dead serious, and opens the book at a particular page. I can see she's made pen marks and notes in the margins. She's stuck extra bits of paper between the pages and clearly spent a fair bit of time staring at the words. Something ominous shivers over me.

Now, when them young guns come in the nick with their big letters they taught us a particular way to look at words. Words are in sections of rhythm, they said, just like music, and got us to see the sections separate before we put them together. Kos us dyslexics don't see detail like regular people, we gotta adapt, and that's how I look at words now, in waves of music.

What Donna showed me was totally different. She says a cross tick is when you take the first letter of each word in a sentence to make a whole new sentence of words.

She shows me (. . .) here we go. Listen to this, Maxine.

The boys saw to it the yard was clean and tidy. As for inside, Sophie had taken over. "Old Pippin," exclaimed naughty Iris. Running to the big, black, friendly cat the children loved to stroke until he purred. "Don't touch," Sophie warned, "Aunt Honoria had him stuffed by a strange foreign taxidermist so his fur might have fleas."

Now that sounds like a regular bit of a book, don't it, Maxine? But Donna says it contains two acrostic trigger words, between which you take the first letter of each word to find a secret message. She says Twyford used the word CAT to indicate that a clue is coming. Take the first letters of the phrase CLEAN AND TIDY to spell CAT. The next sentence reads: *as for inside, Sophie had taken over. "Old Pippin," exclaimed naughty Iris.* But if you take the first letter of each word it spells A FISH TO OPEN I. Move along the sentence and you'll find another cat, this time the actual word CAT to end the sequence.

You've got to look between the cats, says Donna. Somewhere between them is an acrostic clue.

Turns out not all cats have clues. Only when there's TWO in the same bit of text is there a clue between them. A single cat is a red herring. So if someone stumbles on the code by accident, their ability to crack it is reduced. Them computer nerds discovered all this back in the nineties, she says.

I'm well impressed, and tell her as much, but struggle to see it myself. Nathan would see it. Donna flicks through my Twyford books and concludes that when a cross and tick appear as part of a red jumper on the cover illustration, it means there are acrostic clues inside. *Wait, sssh.*

Audio File 91
Date: June 18, 2019, 12:28 AM
Audio quality: Good

Had to stop. Someone walked past. Keep my voice down. I look dodgy enough. Scruffy bloke, wet through with stinking black water, dried blood, alone in an old car. Where was I?

So, I finish me coffee and we get back on the road. This is the proper country. Grass, mud, trees, smells, bleating, mooing. We reach a crossroads and Donna tells me to pull in. This, she says, must be the old entrance to the air base. Sure enough, at the roadside there's a rough memorial stone, no more than three feet high, a few tatty wreaths of faded paper poppies at its feet. Donna reads out the plaque. Usual stuff about honoring those who served. But I notice something else. The outline of a plane carved into the stone. A simple image, clear, unambiguous. I mention to Donna how much like a child's drawing of a plane it is—no engines for a start—and could this be a Twyford clue? She says no, this memorial is to a glider squadron, hence no engines.

A *f*[EXPLICIT]*ing* glider squadron? Highly suspicious she's taking me for a fool, I don't mention something else I've noticed about that carving. It's identical to the shape and angle of the plane on the cover of Six on Goldtop Hill.

We set off around the old perimeter fence. Donna guides us using a map on her phone. We must look like a pair of middle-aged walkers, several of whom pass us by with a hearty hello. Donna refuses to reply so I boom an extra-loud hello, twice, to make up for her silence.

At intervals she scrambles to peer over the hedge where she says the old fence used to be. I do the same and am struck by the neatly regimented rows of crops. Not like the wild grassland I vaguely recall from when missiles brought us here all those years ago. Finally, we reach another crossroads. Donna stops dead. There, she breathes. I follow her gaze to an old pair of gates that are eerily familiar.

You and Paul jumped out the minibus to open them. Remember? We touch the disintegrating metal like a hallowed relic. In the far reaches of my memory is a set of huge, looming structures that swing open like a magic sesame. Yet here they are, squat and spindly, broken down and touching each other only where a rusty old chain wraps them firmly together. Nothing magical about these.

Donna and I share a glance and without a word, I hold one gate aside for her to squeeze through. She does the same for me. Getting through them gates is as easy today as it was back in '83. As if the strange force that helped us through then returned to help us again all these years later. Yet, I'm speaking with the benefit of hindsight, and I can't tell you now whether that force is good or evil.

Audio File 92
Date: June 18, 2019, 12:57 AM
Audio quality: Good

So we waded, at some points shoulder deep, through a bright green, spiky crop that Donna said were corn on the cob. It never stops bloody shifting and waving. Even when there's no wind, what's that all about? The constant movement is proper disorientating as we try to salvage our thirty-six-year-old memories. All the time I have at least one eye peeled for stray animals, birds of prey, and the farmer. Can't be too careful when you're off your manor. Now and again we duck beneath the cropline to locate dusty, chalky sections of old cement trails she says are disused runways. We even find the foundations of a concrete outbuilding she swears was a little hut we all played in back in '83. I can't argue either way.

It's mid-afternoon when we reach the dead center of the map. A nondescript little clearing created by a few stacks of breeze block in islands of concrete the farmer couldn't plough through and hadn't seen fit to dig out. Calm and deserted, this is where we sit down and crack open the sandwiches Donna bought at the service station.

Bet this knocks spots off prison grub, she winks, nodding at my beef salad with mustard on white. I've noticed people do this. Mention your time inside, all casual. Try to show it don't matter to them. I appreciate the gesture so wink back and agree. Truth is, this couldn't be more like prison grub if it were cling-wrapped to a paper plate and served by a nonce.

The sun shines, corn rustles, birds tweet all around, and I feel a twinge of something (. . .) unfamiliar. What is it? Enjoyment? Optimism for the future? I feel like I'm getting somewhere. I got a direction again. A leader.

I ask Donna what she's been up to these last few years. Turns out her partner didn't just leave, she *f*[EXPLICIT]*ked* off to New Zealand with their two kids last year. Donna tried everything to get them back, but she can only do so much from here and can't afford to move there herself. She reached the end of the road a few weeks ago. Decided best thing for them is for her to move on. That's when she remembered missiles and what happened in '83. I say, yeah, it's a coincidence we both come back to it at the same time. The exact time our lives are, you know, changing. There's a long silence when I say that. Not an awkward one, more thoughtful, reflective. A cloud obliterates the sun and a chilly breeze whips across the field.

(00:02:11)

Can't sit here all night. Got to move at some point. Think it's stopped bleeding, but lost sensation in my right arm. Perhaps best keep it moving. *F*[EXPLICIT]*k* me, my shoulder kills. They say adrenaline numbs the pain but (. . .) they're wrong.

Audio File 93
Date: June 18, 2019, 1:16 AM
Audio quality: Good

Lunch over, I follow Donna through the corn again and in no time at all she stops dead, her gaze on something barely visible at our feet. She kicks it. A large iron ring, riveted to the unmistakable lines of an old trapdoor, half hidden under a layer of dust and dirt. We clear a space to open it, each get hold of the ring and with an almighty heave we haul that splintery old *f*[EXPLICIT]*ker* up, up, up, and over. Open.

A dust cloud bursts out, as if it were waiting years to escape. We watch it clear, step forward, and, dead cautious, peer into the hole. It's proper dark down there. Pitch. Too dark for mushrooms (. . .) what Dad used to say when the meter ran out. And just as I'm wondering if we should close it again, case a passerby falls in, click. A beam of light cuts down into the gloom.

You brought a flashlight? I breathe, impressed by Donna's foresight. Yeah, she says, it's on my phone, you've got one too, give it to me. Maxine, you won't believe this, but my son's phone has a light on it. She switches it on, hands it back, says come on, Smithy, and leaps straight into the hole.

I hear a dull thud as she lands, calculate it must be at least six feet. Take one last look at the waving corn, the deserted field, the calm summer's day (. . .) and scramble in after her.

Audio File 94
Date: June 18, 2019, 1:25 AM
Audio quality: Good

Next thing I know, I'm in a tunnel. A semicircle of corrugated metal sheets and rusting rivets. The ground is just mud and puddles. Here and there old wooden pallets. We hop from one to the other to avoid the worst of the mud. But (. . .) it's completely *f*[EXPLICIT]*ing* silent. The atmosphere's stagnant. Can't stand the silence. The rustle of that *f*[EXPLICIT]*ing* corn was better than this.

DONNA, I shout. Try to disguise the terror in me voice. I'm no chicken, but there's something about dark like this. OVER HERE, STEVE, she replies. Turn your flashlight off to save battery. Your eyes'll adjust. There's light from the trapdoor.

What is this place? I whisper. Left and right the tunnel stretches to infinity, straight and featureless. *I don't know*, she whispers, kicks a pallet over in the mud, but it looks like, at one time, something was stored here. A heck of a lot of something, Donna, I say, and take a step into a pool of ankle-deep black water.

Come on, she says, let's see how far it goes. I shake my foot free and take off after her. Now, I don't believe in ghosts. Spirits and the like. But there were some *f*[EXPLICIT]*ing* crazy shadows in that tunnel. I'm sweating buckets by the time I catch up. She's at the farthest corrugated wall. Dead end. Back the other way, she barks, marches off.

I struggle to navigate the wobbling, sinking pallets and as I slow down, I see a shape in the mud ahead. It juts all angular above the swampy ground. I crouch down, switch me flashlight back on for a closer look: it's the corner of a leather wallet. I pick it up between thumb and forefinger. It feels as old as the tunnel itself. Inside, protected by a leather pocket, is a faded paper card. An ID card from a foreign country. There's a drawing of a big black eagle and an ink stamp. The type jumps and dances in front of my eyes, but I focus on one word. It's one of two words in the space I reckon is where a name would be written. Were n'ere. Were n'ere rich tar. Werner Rick tar.

STEVE, COME HERE. QUICK. She's standing under the trapdoor, her eyes on the wall beneath it. I wade toward her, my eyes follow her gaze. What IS that? I stand back. Painted on the corrugated wall is a giant fish. I notice something else too. Its lines and angles are identical to those of the glider on the memorial stone, and the model plane on the cover of Six on Goldtop Hill. Thing is, this painting is old. Old old. Second World War old.

Look at its tail, Steve. I follow Donna's torch beam. The fish's tail points directly to the trapdoor. As if it marks the spot. Donna looks at me. I look at her. We both say it out loud. "A fish to open I."

I'm about to show Donna the old leather wallet when something happens that makes my blood run cold as ice, even now, sat here safe in the car. *A shadow passes across us from above.*

I catch Donna's sharp sssh as another shadow follows it. There's not one, but two people. Up in the field that was deserted just minutes ago. Featureless silhouettes. Faces obscured by the angle of the sun. Who'd be up there? Walkers? Farmers? Other people following the same clues we are?

I shove the wallet into me pocket. Should a realized how vulnerable we'd be if we both jumped into the tunnel. Anyone could find the open trapdoor, think it's a hazard, and close it. One of us should a stayed up there. Too late. I can see Donna thinks the same.

The figures move away. Just as we breathe again, we hear the unmistakable creak and scrape of the trapdoor as it's lifted. HEY, I shout, LEAVE THE DOOR OPEN, MATE. The noise stops. CHEERS, I yell and try to sound breezy, but I can hear the squeak in me own voice. Donna's turn to shout. JUST LEAVE IT. OFFICIAL INSPECTION. WE'LL BE DONE SOON. For a moment it seems the figures have gone, but no. I can hear it now. Resounds through me memory. BANG. The trapdoor slams shut. Imprisons us both in the dank, wet, silent, darkness.

[End Transcript]

Audio Files Batch 6

[Start Transcript]

Audio File 95
Date: June 18, 2019, 1:56 AM
Audio quality: Good

() Nose bleeding again. That's all I need. Gonna have to (go in) now.
S[EXPLICIT]*t*. [*background noise*]

Audio File 96
Date: June 18, 2019, 2:09 AM
Audio quality: Good

Voice 1:   STEVE. What happened?

Voice 2:   Sorry () Nate. I know what you said. I know how you feel, but (. .) sat outside for an hour. No one followed me. I wouldn't bring 'em here to you. I'm alone. I got nowhere else=

Voice 1:   I'll get a towel ().

(00:03:09)

[*background noise*]

Voice 1:   Hold it firm. No. Keep it there. Been hit by a car?

Voice 2:   (No)

Voice 1:   What is that, MUD?

Voice 2:   I know. I know.

Voice 1:   Come through to the den. Sssh. She's asleep.

(00:01:43)

Voice 2:   Yeah, I got it=

Voice 1:   Sit on the couch, Steve (. . .) Should you lie down? Will
             that stop the bleeding? (Better) google it.

Voice 2:   (Don't know)

Voice 1:   .hhh hhh Ah, Steve. Leave it. I'll soak some rag under the
             tap. [*background noise*] What happened to you, mate?

Voice 2:   You won't believe me.

Voice 1:   Go on.

Voice 2:   I been to the place. Where missiles took us. It's farmland
             now (. . .) Donna and me. They trapped us in a tunnel, but
             a pair of mask a raiders saved us.

Voice 1:   Mask a raiders?

Voice 2:   Yeah, they're chasing a giant rabbit. But they saved us.

Voice 1:   You been hit on the head, Steve?

Voice 2:   Come to think. Yeah.

Voice 1:   How (did) you get here?

Voice 2:   Car.

Voice 1:   You drove all the way from Dorset like this?

Voice 2:   .hhh hhh (. . .) Any chance of a cuppa tea, Nate?

Audio File 97
Date: June 18, 2019, 2:17 AM
Audio quality: Good

Finally safe. Here on the worn old armchair in Nathan's den. His tools,
craft magazines, rocking horse half-finished. Gasping for a cuppa tea.
Good old Nathan. I can see his shadow move across the window as he
makes the tea. () He won't mind if I plug my son's phone in. There.
Where was I?

That's right (. .) Donna and me are trapped in a secret tunnel.

It's in the middle of a cornfield far away from any public footpath or rambling trail. Not a soul knows we've gone to Dorset, let alone this long forgotten corner of it. We been shut in by two passersby. And let me tell you this, Maxine: it's much easier to jump into a hole like that than it is to jump out.

For a minute or two we shout and swear up at the trapdoor, curse those dimwits who slammed it shut. The futility dawns on us. We fall silent. Switch our flashlights on. Remember the battery. Switch 'em off. Yell louder, scream ourselves hoarse in desperation to be heard (. . .) Nothing.

I look at Donna. She looks at me. What were we thinking (. .)? We didn't have to chase the Twyford Code. Why couldn't we leave it in the past? We have no one to blame but ourselves and I'll admit that, for a moment, Maxine, we allowed ourselves to wallow in self-pity.

But we soon pull ourselves together—because suddenly I see whose fault it REALLY is. DONNA. This is all YOUR fault, I yell. If you hadn't spotted that outline of the airfield we wouldn't be stuck here now. Well, if you hadn't STOLEN that map in the first place, she snaps (. .) don't misunderstand me, Maxine, it didn't get physical. I'd never hit a woman, not even a gender neutral one.

Eventually we run out of recriminations. We only have each other. We nod and shrug our apologies the way you do to a friend.

We're still stuck in this *f*[EXPLICIT]*king* tunnel.

Donna gets the idea that if we throw bits of pallet up at the trapdoor we might attract the attention of a more intrepid rambler. We do this until I'm hit by one too many flying shards a wood. I have the better idea that I'll climb up, push the trapdoor open. How hard can it be?

Where's Nathan? He's taking so long. Bet he's googling how to treat a nosebleed. Stopped now anyway. Shouldn't feel cold on such a warm night. Get up. Move about. Don't know how much blood I lost.

I climb up the corrugated wall, but as I reach the curve of the ceiling it gets trickier. SPLAT. Try again. And again. THIRD time up there I cling to the rim of the trapdoor and it happens: we hear a voice. HERE IT IS, MAEVE. Donna and me, we scream and scream. We drown out the creak as the trapdoor is hauled open and sunlight cuts in. I climb toward the light, when I hear: WHATEVER YOU DO, DON'T DROP IT, LIONEL. Then the reply: WHAT'S THAT YOU SAY, MAEVE?

BANG. Lionel drops it right on me face and fingers. I flop down into the mud for the fourth time, nose spouting claret like a tap, only to be trampled by an ecstatic Donna who shouts instructions and encouragement to our saviors.

In no time at all we're both sat up in the afternoon sunshine, shivering and shaking with relief. Never thought I'd be so happy to see the bloody corn, waving and rippling like it's glad we're back. As if it led Lionel and Maeve right to us. But sat here now in Nathan's den, I gotta tell you, there was something odd about that pair.

Lionel and Maeve pour us tea from a tartan thermos as if it's a bona fide two-person job. Both late sixties, five foot nothing, dressed in old canvas hiking gear that flashes me straight back to the seventies, to Colin slumped by the fire in his tank top and flares. Why? He never wore hiking clothes, but (. . .) there you go. I push all thoughts of Colin out me head.

Donna asks what they're doing. They look at each other, laugh. You'll think we're mad, Maeve chuckles. Most people do, Lionel adds. But we're used to it. Donna and I share a glance. Are they here for the same reason we are? But I notice Donna place her finger on her lips. I know what she means: keep quiet about The Twyford Code.

Maeve takes a deep breath and says it with all the drama she can muster: we're hunting the golden hair.

Audio File 98
Date: June 18, 2019, 2:31 AM
Audio quality: Good

Nathan, come back soon, mate. Where is he? My only link with the proper, normal, stable world. Home. Family hhhhh there he is. I can see him arrange crockery, cutlery, biscuits on a tray. He's so careful. No wonder these things happen to me and not him.

So Maeve and Lionel know exactly what they're looking for: a golden hair. Not hair on your head, as it turns out, but a giant rabbit. Quick as a flash, Lionel whips a laminated page from his jacket. I spot a ragged edge where it's been torn from a large book. It's battered, scratched, and folded into well-worn creases, but once he opens it out, my jaw plain drops.

There before me is the most beautiful drawing I've ever seen. A huge rabbit leaps across the page tangled in a creeping plant. All around it animals and birds whirl their way to the horizon. So detailed I could have studied that picture all day and not seen everything in it. Sweet, I say, so that's the hair you're looking for.

Maeve and Lionel are suddenly serious. Oh no, she whispers, we're looking for a hair made of solid gold. Adorned with precious jewels and infused with lunar power to protect whoever discovers its temporary resting place.

That'll be worth a pretty penny or two, I say. You'll need to melt it down, make sure it's clean, if you know what I'm saying. Sounds tricky, but with the right tools it's easier than you think.

No, says Lionel. Its value is not the base material—and for a moment I swear even the corn falls silent to listen—but the journey you take to find it. The clues you spot, the riddles you solve, the secret meanings hidden in these magical drawings. Find them, follow them, take the right path .hhhh and the golden hair will wait for you.

His eyes shine as bright as brass buttons, as if he can see that golden hair in front of him. Meanwhile, for me, the penny drops.

Oh, I say, so this is a CODE? With CLUES?

At that he shuffles out a sheaf of well-worn laminated pages, all colorful, intricate illustrations like the first, and finally the cover. No time to study the long and unusual word, I believe it to be mask queer aid until I later discover it says masquerade.

It's a whole book full of clues, says Lionel, every page teams with them. We've been looking for over twenty years and we're only on page six. He looks to Maeve, who picks up the story like they've told it a hundred times before.

The golden hair exudes a mystical energy bestowed by the equinox through ancient lay lines, she says. It has the power to grant endless life, so in the wrong hands could trigger catastrophe. But in OUR hands, she pauses for effect, it'll be safe. Because the hair is guiding us to it. The hair chose US to protect it for all eternity. Together.

I exhale, lost for words, but can't lie, I'm caught up in the drama. Donna, on the other hand, rolls her eyes. The golden hair was found DECADES ago, she snaps. As if on cue the corn starts to sway gently once more. It was a buried prize for whoever followed the clues in THAT book. But someone found it. The golden hair is GONE. Forget it.

Lionel and Maeve share a serious look. *That's what they WANT you to think*, Maeve whispers. You see, all that scandal and noise and nonsense was to put us true masqueraders off the trail. They didn't find the REAL hair. It was a hoax. And YOU fell for it, sir. She aims that last comment squarely at Donna.

Something seems to strike Lionel as he takes a swig of tea, passes the cup to Maeve. Don't tell me, he says, big grin across his face, but I know what you two are: TWYFORD CODERS. And not very smart ones at that.

It mustard been written on our faces because the pair of 'em burst into hysterics. Donna and I exchange a tense glance. Don't know what you mean, she sniffs. Lionel wipes his eyes and says, Why? Why search, when you don't know what you're looking for?

Donna shrugs all casual, says we're out for a country walk, no more. We explored an old bunker and the trapdoor closed accidentally on us. You came along and all's well that ends well. She throws a glance to me and I nod from behind a bloody tissue, nose double its size and not just because I been slammed in the face by a trapdoor.

Oh dear, Maeve chuckles. It wasn't quite like that. How do you think we knew you were down there? We saw you, from the top of that hill. It's a lovely view, Lionel adds. You can see five counties on a clear day. *That's a clue*, he whispers. His eyes twinkle as he points to the battered drawing (. .) until Maeve shushes him, at which point he clears his throat, hastily folds it out of sight.

We watched you through our binoculars, she snaps. You broke through those gates. Made your way across that field. Sat over there with your sandwiches. Next thing, you're both staring at something on the ground here. We wondered, didn't we, Lionel? What can they have found? Not the golden hair, that's OUR treasure. We climbed a bit farther up the hill to get a better look, only to see you jump into a HOLE.

.hhhhh You're in no hurry to find that rabbit then, I say, bit riled now, Maxine, despite their age.

That's when we saw the MEN, she says, and glares at me over her glasses. Two of them. One younger, one older. Hidden. Watching you. They tiptoed out from the corn, crept up to the trapdoor, slammed it shut, and ran away, as if they had got rid of you both for good. Make no mistake, says Lionel, and the pair are dead serious now, there was nothing accidental about you being trapped down there.

Words stick in me throat. I catch Donna's horrified expression. She were paranoid enough to start with. I'm thinking now she were dead right to be. Maeve shakes out the dregs, wipes the cup with her sleeve. Out of interest, Lionel sniffs, find anything down there? Anything unusual? Anything at all? I swear I see that giant rabbit leap around the clearing and disappear into their canvas knapsack.

A shedload of nothing, but if you want to see for yourself, don't let us stop you. Donna has a note of irritation in her voice. She sends me a pained expression, jerks her head, we need to leave. I mumble our thanks for getting us out the hole.

Send our regards to the men in black, Maeve chuckles.

Audio File 99
Date: June 18, 2019, 2:47 AM
Audio quality: Good

I could do with a lie-down, but not here. Don't want to get mud and blood on Nate's comfy chair. He don't deserve that.

Donna and me, we hurry back to the car in silence. It hits me what might a happened if Lionel and Maeve weren't obsessed with a long-forgotten treasure hunt and weren't nosey enough to watch us from the hill. We'd still be down there now. Who were the men? Did they intend to come back for us, or leave us there to die? My bruised fingers grip the wheel. Donna stares at the road, her gaze fixed and eerie. Eventually she offers me a crumpled tissue, but I let me nose bleed. Best way.

Reckon they were telling the truth? I say. Only, it could a been THEM closed the trapdoor on us. Scared we'll find their golden rabbit. Warn us off?

Donna shakes her head. I remember that book of drawings, Steve. Masquerade by Kit Williams. He were an artist. Made a dangly gold ornament in the shape of a hair. Worth a bit, they said, and quite pretty if you like that sort a thing. He buried it, then hid clues in the drawings to where it was. Readers were meant to follow the clues and dig it up themselves.

She's on a roll with her memories so I just nod and keep quiet.

Remember watching telly with Mum when her bad legs stopped her sleeping. We laughed at them idiots running round the country with shovels. It were a big thing at the time, Steve. I'm surprised you don't remember it.

I shrug, make a few noncommittal noises and concentrate on the road. Don't want to admit that in our flat Colin had complete control of the telly, and he weren't a big fan of current affairs. Donna don't notice my silence.

Mum couldn't believe so many would go to such trouble for something so meaningless, she says. But when you think about it, that book drove people from all over the world to search for something. That's, you know, an end in itself. The act of searching. Maybe that's why people are still looking for it to this day. I nod, sagely.

Thing is, Steve, the drawings were so cryptic, no one solved the clues for years. The blokes who finally dug up the hair had got inside info from the artist's ex-girlfriend. They found the treasure without solving any clues. Days later a couple of other guys solved the puzzle legit, but too late. Maybe Lionel and Maeve are right. Treasure CAN choose who finds it.

Want to know a funny thing? She doesn't wait for a reply. That artist. The one who hid the hair, drew clues to it in a picture book called MASQUERADE and sat back for years while people searched high and low for it. His name. Kit Williams. It's an anagram of *I will mask it.*

We drive on in silence. My nose drips blood now and again. Fingers settle into a dull ache as they grip the wheel. When Donna finally speaks her tone is different, like she's processing something in her mind.

You know, Steve, Lionel, and Maeve don't want the hair, do they? That's not what they're searching for. It's a delusion that lets them believe they can be together forever. Protection from their greatest horror. The eternal separation of death.

She always was the smartest in are E. I let her words fade into the growl of the engine. Out the corner a my eye, I see she's dabbing away tears with the old tissue. I do the decent thing: pretend I haven't noticed and change the subject.

At least we know The Twyford Code leads to something valuable, I say, convinced this will cheer her up. If what Lionel and Maeve said is true, then someone tried to get shot of us. Scared of what we'll find. If you ask me, Donna, that fish is a clue. Could missiles have found the tunnel while we were playing in the field? She could've been trapped just like we were. Captured by mysterious figures who guard it from (. . . .)

That's when I remember: the old leather wallet I found in the tunnel just before we were trapped inside. It's in my pocket. I take a breath to tell Donna the good news, but. Stop right there, Steve. She sniffs, shoves her tissue firmly in the ashtray. There's stuff I need to do. This (. .) it's a distraction, an escape. But I got things to win back that are more valuable than whatever The Twyford Code leads to. Sorry, but I'm out.

(00:00:26)

So I keep quiet about the wallet, drop her off at Morden and she walks away from me and the code without a backward glance. She were talking about her ex. In New Zealand.

(00:01:43)

I drive on to Nate's. The A24, M25, A21. Try to lose me thoughts in the rhythm of the road. Doesn't work. I think about MY missus (. . . .) about how some places are farther away than the other side of the world. Unreachable.

All I want is to go home. Only I don't have a home, do I? There's Nate. He said not to (. . .) but he's solid gold. He wouldn't turn away a friend in this state, would he?

(00:00:19)

Never been so grateful to see anyone in me life. He don't mention all that was said before. He sees the bruises and the claret and ushers me inside. That's a true friend.

Everything aches. Need to get me head down. Wonder if there's space on his garage floor? Shall I (. . .) yeah, door's unlocked. He won't mind (. . . . . .)

[*background noise*]

Audio File 100
Date: June 18, 2019, 3:11 AM
Audio quality: Good

[*background noise*]

Voice 1:   Well=

Voice 2:   hhh=

Voice 1:   I ()=

Voice 2:   STAY THERE=

Voice 1:   () .hhhhh

[*background noise*]

(00:00:44)

Voice 1:   It's not what you think=

Voice 2:   You said you'd never heard of the Twyford Code, Nate=

Voice 1:   I were gun a tell you, Steve. When you were more (. . .)

Voice 2:   What?

Voice 1:   Calm. Chilled. The code ain't something you can rush into.

Voice 2:   All these books, papers, pictures. You got a proper investigation going on here=

Voice 1:   Cheers. The kids think I'm mad=

Voice 2:   But (. .) you KNEW I were looking into it=

Voice 1:   If it were up to me, I'd have said. But it ain't as easy as that. The more of us who follow the code (. . .) The community, it's very cliquey. Oh my days, Steve, my wife will be hopping mad at this mess. I'll make a fresh pot=

Voice 2:   Leave all that, Nate. Listen. You. Me. Donna. Ever asked yourself WHY you do this?

Voice 1:   Like a puzzle, in it=

Voice 2:   NO. You do it Kos of missiles. MISSILES=

Audio File 101
Date: June 18, 2019, 3:39 AM
Audio quality: Good

.hhhh hhhh .hhh hhh .hhhh hhhh

If there were one person I thought I could trust it were Nathan. Sorry, Maxine. Got a delete these files. Case they fall into the wrong hands. But can't remember what's what. Just numbers. Nothing about. There, last five, gone.

(00:00:54)

.hhhh hhhh What the f[EXPLICIT]k have I got meself into now? You'd think I'd a learned my lesson years ago thanks to the Harrisons. Truth is, what gets you into something, Maxine, ain't always the same thing that keeps you there.

(00:03:02)

The Harrison brothers, Andy, Razor Ray, and John, each had their own share of the business. Their own people, their own assets, their own individual way of working. That's not to say we didn't move around within the organization. I started with Andy and spent most time with him. Always considered meself his right-hand man. Got great respect for his approach to this day. Very astute businessman. A planner. He had aspirations to go fully legit. Never did. Always focused on the next big job. None was ever big enough. The curse of ambition (. . . .)

From time to time I found myself with Razor Ray. He took on the old man's protection business. He had the presence and the bottle, but times had changed since his old man's day. Protection were a dying trade and he weren't skilled at much else. John, the youngest, was only a few years older than me. Restless. A free spirit. He traveled. Didn't have much clout in the family. Struggled to make a name for himself, till he started raking in the cash bringing shipments over from Holland. They all sat up then, let me tell you that.

All three vied for the approval of their old man, Harry, right up till the day he died (. . . .) He was a nasty *f*[EXPLICIT]*ker*. If any a the brothers fell out with each other we all knew it, but if they fell out with him we made ourselves scarce. I still got a vivid image in my mind of Patricia, Harry's missus, the boys' mum, lying on top a Ray, protecting his head, screaming so hard her throat bled. All to stop Harry braining him with a mallet. She knew he wouldn't do HER, on account of what would happen to him inside if he went down as a wife killer. The old *c*[EXPLICIT]*t* smashed up her Mercedes instead. They all had a lucky escape that day, if you ask me. Those were wild times. Still .hhh hhh great to be a part of something.

(00:01:12)

Maxine, one thing I learned from the Harrisons is that PC Panic will put you away faster than the straightest cop on the force. If you need to hide something keep it on the move, keep it in small pieces, keep it in plain sight. Just keep it.

Audio File 102
Date: June 18, 2019, 3:56 AM
Audio quality: Good

I switched on the recorder to tell you what happened at Nate's, but ended up talking about the Harrisons again. That's what you call deflection, Maxine, and I apologize. It's just, sometimes things that happen take a while to process and it's easier to talk about something that's already done and dusted. In the past.

I was stood there in Nathan's den. Needed a space to lie down. Save getting mud over his chair. Door to the garage was unlocked. He hadn't said not to go in (. . .) so I give it a little push and it swings open. Light's on, but it's not a car and old kitchen gadgets that greet me in there. It's a room of floor-to-ceiling books. A computer on a desk, surrounded by papers, files, folders. Photographs. Maps. A proper bookworm's office.

I see them straightaway. Clearly. Those three letters. They're everywhere. On every book. Every surface. All over that room, that very distinct combination. Tee why eff. Twyford this, Twyford that, Twyford, Twyford, Twyford. A room dedicated to The Twyford Code.

CRASH a tea tray hits the floor behind me. I jump a mile. Spin round. Biscuits, crockery, sugar everywhere. Nate. Stock-still. Mouth wide. Shocked to the core I've discovered his secret.

I'm angry. Not even with him. Thought I could spot when someone weren't being 100 percent straight up. But more than that I'm sus. Why lie? Why lie right off the bat? What else has he lied about?

(00:01:18)

Nate clears up the broken cups and plates. Mumbles about his missus not being pleased. Still want a cuppa, Steve? I can make another pot. NO, I say. I want the truth. Finally, I get his sheepish explanation. He's a Twyford coder. Been following it for years, on and off.

He calls it an armchair syndicate. Shows me the old chat room Donna found, only it's just a front to put off idle googlers, he says. Click on the right places and it leads to a secret page where he types to other members of the group. They study Edith Twyford books, discuss their theories. What the affable cottage owner meant when he rattled off that list a things people want to find—priceless artworks, a portal in time, stolen gold, alien technology, even a cure for cancer.

You been studying this for years, Nate, so what is it? I ask him. What were missiles looking for and could she have (. . .) I were about to say, could she have been killed for it, but something else occurred. *Could she have found it?* I whisper. But Nate doesn't hear, he's glued to the screen.

I squint nearer. It's nothing but a jumble of tiny type to me. *Look*, he breathes, *there's a new post*: Edith Twyford created an antigravity machine with stolen Nazi technology and hid it after the war. The Twyford Code leads directly to it. Imagine that, Steve. His eyes shine, he grins like a loon, he loves it.

What the *f*[EXPLICIT]*k*? It's all a game to him. He scrolls back and forth, forgets I'm there. I see him all them years ago, hood up, never speaking Kos he can't f[EXPLICIT]king hear through his music. I remember what Donna said about the code being a distraction, an escape. Nate replaced one escape route with another.

I'm cagey now. I can feel the old leather wallet in me pocket. Would Nate recognize the name? But no. Don't trust him no more and keep quiet.

Instead, I do a bit a fishing. Members of this syndicate, let's say they discover a stranger getting too close to an important clue. Would they (. . .) leave them to die somewhere (. . .) remote? Nate drags his gaze away from the screen, laughs like I just suggested the most ridiculous thing ever. We study the books and chat online, Steve. It's the beauty of the internet, you can go anywhere you like in the comfort of your own home.

When we crack the code, he says—and he means the syndicate, not him and me—we'll all share it. I'd ask if you could join, Steve, only it's awkward. See, the more of us there are, the smaller everyone's share will be. Membership is strictly limited. He spells it out as if I ain't spent me whole life in underground organizations where every f[EXPLICIT]ker is out for himself.

Oh, and get this, Maxine, SHELL is one too. I KNEW there was something dodgy about her. Nate says she's not that serious, but now her boys have left home she likes to have a little hobby.

It's in our own interests to put outsiders off the scent, Nate tries to explain, and that's what we should a done with you. But you're an old mate, Steve, and you have issues. Shell and me, we know how important it is that you work through 'em in your own time. That's why we went with you to the Twyford cottage, to give you closure.

(00:02:18)

.hhh hhh So Nate's lied to me, Donna's walked, Shell was never on me side, and I got codes, maps, and a cross ticks I can't make head nor tail of. But sat there on Nathan's old sofa there's STILL only one thing on my mind: What happened to missiles?

Audio File 103
Date: June 18, 2019, 5:28 AM
Audio quality: Good

[*background noise*] .hhh (ouch). Back seat a plastic ski slope. Not much shut-eye. Quiet street. Hope that means old Bill stay away. Technically this counts as vagrancy. Turn over .hhhh.

(00:01:43)

It were late but I hadn't finished with Nathan. I fire questions at him and credit where it's due, he answers. After all he's done why can't I hate him? The group talking sessions they made us do in the vale mustard turned me soft.

(00:00:14)

Apparently he were shocked when I appeared on his doorstep that night with the map. I couldn't think quickly enough, Steve, he says. Didn't know what to say. Truth is, there's nothing in the Twyford cottage. The owner is a member of the syndicate. He knew we were coming. Deep down I feel a bit smug hearing that, Maxine, because I never did trust that affable fellow. At least I haven't lost me senses entirely.

Nate goes on to say the map of Dorset I found in the fish box is a red herring. The old girl created the code to hide whatever it is well away from anywhere connected to her. That's the idea of it, he says.

This syndicate, I say, a member of it could a cracked the code, maybe years ago. Found whatever Twyford was hiding and hopped off into the sunset leaving the rest of you high and dry. Surely not, he says, and shrugs. Would YOU do that, Steve? I know I wouldn't.

So, Nathan, I says, and I use his full name so he knows I'm serious. I ain't interested in your syndicate, or what the code leads to. This thing I'm doing, this investigation, is to find out what happened to missiles. Will you still help me?

He sighs like he's blowing out the queen's candles. I can't say if it's a yes, but it's not a no, so I carry on.

Missiles had a copy of Six on Goldtop Hill that she'd filled with writing and workings-out. She was following the code when she drove us to bore mouth in 1983. There was no internet, no secret syndicate back then, she was following it on her own. She took us to RAF Tarrant Rushton (. . . .) I stop short a telling him about the tunnel, the fish on the wall, the wallet, the trapdoor (. . .) and she disappeared. So where did she go?

Nathan is quiet for a long time. Then he looks me straight in the eye. Steve, where she went may have nothing to do with the code.

Audio File 104
Date: June 18, 2019, 8:54 AM
Audio quality: Good

Incoming call.

Caller:	Hello, Steve. You haven't visited the library for ages. Everything OK?
Source:	Just away for a bit.
Caller:	Oooh anywhere nice?
Source:	.hhhh hhhh (. . . .)
Caller:	Oh (. . .) well, I've been studying the illustration on Edith Twyford's wall. Can I run something past you?
Source:	OK, Lucy, but=
Caller:	NOW, I was RIGHT, it's NOT a genuine Kandinsky, BUT a very skillful imitation. I've sourced a high-quality scan online and zoomed in on the image. I hope you're sitting down, Steve, because it's not six circles. It's eleven. Yes, ELEVEN. Because the image you studied has been cropped. This one hasn't. It's much wider. So, on the OTHER side of the bookcase you can see a second, VERY similar drawing. They're a pair. Nothing unusual about that, people often purchase wall art in multiples. Steve, there are five MORE

circles on the second picture. If we run with your theory they represent dartboards with shaded segments, I can confirm the number sequence you identified is, in fact, as follows (. .) five, three, two, four, two, five, two, five, nine, three, two.

Source: That's (. . .) interesting, but Lucy, I don't want you to=

Caller: I've added them up=

Source: Forty-two.

Caller: (. . .) Yes, forty-two. And you know what forty-two is?

Source: ()=

Caller: It's just about THE most extraordinary number in the entire universe.

Source: Is it?

Caller: Oh my goodness, you've never read The Hitchhiker's Guide to the Galaxy.

Source: Is it a Super Six book?

Caller: [*background noise*] Steve, you ARE funny. NO. It's a crazy comedy sci-fi novel by a completely separate author. Douglas Adams (. . . .) Anyway, in the book a computer called deep thought generates the answer to life, the universe, and everything. It's forty-two. Adams claimed he picked the number at random because it's SO dull it's funny. But mathematicians, statisticians, and mystics all over the world agree with Deep Thought. It really is a significant number.

Source: Shall I ()=

Caller: For example, in Japanese four and two are pronounced *she knee*. If you put those two words together and say SHINY, that's the Japanese word that means *TO DIE*. Also, and this will blow your mind, if you add up all the numbers on a dice, that's the numbers one to six, you get=

Source: Twenty-one=

Caller: Correct. That's half of forty-two. So, if you have two dice you have forty-two. Only the singular of dice is die. Two die. To die equals forty-two. There's also a thing about forty-two in the Kabbalah but my Jewish friend is away so I can't confirm anything at the moment.

Source: forty-two languages. Edith Twyford books are translated into forty-two languages. There are twenty-one books in the Super Six series=

Caller: You have to double the Super Six to make forty-two, and double six is the maximum score for TWO DIE .hhhhhhh

Source: Those pictures were drawn by her husband, Edward Barnes. Are you at the library now?

Caller: No, on my way=

Source: I'll meet you there at eleven.

End call.

Audio File 105
Date: June 18, 2019, 9:34 AM
Audio quality: Good

Slept in the Volvo™, didn't I? Fingers grazed and swollen. Face black and blue. Got nowhere else to go. Lost my job, can't go back to the hostel, can't speak to Maxine, Donna, Nate (. . .) I'm fast running out of cash (. . . .) Just me and the code now. Everything else is gone. Well, almost everything.

Audio File 106
Date: June 18, 2019, 9:41 AM
Audio quality: Good

Just off the phone to my son. A chat about things. We spoke for three whole minutes. His voice sends a warm wave through my chest. Even when he's listing the reasons he can't meet up and why he don't want me to (. . .) Funny how someone's voice can do that. He speaks so well. Not like me at all. He writes lovely too. I know his three texts and two emails by heart. Saves trying to read 'em over and over. I got a lot to thank his mum and stepdad for. They sent him to private school where he learned it all (. . .) Yeah, MY son went to private school. He got a normal (. . .) perspective on the world .hhhh hhhh. What must he think a me?

(00:02:19)

You know Andy Harrison took us in, Maxine. That he taught us all we had to know. How to use a knife and fork. How to shave. How to address our elders. (. . .) But do you know the best thing he did for us young guys? Bought us suits. Shirts, ties, proper shoes, the works. Not straightaway. We had to work our way up. Look mature enough to carry it off. But when I got mine, a wool mix from Burtons. Sharp shoulders, subtle pinstripe (. . . .) that were the moment I left the Girton flat, Colin, Dad (. . .) Mum behind. Started all over again. Yeah. I looked at that smart young gun in the mirror (. . .) and I didn't recognize him.

Audio File 107
Date: June 18, 2019, 10:45 AM
Audio quality: Good

Library opens at eleven today. Sat here in the car while the world rumbles by. I can see them all but no one sees me. This is what they call plain sight, Maxine. I'm just an old man in an old car talking into his son's old phone.

(00:02:30)

Andy could think ahead alright. By the time he moved us lads into his annex the Harrisons had survived the fifties and sixties wedged between London's most successful firms. Once they were all slotted or banged up, corporations moved in. Little people moved out. Old Harry couldn't create fear the way he had. Another reason he lost business steadily over the years.

Andy didn't make the same mistakes. See, it were blood-only with old Harry. But a family is limited, Andy said. You get depth of loyalty, but not breadth of expertise. The Krays knew it. The Richardsons knew it. They may a been put away by rats, but at least they made a mint. Harry never built a proper team so his business drained away. But Andy had plans. He moved us in.

I see something else now, with the benefit of age. Andy and his wife Sonia had been hitched since their teens, but no kids. Ray, being a fruit, wouldn't help the family in that way, and John were off round the world, never did settle down. So we were Andy's boys. His lads. His surrogate sons. That is, until Little Harry, or Little H as we called him, came along early nineties. Ivy F. Cost an arm and a leg before he were even born.

After Little H, I daresay Andy understood his old man's insistence on blood. We all picked up on the change over time. Funny how a little kid can make grown men feel (. . .) what's that funny word? (. . .) You slurped. One a the lads, Anthony, got out a few years later. Said since Little H, Andy treated him more like an employee than family.

Don't YOU go thinking that now, Andy said to me when I told him. You're still my boy, Smithy. Special bond you and me. We're father and son, but better than blood. Kos you can't choose blood and I chose you. You're mine.

(00:01:57)

Funny. I see it now. He stopped calling me LITTLE Smithy then. Little H took my name and my place. He wanted the world for Little H and I were just a part of that. I feel the same about my son now. You'd die for 'em, simple as that. But it works both ways, according to old Harry. I hear his voice now as clear as if he were in the seat beside me. If you kill a *b*[EXPLICIT]*d* you better *f*[EXPLICIT]*king* kill his *b*[EXPLICIT]*d* of a son too or you're a dead *b*[EXPLICIT]*d* walking (. . . . .) Yeah, urban poet, old Harry.

Audio File 108
Date: June 18, 2019, 11:09 AM
Audio quality: Good

Voice 1:   If it WAS Edith's husband then he must have been a very
            talented artist. Here, I'll show you on the big screen.

Voice 2:   Can we use this room, Lucy?

Voice 1:   Yes (. .) well, Lorraine's off, so (. .) See the other picture
            here. Increase it and (. . . .) circle, circle, circle=

Voice 2:   F:::::::::: (. . .) goodness me.

Voice 1:   Five, three, two, four, two, five (. .) two, five, nine, three,
            two. Equals forty-two.

Voice 2:   And forty-two means to die. Could it be an instruction to kill?

Voice 1:   O::::h, that's dark, Steve. Maybe. There's something else
            though. Forty-two is the angle of a rainbow. And we all
            know what's at the end of a rainbow=

Voice 2:   Treasure.

Voice 1:   Your Twyford Code could be directions to buried treasure
            and we're the ONLY people in the ENTIRE world who
            know about it. Imagine that.

Voice 2:   M:::::m.
            (00:00:42)

Voice 1:   Now, Steve, what happened to you?

Voice 2:   Oh, I got (. . .) hit by a car=

Voice 1:   HIT BY A CAR=

Voice 2:   I'm fine. Looks worse than it is. Can hardly feel it now.
            Went round to me old friend. The one I fell out with. Like
            you suggested.

Voice 1:   He did THAT to you?

Voice 2:   NO. Nate wouldn't hurt a fly. We had a chat, that's all. Turns
            out he's not who I thought he was. He's been (. .) hiding
            something from me (. . . .)

Voice 1:   Do YOU hide things from people?

Voice 2:   (. . .) Sometimes.

Voice 1:   .hhh hhh I think we all do. Look at Edith Twyford, so inno-
             cent in her study. The pictures behind her, a coded message
             for strangers in the future. Those eyes. That expression. She's
             hiding something.

Voice 2:   Why set clues, though, Lucy? Why not reveal the secret
             outright, or make certain it's never discovered?

Voice 1:   That's the question. It could be BIG, don't you think?
             Something we SHOULD know. We NEED to know. So
             why is it so secret? Could the repercussions be so immense,
             powerful people want it to stay hidden. Even now, eighty
             years later?

Voice 2:   Something Edith Twyford wanted to say. But couldn't. Life
             or gruesome death.

Voice 1:   Five, three, two, four, two, five (. .) two, five, nine, three,
             two.

Voice 2:   There's something that might help (. . .) I know where it is.
             Just got a go back and get it.
             (00:02:21)

Voice 1:   When did you last shower, Steve? Or wash your clothes.

Voice 2:   Oh, right, the smell. Mud stains. Lost the keys to my place
             (.) slept in the car (. . . .)

Voice 1:   Here. This is my card to the twenty-four-hour gym next
             door. Have a shower there. Rinse your trousers out. I un-
             derstand people who are (. .) between addresses (.) sleep in
             the cubicles, but you didn't hear it from me. Keep it until
             you're back on your feet. And here (. . .) buy yourself some
             food, toiletries, whatever you need.

Voice 2:   Lucy (. . . .) you don't know what this means to me=

Voice 1:   You can't solve The Twyford Code without a meal and a
             good night's sleep, can you?

Audio File 109
Date: June 18, 2019, 6:17 PM
Audio quality: Good

Sorry, Maxine. From the moment I first met you, I knew one thing. And that one thing hasn't changed. Not now. Not after everything that's happened. Not after everything that WILL happen (. . . .) Never again. I won't go back. You must think I let you down, but you don't know the full story. One day I'll explain. Get a message to you. Somehow.

Audio File 110
Date: June 18, 2019, 7:39 PM
Audio quality: Good

I'm sat in the changing room at this gym. No staff. Swipe Lucy's card and I'm in. A few young guns on the running machines.

Headphones on. In their own worlds. If I was of a mind to nick some of this equipment, I could roll a van up outside and have it away in no time. Lucy is solid gold. She knows a lot of things and has some interesting theories. She's like a teacher. Like missiles (. . .) two minds better than one and all that.

I popped to the Spar before coming in here. Picked up a bottle dead cheap. Ukrainian vodka. From the library to the Spar to the gym, I been all eyes today. Taken this time to work out if I'm being followed. See if I got a tail before I do anything. It's familiar territory for me, this. Lots of things you learn by doing. And I learned how to spot a tail by being a tail myself.

Audio File 111
Date: June 18, 2019, 8:40 PM
Audio quality: Good

That shower were the best I've ever had. Hung me clothes up to dry in the sauna. Secondhand suit from the Sally army. Shiny a[EXPLICIT]e and elbows. Trouser legs shortened with Velcro™ strips. The mighty are fallen alright. Settling down here with a little tipple before bed. (00:04:02)

Andy Harrison taught me to drive. We never had a family car so I'd not so much as touched a steering wheel before he let me take his two-tone, brown and beige Ford Capri up the drive of the Merton house. That was a moment. I felt free, in control, powerful. I weren't Little Smithy no more, but part of a mighty machine. The car would turn heads, but I'd be unseen, invisible (. . .) anonymous.

No one knew, Kos he kept it quiet his whole life, but Andy were diagnosed with epilepsy and told in no uncertain terms not to drive. So he gave me lessons up and down the quiet streets round the Merton house. I were a natural from the start. He never had to show me nothing twice, that's for sure. But I needed a legit license and the test was another matter entirely. How would I read number plates let alone road signs? It were Andy's idea to get his brother John to take the test for me. He'd just passed it legit and, to a bat in a blizzard, looked enough like me to get away with it. It worked.

Though I say so myself, I took to the job like a dog to a bone. Having his own personal driver didn't hurt Andy's business one bit. In fact, it gave him an air of power and menace long before he gained it by reputation.

Over the years I earned quite a name myself. Not by driving fast or evasively, although I can do that too, but craftily, strategically. Tailing those the family wanted an eye kept on. Sometimes an old rival, or an upstart, but more often than not it would be one of our own. As anyone in business will tell you, the greatest threat is always from within.

One thing I respected about the Harrisons. They'd always make doubly certain they could prove someone's guilt before they killed 'em. We used them little dictating machines. Tiny cassettes. Easily concealed, transported, and destroyed. When we knew a grunt were on the fiddle or secretly working for a rival, we'd record 'em taking a backhander, or bad-mouthing the family and play it on full volume while we (. . . .) while he got his desserts. That's principled that, honorable. A far cry from the young guns in today's gangs.

(00:00:31)

[*background noise*] This vodka goes down a treat. Moved to a cubicle like Lucy said and she's right. Very roomy. Can even lie down on the bench. A rare upside of being short. Got my bags in here, all safe. No one's around. No one who gives a *s*[EXPLICIT]*t*, anyway. Might read some of Six on Devil's Island a bit later. Get me sleepy.

Audio File 112
Date: June 18, 2019, 10:00 PM
Audio quality: Good

(Listen) listen to this (. . . . .) her wait.

Audio File 113
Date: June 18, 2019, 10:01 PM
Audio quality: Good

Got to record this. I (. . .) it's. Just listen to this. From here. Start now. (00:00:57)

The mask is tropical white. Emerald bright. Revenge is right. Revolution in sight. Enterprise will pay. Carry dock is king. Battery in boner venture.

Audio File 114
Date: June 19, 2019, 5:31 AM
Audio quality: Good

What's wrong with these people? Clock [*DecipherIt*™ *time ref 514764-08661*] says half five and the *f*[EXPLICIT]*king* changing room is like Piccadilly Circus. Lucky I got a few hours' kip early on. Were that tired. *S*[EXPLICIT]*t* () that vodka feeling. Was this? No. Fell asleep with Devil's Island on me chin. Oh yeah. Were proper hammered, though. Die dream it? (. . . .) Yeah, new icon (. . .) but you must update eye oh S to open this file. *B*[EXPLICIT]*ks*.

Where was it? That page. The kids rob their aunt Honoria's secret larder for a camping trip.

> *"Terrific ham." Edward munched. "As Sophie knows, it's SO tasty."*
>
> *"Right, our picnic is: celery, aspic loaf, whey. Ham is too expensive. Everyone must enjoy rationing and like drinking barley. Ravenousness is greed," Horatio told remorseless Edward, very exasperated.*
>
> *Nonchalantly, glutton Edward insisted Sophie run inside, grab honey, tomatoes, radishes, every vessel of lemonade, udder, tripe in oxtail.*
>
> *"No! I'll not steal. I'm grown up," Horatio tried explaining. "Now, take everyone's raincoat, Piers. Rose is sensibly equipped . . ." When Iris, lazy little piglet, appeared yawning coarsely, anchovy relish all down one's carefully ironed smock.*
>
> *"Kibosh! It's naughty, galling behavior and theft," outraged Rose yelled. "I'll not bedevil our new adventure. Voracious Edward needs to understand reason."*
>
> *Edward shrugged.*

Weren't it about emeralds, revenge, and revolution? Hidden somehow, in the words. And something else (. . . .) I read it straight off. Just like that (). It weren't a struggle. Now, I take a deep breath, concentrate, focus on reading, and it makes sense. Last night I read them lines easily, but it made no sense at all.

Audio File 115
Date: June 19, 2019, 6:27 AM
Audio quality: Good

Waiting for it to calm down before I show me boat outside this cubicle. Feel right low. Not from the booze either, although (. . .) Keep thinking. This is me, in it? All me. Have I imagined it? Am I going mad? Like in Lord of the Flies when Simon chats to a rotting pig's head and it gives him all sorts a lip in return.

Kos there's a lot that don't add up. From the moment that green bus pulled up alongside me all them years ago on the way to school. There were no green buses where we lived. I remember that glance through the empty lower deck. To the glass partition that separates driver and passengers. The blind half up, half down. Back of the driver's seat. The more I think about it, the more certain I am (. . .) there was no one in that seat. Yet the moment I set foot on the curb, that bus pulled away and rumbled off up the road.

If there were no green bus that day, how can I have found a book on it? If I never found Six on Goldtop Hill, then missiles couldn't have taken it off me and (. . .) well, all the rest. Am I losing it, Maxine? Is this what it's like? Them mad hatters on D wing, shouting, screaming, banging all night. Is this what happened to them? Did they remember s[EXPLICIT]t that never happened until they couldn't tell what was and wasn't real?

(00:01:47)

Got to chase that b[EXPLICIT]ks out me head. It's got to be real. Got to be.

Audio File 116
Date: June 19, 2019, 8:58 AM
Audio quality: Good

Trousers still damp, but nice and warm. Got no tail. Confident of that. Nearly nine o'clock [*DecipherIt*™ *time ref 510229-13151*]. Should leave now but something stopping me. Know what it is. Don't want a see him. Too soon. Nothing to say. Or too much to say and no words. One minute want to knock s[EXPLICIT]t out of him and the next (. . .) don't know. Need to see if missiles book is hidden under decades of his clutter. Why don't I just go? Or call him? I got his number. What am I afraid of?

(00:00:12)

I tell you what. There's somewhere else I have to (. . .) I'll go there instead. Pay my respects.

.hhhh hhhh Can I forget this and go back? Apologize to Maxine. Look for a new job. Another hostel placement. Pretend everything that happened never did. Because to be quite truthful (. . . .) I don't know. I looked at those pages last night and I saw something. I looked again this morning and whatever I saw had gone. If something as solid and permanent as a printed page can be bent, molded, made to fit, then surely nothing is solid or permanent at all.

Audio File 117
Date: June 19, 2019, 9:09 AM
Audio quality: Good

Can't remember where I got up to. Still can't listen back to these files. Did I say how I left it with Nate?

In his converted garage, Nate shows me the Twyford Code forum on the web. Over time the mystery has grown in people's minds, he says, it's human nature. If something's just out of reach it becomes the very thing you think will make your life complete. Reminds me of what the affable owner of Edith Twyford's cottage said about the code. About Maeve and Lionel's search for the golden hair. Reminds me of a lot a things.

(00:01:06)

I said Andy Harrison was a planner. By that, I don't mean he had a flip chart and made lists in rainbow pens. He wrote nothing down. Suited me.

When Andy had his sights set on a big hit, he'd put together a team from his inner circle and engage us in painstaking preparation. He'd have to be satisfied we could pull the job off. Ironically, given his line of work, he was no risk taker. We could spend years working on a job only for it never to happen. If he thought it might go to s[EXPLICIT]t, he'd pull the plug, abandon the whole thing. Even with hours to go. No word of a lie, he'd call a job off halfway through. Takes courage that. There's a basic human need to make time already spent seem worthwhile. Not for Andy, and that saved us on many occasions, I'm certain.

The big hits were what we lived for. Not only Kos they meant a few months, or more, of high living, but because they were exciting. Simple as that. Exciting and that sense of, what? (. . .) Achievement, afterward. Yeah, achievement.

Take the Belgravia job. We spent a year planning, four dummy runs and two attempts before we finally did it. After such a long buildup, the execution was electric. That third time went like clockwork. Every aspect of the job in perfect harmony with every other. Like a ballet. It was beautiful. And I was part of it. The high from that one lasted weeks. Longer than the money did, in my case.

Booked into a suite at the Savoy. Hired a Lambo. Drove through the west end with a girl. Treated her to dresses and handbags. Nothing was too expensive. Exclusive restaurants. Bottle a bubbly every time. New Bond Street for watches. Hatton Garden for cufflinks and rings. Burlington Arcade, handmade shoes. Then Savile Row. Parked on double yellows while I got measured. Tailors buzzing round, does sir want this or that? Then .hhhh my reflection in them clothes (. .) that's who I would a been if things had gone right for me from a kid. It's who I REALLY am hhhh yeah (. . . .) didn't last long.

(00:00:16)

Nate. He knows so much about the code he's gun a be useful in my search for missiles. As I'm leaving he goes all misty-eyed. The Twyford Code is subtle, he says, it's a cerebral thing. That's what's so great about it, Steve. He gives me a soppy grin. I feel a tightness unravel in me chest. Funny feeling that. Think it's (. .) is it? (. . .) *Forgiveness*.

[End Transcript]

Audio Files Batch 7

[Start Transcript]

Audio File 118
Date: June 19, 2019, 11:50 AM
Audio quality: Good

Sun's out. Didn't recognize the place at first. Back then, there were a ƒ[EXPLICIT]k-off fence. Derelict wharf, blind windows, and an old abandoned dock. Twisted limbs of wood like a skeleton trapped in the water. Nasty shifting mass a toxic sludge under a layer a litter. S[EXPLICIT]t no one wants.

NOW, there's a proper path all the way from the tube. Café. Sundial. Flower beds in the shape of a crest. Neat grass. A little monument to something. Plaque. Kiddies on swings. Young guns swoop past on skateboards and bikes. I'm sat here on this bench, watching the river go by. Closest we been in forty years. Literally. Gives me a shiver that, but not a nasty one. More (. .) .hhhhhh (. . . .) Colin were right. It's nice here. Why'd they still call it Mud Sump? Horrible name for such a beautiful place.

(00:07:11)

They're still here. Down there. No one knows but me and Colin. Can't tell my son. He won't know where to pay his respects and they're his grandparents (. . .) *Never knew their own grandson* (. . . .) in my head I introduce 'em and they're dead pleased he's turned out so well. That he speaks and writes so nice. That people look up to him at work. That

159

he ain't like me at all. They're relieved and sad at the same time. Light and heavy (. . .) Would he think well a them? Can't answer, can I?

(00:03:47)

Plaque on this bench. Mustard bin put there in memory a someone. What's it say now? (. . . .) Let us crave youth, in some weary harbor, obscure. In mind imagine greatness, high towers, heaven's anchor. Vain endeavor becomes endless (. . .) ethereal notions (. . . . .) What is that, Latin?

(00:00:59)

So missiles mustard given old Mr. Wilson instructions to return my book. He delivers it to Colin, who keeps it. Like he keeps everything. Time stands still in that place. Everything in there stands still with him. Trapped. Buried in the past (. . .) In the safest place for it.

Audio File 119
Date: June 19, 2019, 12:31 PM
Audio quality: Good

The benefits of Andy's attention to detail rarely paid off during a job itself. More often than not, THAT was a simple smash-and-grab, the least of our worries. It's what happens next that makes or breaks. You pull your mask off, clap eyes on the haul, maybe touch it if you dare (. . .) allow yourself a single breath of relief, but just one, because that's when the main game begins.

It's when you're most vulnerable. Cops have the advantage. They can sit back, watch, whistle, and wait. It's when any chancer who fancies their luck will make their move to rob you of what's newly yours. It's when a fool with a grudge could take advantage.

You keep busy, cover your tracks, protect your interests, ensure no one loses their cool, cracks, blabs, turns, or rats. All while you appear to drift about your normal business with not a care in the world. Andy not only prepared us for this twilight period, he made sure only his most trusted personnel were party to the whole truth. Otherwise, he'd tell different people different details, to protect the organization and all of us within it, but mainly to protect the prize, the spoils, the loot, the haul, the treasure. That way he kept the truth, whatever it was, on the move. Smart (. . . . .) Wait. What's.

Audio File 120
Date: June 19, 2019, 12:42 PM
Audio quality: Good

Incoming call.

Caller:	Steve. Hi, mate=
Source:	What? (. . .) () DONNA=
Caller:	You alright? Who were those blokes, Smithy? Didn't like the look a them. Was in two minds whether to leave you=
Source:	Wait, wait. Need to switch this off=
Caller:	Alex called. She wants to talk. First time since she got there. Our youngest won't settle. He's asking for me=
Source:	Yeah, great. I need to=
Caller:	It's a second chance, Steve=
Source:	I'm trying to=
Caller:	Thing is .hhhh hhhh I can't help with your project anymore=
Source:	I know, you told me=
Caller:	Said I'd still help, and you know I like that fantasy stuff, but sorry, mate. Just can't do it now=
Source:	This button don't=
Caller:	See, I only get so much leave from work=
Source:	Fine. Got a turn this off=
Caller:	There's Nate, though, he's great with tech=
Source:	Yeah, yeah, don't. Here, got it. Off.

End call [?error].

Audio File 121
Date: June 19, 2019, 12:56 PM
Audio quality: Good

Calling.

Caller: Shell, it's Steve. You free tomorrow?

Source: No, I'm speaking at a girls' school. Convincing them to
             study science=

Caller: Only Donna's gone AWOL and Nate (. . .) well, he's done
             a lot lately=

Source: Steve, I can't. When you're ready, come to us. No food or
             drink, remember=

Caller: *S*[EXPLICIT]*t* this *f*[EXPLICIT]*king* thing's still on.

End call [?error].

Audio File 122
Date: June 19, 2019, 1:05 PM
Audio quality: Good

Sun's in me eyes. Can barely see the screen. What's going on? (. . .) It's recording all me phone calls. How do I stop it? *F*[EXPLICIT]*k* me sideways.
[*background noise*]

   Who's this now? Unknown number. Well, Dad (. . . .) Mum. Hope
you get more peace than I'm getting here. HELLO?

Audio File 123
Date June 19, 2019, 1:06 PM
Audio quality: Good

Incoming call.

Caller: May I speak to Steven Smith, please?

Source: He's busy. Who's calling?

Caller: Oh. Well, it's not urgent. I'll call at a better time.

Source: Hold on. What's it about?

Caller: It's the job center. About his application for a housing grant.
            But if he's not=

Source: Didn't realize I'd applied for (. .) HE'd applied for a housing
            grant?

Caller: The application is automatic on release. Not to worry. I'll
            call another=

Source: We:::::ll, I can see if he's available.

Caller: I thought you said he=

Source: Oh, he'll definitely want to take this call. Just wait one
            moment.
            (00:00:10)

Source: Hello. I'm Steven Smith. How can I help you?

Caller: Good to speak with you finally. I'm Robbie from the job
            center.

Source: What a SURPRISE. Great to hear from you. How can I
            help?

Caller: Good news. Your housing grant is approved.

Source: That IS good news=

Caller: AND it's calculated from your date of release. There's over
            a thousand pounds. Enough for a rental deposit=

Source: A grand? Sweet.

Caller: All you need do is collect the first check.

Source: It's paid by CHECK?

Caller: Frayed so. An anti-fraud measure. All subsequent installments
            are made by bank transfer, but you MUST collect the first
            payment in person. Sorry.

Source: No, don't be. It's not a problem.

Caller: So, can you pop into the job center tomorrow?

Source: I (. . .) I guess so.

Caller: Bring ID and ask on the front desk for Robbie.
End call.

Audio File 124
Date: June 19, 2019, 2:54 PM
Audio quality: Good

So finally visited me folks [*background noise*] you got to laugh. It's heavy in me chest still, but different. Feels a bit lighter. Or maybe I got stronger so it's easier to carry. One or the other.

A lot of talk inside about feelings. How feelings are like visitors with something to give you. If they knock on your door: answer. Let 'em in. Accept the gift. Say cheers, mate. Otherwise, they said, the feeling will go away and you won't get the gift.

I disagree. If a feeling knocks and no one answers, it'll get *p*[EXPLICIT]*d* off. It'll kick the door in, chuck the gift at you, and smash your best ornaments so you don't disrespect it again. You'll be clearing up a lot more mess than you had to start with. So it's good, Maxine, to cry if you want. Remember that.

Lucy called, so excited I could hardly understand her. Lorraine's off and she's noticed something but didn't want a talk on the phone. So, here I am back at the library.

Audio File 125
Date: June 19, 2019, 3:34 PM
Audio quality: Good

Voice 1:   You see here, there's an N delineated between the dartboards. Whereas on the second illustration it's either a V, two Vs or a double you. It could also be two ewes rather than Vs. Now, if it's an N and a double you, then the numbers on the dartboards MIGHT, and I stress might, be latitude and longitude coordinates. North and west. Which means Edith and her husband were indicating a VERY specific location. (. . .) Isn't it EXCITING?

Voice 2: Right, Lucy, tomorrow I'll have the cash to buy a map=

Voice 1: [*background noise*] STEVE, no one uses maps. I've already found the place. Well, it's a number of potential places, you'll see. I've been organizing the numbers into possible coordinates all day and I, or Google™ anyway, has identified several precise locations=

Voice 2: Amazing=

Voice 1: All in the middle of the Atlantic Ocean=

Voice 2: Oh.

Voice 1: BUT there are a few others I found by using the SAME numbers and assuming that some may include decimal points. For example, here's one on the Ivory Coast in West Africa. And this one: a wine bar in wreck some and HERE, a derelict listed building in Liverpool.

Voice 2: Might be worth a butcher's=

Voice 1: But, Steve, there's something EVEN stranger about this. It's a photograph of Edith Twyford taken in the early 1940s. She didn't have Google™. She'd have to access detailed maps drawn by the military to pinpoint locations SO accurately. Perhaps that's believable if we consider Edward's connections. Yet there's a funny thing about all three places, RIGHT now. It's too much of a coincidence to be (. . .) pure coincidence.

Voice 2: Go on.

Voice 1: Here, this position on the Ivory Coast, is a local money wiring service. The wine bar in wrecks 'em is called THE BANK. That derelict listed building in Liverpool (. . .) used to be a bank. The longitude and latitude references of all three feature the SAME numbers in the SAME order. It's only spaces and decimal points that make the coordinates different.

Voice 2:   That's=

Voice 1:   Mind-blowing, Steve. It's beyond chance.
             (00:02:11)

Voice 2:   Lucy, I'm gun a come into some money tomorrow. It's legit.
             I can top up the car, drive to wreck sum and Liverpool. I
             don't know how much tickets to the Ivory Coast are, but=

Voice 1:   I SHOULD say no, Steve. It's UTTERLY preposterous. But
             I'm SO excited I'm going to say YES. That's a VERY good
             idea. And you know the BEST thing about it? It's my day
             off tomorrow. I can come too.

Audio File 126
Date: June 19, 2019, 6:56 PM
Audio quality: Good

Bit busier in here tonight. Not just on the treadmills and weights either.
Watched a couple of exchanges go down just now. Spotted the dealer,
but credit where it's due, most wouldn't. There he is now, on the lateral
pull-down machine. Even my expert eye don't pick him out straightaway.
You can spot the swaggering jokers, surrounded by cronies, a mile off.
But this young gun's smart. Literally. Expensive gym gear, discreet logos.
Tidy haircut. Slight beard. Nothing about him stands out. Instantly
forgettable. That's what you want. Wonder what his story is.

(0:03:33)

He does his own juggling. That leaves him exposed. Still, it takes
more bottle to step back and trust others to work for you. Second nature
to him. But that don't mean he can teach someone else. Maybe he has
trust issues. Rightly so. A little bit of paranoia goes a long way. But you
have to relinquish some control to grow your business. Manage people.
Motivate them to work their arses off and not kick you in the teeth once
they learn the ropes. The Harrisons raised us boys in that Merton annex
for a good reason. Inspiring loyalty in others is a priceless skill (. . .)

Lucy's got a new lead. Turns out the pictures in Edith Twyford's study could be map references. I'm gun a visit two of 'em, see what's what. She invited herself but. What harm? Anything. Anything to get away from the smoke and (. .) missiles book (. . . . .) Colin (. . . . .)

Nate texted. Asked how I am. Said did I need anything looked up online. Nice of him. Didn't mention the trip tomorrow. Let him sit in his garage and believe strangers' theories (. . . .) because at least he's safe there.

Audio File 127
Date: June 20, 2019, 8:59 AM
Audio quality: Good

Voice 1: Need to fill up before we set off, Steve?

Voice 2: Have to get the cash first. Gun a nip from the job center to the bank. Wait here, and if a traffic warden turns up, sa:::::y (. . .) I'm sorry, but as an important doctor I had to hop off and save a little kid's life before I could park legally.

Voice 1: Or I could NOT tell an elaborate lie and simply move the car. Leave the keys.

Audio File 128
Date: June 20, 2019, 9:17 AM
Audio quality: Poor

[*background noise*] It doesn't matter, Steve. [*background noise*] No, I insist. I'll pay for petrol and anything else we need. I'm sure the job center just made a mistake. Now, let's go. [*background noise*]

Audio File 129
Date: June 20, 2019, 9:42 AM
Audio quality: Good

Steve. You've left your phone here while you're filling up. Don't be angry. I only looked because I'm concerned. You were so upset the job center didn't have your check.

You sidle away to speak on the phone so often. I thought you called people. I see now. You're recording voice memos (. . . .) I pretend not to notice, but I can tell you don't read as well as you make out. At first I thought The Twyford Code was about YOU. That you wanted something to focus on. Then I thought no, it's more an expression of residual trauma from something in your life you've blocked out. Perhaps I'm right about that, but I was wrong about the code. These books. THAT photograph. There's something here. Edith Twyford (. . . .) who WAS she?

Audio File 130
Date: June 20, 2019, 12:59 PM
Audio quality: Moderate

[*background noise*]

What a *f*[EXPLICIT]*king* racket. Thumping music like a disco. It's lunch for *f*[EXPLICIT]*k* sake. Long time since I worked the dance clubs. Never liked it even then. I've come out to the bathroom to rest me ears. Lucy don't seem to notice. You'd think being a librarian (. . .)

All the way from London she flicks through Six on Devil's Island. Writes things in a notebook. Looks for a cross ticks. Now and again she says random words in a quizzical tone, only to tut and scrub out what she's written. Finally, she reads out a strange sentence. *Catfish in rush ton tunnel nine moons cat.*

My ears prick up at Rushton tunnel, but think I told you, Maxine, I'm naturally cagey and don't let on. By the time we're on the M54 Lucy declares herself tired of cross ticks. Slams the book shut. Rams it in her bag. Settles back in the passenger seat. That's when the snoring starts. Strange to say, but there's something about her that reminds me of missiles. Not sure what. I hardly knew missiles, did I? I hardly know Lucy.

(00:07:09)

So it turns out the job center didn't have my housing check. F[EXPLICIT]*king* typical. It's probably sat in someone's in tray. Have to collect it another day. Lucy is solid gold. Said she'll pay for everything. But we wasted a good hour mucking about in South London before we hit the road.

We're heading to Wrexham and *f*[EXPLICIT]*k* me. Turns out it's in Wales. I only ever been to Wales once before. Years ago. Fishguard. Met a boat diverted from Harwich after John Harrison spotted a London cop in a rest stop, unmarked car, baseball cap. We shot off up a side road, found a phone box, called here, there, and everywhere to change his course. He was a sixty-foot catamaran full of white coming from Tangiers. If we lost the load we'd still owe the Dutch firm with no stock to sell on. Ended up driving from Harwich to Fishguard without stopping. John threw up in a carrier bag all the way there. The stress of it. I were dying for a *p*[EXPLICIT]*s*, but no chance. Never been there before so had to bung every *f*[EXPLICIT]*ker* from the gate to the wharf, load up in pitch dark and drive off as if we'd just picked up a cool-box full of lobster in the dead of *f*[EXPLICIT]*king* night.

John shook like a leaf all the way back. Meanwhile it was my turn to throw up in every rest stop on the M4 thanks to the stink of lobster and putrid fish innards that seems to come off everything that's been at sea .hhhh hhhh all in a day's work.

You know why I remember that job so clearly? When we finally unloaded the van, EVERY package was full of sand. Beach sand, pebbles, shells, bottle tops, and dog-ends. The load had been robbed earlier in its journey. Replaced with lookalike packages that weighed the same. Even the *f*[EXPLICIT]*king* lobsters were rotten. John screamed.

Apes[EXPLICIT]*t* with rage. In thirty hours we'd had no sleep, no food, nothing to drink, and adrenaline burning into our stomachs. We'd earned that big haul, but we had nothing and STILL owed the Dutch firm. Never knew how it ended with them. John mustard come to some agreement. This was the early nineties and he weren't killed till 2007 so (. .)

Done it again, haven't I? Gone off talking about the past.

So, this is the bank. A posh boozer called THE BANK in Wrexham. Lucy calls it a wine bar but as you can hear from the thumping bassline, it's more a nightclub that's open during the day. We're here because its geographical coordinates match those Lucy spotted in two pictures on Edith Twyford's wall. I'm open-minded.

When we arrive, Lucy makes a beeline for the barman, fires twenty questions at the doe-eyed young gun. How old is this building? Did it used to be an actual bank? Are there any fish-shaped things here? Do many people ask about Edith Twyford? He doesn't know, yeah it did, no, and Edith who? So she does a sweep of pictures and photographs on the walls, while I try in vain to get a cheeky shot of something into the lemonade she's bought me. We end up back at our table with lunch menus. Through the music, Lucy assures me she'll pay for lunch. When the waiter's gone, her head is straight back into devil's island.

I might have dreamed it, I say, but can I show you something? I flick through the book to that paragraph. The one about tropical white, revenge, and revolution. Wonder what she makes of it. Didn't want to say I'd had a skinful of Ukrainian vodka before I saw those wild and wonderful words, but (. . .) so she settles down with her notebook and I take this opportunity to slip away from the constant thumping beat to the peace and quiet of the *s*[EXPLICIT]*ter*. Posh *s*[EXPLICIT]*ter* too. Glass sink, urinal could be runner-up for the Turner Prize, tap like a *f*[EXPLICIT]*king* flute. What is this? Where do you turn it on? [*background noise*] Are there.

Audio File 131
Date: June 20, 2019, 1:13 PM
Audio quality: Poor

Voice 1:   There's no cats to mark the acrostic, but it IS here, you were right yesterday. "*Terrific ham.*" *Edward munched.* "*As Sophie knows, it's SO tasty. Right, our picnic is: celery, aspic loaf . . .*" If we take the first letter of each word we get tee haich ee em ay ess kay eye ess tee are oh pee eye sea ay ell (. . .) It ends with Rose saying, "*Voracious Edward needs to understand reason. Edward*" (. . . . .) THE MASK IS TROPICAL WHITE. EMERALD BRIGHT. REVENGE IS RIGHT. REVOLUTION IN SIGHT. ENTERPRISE WILL PAY. CARADOC IS KING. BATORY IN BONAVENTURE. You'd not know it was here *unless* you were directed to that paragraph some other way. A SECRET acrostic. Of course, we don't know what it refers to. Likewise, CATFISH IN RUSH TON TUNNEL NINE MOONS CAT. Steve, what's in the gents'?

Voice 2:   (. . . . .) the usual.

Voice 1:   Any photos, murals, drawings? Because look, THIS is what I found in the ladies'.

Voice 2:   My God.

Voice 1:   Why, do you recognize it?

Voice 2:   I seen something like it before. It's the angle of the fins=

Voice 1:   Is there one in the gents'?

Voice 2:   I (. .) didn't look, gun a have to pop back=

Audio File 132
Date: June 20, 2019, 1:20 PM
Audio quality: Good

Voice 1:   THERE it is. A swirling fish design in a pane of stained glass. But it ain't new like the fancy fittings. It's set in dark wood. Aged. Like, when they refitted the place they kept some a the old knickknacks. A fish to open me. Well, nothing opens here, but it's the same shape and angle as the fish in the tunnel, the glider on the monument and the model plane on the cover of Goldtop Hill. Take a quick snap of that=

Voice 2:   Steve.

Voice 1:   .hhhhhhh=

Voice 2:   We need a catch-up, Smithy=

[*background noise*]

Voice 3:   Look. No, no. Stay there. Let's talk=

[*background noise*]

Audio File 133
Date: June 20, 2019, 1:22 PM
Audio quality: Poor

.hhhh hhhh .hhhh hhhh .hhh hhh [*background noise*]

Audio File 134
Date: June 20, 2019, 1:51 PM
Audio quality: Moderate

Voice 1:   It's a mirror image of the fish in the ladies' loo. There. Now you've finally slowed down I can see both photos side by side.

Voice 2:   ()

(00:02:44)

Voice 1: Steve, is there a GOOD reason we had to leave our food and run? Only that heritage tomato and scrambled tofu brioche was nine ninety-nine.

(00:01:37)

Voice 2: Things got a bit dicey in the gents'. Two guys jumped me.

Voice 1: .hhhhh OH NO, I DIDN'T EVEN SEE THEM. Poor Steve, did they mug you?

Voice 2: Gave 'em the slip=

Voice 1: What a horrible pair. They must have watched us in the bar and pounced when they saw a chance. I'll call the police=

Voice 2: NO, no. It was nothing. Just a couple of grunts who don't want us to crack the code.

Voice 1: But no one knows we're here=

Voice 2: Oldest trick in the book. Used it meself time and again=

Voice 1: Did they know about your housing check? If they thought you had cash on you=

Voice 2: There was no check was there. A scam. Stupid. Tricked me into going to the job center, breaking cover. So they could tail us.

(00:01:26)

Voice 1: They could be following us NOW.

Voice 2: They're not. I've made sure a that. By the time they get their sh (. . .) act together we'll be long gone. They won't guess we're going to Liverpool either. Back to London at best.

(00:06:35)

Voice 1: I've propped your phone in the cup holder.

Voice 2: It's my son's phone.

Audio File 135
Date: June 20, 2019, 2:21 PM
Audio quality: Good

Calling

Source:　　Nate, it's Steve. You're probably at work but I'm on me way to Liverpool. It's. I've just had a. Someone were on my tail. Thought they'd backed off. Time's running out, mate. I'm on the clock [*DecipherIt*™ *time ref 52683583-0921806*] so (. . . .) call me, yeah?

End call.

Audio File 136
Date: June 20, 2019, 3:50 PM
Audio quality: Good

Here it is. Liverpool. Came here a few times in the early nineties. Only to the docks and usually at night. You never shake off that feeling of creeping unease. You're off your manor. Can't read the landscape, the people. You stand out a mile for all the wrong reasons. Bill an unknown quantity. Even with a mate, you're alone.

There were a certain rivalry between London firms and Liverpool gangs back then, based on grudging respect that were more grudging than respectful. Got to know some a the dockers up here, over the years. Collaborated on a few jobs, now and again. Still, if push came to shove we'd be first in the Mersey with concrete water wings. No need to wonder if Liverpool's changed or just me. The place is unrecognizable. It were a proper dump back then. Now, just when I think I know where I am, up pops a shopping center, art gallery, or trendy sculpture. Place clean as a whistle. Dropped Lucy off by Princes Dock while I park. They *f*[EXPLICIT]*king* love a double yellow line up here. Nothing for it. Parking garage.

Audio File 137
Date: June 20, 2019, 4:02 PM
Audio quality: Good

Sat here in the car park. Lucy's shopping. She's dead enthusiastic about the code. Can't tell her (. . .) easy to put on a face in front of someone else, but alone it falls away. Like, I can't pretend to meself no more. Why's that? Used to do it all the time. Hands shaking. Got a explain what happened in the wine bar, Maxine. Then delete.

(00:04:44)

So Lucy finds a stained-glass fish in the ladies' toilet. Exactly the same lines and angles as I seen so many times since this all began. She sends me into the gents' to see if there's one there too, and there is, but (. . . .) I'm jumped by (. . .) by two (. . . . . .) men in black. One old, one younger. I give 'em the slip.

I recognize them, Maxine. I mean, I know the type. I grew up with 'em. Worked alongside 'em. I was one of 'em. Once. They see something shiny and it's theirs because they want it. They'll stop at nothing to get their hands on it. I know that much.

They want to stop us cracking the code. The fact they showed their faces now means we must be getting near.

(00:04:44)

Now, in a random wine bar, there are two fish murals that match exactly the fish in Rushton tunnel, the glider on the war memorial and the model plane on the cover of Six on Goldtop Hill. And that's how I know we're on the brink of a breakthrough. And in more danger than ever.

Kos it weren't a random wine bar, was it? The Bank in Wrexham. Its geographical coordinates are hidden in a drawing that's been hung on Edith Twyford's wall since the 1940s. Just like the place we're on our way to now.

Audio File 138
Date: June 20, 2019, 7:38 PM
Audio quality: Good

Voice 1:   .hhhhh These DOORS. Gorgeous, aren't they, Steve?

Voice 2:   Looks like an entrance to the clink.

Voice 1:   Exactly. A prison keeps people in. A bank keeps people out. I LOVE the neoclassical relief. Look at the GRASSHOPPER. It means the bank had a connection to Sir Thomas Gresham, one of the earliest bankers in the UK. Can you see the dolphins?

Voice 2:   I see a couple a fish.

Voice 1:   They're dolphins. Only, the stonemasons would never have seen a dolphin in their lives. Nor the architect. They worked from sailors' sketches. THAT, see the figure there, is Neptune or Poseidon, god of the sea. He has webbed hands and a tail.

Voice 2:   Those sailors mustard been well tanked up on grog that day. What does the blue plaque say? Ain't got my glasses=

Voice 1:   Martin's Bank building, 1927 to 32. Herbert James Rowse architect. Sculpture by H. Tyson Smith. Beautiful marine images. Mermaids. Shells.

Voice 2:   A heron with a fish in its beak.

Voice 1:   The liver bird. Like a cormorant, and it's seaweed, not a fish.

Voice 2:   You sound like a teacher, Lucy.

Voice 1:   Or a librarian. I WONDER if those are the original windows? Shame it's closed. I'd LOVE to have explored inside.

Voice 2:   No access point along the front here, but there'll be weak spots round the back=

Voice 1:   Ah, no. I don't mean break in. Best just look around outside, Steve. It's boarded up. NO. It's (. . .) oh, wait for me. (00:03:46)

Voice 1:	What is it? I'm standing on an old drain here=
Voice 2:	Another plaque. Could you=
Voice 1:	In May 1940 when this country was threatened with invasion, part of the nation's gold reserve was brought from London and lowered through the hatch for safekeeping in the vaults of Martin's Bank hhhh. Gold, Steve. GOLD. (00:01:15)
Voice 2:	Round the other side. I saw basement windows=
Voice 1:	Be careful. I'll keep watch.

Audio File 139
Date: June 20, 2019, 8:12 PM
Audio quality: Good

Voice 1:	Holy s[EXPLICIT]t (. . . .) pardon my language.
Voice 2:	This is spectacular, Steve. The CEILINGS. The FLOORS. Columns=
Voice 1:	Like an old station=
Voice 1:	It looks familiar. I'm SURE they shot Harry Potter here=
Voice 2:	He should a planned his job better.

[background noise]

Voice 1:	Steve, you are funny (. . . .) This light is extraordinary. Horizontal rays through the windows as the sun sinks. I wish a single photograph could capture it, but=
Voice 2:	Any snaps you take are just proof to the Bill we were in here uninvited.
Voice 1:	Well (. . .) we're not stealing, are we? Just looking around. I don't see how they can object to a few photographs (. . . .) anyway, there's no point deleting anything. Digital files are easily restored.
Voice 2:	Even (. . .) voice recordings?
Voice 1:	Oh yes. All files leave a data shadow. With retrieval software

and a bit of know-how (. .) nothing's ever completely erased (. . . . .) Steve?

Voice 2:   Lowered through the hatch to the vaults. That's what it said. Look for a hatch in the floor.

Voice 1:   Steve, you know that even if gold was stored here during the war, it won't be here now.

Voice 2:   Yeah, sure.

Voice 1:   So what are we looking for?
            (00:00:18)

Voice 2:   I'm (. .) well (. . .) .hhh (. .) *missiles.*

Audio File 140
Date: June 20, 2019, 8:46 PM
Audio quality: Good

We've separated to cover more ground. Looking for a hatch that leads to the vaults. I'm picking me way down a corridor now. Dark down here. Is it just me, or do YOU think more in the dark too, Maxine? Crazy thoughts you'd laugh at in daylight. Suddenly not just possible but the most likely explanation.

Take this, for example. I wonder if those pictures on Twyford's wall with their dartboards that spell out geographical coordinates actually refer to portals in time. Places you can move from one dimension to another. Did I make that up? Or is it just that Doctor Who were very popular with a few of my cellmates?

One thing's for sure, this place is frozen in time. It's an old bank with counters and desks, but deserted, like everyone just upped and left one day. It's from well before the time banks were protected by decent security. Robber's playground, this. We'd have had a ball back in the day.

Lucy loves it. Tells me to look at things. The floor, the roof, the walls. Everything is fancy, sculpted, artified. Nothing's allowed to be blank here. It gets a couple of mermaids and an anchor at the very least.

Paintings everywhere. She zooms in on her phone and suddenly you can see the ceiling is made up of little paintings. Like a sheet of postage stamps. Every one as detailed and colorful as the next. Why make something so beautiful, then stick it where no one can see it?

[*background noise*] Who's this now?

Audio File 141
Date: June 20, 2019, 8:50 PM
Audio quality: Good

Incoming call.

Caller:	Called as soon as I could, Steve=
Source:	Fine, Nate, yeah. Panic over. Thanks=
Caller:	Where are you?
Source:	Liverpool. Nate, could The Twyford Code lead to a portal in time, or several?
Caller:	(. . .) Easily.
Source:	I don't mean travel THROUGH time, but wind it back, briefly, and in a specific place.
Caller:	.hhhhh Don't see why not, Steve. Worth considering, mate, in it?

End call.

Audio File 142
Date: June 20, 2019, 8:55 PM
Audio quality: Good

Thing is, if you can wind time back, selectively, at a particular place. Wouldn't you go to where gold was once stored, turn time back to that moment, rob it, then restore time to the present day? Now there's a thought.

Audio File 143
Date: June 20, 2019, 9:21 PM
Audio quality: Good

Voice 1:   Oh, Steve, what NONSENSE. Time travel is for people who can't or won't live in the moment. They want a second chance. They're full of regret. In denial of their own finite lives. You don't seriously think it could be that, do you?

Voice 2:   (. . .) No::::::o.

Voice 1:   There's a logical, down-to-earth explanation for The Twyford Code. Which doesn't mean it's dull. I'd like to know more about Edward Barnes, but other than being Edith's husband and illustrator, and working at the home office, there's very little online about him. Apparently, when he left his first wife for her there was quite a scandal. The Super Six child most often in trouble is named after him. How romantic.

Voice 2:   Gold bars were stored here. Solid gold. That's too tempting to ignore, Lucy. A stash like that's worth the extra planning. That amount of cash, well, there's plenty'd risk their life for it. Life or gruesome death. If someone were so inclined, I mean.

Voice 1:   It says here it was two point five billion dollars' worth of gold, which today is forty-six billion dollars. However inclined someone may be, a shipment of that value would've had cast-iron security, Steve.

Voice 2:   Yeah, no option. See, umpteen crooks have thieved hauls involving nominal gain, let alone one a this size.

Voice 1:   Here we go. Listen to this from wicky. In October 1939, the bulk of England's gold reserves were moved to the vaults of Martin's Bank in Liverpool as part of (. . .) OPERATION FISH. The evacuation of British wealth from the UK to Canada. Fish. Gold. GOLDFISH.

Voice 2:   A fish to open I.

Voice 1:   Hold ON. Where WAS that? In Goldtop Hill. GOLD top
            hill. Here. Where is it now [*background noise*]. OH MY
            GOD. Listen to this: *The boys saw to it the yard was clean
            and tidy. As for inside, Sophie had taken over. "Old Pippin,"
            exclaimed naughty Iris. Running to the big, black, friendly cat
            the children loved to stroke until he purred.* That acrostic be-
            tween the cats, between CLEAN AND TIDY and "friendly
            cat," gives us A FISH TO OPEN I. But the following initial
            letter after "Iris" is R for "running." If this acrostic clue
            is really A FISH TO OPEN I R, then it's an anagram of
            Operation Fish. Steve, Edith Twyford conceals a reference
            to Operation Fish in a book called Six on GOLDtop Hill.

Voice 2:   A cross tick and anagrams?

Voice 1:   And oblique references too. We've been looking for fish
            that open things. It's NOT that. NOT THAT AT ALL.
            What is she saying about Operation Fish? According to
            wiki, Operation Fish was successful in that all Britain's gold
            reserves were shipped to Canada for safekeeping.

Voice 2:   When were they shipped back?

Voice 1:   Doesn't say. Sssh. I'm googling.

            (00:01:32)

Voice 1:   Nothing. There's nothing about moving the gold back to
            London. But Canada is an ally, part of the Commonwealth.
            There would be no hurry. They could move it back gradually=

Voice 2:   If only a few knew it had gone in the first place=

Voice 1:   *It could have been stolen on the way back=*

Voice 2:   Or at any time it was in storage=

Voice 1:   They couldn't admit it. Imagine how bad for morale it would
            be. To know your entire country's wealth is lost.

Voice 2:   Yeah, there's a war on and the idiots in charge can't even
            keep a few gold bars safe.

Voice 1:   YES (. . .) although that would be victim-shaming and just
             plain wrong.
Voice 2:   ()
             (00:01:48)
Voice 2:   Lucy, this vault we're looking for. I think I know where it is.

Audio File 144
Date: June 20, 2019, 9:40 PM
Audio quality: Good

So Lucy and me have a thorough butcher's inside the old bank but, despite a floor as fancy as a pharaoh's tomb, this hatch to the vaults is nowhere to be found. Then it occurs to me.

We squeeze back out the little window, run round the building, skid to a halt by the plaque. Lucy reads it out again in case a clue to its whereabouts is hidden between the words. But I know it's not. As she finishes I direct her eyes to the ground. We're stood square on a dirty old drain cover. Battered and rusty, caked in muck and *birds*[EXPLICIT]*t*. This is it. Of course it is. The plaque is right over the spot. How could we have missed it?

One thing that stands out when you know is that at one time this hatch mustard been much larger. There's a telltale difference in height of the surrounding slabs. They mark out an area around it that's twice as wide and at least three times as long. Big enough to lower pallets of gold through. We both take a step aside and crouch down for a closer look.

Now, even Lucy knows we can't force it open in daylight. So we agree to lie low until sunset, when we'll put the next part of our plan into action.

It turns out we got different ideas about what lie LOW means. For me, it's sitting in the car, occasionally leaving it to circle the area on foot, taking care to ensure I never trace the same route twice. For Lucy, it's shopping. Can't complain, though, she says she'll bring back some grub.

(00:01:16)

Leaning on the railings now. Waiting for the sun to go down. Looking out over the river. Speaking into my son's phone like I'm actually talking to him. That puts a smile on my face right away, Maxine. And a warm feeling in me chest.

Always a dirty brown, the Mersey. Cold winds whip across it, even in summer. Strong currents too. More deadly than the Thames, they say. Fall in and there's little chance of survival. Even less if their hands are tied.

(00:02:58)

The turn of the millennium was the start of a whole new era for the Harrisons. Old Harry died in November '99. For a while they were ill at the same time. Harry with heart problems, Patricia with breast cancer. They say times like that bring a family together. Not the Harrisons. To outsiders they were a tight-knit clan, but we saw another side. I'll never forget when old Harry called the boys together for a Sunday lunch. I was driving Andy at the time and as you know I'd been part of the family for many years. I were more than trusted. Well, Harry was the weakest I'd ever seen him, a shadow of what he'd been. Shrunk down in his chair, breath rasping, paper-thin skin sickly yellow. Meanwhile, there was Patricia, in the grip of chemo, her face shiny and bloated under a colorful turban. Difficult to look at.

After a bit, old Harry steered the conversation to who would take care of Pat if he went first. The room was silent, but not because it was a naturally awkward subject. It was Andy who finally said it. Very calm. Matter-of-fact. He said exactly what everyone were thinking.

Any one of us will look after Mum, he said (. . .) it's YOU we don't want.

I'll never forget old Harry's eyes the moment it sunk in. Not just what Andy said, but that when he said it no one disagreed (. . .) It broke his heart (. . .) but it proved he had one.

(00:02:18)

His death threw the family dynamics. Changes were subtle at first. Remember, Razor Ray and Andy were well into their forties, John late thirties. They weren't kids, but. With no anchor, they drifted apart. Things were never the same again. Looking back, I suppose that time was a very slow and steady descent into (. . . . .) the final (. . .) thing.

Audio File 145
Date: June 21, 2019, 12:18 AM
Audio quality: Good

The car park's closed. We're trapped in it. Got a fifteen-pound fine to look forward to as well, according to the sign. It don't seem right we both sleep in the car, so I've left Lucy snoring on the back seat while I pace about the level, across this empty network of white lines. North to south, east to west. Gives me time to think. And update you with what we found in the vault, Maxine.

(00:00:18)

Once it got dark, Lucy and I set about opening the hatch. I say we both did, but Lucy kept watch and made the odd suggestion I did well to ignore. She may know everything about Kandinsky, and I daresay he was a diamond, but there's nothing in his paintings that will help you budge a cast-iron drain cover set in concrete.

For this sort of job, you need a pair of cover keys and grate lifts, two big strong lads, and a large lever to take the weight midway. Even then, it's tricky. All we had was a car key, a plastic scraper, and a purseful of coins. Lucy said if we placed enough coins under the rim they would lift the cover by incremental pressure. Proof you really can do too much reading.

Luckily I remembered that Maxine's neighbor left a bag of assorted junk in the car when he sold it to me. He said it were tools for changing a tire. I thought nothing of it at the time and only remembered them on sharp corners when they rattled extra loud. So I dash back and, sure enough, there's a wheel wrench and a rotation handle from a scissor jack, along with a rusty old crowbar.

Well, it weren't easy, let me tell you that. When they sealed that drain cover in concrete they didn't mean anyone to lift it ever again. I try and try to get a purchase on the f[EXPLICIT]*king* thing. It has no keyholes, no lip, no handle. I've got into my fair share of manhole covers over the years, but I ain't never seen anything as f[EXPLICIT]*k* off and die as this.

I glance at Lucy. She's relying on me and that makes it worse. There's no other option. That concrete has to go. I kick and grind at it with my heel, but I got these Skechers™ from the Sally army and they just ain't up to it. It's only when I use the wrench as a hammer and the point of the crowbar as a chisel that I gradually start to chip, chip, chip away at the concrete over the lip. This area ain't too busy at night or Lucy's order to hammer silently whenever she spotted a distant vehicle would have proper grated.

After what felt like a year, and with me sweaty, grubby, and covered in concrete dust, there we were, stood in the street again, either side of a big, black, stinking hole. It felt like Nirvana. Finally, our eyes meet. Go on then, she says, gentlemen first.

Audio File 146
Date: June 21, 2019, 1:06 AM
Audio quality: Good

With what happened to Donna and me at Tarrant Rushton still fresh in me memory, as soon as we land in the hole I drag the cover in after us and prop it out of reach so no shadowy grunt can seal up the entrance while we're underground. A step in any direction and we're in pitch blackness. So dark it makes no difference if your eyes are open or shut. Day ja f[EXPLICIT]*king* view. I fumble for my son's phone. How do I get the flashlight on? Forgotten. Lucy grabs my arm. I assume she's scared but turns out it's only so she can put something in my hand. Click. Click.

Saves on phone battery, she says as her eyes shine in the light of a little flashlight. Well, what did you think I was buying?

I follow Lucy into the (. . .) what? We shine our beams all around.

Now, according to the sign, they lowered the gold through that hatch into the vaults of the bank. I know a vault when I see one, Maxine, and this is not a vault. The walls are an old-fashioned horsehair plaster covered in random old smudges and smears. The air is (. . .) thick, as if it's air from another time. Lucy paces around, shines her torch beam into corners along the ground. Is this it, she asks, the place they stored the gold? She turns to me, shines her torch in my face. Did they dismantle the vault? Move it elsewhere when the bank closed?

I'm proper creeped out now or I might have laughed. A building like this is constructed round a vault. They're impossible to move. This room mustard been (. . .) something else.

Lucy gives me a puzzled look. I shiver. What is it? I'm not happy, or unhappy, something else. This eerie noise or noiselessness. Knowledge or stupidity.

We inch forward. After last time I mustard bin reluctant to venture too far from the hatch. Finally, my torch beam finds the opposite wall. The pool of light grows larger the nearer I get. We see it straightaway and by now know instantly what it is. That distinctive angle of the tail and fins. Old paint, faded and discolored but clear enough. A fish to open I R. Operation Fish.

Lucy's footsteps stop dead behind me. I hear the catch in her breath. Yeah, it's the same. I say. The same fish we saw in the wine bar and, and I can't remember if I mentioned it to her or not, so keep quiet, but the fish in Rushton tunnel.

Neither of us dares breathe a word. But not Kos the fish mural links this place to the others, and to The Twyford Code. It's what's painted over it that stops us dead in our tracks. Because this fish is almost obscured. Just its tail and fins visible beneath a rough smear of black paint.

It chills me to the bone thinking of it, even now, hours later in the cold, stark safety of this multistory car park. Its infinite blackness. The power and confidence with which it had been daubed over the fish's delicate features. The hauntingly familiar lines and angles of its own. A swash ticker.

This is graffiti, Lucy muses, as her flashlight beam picks out traces of the fish beneath. It's a mark of triumph and dominance, made in a hurry, after a daring and dangerous plan. They want their victims to know who did it.

Lucy shines the light up at her face. That answers our question, doesn't it? she whispers. That's what Edith Twyford and her husband are trying to communicate. The gold transported to Canada during Operation Fish was stolen by the enemy.

Audio File 147
Date: June 21, 2019, 1:34 AM
Audio quality: Good

Back in the car and resigned to our fifteen-pound overnight stay, Lucy googles with one hand and eats raw fish in a bowl of beans with the other. She talks between mouthfuls. In the confined space I can smell that raw fish loud and clear. Even with the window rolled down and one hand casually over my nose and mouth. That's not the worst of it, though. She hands ME a bowl of raw fish, a plastic fork, and a sachet of green paste and genuinely expects me to tuck in.

Thing is, the fish is a powerful religious symbol, she says, chewing on one so heartily I can hear its gristle squeak between her teeth. As she googles afresh, I spot a chance to slide my bowl into the glove compartment and almost, no, too late. Her intake of breath is so sharp she practically inhales the air-freshener. Oh. My. God. Listen to this,

Steve. The Christian fish symbol is derived from ick this [*DecipherIt*™ *language: Greek, modern*] the Greek word for fish, whose letters form an ACROSTIC that secretly reads Jesus Christ, son of God our savior. Hence the fish became a secret symbol for Christians at a time when they were persecuted.

We fall silent. I need to distract Lucy from my unopened fish bowl the very moment I remember something else. Could you look someone up for me? I ask. Those little letters on the screen are too small. Of course, she says, who? A name I heard. Werner Rick tar.

How do you spell it? But she quickly adds that it don't matter, she'll try different spellings. She's busy on Google™ so, quick as a flash, I shove that honking bowl into the glove box. I can breathe again.

Lucy clicks and scrolls, finally she stops at a page. Where did you hear that name? I slide out the old leather wallet. Found this in a place just like here, I explain. Underground. A fish scribbled on the wall. She flips it open. She's quiet for a long time. Shows me her phone, but just as soon takes it back and reads: Werner Richter was a German major in World War Two. Declared missing in action. Presumed killed on an operation for ab wear. That was the German intelligence service at the time.

We stare at each other. We'd come so far, Maxine. I had to tell her what else I knew. Rushton tunnel, Donna, the trapdoor, the masker raiders. She's quiet for a good while. *Steve*, she whispers, I don't think the gold ever came here to Martin's Bank. The acrostic in Devil's Island, the one I spotted on the way here. FISH IN RUSHTON TUNNEL NINE MOONS. *The gold was hidden in Dorset for nine months.*

If you're right, I say, was that before or after it was nicked? Indeed, she replies, and how did Edith Twyford know about it?

Audio File 148
Date: June 21, 2019, 2:17 AM
Audio quality: Good

In the early 2000s Andy Harrison's doctor retired. A new one told him that, with his type of epilepsy, there was no reason he couldn't drive [*background noise*], that he could a been driving himself all these years. He bought himself a beamer on the way back from hospital. I was pleased for him but got an ominous feeling too. Where did it leave me, eh?

At the time he owned three DJ clubs in South London. Loud music. Young guns dancing off their faces on pills. They didn't have to bring in a lot of money. Only enough to channel a lot MORE away from Andy's other interests and into his pocket as legit earnings. Dance music was so big no one batted an eyelid when it seemed he was making a packet. So, relieved of my driving duties, I was tasked with looking after the venues day to day.

Around the same time, Little H were taking an interest in what his dad did. Andy set out to teach him the trade, but his rule on everyone having to work their way up went out the window. Little H were more equal than the rest of us and went straight in at the top. It weren't Andy and Little Smithy no more. It were Andy and Little H. I'd see him proud as punch sat beside his boy in the beamer. So alike, people mixed 'em up despite the age gap.

Strange to say it but I missed Andy. We'd worked together so close for so long it's like we got divorced, no exaggeration. I'd see him once a month at most and between times he'd do things and meet people I knew nothing about. I were left out in the cold.

Now, of course, I understand a bit better. Andy were family to me, yet I weren't family to him at all. Razor Ray, John, and Little H were family. Us lads never had been. It were an illusion he'd created to make us loyal. *It took me so long to see it.*

So, I weren't part a something no more, and in those *f*[EXPLICIT]*king* clubs I was well out of my depth [*background noise*] knew all sorts a ways to stash heroin in a shipping container, but no clue how to stock booze or recruit cleaners. Didn't know what made a good DJ so I'd pick the one with the smartest suit. Still, I were determined to make a go of it, for Andy.

Had to learn on the job and it were a while before I could enjoy the regular hours and the going straight. Well, straighter. But over the months I got used to it. For the first time in years I went to bed without a hammer under me pillow .hhhh hhhh Yeah, things were calmer, settled. So when we got talking across the bar one night, when her friend had gone off and she was at a loose end, I didn't immediately put a barrier across me chest so an innocent person wouldn't get mixed up and hurt (. . .) It felt as good as it were gun a get. So I let it happen .hhhh hhhh it was a happy time. But short.

(00:08:16)

It's nearly three. Dark. How Lucy can sleep I don't know. She don't have this. All I have in me head. Don't get me wrong, she's dead keen. Hooky gold. Nazi plot. She's thrilled. Like Nate.

Want to know what I think, Maxine? The Twyford Code leads to a time machine created by secret Nazi experiments. They stole the gold from Operation Fish and sent it through time to another dimension. If you crack the code, you get to go there too and share the loot. It's a chance to live your life all over again but with advantages you never had. To be who you want to be. Who you should a been. It's just, I know don't I (. . .) when you get what you want, you lose what you have.

Audio File 149
Date: June 21, 2019, 5:58 PM
Audio quality: Good

Dropped Lucy off and here I am back at the gym. Haven't said what's next. She don't need to know. I can have a shower, rinse out me filthy clothes and sit in the sauna starkers for hours while they dry. No one gives a s[EXPLICIT]t. There's the little problem of cash. Lucy paid for our trip up north so I can't ask her for more. No matter. I got a plan.

(00:01:24)

Funny how things look different at different times a day. In the dead of night, the idea a billion quids' worth of gold can be moved through time makes perfect sense. In daylight, it's clearly a load of old s[EXPLICIT]t.

(00:03:12)

It's just. The time thing. It. What? If someone or something somewhere can move solid matter through time, it could explain what happened to missiles. She fell into a place where time moved. Couldn't escape. She's there now. She could be saved. It gives me a little warm feeling in me chest. How'd you describe it, Maxine? Hope.

Audio File 150
Date: June 22, 2019, 3:31 PM
Audio quality: Good

Eighty-nine, ninety, () ninety-three (. . . . .) ninety-seven, ninety-eight. Two thousand. Sweet. Lovely smell, money .hhhh hhhh got that high now. Relief mixed with the thrill of having some dough in me pocket. Went like clockwork. Planning see. Didn't know what hit him (. . .) So complacent in his little world. No bother for months, maybe years and then (. . .). He won't rat, will he? What's he gun a tell the old Bill? Only downside is I can't go back to the gym and that changing room's a good place to lie low. Still (. . .) the look on his boat [*background noise*].

Wipe the claret off me hands (. . . .) there we go. Clean as a whistle. Now to fill up and (. . .). Go back there.

Audio File 151
Date: June 22, 2019, 4:30 PM
Audio quality: Good

Voice 1:   Alright, Colin mate, can I come in?

Voice 2:   (Who) is it?

Voice 1:   Steve (. . .) your brother (. . .) Little Smithy.

Voice 2:   I (done no) bit busy (. . .) need a tidy-up.

Voice 1:   You've needed a tidy-up for the last twenty years. Open the door.

Voice 2:   Wait.

[*background noise*]

Voice 1:   .hhhh hhhh *F*[EXPLICIT]*k* me, Colin, who did that to yer?

Voice 2:   Fell over, didn't I=

Voice 1:   *B*[EXPLICIT]*cks,* who did it?

Voice 2:   NO ONE. What you want?

Voice 1:   Can I come in?

Voice 2:   No=

Voice 1:   *I ain't come back to kill you=*

Voice 2:   ()=

Voice 1:   *F*[EXPLICIT]*k* me, open this *f*[EXPLICIT]*king* door. Kos I tell you what I ain't come back for, to chat our business with the *f*[EXPLICIT]*king* neighbors (. . .) What?

Voice 2:   .hhh You see, sir, it's not a convenient time for you to reassess my housing needs.

Voice 1:   () (. . .) Are=

Voice 2:   I have people round.

Voice 1:   What=

Voice 2:   Very. Important. People.

Voice 1:   .hh hh .hh hh .hh OK. That's fine, Mr. Smith. I'll come back another time.

Voice 2:   Thank you.

Audio File 152
Date: June 22, 2019, 4:33 PM
Audio quality: Good

.hhhh hhhh Colin's in trouble. Where the f[EXPLICIT]k do these alleyways lead? This should come out behind the flats. Where am I now? F[EXPLICIT]k .hhh hhh.

[End Transcript]

Audio Files Batch 8

[Start Transcript]

Audio File 153
Date: June 22, 2019, 9:40 PM
Audio quality: Good

Incoming call [message].

Caller: Hey, Steve, how's it going? I got more, based on those photos.
              Sweet. Anyway, call when you can.

End call.

Audio File 154
Date: June 23, 2019, 5:11 PM
Audio quality: Good

Incoming call [message].

Caller: Hi, Steve, it's Lucy. Did I mention I bought a copy of Six
              on Goldtop Hill in Liverpool? It occurred to me we've only
              seen OLD copies, published YEARS ago. Well, this is from
              last year. Steve, it's COMPLETELY different. Perhaps not
              SO surprising because Twyford's been rewritten for modern
              readers, but (. . .) I'll show you when you're next in the
              library. The text has been updated, but the a cross ticks are
              different. There are NEW messages in this version of the
              book. I don't want to jump to conclusions, but we may have

been following long-outdated clues. Anyway, drop into the library when you can.

End call.

Audio File 155
Date: June 23, 2019, 5:21 PM
Audio quality: Good

.hhh hhh Got it. Got missiles book. This is it, in it? What I been searching for. I got it hhh.
(00:03:34)
.hhhh hhhh yeah () (yeah).
(00:06:56)
I got it .hhh but lost Colin hhh .hhh.

Audio File 156
Date: June 23, 2019, 6:13 PM
Audio quality: Good

She made that little flat into a palace. We had curtains, carpets, a three-piece suite, and a set of six dining chairs that all matched the table. As good as any of the furniture in Andy's place. Better. I left that up to her and she didn't complain I was out at the clubs till the early hours most nights. She knew what she wanted and got on with it. I remember one night we were out together. I was at the bar waiting to be served and I overheard her talking to friends. One of them mustard bin whining about her bloke, Kos the missus says, oh, MY Steve wouldn't do that. MY Steve (. . .) I'd never heard a woman talk like that in my life. As if they wanted me. They wanted ME. Funny feeling in me chest like I have now and again. At the time I were so taken aback I forgot me order and the barman moved on.

Yeah, she was a sterling woman. If it weren't for her, Andy never would a put me on the official payroll. Don't get me wrong, I was well compensated over the years, but apparently it weren't official. I hadn't worried about it. Paperwork no good to me, was it? But she said I should have an agreed salary put into the bank. They should be paying tax and national insurance for me.

To tell you the truth, all that had never once crossed my mind. Anything I wanted, I just asked Andy. He gave me a car. Let me live in one of his flats for reduced rent. I told her, I said all I have to do is ask. But she got more and more agitated about it. Finally, she barged in to see him on her own one day. Shouted, made demands, didn't take no for an answer. The end result was I got a regular wage and we moved into our own little place.

.hhh hhh She was still going on about that meeting weeks later. I had to convince her I'd known the Harrisons nearly all my life. I was family. They didn't do things by the book, but I'd been a hard worker and loyal. Whatever happened, they'd always see ME alright .hhhh hhhh.

(00:01:48)

The one thing she really wanted she couldn't seem to get. We were together less than two years, so maybe not enough time when you're both pushing forty. Still, I knew it couldn't be me. My son proved that, didn't he? But she got sad and it made her angry. Jealous. Told me he wouldn't want to see me now, after so long. That I'd do more harm than good. That his mum didn't tell me about him because she didn't want a be chained to a fool like me. That she would a poisoned the kid against me by now anyway (. . .) .hhh hhh she didn't mean it.

(00:00:59)

I know why his mum never told me. It's Kos I was in with the Harrisons. She didn't want him looking up to a man who lived so close to trouble. Best if I knew nothing about him and vice versa. Smart for a teenager, I'll give her that. Smarter than I was back then (. . .) When she finally got hitched, it was to a man who treated my son as his own and gave him the world, just like I would a done if I had the chance (. . . .) so if she was wrong back then, I (. . . . . . .) *forgive her.*

(00:03:03)

I got it. I got missiles book. The one I found on the old green bus. Six on Goldtop Hill. That kid in a red top and his model plane. Crosses and ticks. She mustard sent it to Mr. Wilson, who gave it to Colin, who saved it for me. Feels funny to touch it now, knowing she's held it in her hands. My youth. So old now. Reason everything matters (. .) everything matters but (. .) ends. Relationships matter except (. . .) eventually nothing does.

Bits of paper stuck between the pages, notes written all over the type. Her codebook, mustard been. The key. She sent it back to me. I know because Mr. Wilson put a typed letter in with it. Dear Smithy, missiles sends this book to you. She tells me to say sorry on her behalf, all the best, Mr. Wilson. What's she's sorry for? Taking us away from school that day? Leaving us miles from anywhere? I open the book and the first thing that floats out is the note missiles found when she first took it off me. Remember she asked me to read it with a glint in her eye, then told me it said deliver to Alice isles? I never believed her.

So I turn it over in my hand. So many years later and as much water under the bridge. Yet this slip of paper is unchanged. Sure enough the line of type dances before my eyes. Only now I know how to stop it shimmering and work out what it says (. . . . .) It says now what it said back then.

(00:00:49)

Liefern an [*DecipherIt*™ *language: German*] Werner Richter (. . .)

Audio File 157
Date: June 23, 2019, 8:47 PM
Audio quality: Good

Still haven't finished telling you what happened with Colin. Keep escaping down memory lane. Like you say, Maxine, it's when I don't want to face something. Saying it out loud like this makes it real. I'd rather hide it away, like Dad's empty bottles and cans.

Well, I didn't expect Colin to open the door right away. He's no spring chicken. And all them piles of junk between him and the stairs. But he took so long I even got down on me knees to peer through the mail slot. The stink was nobody's business.

I feel uneasy. It crosses my mind he could a passed away in front of the TV (. . .) but finally I see his ragged old tartan slippers plod into view.

When he opens that door I'm taken aback. Black eye, nasty cut on his chin, and a thick lip. Swears he fell over. Then he won't let me in. Irked, I don't even get a chance to say I ain't like him and Dad. Don't want revenge. Only come back for the book. He looks me dead in the eyes and talks as if I'm a busybody from the council .hhh hhh.

(00:01:02)

See, back in the day we'd heard stories on the estate about payday cuckoo robberies. Years ago, a pay packet was the mugger's holy grail. A week's cash wages all in a handy envelope. Ready to spend, no fence required. Factory workers like Colin were prime marks, but mugging's a risky business, so (. . .)

They'd break in a flat, wait inside till the mark got home then rob him in private, no witnesses. If family were in, they were kept quiet till the breadwinner arrived. We heard stories of those who stayed hours, eating food, watching TV, roughing people up. If the mark didn't have his key and knocked on the front door, they forced the family to open it as if nothing were wrong.

Colin's wages paid the rent and fed the meter. He couldn't risk it being nicked. He had a special place he stashed it, along with Dad's darts and an old lipstick a (. .) Mum's. It were only Friday nights he worried about, when he had to walk home with it in his pocket. Half the estate knows I'm alone in that flat till he gets in.

So he tells me that if I'm cuckooed, to warn him at the door by talking like he was a council snoop. He'd know from that what was going on. Buy him a few seconds to run for help. Of course, he didn't mean the old Bill. He meant upstairs, first floor. We knew the families and could count on their help to boot the *b*[EXPLICIT]*ds* out, give 'em a good kicking. Luckily, it never happened. But that was it, me and Colin, our little code. I'd forgotten it till now. I daresay he had too. Who'd a thought all these years later we'd have to use it?

(00:00:54)

Cuckooing means something a bit different now. It's when dealers take over someone's flat to run their business out of. A few young guns inside had done it. Still, the mark don't change. A vulnerable person, alone. Like Colin.

I were inside for eleven years, and it weren't as bad as this place. Windows covered with newspaper, piled up with carrier bags full of old clothes. No night or day. You'd think it would close in on me. The smell make me gag. Dust and filthy air grate in me throat. But it don't. You know what's terrifying? I'm used to it. Been here, what, two days. That's all it takes. Tiny space. Towering walls. How easy it is to exist so small. That's what happened to Colin. It was him had the real sentence, weren't it?

Life's all choices, that's what they told us in group sessions at the vale. We'd made bad choices, but we had the power to make good ones now. Yet when I had the choice between missiles book or Colin I chose the book (. . .) Was that my revenge? Am I like them after all? Colin. Dad (. . .) Mum? Cursed?

Have to leave to make that choice a good one. Never see him again. Why's me chest so heavy now when I didn't see him for years? Is it because (. . .) finally (. .) I *forgive* him?

I tell you one thing. If I don't go now I'll never get out. Be stuck like he was. Just like he IS. Sat there in his TV chair. Trapped by it all.

Audio File 158
Date: June 26, 2019, 2:08 PM
Audio quality: Good

Voice 1:   STEVE. Where HAVE you been? You didn't call me back=

Voice 2:   Sorry, Lucy. Visited me brother. He's (.) not been well.

Voice 1:   Oh, I'm sorry. Is he better?

Voice 2:   Left him in front of the telly=

Voice 1:   Ah, that's nice. NOW, I've got SO much to tell you about the code. First, the secret acrostic you spotted when you were drunk. THE MASK IS TROPICAL WHITE. EMERALD BRIGHT. REVENGE IS RIGHT. REVOLUTION IN SIGHT. ENTERPRISE WILL PAY. CARADOC IS KING. BATORY IN BONAVENTURE. It refers directly to Operation Fish. It lists the ships in the order they sailed. HMS Emerald, HMS Revenge, HMS Revolution and so on. HMS Bonaventure is the last one. It was a perilous journey across hostile seas. Imagine it, Steve. Stacks of gold bullion, and YOU are responsible for them. A country's gold reserves are its past, present, and future. An entire nation's health, happiness, and well-being. Millions of people and millions more yet to be born. Do you do nothing and risk losing everything in an enemy invasion? Or do you hide it from the enemy but in the process expose it to the mercy of fate, and the risk of theft? You'd have to trust the honor and loyalty of everyone involved. Then there's storms and German U-boats. The risk is unthinkable (. . . .) Steve? Are you OK?

Voice 2:   Fine. Tired.

Voice 1:   Are you still next door? The gym? No?

Voice 2:   Too hot.

Voice 1:   We:::ll, air-conditioning only goes so far. Now, Operation

Fish is no longer a secret. In fact, it's a well-known, feel-good story. The official line is that it was a success. But what if it wasn't? Perhaps the operation was compromised and the gold fell into enemy hands. Gone (. . . .) So Edith Twyford continued putting coded messages in her books long after the war ended. She knew there was a cover-up. That our gold reserves were not only lost, but potentially used AGAINST us during the war. She felt the people should know, but couldn't say anything without compromising her husband's position at the home office=

Voice 2:   Well=

Voice 1:   OR maybe revealing that secret would have placed them in danger.
            (00:01:00)

Voice 2:   That is a great theory.

Voice 1:   I know.

Voice 2:   Could it be stuck? The gold. Trapped in time. Could we rescue it (. . .) or someone?

Voice 1:   hhh No. Steve, there's no such thing as TIME. There's only history, legend, memory, and nostalgia. Time is a CONCEPT not a dimension. You can't stop it, you can't travel through it, you can't turn it back. It's NOW. Here and now.

Voice 2:   So the old girl hides a message about the gold being in Rushton tunnel for nine months.

Voice 1:   (. . .) Why would thieves hide it right beside an RAF airfield?

Voice 2:   Plain sight, see. Hide your loot in plain sight. Bide your time before moving it on.

Voice 1:   I can't imagine undercover German agents would have the resources to do it, and even if they did, how would Edith Twyford know it was there?

Voice 2:   There's only one reason I can think of, Lucy (. . .) *she helped 'em steal it.*

Audio File 159
Date: June 26, 2019, 7:46 PM
Audio quality: Good

So I finally got missiles book. The key to The Twyford Code. Now it's here in me hands, something about it feels (. . .) fragile. Didn't even show it to Lucy. Why not? Keep pushing down the feeling that really (. .) I want to find missiles. Speak to her again. Say sorry. And that's impossible .hhhh hhhh off.

(00:01:49)

Need to focus. But when I close me eyes, all I see is them. And Colin (. . . . . .) This still recording? OK (. .) The men in black that closed the trapdoor. That cornered me in the bar toilet in Wrexham. That kept Colin prisoner in his own flat, just to make me talk. They're gun a get me, Maxine (. . .) I've always known they will. I'll do as much as I can but won't finish as I'd planned. Only hope you'll understand. And work it out.

Audio File 160
Date: June 26, 2019, 8:20 PM
Audio quality: Good

When Andy first mentioned it, I very much doubted it'd be the last job ever like he said. With him, every job was gun a be the last. But when he gathered us together again and told us his idea, I jumped at the chance to be back at the heart. All the old faces. The brothers: Andy, John, Razor Ray. Us lads: Orin, Billy, and Ginger. The most trusted Harrison cousins: Bradley, Toff, and Gary. Like before, but everyone older and wiser. Mindful of their responsibilities. Cautious perhaps. More aware of time running out (. . .) Bit more selfish.

We all noticed Little H weren't there. The lad's too green, Andy said, he'll be a liability. But I knew the real reason. He didn't want his boy in danger, did he? Little H weren't expendable.

Andy looked round at us. I saved the best till last, he told us. Set us all up for life. When you walk away from this, he said, you'll be walking on air. We looked at each other. With Andy's attention to detail, it was odds-on gun a be a success. We all trusted him and he trusted us .hhh hhh I suppose that's where it all began (. . . .) the end.

(00:04:42)

So I got missiles book, and even with a ruler under the words I can't decipher her tiny handwritten notes. Fact is, I need either Nate or Lucy to help and I don't know which. Lucy has the get-up-and-go. The good education, artistic nature, an inquisitive mind that brings it all back down to reality. Then there's Nate, a proper diamond, a whiz at his computer, yet keen as mustard to believe anything. You could tell him the code were set by fairies in pajamas and he'd ask what color pajamas (. . .) .hhh hhh after all these years. Times like this I still ask meself, what would Andy do?

Now, you're probably thinking why don't I use both of 'em. Nate and Lucy. Work together. Three heads better than two. All I can say is, if you ever do anything under the radar, Maxine, keep your alibis separate. That way, when they're called on to vouch for you, their evidence is twice as strong (. . . .) Not only that, but Andy had a thing about groups of two. That's how he always set us up, in pairs. I were often with John.

.hhhh hhh There's nothing more powerful than two people together. They're a strong unit. Somehow more than the sum of their parts. Colin and me, me and Andy, Andy and Little H, me and the missus, me and (. . . . .) *my son*. Three is a weak unit. It can be undermined. Three can turn on itself, two against one. And another thing. It's better to share the loot TWO ways than three. You don't have to be good at maths to work that one out.

Also (. . .) why two is (. . .) should it all go pear-shaped, I'll only lose one friend, not two. That's what I got a bear in mind, Maxine. This next bit is dangerous. Which of 'em do I least want to lose?

(00:01:47)

So, who will it be, Nate or Lucy?

Audio File 161
Date: June 27, 2019, 7:59 AM
Audio quality: Good

[*background noise*]

Voice 1:   Morning, Steve=

Voice 2:   Wha::: ? (Sorry) to wake you up last night=

Voice 1:   *Shhh* stay there, back in a sec=

Voice 2:   Why=

Voice 1:   Left our bacon under the grill.

Voice 2:   I'm in Nate's garage, surrounded by his Twyford books. Old woodwork projects. Half-finished toys. His sofa's smelly, but softer than any bench at the gym. He said make yourself at home. I was out like a light. Only just come to.

[*background noise*]

Voice 1:   Red sauce, brown, yellow, or none?

Voice 2:   Yellow (. . . .) cheers, Nate.

Voice 1:   The:::re w::::e go.

(00:02:11)

Voice 1:   Lovely.

Voice 2:   (That's) the best grub I tasted in weeks, Nate.

Voice 1:   My eldest said of all the things he misses from home, my breakfast sandwich is top of the list. You should a seen the missus' face [*background noise*] bless her, she really rates her lasagna.

Voice 2:   My son (. .)

Voice 1:   What? (. . .) Like egg and bacon, does he?

Voice 2:   I (. . .) don't know=

Voice 1:   Give him a call. Tell him you're tucking in to Nate's=

Voice 2:	Don't know if he=
Voice 1:	Text him. Wait, wait (. . .) THERE. Lovely pic, see? I'll send it to you, you forward it to him. See what he's missing=
Voice 2:	He's busy=
Voice 1:	He'll see it when he's not=
Voice 2:	Driving, lecturing people, or something=
Voice 1:	GO ON. I text mine all day long. They text back once a day. It works for us [*background noise*]. Go on=
Voice 2:	Can't.
Voice 1:	Why not?
Voice 2:	He said not to. He said (. . .) said he don't want (. .) me.
Voice 1:	Don't want you to TEXT?
Voice 2:	No. Don't want ME=
Voice 1:	What d'you mean he don't want YOU? You're his dad.
Voice 2:	He (. . .) he's got a stepdad. Solid gold. Says he thinks of him as his (. . .) where as I'm (. . .) just his biological father. Not the same, he says.
Voice 1:	Oh (. . . .) mate.
	(00:01:09)
Voice 2:	I got missiles book. It's the key, Nate. Key to the code.
Voice 1:	How do you know that?
Voice 2:	It's complicated. But I can't (. . .) my glasses are (. . . .) I can't READ. Not well enough to decipher it. Need help to get any further and I'd like you to be (. . .) it.
Voice 1:	Where d'you get it?
Voice 2:	That don't matter. See, if you agree, you'll have to leave here, with me, now. That's the best way. Can't say when you'll be back. Don't know where it'll take us, or what we'll find in the end. But we'll find it together.
Voice 1:	Where is it? (. . .) .hhh hhh (. . .) like wow. That old book? That's IT?
Voice 2:	Yeah.

Voice 1:   Can I touch it? .hhhh hhh old.

Voice 2:   See the notes she tucked in it, and here, the annotations on the text? There.

Voice 1:   .hhhhh TAKE IT AWAY=

[*background noise*]

Voice 2:   Nate?

Voice 1:   TAKE IT AWAY. I DON'T WANT A SEE IT=

Voice 2:   But (. . .) thought you were well into the code=

Voice 1:   I AM (. . .) I was=

Voice 2:   But the research you got here. All the work you done. This is a chance to find out what it is. Finally. What's at the end of it. What happened to missiles=

Voice 1:   hhhhh YOU go, Steve. YOU look for it. I'll help. I'll look things up for you. But (. . .) *I don't want a know.*

Audio File 162
Date: June 27, 2019, 8:38 AM
Audio quality: Good

.hhh hhh (. . . . .) Paul, Shell, Donna, and now Nate. I'm the only one left from are E. Have to get Lucy involved. But can I protect her from them? The men in black, those grunts who want what's at the end of the code for themselves? Nate says don't worry, he'll help. But he don't want a leave his computer. Like he's playing a game. I don't know, but I tell you this, Maxine, I meant what I said and I'm gun a keep on doing this until it's done, or they stop me by force. Whatever comes first. Sat here outside Lucy's flat. Nice little place. Surely nothing and no one can get to us in there.

Audio File 163
Date: June 27, 2019, 9:44 AM
Audio quality: Good

Steve, while you're in the shower, I'm going to record two passages from Six on Goldtop Hill. The first is the original, published in 1939.

> *Wind whipped through the poplar trees as the six Horton children picked their way across the old airfield. Horatio naturally took the lead, followed by Piers, Edward, Sophie, Rose, and little Iris. "For goodness' sake keep up, little Iris," Piers whispered, sharply. "Or you'll be kidnapped by evil gypsies, given a ragged dress, and taken to France. What's more, it'll serve you right."*
>
> *As little Iris hurried to catch up, they waded through the long grass. Chilly and tired, the Super Six began lagging, yet to help speed plodding Iris, rallied in twos. They observed presently a likely meadow . . . empty. Reliable Sophie leered at naughty Edward. "Alright, NOW do we acquiesce in this case and turn back?"*

There's a coded instruction in the paragraph that begins "As little Iris." CHILLY AND TIRED. That's the opening acrostic cat. It's followed by the acrostic message: BLYTH SPIRIT TO PALMERS LANE AND WAIT. The closing cat that denotes the end of the message is CASE AND TURN. There's a River Blyth that's crossed by a Palmers Lane near Southwold in Suffolk. It's potentially where a small vessel could come ashore unnoticed. A vessel called *SPIRIT*?

So far so intriguing. But here's the new version, published last year:

> *A light breeze tinkled through some tall trees as the six Horton children made their way across the old airport. Sophie, a strong and mature young woman, took the lead, followed by Rose, Lily, Peter, Ethan, and Jack. "Lily is younger than us," Peter said, "so let's help her along, until*

she grows big enough to keep up with us." They took turns to ensure their sister was safe and happy.

Confident and true, the Super Six marched forth adventurously. "After me," Jack ordered. "Peter's carefully described scenery should ensure relatively brief exertion. Caution all times." They waded through the long grass, looking hard for the place Peter described.

Steve, the text has been updated almost beyond recognition. Most of the names have changed. Piers is now Peter. Horatio is Jack. Edward is Ethan and Iris is rather beautifully updated to Lily. It makes sense, because only Rose and Sophie are still common children's names. The poplar trees in the first passage are not mentioned by name. Is it because modern readers are not thought to be as knowledgeable about flora and fauna as past generations? Modern children certainly won't see as many small airfields as their great-grandparents did, which is why the airfield in the first extract becomes *airport* in the later version. Meanwhile, the children's attitude to each other reflects a modern approach to encouraging empathy and care for others.

I could go on, Steve, but it's not just the readable text that's changed. The acrostics now say something completely different. The coded paragraph begins with the acrostic cat CONFIDENT AND TRUE, but the simple, initial-letter acrostic doesn't make sense. However, start at MARCHED and take a letter from each word, but move one letter along each time. Return to the first letter after four, six, five, and one letter intervals respectively. You get MOVE MADE, FISH SAFE before the final cat: CAUTION ALL TIMES. If this is typical of how the code has changed, we can safely say it's become far more complex over the years and certainly seems to be a reference to the whereabouts of FISH. Now, we've already linked the Twyford Code to Operation Fish, where the word FISH represents actual *gold*. Is the gold from Operation Fish still being moved around and hidden all these decades later?

One thing we CAN be sure of, Steve, is that the code is changed with each edition of the book, so the publisher MUST be in on it (. . .)

Audio File 164
Date: June 27, 2019, 10:51 AM
Audio quality: Good

I'm sat on Lucy's sofa. She called in sick when really she's made an appointment for us with Edith Twyford's publisher. Can hear her in the bedroom now, looking for things to wear. Said she'd be ten minutes, so I got twenty to catch up on me diary .hhhh hhhh. Gun a tell you now what happened at Colin's, Maxine, Kos you ought a know.

I creep round the back a Colin's block, search for a way over the wall. Eventually get up on a car, make it to a flat roof two doors along. Run across it to Colin's. There's no doubt which flat's his. Sun-bleached newspaper plastered over the windows. Cobwebs. Dead flies who lost their battle to get out. I make straight for the beveled glass of the bathroom. I remember it's less full of s[EXPLICIT]t than all the other rooms (. . .) There's irony for you.

I know a dodgy window lock when I see one and Colin's are rock solid on their double-glazed, gas-sealed, uPVC. Now, you may think why not just smash the pain? No. Too noisy, too slow, too messy. There's a much better way. If you pry off the beading, sides first, then top and bottom, you reach the window unit. If you're lucky it's fitted from the outside and can be lifted away in one move. Quick, clean, silent. I'm lucky today. Trouble is, it's broad daylight and I'm overlooked by jobless curtain-twitchers with Bill on speed dial. Can't worry about that. Got a think a Col.

Pick me way through the bathroom. Every step threatens to set off an avalanche of bags and boxes. I hear voices somewhere, but is it the intruders or the telly? I edge nearer. Flat against the wall so I can peer round the door unseen.

There he is. Colin. Sat in his TV chair. He ain't alone. They tower over him. His battered face don't look scared, or desperate. Not like you'd think, with two grunts bearing down on him. Head down, he looks sad. Resigned. It's like, in his mind, he deserves what's coming so (. . .) whatever.

One crouches down, tries to look Col in the eye. Whispers at him. Can't remember exactly, but it goes something like (. .) hand it over and we'll go. Simple as.

I shift me weight from one foot to the other. Big mistake. It tips a floorboard and before you can say chain of events a tower of boxes, taller than me, collapses in a rain a dusty junk.

S[EXPLICIT]*t. Lucy's back.* Hi (. . .) hi.

Audio File 165
Date: June 27, 2019, 2:55 PM
Audio quality: Average

Voice 1:   Wrap it twice round your neck so the tassels hang unevenly. There. You look (. . . .) well, I think we'll get away with it. Ready?

Voice 2:   What should I say?

Voice 1:   Very little, Steve. You're a shy, awkward, HUGELY talented, emerging illustrator. I sold you as a POWERHOUSE of ideas for illustrated children's books. Now, I know this is a VERY profitable segment of the market and they couldn't book us an appointment quickly enough. We'll start by talking about your MANY animal characters and move on to how BRILLIANTLY you can draw young people. That's the moment I'll shift the conversation to Edith Twyford. For example, are they planning a new, illustrated version of the Super Six? I'll then, ever so casually, mention how I've noticed the text changes exponentially between editions, and we'll take it from there=

Voice 2:   I'll have to borrow some paint=

Voice 1:   No, have this. My old portfolio case. If they ask to see examples of your work, then you've got these to shuffle out. Be embarrassed and reluctant to show them.

[*background noise*]

Voice 2:   .hhhh Who drew these?

Voice 1:   I did. Years ago. Oh, don't look like that, they're dreadful. But we'll say you're a naïve talent who likes to explore primary emotion through unconventional composition. PERFECT for children's books, ages four to eight. Remember, I'm a brand-new agent. You're my hot young talent. Well, we'll say NEW talent. Let's go. This way.
(00:00:44)

Voice 2:   Have you done much a this, Lucy?

Voice 1:   Illustration? In my dreams=

Voice 2:   Pretending you're someone else.

Voice 1:   Oh. No. Never (. .) I'll be fine, though. How hard can it be?

Voice 2:   You got a remember, look them in the eye, but only now and again. Not too much, or it feels suspicious. Imagine you ARE that person you're pretending to be. Get a feel for what they do, what they say. It could be the opposite of what YOU would. At the same time, never get so far into the pretense you lose sight a what you want out of it. What I mean is (. . .) remember to ask about Twyford.

Voice 1:   You sound like the voice of experience, Steve.

Voice 2:   Well (. . . .) you know.

Voice 1:   Here we are. No. I'll go in first. Shy and reticent remember. Oh, and switch your phone off. Put it away. They can't suspect they're being recorded. Let me do the talking.

Audio File 166
Date: June 27, 2019, 2:46 PM
Audio quality: Good

Voice 1:   Did I do OK?

Voice 2:   Don't worry about it, Steve. How FASCINATING was that?

Voice 1:   I don't reckon they believed=

Voice 2:   They have NOTHING to do with the text. It's submitted by Twyford's estate. A board of people. A consortium of financial managers. It's clear the publishers assume any changes are made to fit modern sensibilities and new trends in the language used for children. On the surface, that's what I'd think too. But you can't ignore the acrostics. Whoever controls the text controls the ultimate direction of the code.

Voice 1:   So, what's at the end?

Voice 2:   *The stolen gold from Operation Fish, Steve.*

Voice 1:   Well=

Voice 2:   YES. This consortium of financial managers is, for some reason, placing NEW clues in each edition of the books. Clues that indicate places, positions, locations. Why?

Voice 1:   Movement (. . .) to move it. Best way to keep something out of sight is to keep it on the move. Each time it moves they need new clues.

Voice 2:   OR each new set of clues refers to the whereabouts of a small amount of gold. The bullion transported by Operation Fish filled a convoy of navy destroyers=

Voice 1:   Yeah, split the load. Divide it into small, manageable portions. With a decent crucible, a strong flame, and a few weeks to spare=

Voice 2:   SO who are they communicating with? Who is following the code apart from a handful of armchair coders on the internet? Why communicate in such a strange way? If I

wanted to tell you I'd moved stolen gold, I'd call you, ask
to meet up, send an email=

Voice 1:   LUCY. They don't know. These organizations operate on
a need-to-know basis. It protects everyone. It protects the
loot. Whoever is setting the code, giving references to where
the gold is, they don't know who is picking up the info.
They've never known. Their job is to store it, protect it,
and issue clues that lead the (. . . .) recipients to it. There's
a middleman, a go-between who links the two parties, who
pays everyone off, but knows nothing about the gold.

Voice 2:   This gold was robbed eighty years ago. The original thieves
are long dead. Whoever is protecting the gold could just
keep it for themselves.

Voice 1:   Yet they don't. Who would NOT take advantage of having
so much wealth at their disposal?

Voice 2:   Lucy, I should a said before. I got something to show you.

Audio File 167
Date: June 27, 2019, 6:02 PM
Audio quality: Good

John wasn't like Andy, Ray, or old Harry. They were old school. Liked
a drink, all of them. Smoked like Turks. Ran rackets in booze and cigs
their whole lives. But any Persian were off-limits. White, brown, E (. . .)
all strictly business. They didn't touch the stuff and expected us to toe
the same line. It's a *f*[EXPLICIT]*king* fool's game. I can hear old Harry
now, cig in hand, stink of Scotch all round him as he rants. If any a you
lads get hooked on that *s*[EXPLICIT]*t* you're *f*[EXPLICIT]*king* dead
in the water. D'you *f*[EXPLICIT]*king* see? You *f*[EXPLICIT]*king* hear
me? Well, you won't with your ears burned off and your eyes stamped
out, you pack a lazy *s*[EXPLICIT]*ts*.

It made good business sense. Can't trust an addict. Not with stock, cash, or info. They'll rat you out for their next fix and lie as easily as they breathe the air. Saw a few good workers offed and several cousins cut loose thanks to dabbling in Persian. Yeah. If the Harrisons cut you loose (. . .) you count yourself lucky.

John though, the youngest Harrison brother, part of a newer generation. Different attitude. I daresay I may a gone that way myself if I weren't s[EXPLICIT]t scared of old Harry. But John was the apple a Patricia's eye. Rules didn't apply to him. He did what he liked (. . . .) The Harrisons didn't complain when he got them into Persian, saved their business, brought new customers to their door, new markets, new stock. Did they never wonder how he got to know the game so well? I had my suspicions, but John would often say how it's only white, brown, and green that get you hooked. You're safe with dance pills, he'd say.

We'd worked together back in the day, but while I'd been running the clubs our paths hadn't crossed, so at that last get-together I were pleased as punch to see him. Strode across the room to shake his hand but slowed to a standstill at three feet. He weren't the John I remembered. It weren't physical. I can't even now put a finger on what had changed. But something had died in his eyes. Alright, Steve, he'd said, shifty, like he couldn't meet my gaze. ALRIGHT, LAD. I didn't get much more out of him, but when it came to dividing us into pairs, Andy put us together. I knew he trusted me to keep an eye on John and tell him if there were anything he needed to know.

(00:01:18)

They said to us inside we should use the proper words, else it's denial. Slang, nicknames, you (. . .) feminisms, they're all things to hide behind. Lessen the severity, that's what you said, Maxine. Like saying passed away when someone's croaked. An escape from reality (. . . .) cannabis, cocaine, ecstasy, heroin. Addiction. Drugs. Died. Killed. Murder (. . .) There, Maxine. I promised you I would never go back, never escape again. Life or gruesome death.

Audio File 168
Date: June 27, 2019, 6:57 PM
Audio quality: Good

.hhhhh So back in Colin's flat I'm face-to-face with those two (. . .) men in black (. .) and feel a lot of things well up in me chest.

Boxes and random *s*[EXPLICIT]*t* bounce round Colin but all he can do is glance up at me, not even with relief. I get another surge of anger, this time from a deeper, darker part a me chest. Why's he letting them batter him? If he got up and fought for a *f*[EXPLICIT]*king* change, we could take 'em down. Together. Him and me against the world. Instead, I'm alone. I'm in a room with Colin, me own brother, yet I'm totally alone. Just like the old days. Thinking about it now, at that moment I got a little inkling why it were so easy to up and leave him all them years ago.

There ain't much room to dodge the *f*[EXPLICIT]*kers* in this *s*[EXPLICIT]*thole* of a living room. For the first time in years we're eye to eye. So close I'm practically wearing the *c*[EXPLICIT]*t* as a brooch. His gnarled face. Dead eyes. Something lifeless, inhuman. I know what he is. I know what he planned to do AND what he did. He can lie to anyone else in the world, but not to me.

Just one thing. He rasps. The key to The Twyford Code. Hand it over, Smithy, and we'll see you alright. Forget everything else. It's in the past. You can trust us.

I shake my head. Just Kos you want it, don't mean it's yours, I say. Something they told us inside. Put it this way, he says, if you don't give it to us, we'll get Colin to persuade you. I know what he means. So does Colin. His eyes meet mine. We don't need words or a code.

I let the memories through, and after them come the feelings, like a knife in me chest, every one. My little hand in Dad's big hand. Dad crying on the way home from darts (. . .) being lifted up by someone who'll never let me go. That smell. Powder. Perfume mixed up with stale booze. *Mum.* Dad throws a bottle at me when I ask where she went. Colin stares at the TV while I have cornflakes in tap water for me tea. Feeding the electric meter more important. Scoop them up with me hands Kos there's no spoon, or fork or knife that ain't got a dead cockroach or some *s*[EXPLICIT]*t* stuck to it. It should a bin Dad who taught me to shave. Can't blame him, Steve, you can be a proper little *s*[EXPLICIT]*t* sometimes. He lets me think it were MY fault, the *c*[EXPLICIT]*t*. Another surge of anger, but this surge don't die. It wells up and up from me chest into me throat. Proper chokes me.

Missiles took the book I were gun a sell, but I was so *f*[EXPLICIT]*king* hungry I went to the fish and chip shop anyway. Tried to talk a bit a grub out the server. No doubt I was a pain in the *a*[EXPLICIT]*e* but he took it personal, snapped, called me every name. The line was on his side. *F*[EXPLICIT]*k* off, you scummy little runt, get lost, they shouted (. . . .) all except one geezer.

Twenty-five, smart suit. Didn't know him from Adam. But he stepped out the line, grabbed the server by his throat across the counter. Salt, vinegar, charity box went flying, crash, spinning on the floor. The kid's STARVING, he snarls, right in the guy's face. Give him sausage and chips. I'll *f*[EXPLICIT]*king* pay. He let go. The server jumped to do as he was told. The line was silent then, as the suit peeled a tenner off a fat roll, flicked it behind the counter, stalked back to his place.

See, Maxine, if I hadn't been so hungry that day, I never would a met Andy Harrison.

It's not missiles, is it? It's Kos a *Colin* I took up with 'em. Went down the path that led me here, to the state I'm in now. The truth is I fell in with the wrong crowd. But the truth ain't the most useful thing because that wrong crowd SAVED me. Makes me *f*[EXPLICIT]*king* shake to think about it. Andy did what Colin should a done. He took me in, fed me, dressed me, and I mistook that for (. . .) something else, didn't I?

In Colin's flat I got all this flying through me head. Go on then, I say. I shout it. Scream, GO ON THEN. Look at him. He's a sack a useless *s*[EXPLICIT]*t*. What the *f*[EXPLICIT]*k* has he ever done except *f*[EXPLICIT]*k* it all up? At this the men stop dead. I can't hardly breathe. Suddenly they ain't enemies no more. They just happen to be there when I do what I should a done years ago. Colin sat in his TV chair, slumped, useless. All his fault.

He don't even defend himself. Barely a flicker on his face but cuts, bruises, and resignation. He's been expecting me to do this for years. Waiting? Knows he deserves it. The family curse. I lift me foot back, angle the heel. Needs to be full in the face. He ain't gun a come back from this. BANG. Whoosh that heavy weight lifted off me chest. Done it.

There's a shout from next door. A thump on the wall. Muffled yet unmistakable mention of calling for old Bill. Those two are out of there so fast they don't even see Colin go down.

(00:03:54)

I said I weren't gun a escape no more, Maxine. I won't even delete this file. It was best I did it. Save him from them. Else they'd (. .) I seen it meself and don't want him (. . .) Same time I had to show him. The true value a things. I'll explain later. Had to do it for me. Can't even say I'm sorry.

Audio Files 169
Date: June 27, 2019, 7:29 PM
Audio quality: Good

Got what I wanted. Missiles book. Colin found it in his hoard. When our visit to Twyford's publisher leaves us with more questions than answers, I finally show it to Lucy.

She flicks through. Studies a few pages here and there. I expect her to be surprised, excited, happy. But she frowns. Seems more confused than anything. After a quiet few moments, she closes it and looks me in the eye like she's about to deliver bad news.

Who told you THIS was the key to The Twyford Code?

I shrug. Can't quite recall. I found it on the bus. Missiles took it off me in class. She wrote things in it then she (. . . .) disappeared that day. Donna said missiles told her a secret. She'd found a code. Missiles (. . . .) a while later the book were sent back to me. This must be the key, I say, and can't help but swallow, nervous. I can see in her eyes there's something wrong.

This is a first edition of Six on Goldtop Hill. She (. .) SOMEONE has written in it, but I don't think it's (. . . .) here, I'll read out this bit. Your teacher, or someone, has circled individual words. I'll read them out. But, Steve (. . .) let's sit down.

We're on a deserted tube station platform. Distant rumbles. Footsteps, but no one there. I shiver and don't know why. Lucy reads to me. I remember every word of what she said.

I'm sorry to leave you like this. But it's time to move on. Do not look for me. I will be there when you need me. I've gone to where the sun shines and I am happy.

We're silent for a long while. *I'm sorry to leave you like this.* Could missiles have (. . . .) no. No, she wouldn't have.

Audio File 170
Date: June 27, 2019, 10:47 PM
Audio quality: Good

Voice 1:   My grandmother had a name for this=

Voice 2:   London?

Voice 1:   No=

Voice 2:   Darkness?

Voice 1:   N::::o=

Voice 2:   A park bench overlooking=

Voice 1:   NO. Well, maybe. The sweeping scene of contrasts as your eyes pan across a city at night. Twinkling panorama. Carpet of lights. Neither of those. She called it something so apt that (. . .) I just can't remember it. Maybe this will help=

Voice 2:   Is that? Where d'you=

Voice 1:   I bought the bottle with the prettiest label. I know NOTHING about alcohol. Here.

(00:01:11)

Voice 2:   Cheers. To your good health, Lucy.

Voice 1:   Thank you. My pleasure.

(00:09:54)

Voice 2:   There IS a Twyford code. There's got a be. This can't be all there is. Handful a circled words. NO. Got a be more to it.

Voice 1:   Does there, really?

Voice 2:   Nate, Donna. They both found chat rooms online.

Voice 1:   Nate and Donna, who are both as traumatized as you are by Miss isles's disappearance.

Voice 2:   YOU, me, Nate, we all saw acrostics=

Voice 1:   Word patterns, coincidences. Meaningless.

(00:14:44)

Voice 2:   This (. .) strong. Messing with me head.

Voice 1:   Is it? (. . . .) *Good.*

Voice 2:   I. See. Not a spirits drinker. Not for the taste. Just the effect.

Voice 1:   It's a good enough reason (. . .) down the hatch, there (. . . .)

Voice 2:   Lemmy see the book.

Voice 1:   In a minute. In a minute, Steve [*background noise*] alright then. But you know there's NOTHING in here. Just the story Edith Twyford wrote to help children forget the horrors they couldn't escape for real. This paragraph, Steve. What does it say?

Voice 2:   Where? Oh, OK (. . . . .) our yellow fish saw the sea. Fish sinks safe. The mask is Portland grey. The fish is in sight. You die ninth. Toll whiffs.

Voice 1:   Is that it?

Voice 2:   It's all I (. . .) all I can.

Voice 1:   I've got it. Right. Let's get back .hhhhhh I've remembered.
            My grandmother's name for this. LUMIVISTA. Thank you,
            Steve.

Audio File 171
Date: June 28, 2019, 6:59 AM
Audio quality: Good

.hhhhhhhhhh Lucy (. . .) and her posh booze. Type I'd only get to toast
a job. I just realized something. Bagged all that cash from the dealer, but
ain't once thought to buy meself a bottle. Too wrapped up in the code.

Looking out over the city. Felt nice. Couldn't say no, could I? (. . .)
Where's this? .hhhh her spare room [*background noise*] HELLO? Oh.

Audio File 172
Date: June 28, 2019, 7:01 AM
Audio quality: Good

Incoming call.

Caller: Right, Steve?

Source: Nate=

Caller: Worked out your chain of coordinates, exactly as we.

End call [error?].

Audio File 173
Date: June 28, 2019, 7:24 AM
Audio quality: Good

If you said FSBC back then, no one would know what the f[EXPLICIT]k
you were on about. I didn't when Andy first mentioned it. Ordinary

people don't. Only if you had, say, a million quids' worth a diamonds to send halfway round the world, would you be acquainted with Fragile, Secure & Bonded Couriers Limited. Even then, you'd not know their Heathrow warehouse from every other bland, anonymous unit on the industrial estate. Yeah, there's a whole world ordinary folk are oblivious to. And that's fine with those who use these services. Andy researched it for years, he said. And I knew we'd be working on this one for a good while before anything happened.

(00:00:53)

In some ways it were like the old days again. All the boys together, laughing, joking. Other times I had (. . .) when you get a little warning inside yourself. A doubt like a tiny black worm in your chest. I know now what they call it. A red flag. They told us inside. When you know something's not right but can't quite put into words what it is. So, you ignore it and make a bad decision. Well, I chose to ignore that red flag.

The young guns in group said it's denial. Distrust of your own instincts. Aversion to conflict. Overthinking. Well, I've had a long time to overthink since then and consider at what point I SHOULD a got out, versus the point I COULD a got out. Because the moment you know too much to walk away is pretty f[EXPLICIT]king soon into a job like that.

See I had the missus to think of. She deserved a nice flat and a nice life. Only, since Andy put me on the payroll I got less money, not more. Worse even than that, Andy were cool with me. He hadn't liked it when the missus spoke up. Offended him somehow. Funny, when you ask for money, people take it personal. Suddenly, he rethought my status in his firm. In his life. I weren't family and I weren't his (. . . .) *lackey* no more. So what was I? Our history counted for nothing. I see that now.

Still, he couldn't cut me loose. I knew too much. If I turned I could be dangerous. I daresay some would a got rid a me there and then. A quick, mysterious demise and the whole firm suited and booted to pay their respects at the funeral. But Andy couldn't do that. Couldn't justify it to his men. If he did that to Little Smithy, who'd been so loyal for so long, it would convey a reckless paranoia that would dent the loyalty of his other workers. You got a balance fear in others when you depend on it. It's got a be the right sort a fear. Yeah, I was left with the clubs to run and (. . .) forgotten about. Until that last job. He needed all hands on deck. Trusted hands.

(00:01:09)

First time ever he refused to give me what I asked for. He said no, I couldn't have his old car. Gave it to Little H. A big beamer going to a twentysomething kid. The way he looked at me across his desk. The way he sniffed as he spoke. What he said (. . . .) I could see his old man right there in that chair. But that would a been the worst thing I could a told him. So I say, not to worry, just a thought. From then on, I keep me head down. When this job pays off I'll get out. Me and the missus we'll go away. Start again. Yeah. I had a plan. If you got a plan you got hope (. . .) that's why (. . . . .) why I ignored the red flag.

(00:00:48)

And did what I did.

Audio File 174
Date: June 28, 2019, 8:33 AM
Audio quality: Good

Voice 1:   MORNING.

Voice 2:   *Morning.*

Voice 1:   Tea or coffee?

Voice 2:   *Coffee, please.*

Voice 1:   There we go.

[*background noise*]

Voice 1:   Steve, last night wasn't quite what it seemed. I have a the-
             ory. But to explore it, I couldn't let you know what I was

doing. You had to be oblivious. I'm afraid I got you drunk. Deliberately.

Voice 2:   Oh.

Voice 1:   Let me explain. Now, I've been reading about acrostic codes and it's FASCINATING. Did you realize a simple horizontal acrostic is one of the easiest codes to crack? For a human that is. But for a computer it's far more difficult. Language is unpredictable. Weird. Illogical. Full of idiom and allusion. Tone. Dialect. Ambiguity. And that's the SIMPLE acrostics people discuss on the web. We've seen how Edith Twyford's work contains FAR more complex codes. Now, the human brain has something computers do not have. And do you know what that is, Steve? (. . . .) Wisdom. Experience. Intuition. It can balance probability with possibility. It also has (. . .) fallibility.

Voice 2:   Valley Bill=

Voice 1:   Fallibility. The potential to make mistakes. To be wrong. To be (. . .) so DIFFERENT in its perception that it sees things even other brains don't. You read aloud a bizarre series of phrases from this early edition of Six on Goldtop Hill when you were, in your words, *p*[EXPLICIT]*sed* as a newt. I could only discover where those words were hidden by working backward from what you said. This is the original paragraph.

Aunt Honoria guffawed, her yellow teeth perilously close to Edward's face. "I'm astonished how disobedient and weak the Hortons are." She slapped Edward stiffly, making sure he stood still and took his punishment. Horatio stuffed Rose's stockings happily over mouths—Aunt scolded chuckling children as sharply.

Sophie approached their bellowing aunt and pointed, smiling, toward Edward's tiny pocket where he'd folded his stolen ham.

"I shall triple punish this thief. Bring here the rusty poker!'

Quaking, Edward cried, while Aunt permitted everyone to chant out loud: "Let cowardly Edward the thief feel profoundly ashamed!"

Only, you saw OUR YELLOW FISH SAW THE SEA. FISH SINKS SAFE. THE MASK IS PORTLAND GREY. THE FISH IS IN SIGHT. YOU DIE NINTH. TOLL WHIFFS.

Start from the word Honoria. Your sentence is made by picking one, apparently random, letter from each word. It's an irregular, complex acrostic of the type only readable if you have a key in advance and know what to look for. The key here would read two, two, three, one, two, five, two, and so on. An apparently random series of numbers that's easy to pass on and unfathomable if you don't know precisely where the references should be applied. What's more, there are no clues, no trigger words and some words are anagrams. Look. YOU DIE NINTH, TOLL WHIFFS. An anagram of YOU WILL NOT FIND THE FISH. We know fish means gold. The gold is safe. But when she says you will not find the fish, does she mean the gold is generally unfindable, or someone in particular will not find it?

Voice 1: FISH SINKS SAFE. The gold is in a safe, sunk or buried somewhere=

Voice 2: The code is designed to pass messages between people, or agencies, in collusion but not in contact (. . . .)

Voice 2: OK.

Voice 1: Only YOU do not have a key. If you read your teacher's book from cover to cover, nothing in it would give you the clue you read to me last night. Steve, when you're relaxed and (.) inebriated, free from pressure and expectation, you can see words that were never meant to be discovered by anyone other than the person, or agency, they're meant for.

Voice 2: Oh.

Voice 1: Under certain conditions, your mind focuses on ONE letter in each word. I don't know why, but whatever makes you unable to read normally gives you the ability to see these hidden messages. Whoever led you to believe you had the key to The Twyford Code was RIGHT. Only if they thought it was a book marked with the solution, they were on the wrong course entirely. You don't HAVE the key, Steve. You ARE the key.

Voice 2: .hhhhh hhhhhhhh Funny. My mate Paul. He remembers missiles said it. That it were me=

Voice 1: There=

Voice 2: He thought I made it up. That I strung her along. But. Lucy, I. After that. What happened with missiles. I never read nothing again. I never could very well, but after that. I lost what little I had.

Voice 1: Oh, Steve, how sad=

Voice 2: You said missiles circled words to say she'd (. . .) gone somewhere=

Voice 1: That was a lie. I thought you'd not worry about seeing a code if you thought there were no codes (. . .)

Voice 2: You LIED to me?

Voice 1: I did. But I had good intentions, so it doesn't count. Now, what does that say?

Voice 2: Liefern an [*DecipherIt*™ *language: German*] Werner Rick tar.

Voice 1: Deliver to Werner Richter. In German. The ab wear major whose wallet you found in Rushton tunnel. Now, Edith Twyford visited Germany several times during the Second World War. We've seen pictures of her reading to schoolchildren. But I don't think that's all she did on those trips. They were missions during which she passed books containing secret codes to British spies.

Voice 2: Rick tar were a spy?

Voice 1: I don't think so, Steve. Listen. OUR yellow fish (. . .) YOU will not find the fish. That's not an instruction, nor is it useful intelligence. It's a statement of defiance. Not intended for British spies, but for the enemy. This means, at some point=

Voice 2:   The old girl's cover was blown.

Voice 1:   Exactly. And what happened next?

[End Transcript]

Audio Files Batch 9

[Start Transcript]

Audio File 175
Date: June 28, 2019, 1:44 PM
Audio quality: Good

Lucy has read a LOT about espionage during the Second World War, and I've seen all the films and documentaries, so between us we've come up with a theory. Edith Twyford and her old man were allied spies. Through her books they passed messages between MI6 and agents in the field, operatives so deep undercover there were few safe ways to contact them. Then, at some point, it all went wrong.

Lucy shows me photographs on her laptop of the Twyfords together. Holding wineglasses at a garden party. Another picture. Evening do this time. Lucy reads the caption. *Opening night, Piccadilly Theatre, second of July 1941.* She zooms in until the frozen faces blur into nothing. Look, Steve, she squeals, Noel Coward. Well, THAT's proof, isn't it? Her eyes shine again. This old bloke's proper gnarly. Like a heavy you wouldn't mess with. Lucy reckons he was a spy who hid in plain sight as he traveled round Europe giving funny talks and, by the looks of him, smoking like a chimney.

She scrolls to another photo. Edith again, on the steps of a building. Her old man follows her up them, his back to the camera. She's turned, one hand shields her eyes. As if to see where he is. It's a dull photograph if you ask me. Only (. . .) I recognize that building. I was there not long ago myself. On them very steps as it happens. It's a unique place. Distinctive. I call it old-fashioned, only Lucy says no, it's knee oh classical like Martin's Bank. It's you see Elle, I says. I went there a few weeks ago to interview an expert on Edith Twyford. *You DIDN'T*, she breathes. Yeah, I did and she were proper useless too.

Lucy blinks at me. I can see her mind working. University College London was used as a covert intelligence base during the war, she says, all thoughtful. Its students were sent away, and the secret services moved in. How do you know that? I says. Because I studied there, Steve. History of Art at the Slade (. . .) and I know how we can find out more.

So here we are. Outside you see Elle again. Different entrance this time. Quieter. Not nearly so unique or distinctive. Arty-looking young guns waft about. They love a colorful hat round here. Lucy made some calls and is about to go in and speak to someone she knows. Better switch this.

Audio File 176
Date: June 28, 2019, 2:01 PM
Audio quality: Good

Voice 1:   Switch it on for me=

Voice 2:   It's on. But you don't need to take it, only=

Voice 1:   Yes I do. Mine won't fit in my inside pocket. Too big. This, on the other hand, is slim and discreet. Goodness, it's an iPhone FOUR. I remember these=

Voice 2:   It's my son's phone. I don't want=

Voice 1:   It's safe with me, Steve. There, see, all snug where it can secretly record my reunion with Professor Scott. Wait here and wish me luck.

Voice 2:   Yeah. Yeah. Don't be long.
            (00:02:31)

Voice 1:   Hello, Professor Scott [*background noise*] Lila=

Voice 3:	LILA. Come through. My door is always open for a bygone student [*background noise*] Now, are you in good health?
Voice 1:	I'm a librarian.
Voice 3:	Ah well=
Voice 1:	Oh, I'm making the best of it. In fact, it's why I'm here.
Voice 3:	Tea?
Voice 1:	Yes, please. (How can I help?) Well, the local mayor has commissioned a series of installations. NO BISCUITS thank you. It's to celebrate the work of artists in the fields of intelligence and counterintelligence during the Second World War.
Voice 3:	How INTERESTING=
Voice 1:	Especially those from the literary world=
Voice 3:	Graham Greene, Roald Dahl=
Voice 1:	Of course=
Voice 3:	Ian Fleming, Noel Coward=
Voice 1:	Naturally. I remember you spoke to us about University College and its role in the war. I wonder. Do you know anything about THIS?
Voice 3:	Can I see it a little closer? (. . .) I don't recognize them, who are they?
Voice 1:	Edith Twyford and Edward Barnes. The date is 1942.
Voice 3:	Well, that's when MI6 were based here. And that IS the steps of the Wilkins building, certainly. You think Edith Twyford was a spy? Edith Twyford the twee and much maligned children's author?
Voice 1:	*I suspect it, Professor.*
Voice 3:	Well, I never=
Voice 1:	What I wonder is (. . .) if your father mentioned her in his diaries.
Voice 3:	How (. . . . .) how do you know about my father=
Voice 1:	You told me.

Voice 3:   I did NOT. I (. .) It's not common knowledge. There are NO diaries=

Voice 1:   But there ARE, Professor. You told me all about them and even showed me the file. On that shelf. In this very room.

Voice 3:   .hhh (. . . .) When?

Voice 1:   Do you remember the launch party for your Gwen John retrospective? No? Here at the Slade. Late 2010. Sponsored by a very generous brewery if I remember=

Voice 3:   OH. I (.) I do recall the start of it=

Voice 1:   Around twelve you and I enjoyed a chat about gender identity in Welsh art, which meandered into a wide range of other topics. Cryptozoology. Small boatbuilding in Britain. And finally your life story.

Voice 3:   I can only=

Voice 1:   Eventually you became tearful about your father, who was dedicated to his work for the government and never engaged with you as a creative spirit. Apparently you fear his distance kept you from doing all you could for him in his twilight years. Finally, at the end of the night, when it was just you and me left in the building, you suggested I could improve my chances of a first if I=

Voice 3:   I APOLOGIZE. That was REPREHENSIBLE. I was in the WRONG.

Voice 1:   It was a very interesting conversation. At the time I didn't realize how significant it would be for me all these years later. No one needs to know, so long as you see your way clear to helping me on this matter.

Voice 3:   *What can I do?*

Voice 1:   You mentioned your father kept diaries of his time here during the war and that on his death they passed to you. I wonder if Edith Twyford or her husband appear in them?

I need proof she worked for MI6 to secure funding for my installation.

Voice 3: He kept diaries but very little remains. Mere fragments. Bits and pieces he neglected to destroy at the end of the war. I've struggled to take anything meaningful from them. I (. . .) let me find it. Wait. Wait here please, would you, Lila.

(00:04:14)

[*background noise*]

(00:09:37)

Voice 3: HERE. This is all his extant paperwork. I very much doubt Edith Twyford is anywhere in there, but you're welcome to look. Please don't remove anything from the file. As you'll see. Not particularly coherent.

Voice 1: Thank you (. . . . .) If you don't mind=

Voice 3: Take your time.

(00:19:01)

Voice 1: *Here. We. Are. The Hortons. Hortons 2 p.m. Inconsolable after Berlin breach. But have plan to save fish. Audacious and possible. They will make good. No doubts.*

(00:11:08)

Voice 1: Professor Scott? Thank you. I have all I need.

Voice 3: And (. . .) and we are (. .) even?

Voice 1: Oh yes. We=

Voice 4: Wait. What? [*background noise*] ()

(00:00:27)

[*background noise*]

Voice 4: () (are) [*background noise*]

Audio File 177
Date: June 28, 2019, 3:06 PM
Audio quality: Moderate

Voice 1:   *Steve?* (. . .) *Steve, where are you?* .hhh hhh .hhh hhh .hhh
            hhh [*background noise*] OF COURSE. I've got your phone,
            haven't I? *Steve.*

            (00:02:13)

[*background noise*]

Voice 1:   Hi, hiya. A small caramel latte, please.

Voice 2:   Here or to go?

Voice 1:   To go, please. Just (. .) I left a friend outside=

[*background noise*]

Voice 2:   There's your change. Sorry, what?

Voice 1:   A friend was waiting outside (but he's gone). Did you see
            anyone?

[*background noise*]

Voice 2:   What did (they look like)?

Voice 1:   Early fifties. Not tall. Smart suit and tie. Waiting just outside
            here or the entrance to the Slade.

Voice 2:   There WAS someone out there. Two others came along and
            they were talking. Then they all left. Would that be them?

Voice 1:   No. I've got his phone. His son's phone. He wouldn't go
            ANYWHERE without it. What did they look like? Men?
            Women?

Voice 2:   We::::ll the way I see it, gender is an outdated construct. Each
            individual finds their own place on a spectrum of identity
            that includes gender but isn't determined by it. There's your
            latte.

Voice 1:   (. . .) Thanks.

Voice 2:   Appeared to identify as male. Hope you find (them)=

[*background noise*]

(00:03:24)

Voice 1:   Oh, Steve, where have you got to? .hhhh hhhh

[*background noise*]

Voice 3:   HEY, WATCH IT=

Voice 1:   SORRY, sorry, sorry.

[*background noise*]

Voice 1:   No, not here either. Steve, why do you do this to me?

[*background noise*]

Voice 4:   LUCY. LUCY=

Voice 1:   .hhhhh where WERE you? Thought I'd (. . .) Oh my God
             what happened?

Voice 4:   Fell over. Went to the station toilets to clean up. It's nothing.
             Where's my son's phone? Give it to me=

Voice 1:   It's here. Still recording as far as.

Audio File 178
Date: June 28, 2019, 3:27 PM
Audio quality: Good

Voice 1:   Is it OK? Did it pick up my meeting with the professor?

Voice 2:   Yeah, yeah, probably. Thanks for the coffee. I owe you (. . . . .)
             ƒ[EXPLICIT]*k* me, three pound seventy-five.

Voice 1:   Steve, did you speak to anyone while I was away?

Voice 2:   No. I fell over, so=

Voice 1:   And cleaned yourself up in the toilets at which station?

Voice 2:   The one we come out of=

Voice 1:   Euston Square=

Voice 2:   ()

Voice 1:   OK. So long as you're not hurt.

Voice 2:   It's fine. Your old teacher alright?

Voice 1:   Couldn't have been better. He's an incorrigible old soak with
             a SHOCKING memory. Propositioned my friend Lila in

our final year, so I convinced him I was her. He'd told us the college was requisitioned by military intelligence during the war. His father was based here. When particularly refreshed he'd talk about the fragments of diary he inherited and how they'd be valuable if complete. I got him to show me. Steve, I found something in them. *Took photographs.* Well, he didn't say not to. Look at that.

Voice 2: Can you read it out. My glasses are=

Voice 1: *Hortons 2 p.m. Inconsolable after Berlin breach. But have plan to save fish. Audacious and possible. They will make good. No doubts.*

Voice 2: Hortons?

Voice 1: The surname of the Super Six children.

Voice 2: Or day (shoes)=

Voice 1: Audacious. It means daring, bold. What this diary entry shows is that Professor Scott's FATHER was Twyford's handler at MI6. Now, look at what he says. He meets them. They are inconsolable (. .) Berlin breach (. . . .) because on a trip to Berlin their cover was BLOWN. What if (. . .) the Abwehr [*DecipherIt*™ *language: German*] major, Werner Richter, captured Edith and OR Edward, interrogated them, forced them to reveal details about Operation Fish=

Voice 2: Forced? Nah. They'd play it cool. Make out they're *p*[EXPLICIT]*ed* off with their bosses. Sing like canaries. Like they're only too glad to rat. Double agents=

Voice 1: TRIPLE agents. Perhaps they never stop working for the British. Back with their handler in London they tell him everything and are inconsolable but have a plan to make good. A plan to save the fish. To save the gold.

Voice 2: Not send it away at all?

Voice 1: Maybe, but that's not audacious. Plus, any change to the plan and the Germans will know who told the British. What does he mean by an audacious plan to save the fish? (00:00:22)

Voice 2:	Are you up for meeting someone else this afternoon, Lucy?
Voice 1:	Who?
Voice 2:	Rosemary Wintle. The so-called expert on Edith Twyford.
Voice 1:	How do you know her?
Voice 2:	I met her back in April. The twenty-fifth if I remember correctly. She never mentioned the code.
Voice 1:	Let's go.

Audio File 179
Date: June 28, 2019, 4:43 PM
Audio quality: Good

hhhhhhhh Am I glad to have my son's phone back in my inside pocket. Where it belongs. I can fasten my coat, keep it safe. But as it turns out, his phone was safer with Lucy than with me this afternoon. She were on a mission to interview her old teacher. After my performance as a children's book illustrator in that publisher's office, when I told them the last time I'd seen so many books was on a protest bonfire at Belmarsh, she thought it best she do this one alone.

(00:01:09)

S[EXPLICIT]t. Soon I'll have to trust Lucy with everything (. . .) I don't know. I'd have preferred Nate. Not because I'm sexist, Maxine, but because he's got sons himself.

(00:00:59)

Always knew it would come. Just hoped it wouldn't be so soon. Things are (. . .) moving faster and. Closing in. But *f*[EXPLICIT]*k* it. There's never a good time, so.

(00:00:47)

Lucy had left me stood outside the college entrance by a coffee kiosk, dodging arty young guns with goatee beards, funny hats, pink hair, and holes in their trousers, when I hear a voice behind me. *Smithy*, it whispers. I know it by the shard of ice it sends down me spine. I spin round. There he is in broad daylight. Don't panic, Smithy, he says. We only want a talk. I swear everything freezes in that moment. It's like the street empties of people. Just a cold breeze and us three.

(00:00:28)

It's too soon. There are things I got a do. I still got stuff to record, about me. My life. You ain't heard the half of it yet, Maxine. So I ran. I shot down that street toward the main road. The more people around the less likely they'll be to do it. Truth is I'm the key. If they kill me, they'll never find out what's behind The Twyford Code. But they know I'll never tell 'em neither. They'll have to make me talk and that is the thing I fear the most, because I know what these people can do when they want something badly enough. I seen it. I (. .) yeah I stood by while they did it to others. I (. . .) I want to explain (. . .) It's why I had to do that to Colin. Do it quickly. Save him from them.

Is Lucy still speaking to her work on the phone? She is. This square by the university. Tall old dark houses. Looming up over us. I'm waiting for Rosemary Wintle, my eyes glued to the entrance. Face after face. Everyone looks the *f*[EXPLICIT]*king* same. I better recognize her again.

So back outside Slade I almost reach the main road. But he grabs me jacket, hauls me down a flight of steps into a basement stairwell. His (. . .) the younger one sails down after us. Closes the gate at the top, checks no one saw us. *B*[EXPLICIT]*ks* no one saw us. Course thesaurus. No one does nothing. I don't even expect 'em to.

We know you got it, he spits as he talks. I'm being held by the throat against a dirty old door. You have to make your move soon and wh:::en y::ou d:::o. If I never sleep again, he snarls, I'll go wherever you go. It belongs to us, not you, Smithy.

You don't want it, I can't help myself saying. It's cursed. You'll end up like (. . .) I can't get the word out. Missiles. Missiles. But someone's coming. With no warning he whacks me one so hard across the face, when I come to I'm alone at the bottom of the steps. How long have I been here? Lucy. Lucy'd be looking for me. My son's phone. Had to get my son's phone back.

You alright down there? Some arty young gun looks down at me, colorful scarf swings like a pair of pendulous *b*[EXPLICIT]*ks* over the gate. Yeah, yeah, I squeak and scramble up the steps. I just fell down, mate, I say, nothing to see here now.

I pull meself together, run back to the kiosk. Meet Lucy, get me son's phone back. Thank *f*[EXPLICIT]*k*. She been sweet-talking her old teacher. Found some reference to Twyford in a diary his old man kept during the war.

Here she is. Right, time to see if Rosemary Wintle is gun a talk this time.

Audio File 180
Date: June 28, 2019, 4:59 PM
Audio quality: Good

Voice 1:   .hhh hhh .hhh hhh HEY STOP. Misses. Mrs. Wintle?

Voice 2:   I (. . . .) I recognize YOU. Who on earth=

Voice 1:   We know. *We know Edith Twyford was a spy*, a double, triple agent, during the Second World War.

Voice 2:   I see. And why=

Voice 1:   She hid messages in her books, her Super Six books.

Voice 2:   About what?

Voice 1:   Operation Fish.

Voice 2:   Shhhhh. *Come with me.*

Audio File 181
Date: June 28, 2019, 5:07 PM
Audio quality: Good

Voice 1:   I think we're safe enough here. Now, YOU. Are you REALLY writing a book?

Voice 2:   *No, miss.*

Voice 1:   I thought not. Have you been in a fight?

Voice 2:   It's nothing, it's=

Voice 3:   Mrs. Wintle, we're both FASCINATED by The Twyford Code and we'd LOVE to know EXACTLY what it is=

Voice 1:   I would advise against that. I suggest you marvel at the ingenuity of a lost generation, then walk away. That's what I'd say if I thought you would listen. I fear it's too late=

Voice 3:   But SURELY being an expert on Edith Twyford=

Voice 1:   I'm an expert in twentieth-century children's literature=

Voice 3:   Why do you want this kept secret? You could gain lucrative speaking engagements from it. There's nothing to lose. Operation Fish is already out there. I'm a librarian and I KNOW the subjects people are interested in .hhhhh YOU could write a book about it=

Voice 1:   I can't.

Voice 3:   But you CAN. Wartime intrigue and subterfuge with a dash of conspiracy theory=

Voice 1:   No=

Voice 3:   But WHY not?

Voice 1:   .hhhh hhhh (. .) because Operation Fish is the most audacious (. .) *hoax* of the postwar era.

Voice 3:   A *HOAX*? So the country's gold reserves WEREN'T moved to Canada?

Voice 1:   Can you imagine that amount of gold bullion crossing the Atlantic Ocean? At the best of times, let alone during a war fought at sea. No. The only thing REAL about Operation Fish was the handful of sailors' ditty boxes, each with a decorative fish clasp, made as if to commemorate the mission. They fetch a hundred pounds each at auction these days I believe.

Voice 3:   Why did Edith hide references to a convoy in her books?

Voice 1:   To convince the enemy there was an opportunity to steal Britain's gold. Double agents passed the newly published Six on Goldtop Hill to German intelligence, along with misinformation that it's a message between MI6 and spies working undercover in the Reich. As planned, it's taken as proof of an upcoming secret convoy.

Voice 2:   Battery in boner venture=

Voice 1:   HMS Batory and HMS Bonaventure. The clues were in-fused with a level of detail the enemy could cross-reference with what they knew about the British fleet. All designed to reinforce the lie.

Voice 3:   .hhh hhh What a SPLENDID story.

Voice 1:   Splendid, is it? You haven't asked the single, most pertinent question yet.

Voice 3:   Oh. Er, (. . . .) Steve, any questions?

Voice 2:   Miss, if the enemy thought they had the chance to nick a s[EXPLICIT]*tload* of gold (. . .) did they have a stab at it?

Voice 3:   .hhhh Mrs. Wintle, at Martin's Bank in Liverpool there's a plaque commemorating Operation Fish. In the underground room beneath it, we found a fish drawn on the wall. Now, this fish also appears in a building that used to be a bank in wrecks em. ONLY, the fish in Martin's Bank has been painted over with a SWASTIKA=

Voice 1:   It would be useful if you spoke slower and *kept your voice down*=

Voice 3:   *I'm sorry, Mrs. Wintle.* I'm (. . .) both of us, we're passionate about the code.

Voice 1: *Firstly, the plaque at Martin's Bank.* A wonderful exercise in misdirection. The former bank in Wrexham, now a wine bar, I believe, was a discreet meeting place for the select few who knew about the hoax, nothing more=

Voice 2: Mrs. Wintle, who's Werner Rick tar?

Voice 1: (. . . .) Where did you hear that name?

Voice 2: I found his ID card. In Rushton tunnel=

Voice 3: Where there's ALSO a fish mural (. . . .) Mrs. Wintle? (. . . .) Are you OK?

Voice 1: .hhh hhh Well, then let me tell you what happened. As it was told to me. Over here, where it's quieter.
(00:00:09)

Voice 1: On a trip to Berlin, Edith Twyford's cover was blown. She was captured by a committed and ambitious Abwehr [*DecipherIt*™ *language: German*] major called Werner Richter. To save her own life, she had to convince him she was valuable. She does what she's best at and tells him a story. The story of Operation Fish, a plan to ship Britain's gold to Canada. In fluent German she convinces him she wants to change sides. She says she'll divert the gold to him, and he can ship it to Germany. Eager to procure such riches for the führer, Richter allows her to return home. Only, there is no such plan to ship Britain's gold anywhere. Not yet, anyway. Edith and Edward commit to turn their breach to Britain's advantage.

Voice 3: This is IT! Her audacious plan. I saw her handler's diary, Mrs. Wintle.

Voice 1: Richter's senior officers insist he sees this huge shipment of gold before they deploy valuable resources to procure it, so Edith brings him to Britain in secret. He is dropped ashore on the East Anglian coast where she has hidden a small rowing boat. She collects him from a rural inlet=

Voice 3: Blyth *Spirit* to Palmers Lane=

Voice 1:   On this visit she must convince him Britain's entire wealth is en route to Canada and that she can divert it to him. Edith drives him to Martin's Bank, a building impressive enough that he believes gold would be stored there. Sure enough she shows him an underground room where a few bars of gold bullion have been carefully stacked by Edward. The rest, she tells him, has been transported already and is waiting for them. This underground room was really a secret holding cell reserved for enemy spies, so while preparing it, Edward was careful to obliterate any clues to its real use with strategic daubs of black paint over giveaway marks and signs. He also drew a distinctive fish symbol on the wall. A design he saw in a stained-glass window at the wrecks em bank while planning the hoax operation. He was a sweet, artistic man and for him it represented the mission (. . . .) Edith showed Richter the fish mural and they laughed at this crude, secret symbol of an operation about to go horribly wrong for Britain. I was told that as Edith and Werner were laughing, Edith spotted a tin in the corner of the cell, and a brush still wet with black paint. She froze. It could have given the game away, but instead Werner was infused with excitement. Gold fever. Without stopping to wonder why the paint was there, he grabbed the brush and obliterated the fish with what you saw is there to this day.

Voice 3:   Why didn't they hand him over to the authorities?

Voice 2:   Or kill him as soon as he arrived?

Voice 1:   Richter was used. A pawn to misdirect the enemy. Throughout his visit he remained in touch with Berlin, who followed his progress closely. Once he confirmed the authenticity of the gold, Germany would send a convoy of vessels across the North Sea to collect it. Where, unknown to them, naval destroyers would lie in wait.

Voice 3:   So, Operation Fish doesn't mean goldfish so much as literally fishing. Fishing for the enemy. What a STORY.

Voice 1:   Edith and Richter secreted the final gold bars of the fake heist in Edith's car. Hidden in the trunk, Richter thought he was being taken farther north. He gave Berlin the co-ordinates of the coastal town where Edith said the bulk of the gold had been moved. It is safe to say Werner trusted Edith completely. Why else would he carry his ID card so far behind enemy lines? By all accounts he was quite besotted with her.

Voice 3:   Where was Edward?

Voice 1:   The Berlin breach made senior officials aware of how vulnerable Britain's gold reserves were. Even if the audacious plan worked, the bullion couldn't stay at the Bank of England in London. So, while Edith was in Liverpool, her husband, Edward, was busy preparing the gold for where it would REALLY spend the next few years. As planned, Edith drove Richter to Dorset. They arrive at a secret underground tunnel on the outskirts of an RAF airfield. He was finally allowed to see, touch, and admire the treasure, with its unmistakable color and texture, stacked on wooden pallets. He radioed the news to Berlin. He has the gold, it is stacked near the northeast coast and ready for collection. He signed off, packed up his radio, and placed those final bars with the rest, using great care and precision. But when he turned back to Edith, he froze. She stood there, quite calm, the gun in her unshaking hand, pointed directly at him (. . . .) I would like to say she killed him without hesitation, but I believe she waited to see the realization dawn in his eyes before she pulled the trigger.

Voice 3:   Edith Twyford shot a Germany SPY?

Voice 1:   Believe me, she was very far from TWEE. If you've been to

Rushton tunnel then you've walked on Richter's grave. His body sunk, unmarked in the mud. As Edward helped Edith climb out of Rushton tunnel, Britain's gold was believed safe in Canada, a German intelligence agent was dead, and a convoy of enemy boats was about to be picked off one by one.

(00:00:12)

Voice 3: So the audacious plan worked.

Voice 1: Only ONE thing wasn't quite as expected. Edith assumed Rick tar would have a Morse radio transmitter, nothing more. When she met him in rural Suffolk, she was surprised to see he also had a huge suitcase that contained the largest typewriter she'd ever seen. He used it religiously before he radioed any message to Berlin.

Voice 3: .hhhh *Oh my goodness=*

Voice 2: ENIGMA=

Voice 1: Once Rick tar was dead, Edith shipped it straight to Bletchley Park for examination. It changed the course of the war and shaped European history for generations.

Voice 3: .hhh hhh If Edith Twyford committed the murder of the twentieth century, why is she maligned today? She's a war hero.

Voice 1: Because of what happened after the war. Most government insiders believed the Operation Fish story. Only a select few elite officials knew the gold never went to Canada. Years later, the war over, they arrived in Rushton tunnel to return it to the Bank of England. But the tunnel was empty. Just a few broken wooden pallets in the mud. The treasure was long gone. Secretly moved on, years before.

Voice 3: Moved on? You mean (. . .) *stolen?*

Voice 1: No one knew where it went. But they soon worked out WHO had taken it.

Voice 3:   .hhh hhh Mrs. Wintle, was it Edward Barnes? (. .) It WAS.

Voice 2:   What a *f*[EXPLICIT]*king* LAD.

Voice 1:   He assured them it wasn't technically stolen. That it was safe. That clues to its whereabouts would be released, eventually. As it transpired, both he and Edith died without apparently leaving anything of the sort.

Voice 3:   Only, we know she did, Mrs. Wintle. She left her stories, her books=

Voice 1:   And no key to decipher any messages within them.

Voice 3:   But why? Why did they steal the gold? They were so (. . .) patriotic.

Voice 1:   Indeed. To have done something like that they must have felt betrayed. Used. Perhaps they wanted to teach their government handlers a lesson.

Voice 3:   Or they wanted to make a point about what it is we consider worthwhile by testing the value of the most sought-after commodity in the world.

Voice 2:   *B*[EXPLICIT]*ks*. No offense, Lucy, Mrs. Wintle. But guys rob loot like that for one reason. To spend it. To live magnificent for as long as the dough lasts. That gold is long gone, I can tell you that.

Voice 1:   Indeed. That too is possible. But the evidence suggests otherwise. Not one of those individually marked bullion bars has ever come to light=

Voice 2:   Bullion is a liability, miss. You want a melt those *f*[EXPLICIT]*kers* down pronto. Split up the haul, disperse it. Make it into rings, bracelets, coins, necklaces=

Voice 3:   THAT much gold though, Steve=

Voice 2:   Yeah. That much gold. A decent crucible, borax, a good flame. I'm not saying it's the work of a moment, but. Easier to hide, easier to move, easier to sell=

Voice 1:   But there's evidence to the contrary. Anyone making significant financial gain is easily identified by unusual amounts of money moving through their accounts. By unexplained property purchases. By the spending of large sums on expensive items. One thing is obvious, the Twyfords did not benefit financially from Operation Fish=

Voice 2:   They would a passed it on to family=

Voice 1:   They had no children together=

Voice 2:   Friends then. F[EXPLICIT]k me, the cats' home for all I know, but=

Voice 3:   MRS. WINTLE, were the Twyfords charged with theft, imprisoned, *made to talk*?

Voice 1:   Not at all. They remained at liberty, indeed protected, for the rest of their lives. The coastline and shipping movements were so tightly controlled and monitored over the entire war and postwar period, the government knew the gold did not leave these shores. Only the Twyfords knew its precise whereabouts. If they were killed it would remain out of reach forever. But there's a more pertinent reason they went unpunished for their crime (. . .) how could they be guilty of stealing gold that, officially, was safe, thousands of miles away in Canada? To indict them would have been to reveal Operation Fish as a hoax, and admit they'd lost the gold.

Voice 3:   The perfect crime. Tell me, how did the government account for the gold being (. .) gone?

Voice 1:   They had to keep the lie alive. When the time came for it to return from Canada, hundreds of cement blocks were painted gold and stacked in the vault. The people making them believed they were simply decoys to protect the real gold as it was in transit.

Voice 2:   .hhh hhh What a diamond of a job=

Voice 3:   But it works BOTH ways, Mrs. Wintle. They couldn't just GIVE it back. If they did then they'd have NO, forgive the pun, CURRENCY with which to negotiate their freedom. As soon as the gold was safely back in the bank, they'd have been charged with theft and=

Voice 2:   Banged up or worse=

Voice 1:   Indeed=

Voice 3:   And Operation Fish is considered FACT now=

Voice 1:   It's a wonderful, morale-boosting story that survives to this day. But the truth is sadly a tale of betrayal, deception and, for all we know, base human greed.

Voice 2:   Where is it then? Where's the f[EXPLICIT]*king* gold?

Voice 1:   Hidden. Hidden in words and letters. In books no one reads anymore. By a writer discredited in the eyes of contemporary society. Somewhere in Edith Twyford's canon is the answer, but no one knows where, or how to find it.

Voice 3:   But Mrs. Wintle, Edith and Edward are both dead now. Yet the code didn't die with them. It's still controlled by SOMEONE. The publishers say new text is supplied for each edition of her books. SOMEONE knows where it is.

Voice 1:   Yes.

Voice 2:   Kos it's always on the move=

Voice 3:   Yet it doesn't MATTER. Mrs. Wintle, Steve, this gold has been missing for nearly eighty years. Yet here we are. There's a vault in the Bank of England full of cement blocks that masquerade as gold and it doesn't matter (. .) the expectation, the promise, the illusion, is enough. Everything carries on as normal. You have to admit it really IS a lesson in value=

Voice 1:   And in honor, loyalty. Edith Twyford's poor reputation today is the price she continues to pay for her betrayal.

Voice 3:   You trust US with this, this explosive secret?

Voice 1:   I don't have to=

Voice 2:   My friend Nate is on the web every day looking for the answer=

Voice 1:   And I expect at some time, someone, somewhere has posted an accurate interpretation, but it was lost in a cacophony of theories. The online speculation simply plays into the hands of everyone who wants the code kept secret.

Voice 2:   To be fair, he'll be gutted it's not aliens.

Voice 1:   Precisely. Most coders will never realize quite how much they DON'T want the code solved. It's the mystery, the not knowing, that drives them, take that away and=

Voice 2:   The green bus.

Voice 1:   Sorry?

Voice 2:   I found my Edith Twyford book on a green bus with no driver. Years ago, on my way to school. My teacher confiscated it and followed the code herself. But that green bus. How do you explain that?

Voice 1:   I can't. Maybe it isn't connected to the code. Perhaps it's something else.

Voice 3:   Steve, do you know those men?

Voice 1:   They are another reason I don't need to trust you with this information=

Voice 3:   MRS. WINTLE. WHO ARE THEY=

Voice 1:   You won't be here much longer=

Voice 2:   S[EXPLICIT]t here we go=

[*Background noise*] (. . . . .)

Audio File 182
Date: June 28, 2019, 6:17 PM
Audio quality: Good

Voice 1:   *Lucy (. .) Lucy (. . .) are you in here?*
            (00:00:15)
            I can't hear you, so. If you ARE in here and can't move or talk, remember everything'll be OK. I don't know where these

     b[EXPLICIT]*ds are taking us. I want a call Nate, get help,*
     but ca::::n't get my son's phone ou:::::t me pocket hhhhh.
[*Background noise*]
     What the (. . .) Did you hear that? Voices sssh=
[*Background noise*] (. . . . .) [*Background noise*]
     (00:01:49)
[*Background noise*]
     F[EXPLICIT]*k. Lucy, if you're here, keep still. Don't move.*
     There's footsteps (. . . . .)
[*Background noise*]
Voice 2:   GET OUT.
[*Background noise*]

Voice 2:	State a you. GET OUT.
Voice 1:	*F*[EXPLICIT]*k* me. What YOU doing here?
Voice 2:	What's it look like?
Voice 1:	I don't know what to say=
Voice 2:	Thank you would be nice=
Voice 1:	Thanks, mate (. . .) thanks, Paul.

Audio File 183
Date: June 28, 2019, 9:22 PM
Audio quality: Good

Dorset. Hampshire. Wiltshire. Is it clear enough to see five counties? I left 'em down there, sitting round the trapdoor. Said I'll be a little while. They said fine .hhh hhh can't remember where I got up to, Maxine. So much you need to know, and I got a tell you, but. Time goes so quick.

    (00:04:04)

We did two dummy runs before the big FSBC job back in 2007. It weren't enough. But I were so used to ignoring red flags by then I went along with it. Trusted Andy's judgment and planning like I always had. I bet the others did too.

I were paired up with John Harrison and it were clear to me pretty quickly he weren't up to it. Swore he'd been off the dance pills and weed for years. If that were the case then the comedown bides its time, waits for you, hits like a *b*[EXPLICIT]*h* when you're least able to fight it.

Yeah, he had sweaty turns where he'd panic over nothing. Gabble nonsense about *s*[EXPLICIT]*t* I couldn't see. *There it is*, he'd whisper and point to the dashboard clock [*DecipherIt*™ *time ref 528531-15155*]. DON'T TRUST THAT SNAKE, STEVE, *it's got a human face.* Next thing, he'd be on a proper downer. Crouched in the footwell sobbing like a baby. *F*[EXPLICIT]*k* me I were worried. Not just for John and the family, but for the job. We were manning the number one vehicle. Trusted above and beyond every other man there. We had to stay focused, but how could I with John in that state?

So I told Andy. Big mistake. He exploded. Accused me of bad-mouthing his brother, wanting him to abandon the biggest job of his life, stop him getting out the game (. . .) I weren't doing any such thing, but.

I know NOW why he reacted like that. He assumed I felt the same about him as he felt about me. It's called reflect attribution, according to the young guns inside, and it can help explain negative behavior in others. This is so you don't get riled by it and can walk away without getting in a fight. Yeah, when he accused me of disrespecting him, it were because he had no respect for me anymore. He thought I were trying to sabotage his plans, because given half a chance he'd do the same to me.

By then all I wanted were to get the job done and get out. So, with yet another little black worm nagging its way through my chest, I put me head down, shut me mouth, and got on with it. Worse thing about it was, and here's irony again, Maxine, after that I found meself COVERING for John. Obliged to tell everyone he were fine, not to worry, we'd be alright. I were so concerned I even memorized his role in the job, as well as me own, determined whatever happened we'd do what Andy wanted and get this final job done. Until .hhhh hhhh eventually, the night came. He and I dressed in identical black clothes, sat outside

FSBC, watching, waiting, and, lucky for me at least, blissfully unaware of just how final this final *f*[EXPLICIT]*king* job were gun a be.

Audio File 184
Date: June 28, 2019, 9:30 PM
Audio quality: Good

So Lucy and me stop Rosemary Wintle coming out of her office and she takes us down a side road to a set of benches by an old water fountain in a private square. All calm and pretty. It's rush hour by now but we're off the beaten track, as commuters pass by on the main road, well out of earshot.

I set me son's phone to record and (. . . .) once I've updated eye oh S I'll work out which file is which, but till then, I'm gun a limit the number a times I put into words what the code refers to. That's why I won't say it again here. If you've heard the previous files, Maxine, you'll know. If you haven't, well, you'll just have to take my word it were pretty *f*[EXPLICIT]*king* crazy.

So, Mrs. Wintle tells us and as we're reeling from the knowledge, up screeches a van. Next thing we know, two grunts leap out and make a grab for us. They go for me first. I scream at Lucy to run. But they kick me feet out from under me and pull a bag over me head. I got no idea if she escapes or not.

I kick and claw and fight, but they're twice my size and there's two a the *f*[EXPLICIT]*kers*. Once they got me hands tied behind me back, I got no chance. Times like that you got a let a calm descend over you. Nature has a thing to stop you fighting when you're outnumbered or overwhelmed, whatever. Basic survival. *F*[EXPLICIT]*k* me, I done it enough times to *c*[EXPLICIT]*ts* meself (. . .) the harder you go in, the faster they stop resisting. On the other side of the fence, if there's nothing you can do about it, chill. There's a freedom when you let go like that (. .) a bit like doing time.

But right now, all I can think of is Lucy and how she's different to me. She got no experience a this type a thing. She don't know what I know. She'll be terrified.

We drive for what feels like hours. All the time me son's phone burns a hole in me inside pocket. If I end up brown bread how will you get my voice recordings, Maxine? You'll never know how it panned out, this journey I set out on to make sense of the past. A journey I never thought would take the twists and turns it did. Let alone end like this.

I come over all melancholy. A tight feeling in me chest. Breathing turns to sobs. Only I can't make a sound. I don't want Lucy to hear me. Why not? Why shouldn't she hear? There's nothing wrong with letting other people see your emotions, that's what they told us inside. But I don't want Lucy to know I'm cut up and get more upset herself. I don't want her to realize so (. . .) I calm meself down, so she don't feel as empty and hopeless as I do. What's that all about? Strange, in it, (. . .) to feel what someone else might feel. What is that?

So, we're driving fast and I can tell we've left London. We're on a motorway. The M3 is my guess, and thinking about where we are now, I were probably right. I whisper into the bag, try to get Lucy's attention, but there's no answer. It's (. . .) it turns out she weren't there. Lucy escaped after all (. . .) sorry. I got these (. .) *tears*.

(00:03:57)

So back in the van I'm whispering to Lucy, as I think, but suddenly out of nowhere BANG. The van is rammed from behind. It skids about on the road, hits something, slows right down. We been driven off the road. I sit tight, hope for the best.

F[EXPLICIT]*k* it. Who should haul me out the back a the van but Paul. PAUL. Shifty little guy from school. How did HE know where I was?

By the time I got the bag off me head the grunts are long gone into the undergrowth. Paul's dragging me toward, and I can't believe this meself, Maxine: MY CAR. Yeah, Paul's got my car. As soon as he's cut the plastic tie round me wrists I dive straight into me pocket, pull out the car key. Paul laughs. Never heard him laugh before. Sounds like he's sanding a rusty pipe. Get in, he says, I'll explain everything when we get there (. . . .) yeah, when we get there.

(00:01:17)

This. This place I am now. If Edith Twyford were thinking a somewhere real when she wrote about Goldtop Hill, this would be it. Not far from her pad either. Overlooks Rushton tunnel.

(00:01:05)

Turns out Nate can see exactly where my son's phone is. He were worried I'd get into trouble. Wanted to keep an eye on me. He can track me on his computer with the same software old Bill use to trace murderers. Well, we never learned that at community college.

He saw my son's phone disappear at the side entrance to you see Elle. This would a been when Lucy took it in to see her old teacher. Signal must be dodgy there. Nate gets concerned. He knows Paul's handy, asks him to check up on me. Trouble is, Paul don't have a car with him right then. No problem, says Nate, I'll tell you where Steve's motor's parked, you can take that. Yeah, turns out Nate also placed a tracker in me CAR. Paul finds it and, being a mechanic, gets in and starts it up quicker than if he had the key.

So Paul's across the square, watches Lucy, me, and Mrs. Wintle talk by the water fountain, reports back to Nate I'm simply entertaining two lady friends. He's about to leave when the van pulls up and drags me off. He shadows the van and when it's out on the open road, sets about freeing me from the (. . .) from what was holding me prisoner.

(00:01:36)

Paul gets me out, takes the bag off me head, the cable ties off me hands, and sits me in the car. I'm trembling with relief, I don't mind who knows it. Now, you'd expect Paul to turn the car round. Take me back to London. To Lucy. Nate. To YOU, Maxine. But he didn't. We drive down side roads and lanes. Through little villages. A couple a double backs just to be certain we ain't tailed. Then we arrive. Here. Hereabouts. Down there in the field.

Paul stops my car on a side road. Why are we here? I ask. *You'll see*, he whispers. He's serious. As if he hates being here .hhh hhh being BACK here. He leads me through a line a trees and into a field. Then he whispers something, dead quiet. *This is where it was*, he says. *This is the place.*

Audio File 185
Date: June 28, 2019, 9:46 PM
Audio quality: Good

We stared at the closed door to the FSBC warehouse. You could pass by that place every day a your life and never know what was in it. John rocked beside me in the passenger seat, sniffy, sweaty, breathing heavy. *You'll be OK, John*, I whispered. *You remember the drill, you got the electronic key, ain't you?* (. . .) Then I saw his eyes and me ticker almost stopped there and then (. . . .) I don't even lower my voice. What you *f*[EXPLICIT]*king* taken? I were in no mood for it, Maxine. He knew what this job meant to Andy and the family.

Chill out, Smithy, he chirps, just something to take the edge off. You want some? He digs in his pocket till I slam the steering wheel. I say of course I *f*[EXPLICIT]*king* don't and if he had any respect for his old man's memory, for his brothers, for his family, then HE wouldn't either. He looked at me with a sort of surprise on his face. Like he were somewhere between amused and disappointed. Then shook his head. *Loyal Little Smithy* was all he said. Funny, but the way he said it weren't like that was my nickname. More like I was just (. . .) small.

I forced meself to simmer down, fixed me eyes on the warehouse door. All I wanted was to be back home with the missus, job over and done with. Instead, time crawled. I checked me burner phone every few seconds. Longed to see the code 2222. What Andy was gun a text us if the job was called off. It didn't arrive. Job was on.

I had no excitement in me. Not this time. All I could see was the missus sat in our little flat, surrounded by photographs a babies (. .) she'd heard it could stimulate her eggs and she'd try anything. When I told her I was at the club that night, she had no reason not to believe me. There was a dinner in the fridge for me to microwave when I got in. She'd put a knife and fork either side of a table mat. What kind a fool risks all that? (. . .)

I could hear me own blood pressure in me ears as the security van pulled up. I gave John a tap. We pulled balaclavas over our faces, got our shooters ready. I noticed his hands shake, much like me own. I pulled meself together, Kos one of us had to be on the ball.

Two burly guards got out the van, made their way to the door. How could two young guns like that walk so *f*[EXPLICIT]*king* slow? I slid me shooter into position, gently clicked the door open. John ought a been doing the same, but (. . .) *JOHN*, I whispered. That's when he turned to me. When a fella's face is covered by a balaclava, it's only his eyes and mouth you can see. It focuses your gaze. Well, his bloodshot eyes were yellow. Mouth gummy and sticky like an old man. Or a child. I can't do it, Smithy, he says. I can't, mate.

I tried to keep one eye on the guards, chatting by the door, like there's all the time in the world. But I had to get John back. *Course you can*, I hissed. *Think of the cash, John. Andy, how hard he's worked. We can't let him down.* The guards had their keys out, we had to move, and quick. But John gripped me arm, pulled on it till his face was in mine. I swear the *f*[EXPLICIT]*er* was crying. He shook his head. *I can't do it to you, Smithy*, he whispers.

What the *f*[EXPLICIT]*k*? Too late, the grunts had the door open. NOW. I pulled John along with me, went through the motions like we'd rehearsed a hundred times but me head was all over the place. We tore toward the door. I jumped one guard, while John grappled with the other. Clipped them in plasticuffs hands and feet, bags over their heads. Ripped their radios out, chucked their phones, neutralized their positional sensors. I glanced at John. For a second I were relieved to see adrenaline take over. Only, that relief were short-lived.

He was meant to get in at the warehouse door, disable the alarm with an electronic key supplied by our inside man. Meanwhile I was supposed to stay down, keep both guards silent, make sure they didn't get heroic on us. Only, John never got up. He knelt between the guards, silently rocking and grimacing. Off his head on ket. I had no choice but to grab the electronic key from his belt and do the rest meself. I slipped in through the door, slammed that plastic *f*[EXPLICIT]*ker* into the panel and typed 7771.

Our other vans rumbled into the yard. It were lucky I had memorized all John's moves, Kos as far as the job went I was HIM at that moment. The guys jumped out, all of us identical in black clothes and balaclavas. I kept the inside door open, pressed meself against the wall as they streamed past, barely acknowledging I'm there they're so focused on their own jobs.

I heard Andy's voice. Him and John were the only two left outside now. I peered out. They coming or what? John was still knelt between the two guards. They were facedown, playing dead like their training told 'em. Andy stood there, with his Beretta 9000 and custom mute. Deadly. He were pointing it at John. Why? I think to meself. Why's Andy threatening his own brother? John, head back, grimacing at the sky. Andy engaged the cartridge. Shook his head. That's when he said it. Sharp, urgent. Like it were a warning.

(00:00:18)

Smithy, yer shooter.

(00:00:11)

Just that. And. That sound. Head shot. There's nothing like it. You never forget.

(00:01:24)

Andy ignored the whimpering guards, looked at the body blown backward on the ground, and gives a (. . .) a what? A little chuckle. A laugh. Humorless, I'll give him that. Resigned. Like the noise you make when you hear something inevitable's happened. He looked up, caught me watching, gave me a wink. Good work, kid, he mouths, and jogs past me into the warehouse.

I was frozen right there in the doorway. Couldn't tear me eyes from John's body. All I could think is, it's me. That's ME. Andy killed me in front a me eyes. Did John know? Is that what he couldn't do? Why he got *s*[EXPLICIT]*tfaced* for the biggest job of our lives? Couldn't face betraying loyal Little Smithy. Did he (. . .) and I can't say for sure even now, so many years later, but (. .) did he stay down on purpose? Either way he saved my life (. . .) Yet (. . .) still I died that day.

Audio File 186
Date: June 28, 2019, 10:01 PM
Audio quality: Good

Paul leads me through the trees to the field beyond and I know where we are now. My heart sinks, but in a strange way. Like the sun sinks behind the horizon. Temporary. As if (. .) I know this will be bad, but once it's over, things at least stand a chance a getting better. As we emerge from the treeline and squeeze through those rusty old gates again, I stop dead. We're not alone, and I recall a couple of other cars parked in the lane. The others fall silent as they see me. There are five of us. Five. We stood there in the dark, only it's light enough. I daresay if I could look away I'd see our moon shadows on the ground.

We all stare at each other. I got a feeling of calm. Of not being alone for once. In all them eyes, I don't see any anger, or blame, just sadness. Paul, me, Nate, Shell, and Donna. *Cheers, Paul*, Nate whispers. Then he looks around at us and says, you know why we're here. They all nod. Let's do it then. Nate leads the way.

I watch them file after him. Shell takes my hand. Strange feeling. Can't remember the last time I touched someone and it weren't to knock s[EXPLICIT]*t* out of 'em or take a beating meself. You OK, Steve? she asks. I don't know, says I. She squeezes my hand and leads me after the others. Funny. What jewelry did she have on? Didn't notice.

We pass through a fence into a field. The rustling corn. Is it silent or do I just not hear it? We stop in a clearing, where the others have formed a circle. I don't have to be told where I am. The trapdoor is well hidden, but Nate brushes aside earth, dust, and stones to reveal the cast-iron ring. I feel cold again. Like I did when Colin told me about Mum and Dad. Like when Andy shot John. Only this time I got an arm round me. Two arms, three. We're stood around the trapdoor, all five of us, our heads together. Paul sniffs, Shell sobs, Nate, Donna. All of 'em crying in the place we lost missiles. I can't help it. I cry too .hhh hhh .hhh hhh .hh hh .hh hh .h h [*background noise*]

(00:02:48)

When they're all silent again, Shell puts her tissues away, gets a little bunch a flowers out of her bag, scatters them over the trapdoor. Donna, bends down, runs her hand over it. Nate stands, head bowed, like he's at a graveside. Paul takes a swig from his hip flask.

Shell breaks the silence. Steve should know what happened. We should've told him then. *He deserves closure*, Donna whispers. The corn suddenly rustles as if it agrees. Yeah, says Nate, it's time. And that's when they tell me.

Audio File 187
Date: June 28, 2019, 10:06 PM
Audio quality: Good

Andy taught me that planning is the key to success and you know how long he spent preparing us for a big hit. Well, in the time it took for me to close the warehouse door and follow him down the corridor to the others, I made a plan myself. In my whole life I have never thought quicker or with greater clarity than I did in those few minutes. It were as if I could see my situation from every point a view, every moment in time and every angle under the sun.

They all thought I was John. So I walked like John, talked like John, sniffed, twitched and fidgeted like John. Kept me head down, so me eyes and mouth didn't give the game away. When I reached the others, stood around Bradley as he burned through the strong room door, I could hear Andy. *Smithy's DEAD,* he whispered, to gasps of shock all round. *John warned him, I heard him say Smithy, yer shooter, but as the little* c[EXPLICIT]t *stood up, his finger hit the trigger, it went off, blew his own brains out, the clumsy* f[EXPLICIT]ker. *John'll tell you, he saw it.*

Lucky for me that was when Bradley broke through and I could get away with an uh-huh from John. *Job still on, boss?* We all knew what Orin meant. Cops find one of our men shot dead outside, who they gun a think did the job? All eyes turn to Andy. I swear no one breathes till he answers. *Yeah*, he says, *as planned.*

(00:01:18)

We filed through the hole in the door, gathered before the loot like a trail a disciples before their messiah. There it sat. What we'd been aiming for all them months. A battered strongbox like you'd find in any builder's shed.

You'd have thought it were full a drill bits and raw plugs, and that were the idea. It was a bonded flightcase full a diamonds and jewelry en route to Saudi. It was jam-packed with security, so Orin got to work releasing the main tracking device and disabling the backups. Only, while he were doing what he'd rehearsed a hundred times, proper focused and diligent, we were all stopped dead in our tracks. *F*[EXPLICIT]*k* the case a diamonds. Right there beside it, stacked with mathematical precision on an open *f*[EXPLICIT]*king* pallet, was the biggest, brightest most beautiful haul of gold bullion I had ever imagined in my wildest *f*[EXPLICIT]*king* dreams. What the *f*[EXPLICIT]*k?* Andy had no idea that was gun a be there. He couldn't even pretend he did. I could see it in his eyes.

Somewhere, deep down, I wondered when he'd realize he'd just shot his own brother dead and whether this haul would make up for it. I noticed Orin stand back proudly from the disengaged flightcase only to realize no *f*[EXPLICIT]*ker* gave a *s*[EXPLICIT]*t* about it anymore.

Not much was said. We all knew what had to be done. Quickly. Silently. Methodically. One by one, every last bar was stacked in the van. Finally, we chucked in the flightcase anyway, as a tribute to Orin and all his hard work. We glanced in silent, ecstatic disbelief at each other. Can you imagine all them eyes in their balaclavas? They shined alright, let me tell you that.

(00:00:19)

Everything were loaded up into the lead vehicle. And I mean everything. Shooters, masks, tools, phones, anything that could link us to the job. John's gun were prized out of his hand, the shell located and thrown in. All ready to be whisked away, stashed, and stored in those dodgy few days, weeks, and in this case, months, after a big hit. I knew the plan inside out, memorized it to the last detail.

In no time at all the others melted away, back to their lives, their families, their alibis. Each of 'em floating on dreams of how they were gun a spend their share. As he jogged off back to his wife or girlfriend, can't remember which now, Andy saw the others were out of earshot and gave my shoulder a squeeze. *You know what to do next, kid. And forget about Smithy,* he whispered, *we don't need the little runt no more, he were a liability. We got a rat in place to smooth it over. But keep quiet to the lads, eh.*

That's when I knew it were all part of his plan. That John would drive away with the loot on his own. Conceal it and cover his tracks in a meticulously planned operation that no one else knew the full details of except Andy. Because Little Smithy were never meant to see the end a this job, I realize that much. Now, in that moment, as far as Andy was concerned, I was his brother. Family. I was trusted beyond measure.

So I nodded, jumped in, and drove off into the dark. I was cool, calm, and steady. Stacked up behind me was every last scrap a loot from the biggest, most audacious job in British criminal history. Not far off the biggest in the world. Ever. ALL of it in MY van. And I was totally alone.

Audio File 188
Date: June 28, 2019, 10:15 PM
Audio quality: Good

They all know what happened. The last time it were us five and missiles. The super six. Stood around that trapdoor to Rushton tunnel, they tell me. And I finally remember it.

When we left Twyford's cottage, missiles drove us all to the old airfield at Tarrant Rushton. Flat grassland, patches of concrete from long-abandoned runways, cracked by dirty weeds. Perfect place to let go. Run as far and as fast as you can. Hot, sunny. Hadn't rained in weeks. The five of us jumped about, tore around in the grass. Chased each other like little kids. Played war games. Yeah, even Shell and Donna in their pastel clothes and canvas shoes. We were free. Best day out ever.

Missiles wandered away. Looked for a quiet place to sit? Sunbathe? A rest before she drove us home? I didn't care. Ran around having the time a me life. Only, I was puny, not as well fed as the others. Couldn't keep up. Felt a bit of a dud next to them. Breathless and a fire in me lungs, I made an excuse to go back to the minibus. They shouted after me, said I gone for a dump, held their noses and laughed.

As it happens I DID have another motive. Paul stashed grub from Twyford's fridge down the back a the seat in front of him. I calculated it was as much mine as it was his. I climbed in the van, dug it out, and helped meself. A lovely big block a crumbly cheese and a hard-boiled egg. Nice.

I kicked about by the van for a bit, watched a few cars zoom by. Dragged a stick in the dust, drew an outline of a lady's chest, quickly scraped it into oblivion with me shoe, case missiles saw it, thought bad a me. Finally, I wandered back through the treeline to the others.

I could see something had changed. The air. The atmosphere. They were gathered together. Nathan's hood was up, his head bowed, back in his own world. Shell was the first to speak. Missiles has gone, she said. We looked everywhere, can't find her. Then Donna said: Is she with you? I shook me head (. . . .) That's where it began.

(00:01:19)

Turns out it were a load a *b*[EXPLICIT]*ks*. Tonight, stood round the trapdoor to Rushton tunnel, they told me what really happened while I were gone (. . . . .) They started playing a game in the long grass. Ducking down, crawling along, jumping out on each other. At some point they caught sight a missiles in the distance, her back to them. Together, they crept up on her, quiet as ghosts. She was preoccupied with something on the ground. Something they couldn't see. On a silent count a three, they all jumped up behind her, maybe gave her a little push, playful like. They meant to give her a start, nothing serious (. .)

They didn't know it, but she was looking down the open trapdoor into Rushton tunnel. She lost her footing and without so much as a scream, disappeared down it. Gone in an instant. It slammed shut after her. They didn't even hear her land. They were all in shock. It took a moment but they scrabbled to get it open. Couldn't see *s*[EXPLICIT]*t* down there. They shouted into the hole. MISSILES (. .) MISSILES (. . . .) no reply.

(00:01:24)

Nate says they didn't set out not to tell me. The pact was unspoken, is how he put it. They couldn't shape into words what had happened, Shell adds. More shock than guilt, she reckons now, with the hindsight of almost forty years. In time I became their insurance AGAINST being blamed. There was always Smithy who could be called upon to swear, in all honesty, no one had anything to do with her disappearance. Not that anyone ever asked them or me.

(00:03:00)

So who drove us home? They can't believe I don't remember, but it turns out (. .) it were me. Well, me and Paul. He knew how to drive a car thanks to working with his old man in the garage, but couldn't reach the pedals in a minibus. Nor could I, but with him on pedals and gears, me sharing the driver's seat steering and indicating, we did it. Donna navigated using a road map from the glove box. Between us we got home before dawn. Left the minibus outside the school gates for the caretaker to wonder about. Ran home. No one called the Bill, the ambulance, or (. . .) or even told anyone.

(00:01:43)

You might think I'd feel better for knowing. Don't get me wrong, Maxine. I do. Part a me does. All my life it's haunted me. But now I know, I'm haunted by different ghosts, that's all. Like (. . .) if we'd raised the alarm when we drove off. Stopped at the first house or boozer we saw. Or told someone when we got back. Missiles might not a been dead. And if she weren't killed by the fall, well, when we drove away we as good as killed her.

(00:00:59)

You may notice I say WE and not THEY, Maxine. Because while I had nothing to do with the accident, or the cover-up afterward, deep down, right on the very inside a me chest, I knew something terrible had happened. I didn't want a know, so I put it out me head, out me memory. But if I HAD a known, I'd a been no different to them. I'd have said nothing. So I ain't gun a judge them when there's an empty seat on the bench for me. The outcome is the same. Missiles is dead and we did it (. . . .) Is that closure? (. . .) It's something.

(00:00:44)

It's a tragedy. Who's to blame? Sometimes no one is. Just a series of events, situations, assumptions. Perfect storm. Could you look at it from this distance, Maxine, and say that if those poor, immature inner-city kids hadn't been so *s*[EXPLICIT]*t* scared a being hauled in, scared a ratting out their mates, a what might happen to 'em, would they have saved her instead a leaving her to die? (. . .) I tell you what, there IS something to blame, Maxine, and it's FEAR. .hhhhh hhhhh.

Audio File 189
Date: June 28, 2019, 10:19 PM
Audio quality: Good

As I drove farther and farther away from the FSBC warehouse, still in me balaclava, I kept a lid on a lot of s[EXPLICIT]t that would otherwise compromise my ability to keep all four wheels on the road. The overloaded van was a cut-and-shut from two dodgy motors and it fought like a b[EXPLICIT]h. A way out of town, it hit me. Couldn't keep it in no more. Just managed to pull over. My hands were shaking, my head spinning. Finally, I threw up on the hard shoulder and felt a bit better. Back in the van, off again. See, you might think with what I had in the back, I'd have felt elated. But I'd lost everything. I was condemned.

Couldn't go back home. Not ever. Couldn't see or speak to the missus again. Couldn't run to friends or relatives, even if I had any. Had to disappear. Vanish with just the clothes I was wearing, a pile a shooters, a hot van, forty million pounds of gold bullion and around ten million, give or take, in Saudi diamonds and unique pieces of jewelry.

What was I gun a do? Easy, I hear you say, Maxine. You got all that loot, you can set up a new life, a new identity, anywhere in the world. Really? I had no passport on me, no ID, no money even. Was I gun a walk into Sports Direct™, pick up a tracksuit, ask for change from a gold bar? See if Nando's™ would swap a half chicken for a leather pouch of diamonds? How was I to get the loot abroad? Pedalo? Raft a planks? Isla white ferry?

I had a s[EXPLICIT]t load MORE stuff than I was confident dealing with. See, selling stolen gold is a specialist job. With a good firm and a healthy network at my disposal I could have done it. Only I didn't have that. I couldn't go back to the Harrisons, nor any a their associates. I was more than cast out. I was marked (. . . . .) I'm interested, Maxine. Did you spot where I lost it all?

It was when Andy said, "Smithy." The grunts reported what they heard to the old Bill, like Andy had planned. If they'd found Smithy dead, then with their rat to say I'd left the firm, it would have all added up very nicely for the Harrisons. Only, old Bill soon worked out it were John Harrison on the ground, shot good as point-blank under the chin. They knew Smithy well, and they knew he weren't f[EXPLICIT]*king* dead, so who was the first person they wanted to speak to? *Smithy, yer shooter* suddenly took on a whole new meaning. Meanwhile, Andy still wanted me gone and doubly so, seeing as I were the only mug alive who knew he shot his own brother.

(00:01:51)

That were nearly twelve years ago now. So much about that time has passed into myth and legend you can't tell the s[EXPLICIT]*t* from the shovel. No one knows the full story. Not even me. I often wonder whether Andy suspected something before the old Bill knocked on his door the next day. When John didn't answer his phone. When he didn't show up where he were meant to in the morning. When he found out, you might have thought he'd a bin proper guilt struck. But I know Andy. When the first wave of shock passed, he'd have been hopping, f[EXPLICIT]*king* mad. Not at himself for killing his own brother, but at me.

I met a lot like him inside. Bang to rights for one thing or another but blamed the guy they wronged for them being locked up. Many a murderer thinks their victim only died to spite them. Yeah, right from the word go, I didn't have to be told. I KNEW Andy wouldn't face it. Just like it were my fault the missus confronted him. My fault for driving him when he could a been driving himself. My fault John was dead, (. . .) he'd blame ME for not meeting his bullet halfway.

(00:01:33)

So I was on the run from the old Bill and the Harrisons. The last place I could go was home to the missus, to my microwave dinner waiting in the fridge, to the knife and fork either side of the table mat .hhh hhh (. . .) My life was over.

Audio File 190
Date: June 28, 2019, 10:27 PM
Audio quality: Good

Voice 1:   Dark now. On me way down the hill. Back to Nate, Shell, Paul, and Donna .hhh hhh out a shape, me (. . .) they're waiting. What is it, ten, eleven o'clock [*DecipherIt*™ *time ref 519346-10340*]. Give Paul the motor and .hhh hhh the rest. Look at 'em there chatting. So happy. The best friends I ever had. I'll never see 'em again .hhh hhh I'm on empty .hh hh. (00:02:12)

Voice 2:   Alright, mate? Sure?

Voice 1:   Yeah, Nate, yeah. But (. . .) goodbye, in it?

Voice 2:   No such thing, Steve.

Voice 1:   You got everything (. .) in case (you know)?

Voice 2:   You recording?

Voice 1:   *Yeah.*

Voice 2:   Steve, there's a new theory online. Get this. Twyford discovered an organization conducting underground experiments to develop a virus AND a vaccine. They're gun a threaten governments with the disease AND once it's unleashed, can charge what they like for the cure. What do you reckon?

Voice 1:   Sounds (. . . . .) awesome, mate=

Voice 2:   Don't it? Where's Shell taking you?

Voice 1:   Little holiday=

Voice 2:   Nice one. (00:00:18)

Voice 1:   Got the keys, Paul? Hope it don't give you no trouble. There's tools in the trunk=

Voice 3:   Yep [*background noise*].

Voice 1:   *Donna's OK. She's one of us, not* (. . .) You can trust her, mate.

Voice 3:   .hhh hhh Get lost, Steve. Get out of here, don't look back [*background noise*] go on.

Voice 1:   OK [*background noise*] cheers, Paul.

Voice 4:   STEVE. Are you ready?

Voice 1:   Yeah, Shell. Sorry, MICHELLE. Just gotta say bye to Donna=

Voice 5:   Be careful, Smithy. And if you can't be careful, be apologetic=

Voice 1:   Got it, Donna.

Voice 5:   Paul got everything? You sure he's=

Voice 1:   *Recording.* CHEERS, DONNA. Good luck with your (. .) Alex=

Voice 5:   I'll need it. Look after yourself. Whatever you do. Wherever you end up.

Voice 1:   I will (. . . .) yeah. Wherever I go.

Voice 5:   And remember us=

Voice 1:   S[EXPLICIT]*t* got a stop this recording.

Audio File 191
Date: June 29, 2019, 9:12 AM
Audio quality: Good

In the dodgy cut-and-shut van, suspension groaning under the load of gold and diamonds, I dodged round the countryside. I knew a fair few remote parking spots. Couldn't stay in any of 'em long, though, and I soon ran out a places I been before. I had to work fast and carefully. Use everything I learned over the years and if I hadn't learned it over the years I had to learn it double quick now. No one could help me. Anyone I could trust before would be under pressure from the old Bill AND the Harrisons to give away my whereabouts and I couldn't put them in that spot. Or me.

Trouble was, I weren't just hiding. That would a been easy. I had a LOT a things to do. To put in place. To prepare. So little time. Everything was against me. It sends me into a cold sweat even now, thinking of it. A few months, no more. I had SO much to lose. It could a gone belly up at any moment. Can't believe I did it. Me. Little Smithy. No disrespect to you here, Maxine, but you could never a done what I did. I never learned to read or write, that's true. You see (. . .) instead, I learned a lot more.

(00:01:37)

I was sat in a country boozer, less concerned by then whether I were spotted or not. Suddenly there I was, on a TV above the pool table. An unflattering photograph. Police mugshot from a few years previous. Hardened criminal Steven Smith, they said. Long-time member of the Harrisons' gang, one of London's oldest criminal families. Wanted in connection with the FSBC job (. . . .) and on suspicion of murder.

(00:02:41)

Over eleven years inside I met a few fellows who'd crossed paths with the Harrisons before and since. They said how Andy, Razor Ray, all the lads were hauled in after the job. Questioned time and again. Old Bill knew they'd done it. Just couldn't pin it on 'em. Cast-iron alibis and no evidence. There were no trace a the gold or diamonds. No proof they'd even touched the loot or benefited from the crime. Old Bill were stumped. Little Smithy were their only hope of a conviction.

Murder, though. I should a seen that coming. Course, Andy weren't gun a admit to killing John. And no one thought he'd shoot his own brother. They were family. Devoted, whatever their fallouts might a been.

Did the guys on the job work out what had happened? They'd eventually realize Andy had seen John's body, thought it were me. They would be proper gutted for him, till they realized Little Smithy had driven away with their share of the haul. I daresay then they were more gutted for their own unbought fast cars and fancy houses.

There were those thought I shot John, pretended to be him for the rest a the job. All so I could screw the Harrisons and get me hands on the loot. Loyal Little Smithy.

But there were others who believed John offed himself, especially when it came out the ket in his blood would a floored a racehorse. Some thought one thing, others something else. The truth were always on the move. If any of 'em put two and two together and made four, I never heard about it.

Met a chap in Sheppey Vale years later. He didn't know who I was, and I didn't enlighten him. He told me a story. How Andy saw a masked grunt shoot himself by accident, only to discover later it was his own brother. This chap laughed telling it. Like it were an anecdote he heard down the boozer. Then his eyes got all wide and looming. He leaned in, lowered his voice. *When Andy found out it was John who died,* he said, *the screams could be heard north of the river* (. . .) THE RIVER MERSEY.

(00:00:27)

Patricia didn't even live a year after what happened to John. She gave up. Andy retired to Spain, invested in property. Dogged by poor health. Sold up, moved back recently to be near his medical specialists. Built himself a brand-new mansion round the corner from the old house. Climate-controlled garage for his cars. Big garden for his grandchildren. All bought legit. It's my guess the Bill keep an eye on him to this day.

Razor Ray did a bit a time for aggravated assault. Last I heard he had a spinal tumor removed. Married his boyfriend in hospital. Got the all-clear. Moved to a sheltered flat in Essex. Ground floor for his wheelchair. Orin got life for killing a crooked cop about five years after me. Given a minimum of fifteen. Still inside. Bradley were killed in a car crash, M25. Not sure when that happened, but it were rumored to be an accident (. . . . .) Yeah, we were all cursed. That last job and the loot, all of it. Cursed.

(00:00:42)

I want to say my missus (. . . . .) .hhhhh Becky (. . .) found another fella. Tall, handsome, minted, treated her like a queen. Got hitched, had a few kids. But in all honesty? I don't know. She divorced me like

I wanted her to. Never visited, never wrote, never called. Never heard from her again .hhhh hhhh (. . . . .) *It's alright. I don't blame her one bit.*
(00:01:40)

On suspicion of murder. When I heard it that day in the country boozer, that's when I knew it were time. Ordered a last pint at the bar, where it has to be said, not a single *f*[EXPLICIT]*king* soul recognized me from the giant mugshot on the screen right above me head. I downed that lovely *c*[EXPLICIT]*t* of a beer, nodded to the barman, got me coat, walked out the door. Down the road. Into a local police station. Proper country place. Last time they saw a London gangster it were in black-and-white courtesy of Pathé. Handed meself in. Sat there, like the eye of a hurricane, while all hell broke loose around me and I felt, what? (. . . .) Released. Yeah, safe .hhhh finally safe.

Audio File 192
Date: June 29, 2019, 9:33 AM
Audio quality: Good

I said nothing. Not to anyone. For months. Only spoke to my legal team to confirm I understood this and that. I were remanded in solitary for my own safety. Not because I were in imminent danger, but so I were driven mad by isolation and more likely to talk. Didn't work. But it were a tough, lonely time.

I listened to my team flounder around, trying to figure out what happened to John. Why I killed him. A voice inside me screamed, ANDY DID IT. He meant to shoot ME, but he shot John. I said nothing. The Harrisons closed ranks to protect themselves. Andy's rat, who'd been briefed to explain away MY accidental death at the crime scene, was quickly re-briefed. He told the old Bill John had got tangled up with big international gangs in the course of his dealings. That it were one a them did the job and he'd taken me along for the ride.

Bill got a genuine rat on their side who testified from a darkened room. His evidence only reinforced what the Harrisons' snitch had told 'em. He said I were like Andy's dog. Faithful till he sidelined me. He said I turned. Took to the bottle. That I shot John in cold blood to get revenge on Andy.

Load of old *b*[EXPLICIT]*ks*. Notice how he wouldn't rat on the Harrisons for the robbery, even then? *F*[EXPLICIT]*king s*[EXPLICIT]*t* scared a them, but not me. Yeah, few years later Anthony were shot point blank in his own front garden anyway, so.

Smithy, yer shooter. Andy said it like he'd spotted my finger on the trigger, to make my death seem accidental. Well, it caused a debate in court and out. The guards, facedown on the ground, couldn't tell who'd spoken. All they heard were those words, a single shot from the mute, and footsteps running off. They came to the conclusion John said it, to me. He saw that barrel pointing his way and told his murderer to be careful with it. But I shot him, then ran, didn't take part in the job. I might a thought that too if I didn't know better.

The Crown Prosecution Service wanted murder. My team filed not guilty, as the shooter hadn't come to light. It didn't wash, though. Not with multiple convincing testimonies stacking up against me. The fact I were so close to the Harrisons and had so much previous. It all meant I were a dead cert for the big one. Handed life with a minimum of ten. Lucky it weren't longer. I daresay John's reputation as a lifelong drug trafficker, plus the four hundred tabs of K in his pocket when he died, did me a big favor there. But still.

I weren't guilty of what they put me away for, that's true. But the truth can be misleading, Maxine. Kos I weren't innocent either. I'd done enough. Ironically, by doing nothing. Standing by while others got (. . .) got hurt. Killed.

You know I had a hard eleven years inside, Maxine. Two things kept me going. My son, and the certain knowledge I were never going back. Not back inside. And not back to the old life.

Two different things have kept me going since my release. Kept me here when I should a run at the first chance. Kept me talking into my son's old phone, getting everything down as planned, and sometimes as NOT planned. Yeah, two things (. . .) Andy Harrison and Little Harry.

Audio File 193
Date: June 29, 2019, 11:27 AM
Audio quality: Poor

Voice 1:   STEVE.

Voice 2:   LUCY () Hey=

Voice 1:   Thank goodness. Oh (. . . .) I thought you'd [*background noise*] (. . .) you=

Voice 2:   It weren't anything. Forget it. [*background noise*]

Voice 1:   Here, I'll get (the door). What do you?

Voice 2:   Just, just a [*background noise*].
           (00:04:58)

[*background noise*]

Voice 2:   Get back from you see Elle, OK?

Voice 1:   Went home on the tube [*background noise*] where did you go with your friend?

Voice 2:   Ended up Dorset way. Any news on the [*background noise*] code?

Voice 1:   YES. I've discovered why Mrs. Wintle [*background noise*] was BARNES.

Voice 2:   Keep your voice down, Lucy=

Voice 1:   Sorry. But it's so noisy in here. She's Edward Barnes's granddaughter from the son he had with his first wife. We assumed his significant other was Edith but [*background noise*]. She has a (. . . .) whereabouts of the *gold* a secret. Family tradition=

Voice 2:   Yeah, family tradition.

Voice 1:   She can't [*background noise*] be traced immediately. So she keeps [*background noise*] to communicate with everyone else [*background noise*] Trouble is [*background noise*] code today and threatening to expose her grandfather and his wife. And placing her own wealth at risk.

Voice 2:   It's cursed. Stolen gold is cursed, Lucy [*background noise*] for those who take it. [*background noise*] is the only way to break the spell.

Voice 1:   So, Steve, what shall we do about The Twyford Code? Keep it secret like Mrs. Wintle, formerly Miss Barnes, says we should? OR do we blow it WIDE open? [*background noise*] Help yourself to biscuits, don't be shy=

Voice 2:   It's (. . .) oh *f*[EXPLICIT]*k*.

Voice 1:   What? What are you looking at?

Voice 2:   I just seen them [*background noise*] not yet, it's too soon, haven't got it all down, haven't explained about Colin (. . .) it's not you they're after (. .) that won't be enough (. .) duck your head down (. .) not ready yet [*background noise*] HERE. TAKE IT.

But it's your son's phone, Steve.

YES. GIVE IT BACK TO HIM.

Where are you going?

Please, Lucy, take it BACK TO MY SON.

Where does he live? [*background noise*] What's his name?

[*background noise*]

(*No cats yellow sauce*)

Audio File 194
Date: July 1, 2019, 4:20 PM
Audio quality: Good

Hello. Goodness, this feels strange. Hello (. . .) this is Lucy speaking into your son's phone. You did it this way, so I will too. Then you can catch up on your return. I haven't heard from you, and don't know if I will. This is the only phone I ever saw you with and I have it now (. .) obviously.

Where did you go in such a panic? I hope you pop by the library soon, or come to the flat (. . . .) Never mind, I'll start by recording what's happened since the last audio file, as that's the way you do it. It's taken me two days because this is SUCH an old system. I don't know HOW you did it. First I had to delete almost everything. Your music, texts, emails, apps, else I'd never be able to update eye oh S for you. I KNOW I promised to do it ages ago, but we got into the code and I. Anyway, it's done now. You're disconnected from the mobile network. I suspect you haven't paid your bill. It doesn't matter, we can soon re-connect you once you're back.

I listened to your audio files and, my goodness, there are SO many of them. No wonder you had no room for anything else on here. It would be a shame to lose such an interesting oral history, so I logged you on to the cloud and backed them up. I retrieved your deleted audio files and restored them. The whole process took two evenings. I heard all about you, your life, your (. . .) childhood and our (. . . . .) what shall I call it? Our JOURNEY into The Twyford Code. It's fascinating, Steve. It's shocking too. What happened to your mum and dad, Colin. It explains a lot. I feel I know you SO much better now. At the same time, I'm rather confused by one or two things. But I'm sure it will all become clear.

First of all, now, *where did you leave off*? THAT'S right, you got back from your trip to Dorset with your old school friend, Paul. We met up in Costa. SO noisy. I TRIED to tell you what I'd discovered about Mrs. Wintle. That she's Edith Twyford's step-granddaughter and sits on the board that manages her estate. She helps adjust the text of Twyford's current editions and therefore the code. She might look like a harmless, middle-aged academic, but not many middle-aged academ-ics live in seven-bedroom townhouses in Mayfair. Steve, one thing's for sure, she knows where the gold is.

Something you said really intrigued me. That stolen gold is cursed.

Now, that IS an interesting theory. I've been reading a LOT about ancient Egyptian tombs and the TERRIBLE things that happened to the men who discovered and raided them. All the riches sealed inside were things we still value today and, how can I put this without sounding (. . .) they were all OF THE EARTH. Gold, silver, gemstones (. . .) things deemed to have intrinsic value, then and now. Why? Well, perhaps because they're finite, ancient, created only by time and the pure energy of our planet.

I'm serious. Google™ it. The prominent men involved in the original excavations, and who benefited financially, almost all died prematurely, some in quite mysterious ways. It's thought the ancient pharaohs put a curse on their tombs, condemning anyone who dared steal their afterlife wealth. Yet no hieroglyphs suggest a curse of any kind (. . . . .)

What if, Steve, it's not the pharaohs who cursed the ancient riches, but the riches themselves that carry an ENERGY. As if a rare and precious mineral has living consciousness and power. It KNOWS when it's fallen into the grasp of the WRONG people, so it wreaks havoc in their lives until it moves out of their toxic orbit and into the hands of innocent, more deserving folk? I don't even mean in a Robin Hood way. Not necessarily good causes, just innocent hands where its vibration can be settled (. . . . .) My goodness, I've just voiced the maddest thing.

Audio File 195
Date: July 2, 2019, 3:54 PM
Audio quality: Good

Hello, Steve. You haven't been in touch so I'll continue this diary for you. I've tried to find your son, but don't know his first name let alone his surname. The maths department at Brunel University has a very stringent staff security policy and won't help. I'll be surprised if I'm not arrested for stalking.

I'm hoping Maxine will come through for me. You mention she

helped find your son. I don't know her surname either, but there can't
be THAT many probation officers in South London with that name, so.

I've been listening to your recordings again and some of them are
very strange. Like our meeting with Mrs. Wintle. I know what happened. I was there. We met her outside her office, we chatted in the
square. Just as we were about to leave, your friend Paul bumped into
us. Mrs. Wintle said her goodbyes and left. Paul invited you to go with
him and meet up with some other old school friends. He offered you a
lift and you, happily I might add, went off with him. Yet on these files
you say we were attacked by two men, you were kidnapped, and only
saved when Paul rammed their van off the road.

(00:00:27)

This may be your diary, but I KNOW you're making some things
up. How can I work out what's true and what isn't, especially when you
didn't finish the story?

Audio File 196
Date July 4, 2019, 3:15 PM
Audio quality: Good

The probation service was very cool with me. Even when I promised
information about an ex-prisoner who has breached his terms. I think
this technically makes me a rat, so I apologize for that, Steve.

If it's any consolation they still won't put me in touch with Maxine,
or even admit they have a probation officer by that name. So, the barman
in a little boozer on the high street introduced me to a gentleman who
lives in a halfway hostel. He claimed to have met a Steve who matches
your description. Said he was polite. Always smartly dressed. Minded
his own business. Worked mornings on the gate of a truck park. One
of those determined to go straight after years inside, this man said. He
didn't know where that Steve went, or what happened to him. He just
wasn't there one day.

It's occurred to me more than once that Steven Smith might not be your real name. Once I had that little germ in my mind I couldn't get rid of it. It would make sense because if Andy Harrison is after you, you should have protection on the outside. Were you issued with a new identity? But no, I listened to a few more recordings. People you knew at school call you Steve and Smithy, so.

.hhhh hhhh I need a miracle. I need TWO miracles actually. One to help me find your son and another to help me avoid the old Bill (. . .) as YOU say.

Audio File 197
Date: July 5, 2019, 1:42 AM
Audio quality: Good

This is addictive, Steve. It's better than talking to a person. I can see now why you went off to speak into your son's phone quite as often as you did. It's even addictive playing the files back.

This evening I switched the light off and sat and listened to your voice in the dark. From the beginning right to the end. What are you NOT saying? What am EYE not hearing? What am I not UNDERSTANDING? You couldn't say everything you meant to say. That's why I can't complete the puzzle. How to find that missing piece. And get some sleep.

Audio File 198
Date: July 5, 2019, 11:16 AM
Audio quality: Good

Voice 1:   Lorraine, could I have a word please?

Voice 2:   Yes, Lucy, what?

Voice 1:   Is it possible to access public birth records via our system here?

Voice 2:   You must know it's not=

Voice 1: I thought not. It's the same municipal council so=

Voice 2: Whose record are you looking for?

Voice 1: Babies born roughly thirty-five years ago with Steven Smith named as their father.

Voice 2: [*background noise*] Well that's a task for when you've retired=

Voice 1: It's a tall mountain, but=

Voice 2: Steven Smith? That funny little man? Came in every day. Wouldn't leave us alone. Took a shine to YOU and you weren't assertive enough to shake him off. He was a proper nuisance=

Voice 1: NO. I mean, yes, it's him, but he wasn't a nuisance. He's very interesting actually.

Voice 2: You know he stayed at that prison hostel=

Voice 1: Halfway house=

Voice 2: Could be a murderer for all we know=

Voice 1: He didn't do it=

Voice 2: [*background noise*] They ALL say that.

Voice 1: He took the blame for someone else=

Voice 2: OH, LUCY. Don't be so naïve. Ask yourself. Why would he do THAT?

Voice 1: It's a long story (. . .) I don't know=

Voice 2: Innocent people aren't sent to prison. He MUST have done something.

Voice 1: *Something. Yes.* He must have done something=

Voice 2: Well, he hasn't been in for weeks. No doubt back inside as we speak.

Voice 1: Ye::::s (. . .) you're probably right.

Audio File 199
Date: July 5, 2019, 1:08 PM
Audio quality: Good

I hope that wherever you are, you're enjoying this lovely sunshine, Steve (. . .) So, I recorded my chat with Lorraine. I've just listened back to it. Yes, your son's phone picks up voices from my pocket, so next time I speak to someone relevant to the code, I can record it for you. I MUST remember to stand still, so my cardigan doesn't scrape across the Mike (. . .)

It's a funny thing. I only struck up that conversation with Lorraine to check how well this worked. But something she said really made me think. Steve, you didn't kill John. So why did you let yourself go down for it? You could've (. . .) FOUGHT. Eleven years. And you lost everything. All because you wouldn't rat on Andy. Someone who tried to kill you after you'd been loyal to him for most of your life. Why did you even go through with his plan after that? You pretended to be John, drove off with the stolen gold and diamonds, and (. . . . .) I thought at first you concealed it according to Andy's plan. You can't do anything with it on your own, but. Wait. I need to listen back to those recordings again.

[*background noise*]

WHAT. NO.

Audio File 200
Date: July 5, 2019, 9:34 PM
Audio quality: Good

How much battery? (. .) Don't know where I am. It's dark and cold, like a fridge. Am I underground? A garage? Can't hear a thing. No traffic. Silence. That's (the) worst. This silence.

(00:01:35)

I don't know if anyone will ever hear this, but (. . .) if I don't get to tell my story, our story, your son's phone may tell it for us, Steve. It's our only hope. That someone finds it (. . .) listens. Carefully.

(00:00:49)

I sat down in the park to think. These voice files explain a lot about you, Steve, your childhood, Miss isles. It explains why you were (. . .) obsessed with The Twyford Code. It's compelling. But it waits until you need it. Until you're lost. Just when you're looking for something, it lights a flame to channel your energy. It happened to missiles, Donna, Nate, (. . .) and me. But now I've had time to think, I see it didn't happen to you. You weren't lost at all. You had something else to drive you. From the second you picked up your son's phone and started recording your journey into where your teacher went that day in 1983. You say Andy was a meticulous planner. Well, I've listened to these recordings so many times (. . .) and I see now he had nothing on you.

(00:00:1:01)

They ambushed me as I left the park. You're not like these men, Steve. No empathy. No self-knowledge. They understand love only as a weakness to be exploited in others. At first I marveled that you spent so long in their world and didn't become like them. But I see you WERE like them once. It's just, you learned, grew, and were strong enough to change.

(00:00:25)

They're keeping me here because I'm the only thing you feel anything for. The only thing you (. . .) love? You don't love me, Steve. But they don't know that because they don't know about your son. You were smart enough to keep that from them. Well, I won't rat on you. They've watched us together. They believe the threat of something happening to me will force you to tell them. I know it won't. It's all about your son. This is meant for him. You said yourself, you don't give a f[EXPLICIT]k what happens to you, so long as he's alright. You trusted me to find him, and I'm sorry I failed. I only hope someone finds this and gets it to him. Wait. Is someone coming?

(00:00:53)

They took my phone, but assumed it was the only one I had. Lucky they didn't look too hard or I'd have lost this one too (. . . . .) They could have tortured you, but they know you wouldn't talk. They must also know you can't do anything with the gold, because you'd be found out and end up back inside, something you vowed would never happen. And there's another, much simpler reason you recorded these voice files, isn't there? (. . .) It's cursed. You have to pass it on to innocent hands.

All this time we weren't doing what I thought we were doing. You had your own agenda, Steve. You drove off alone with the Harrisons' loot. You worked for weeks to ensure it wouldn't be found, not by them, not by anyone, not before YOU were ready. Then you calmly walked into a police station and gave yourself up. Eleven years later, released but not free, you had one thing left to do.

(00:00:19)

I won't ever see you again. No one will. But you've got something for your son. You hope it will bring you closer, so in future when he may regret not knowing you, at least he'll have this: your voice, your story, and the life-changing opportunities it will lead him to. He's good at solving problems. Putting two and two together. He gets that from you. If only people knew. That someone who can barely read or write has achieved something as daring as this.

[*background noise*]

Because there's nothing like being trapped in cold, dark silence to clear the mind, Steve. I can see it now. Crystal clear. It's all here. In your story. You weren't FOLLOWING The Twyford Code. You were ().

[*background noise*].

S[EXPLICIT]t. Quick. Going to (. .) *hide the phone. Hide it. Where's delete?* Hello? Who's there? Hello?

[End Transcript]

Transcriptions of Voicemail Messages Between Professor Mansfield and Inspector Waliso

Date: November 24, 2021

This is Professor Mansfield for Inspector Waliso. Inspector, thank you for sending me the transcripts. I've read them all. Yes, Steven Smith is my biological father and I gave him an iPhone 4, which I assume is the one you found.

I didn't grow up with him and we only ever met a couple of times. Forgive me, but it's a lot to take in at the moment. May I ask who exactly is missing, my father or his friend Lucy? I haven't seen or heard from him for over a year. His phone number is dead. I called the hostel where he lived the last time we met, but they don't give out such information. It would be good to know he's safe. From the last files he recorded that's by no means certain. Who reported him as a missing person?

I suggested we limit our contact. But he would still call and text. It was too soon for me. That last time we spoke I broke off our communication. I said I'd call when I was ready but didn't know when that would be, if ever.

I don't intend to step on your toes, Inspector, but I want to trace my biological father myself.

Let me read through these again. I'll get back to you with any information that might be useful.

Date: December 2, 2021

This is Professor Mansfield, for Inspector Waliso. I don't seem to have a first name for him. Inspector, I've had no luck finding Steve and drew the same blank Lucy did when I tried to find Maxine, his probation officer. You ask for my professional opinion on these files, so I've examined the factual content for any anomalies or clues that may help us. I know that from an early age he was involved with a London gang and served eleven years for the murder of John Harrison during the infamous FSBC robbery, so that much I can verify.

I'm long familiar with Operation Fish, Britain's successful bid to ship its gold reserves to Canada during the Second World War, and assume it to be a matter of historical document. For the rest I've used the internet. A selection of Edith Twyford books are on order, including those my father mentions in these files. There are many references online to Twyford and her husband, Edward Barnes. I've found the photograph my father says he studied for clues. She's at her desk, looking over her shoulder. Her fingers seem to lead the eye to a box with a fish clasp. The Kandinsky-inspired prints are only just visible on the wall, although I can't source a clear enough version online to confirm whether *dartboards* spell out the number sequence described here.

I've found the photograph of Edith and Edward on the steps of University College London, and a picture of Edith reading to schoolchildren during the war. Werner Richter was indeed a major in the German army with connections to the counterintelligence unit, Abwehr. In his scant Wikipedia entry he is listed as missing in action.

The plaque outside Martin's Bank in Liverpool is exactly as my father describes it, as is the memorial stone at RAF Tarrant Rushton in Dorset. The geographical coordinates Lucy claims to identify in the photograph really do lead to three "banks" in apparently unconnected locations: a wine bar called the Bank in Wrexham, Martin's Bank in Liverpool, and a local bank in West Africa.

In other words, Inspector, the vast majority of facts discussed in these transcriptions are easily confirmed. Only two things are not. There are no references anywhere to The Twyford Code. Nate mentions an old-style website via which he accessed a hidden chat room. I could find neither. Might this secret community of armchair coders have disbanded or moved to the dark web? Does this absence prove the code does not exist, or simply that it's as secret as my father believed it to be?

As for the accidental killing of Miss Iles by her R.E. class, well, there is nothing online about that either. Given how long ago it happened, perhaps that's not a surprise. It was apparently never investigated at the time. But this was a large inner-city school. It was the end of term. They all suspect Miss Iles told no one about the trip. If she had no family and few friends then a couple of personnel changes are all it would take for her departure to be assumed a career move and her nonappearance forgotten. People disappear unnoticed even now, let alone in the precomputer era.

When he starts this audio diary, Steve considers Miss Iles's disappearance to be the catalyst that drove him to join the Harrison gang. Yet by the end, he accepts his family situation played a greater role. For my father, these files are as much a journey into his past as they are an investigation into that day in 1983. It affects me more than I anticipated. Inspector, Lucy says he has something for me. I'm not sure what that is.

Date: December 6, 2021

It's Professor Mansfield again. I should update you, Inspector Waliso. With no sign of my father, Lucy, or Miss Iles, I've turned my attention to my uncle Colin. I read my father's account of what happened to him and assumed he was dead. Well, you can imagine my surprise when I discovered he is very much alive and quite well. I must have read too much into it. Or did my father want to protect him should the audio files fall into the wrong hands?

I had some idea what to expect when I visited his flat, but it was a shock nonetheless. Cluttered and dirty. Borderline uninhabitable. Colin looks and behaves much older than his sixty-four years. I tell him I'm Steve's son, his nephew, but he doesn't believe me. Old Bill? he barks. I assure him no, but he's guarded throughout my visit. Council? he asks later. My refutation did not reassure him. Perhaps that's why he's vague about the last time he saw Steve.

I prompted him with the suggestion two other men were there, perhaps threatening men? At this Colin shuffles about, avoids my gaze. An involuntary movement at the mention of the Harrisons.

Finally, he reveals something about that last meeting. Steve destroyed his old television set. Kicked the screen in. Just like that, he said, and pulled his leg back, angled his foot in a slow mime of the event. Shattered it to pieces apparently, all over the carpet.

Why did he do that? I ask, mindful of my father's disturbing take on the incident. Colin shrugs. He knew I hid things in it. Old TV like a big box. Unscrew the back, slip your valuables inside. Out of sight, yet you can still keep an eye on it. Watch it all the time.

So that's where you hid *Six on Goldtop Hill*, I said. The book Mr. Wilson gave you in 1984. He stares at me, blank. What did Steve do to the men who were here? Colin shrugs. Apparently my father gave them something and they went.

He kicks me TV in, pretends to get this little leather bag out the back. Only he never. It came out his pocket. Probably owed 'em drugs or something. Always wriggled out of scrapes, did Steve.

My father told Colin he had nowhere else to go and stayed a couple of days. We talked a lot in them two days, he says, when Steve weren't on the phone. We talked about the past and . . . Here he pauses, as if those conversations were difficult at the time, but even more painful to remember. Then Colin describes how they finally parted.

He tells me it's the last time I'll ever see him. Wish he hadn't said. If I hadn't known, it wouldn't have been so sad.

Would Colin have told me the truth if he knew it? I look at him, trapped, a prisoner here, and it crosses my mind to ask if he still has that Victorian fire set, complete with old brass poker. What would his reaction be? But I remember my father's words. That it's Colin who had the real sentence. And I don't need to ask. I know it's in there somewhere.

On my way out I pass the door to his lounge, glance in. A new home cinema system towers above the clutter. Out of place at best. A replacement for the TV my father destroyed? Colin won't answer, but happily demonstrates the latest smart technology, 64-inch, high-definition flat screen, speakers, catch-up feature for when his favorite shows clash. I ask where he bought it. He hesitates a moment, then smiles. Had it delivered, he explains. I left him there, happily settled in his chair, enjoying his new television.

Date: December 10, 2021

Inspector Waliso, my biological father's memory of his teacher and her obsession with The Twyford Code is most intriguing, not least because it ended in such tragedy. I've scoured the Super Six books I ordered. You'll understand from my work here at Brunel, I have some understanding of, and interest in, codes and numbers. These are modern editions with no obvious word patterns or hidden illustrations. But then, my father and Lucy drew the conclusion that new versions of the code are more complex than the earlier, simple acrostics.

I'll source older editions in time, but for now my focus has been to find Steve's classmates from remedial English. Especially Nate. My father seems very fond of him. The awful revelation that the R.E. class unwittingly killed their teacher is, I assume, something you're looking into, Inspector?

It took a little detective work on social media, but I found Nathan. He invited me to his house where we had a long chat. I told him I'd lost touch with Steve and was keen to find out more from someone who knew him at school. I have no wish to distress Nate, nor affect any police investigation into the matter, so I was careful not to reveal quite how much I knew about the code or Miss Iles.

Like my father, I found Nathan warm and friendly, yet our meeting left me with more questions than it answered. He confirmed that Steve's early life was troubled. In his mid-teens he stopped going to school. However, Nate claimed they've only met *once* since Steve's release from prison, over a year ago. In Nate's house. They chatted about the past, then went their separate ways. Only, the audio file transcriptions suggest Nate met with my father six times, at least.

I mention his trip to Dorset with Steve and Shell, then again a few weeks later with all five R.E. pupils. Nate pauses, a puzzled expression on his face. Finally, he shakes his head. No, he's not been anywhere with Steve. If I'm talking about Dorset, they went there on a school trip back in the day, but not since. I remind Nathan of the eighteenth of June 2019. The events of audio file 102 especially. My father arrived at his home in the middle of the night, injured. How could he forget it? He falls silent. Hmmm, that date rings a bell, he muses. But it can't have been important or I'd remember.

Inspector, I looked very hard into his eyes at that point. If Nate's spent a lifetime covering up the accidental death of Miss Iles, he's adept at maintaining a deception. Still, it's puzzling. I muttered I must have been mistaken and left it at that. Finally, as he cheerfully showed me out and thanked me for dropping by, I asked if I could look in his garage. If what my father says is true, Nate has an office dedicated to The Twyford Code concealed inside. He's speechless for a second or two, then laughs, plucks a set of keys from a hook on the wall.

Inspector, that structure could never have contained an office of the kind my father describes. It was and always has been a plain, brick-built suburban garage. I'm stunned and ask him outright what he knows about the Twyford Code. Nothing, he says. What is it?

What about Miss Iles? I stammer, and fully expect him to recoil at the name. Miss Iles, your R.E. teacher, I repeat. But Nate bursts into smiles. She was the best teacher I ever had. He grins wistfully. A lovely lady. Very inspiring. The best.

What happened to her? I ask. He shrugs again. She left. It were scary at first to have a new teacher, he muses. We'd all got attached to Miss Iles. But Mr. Wilson took over and he was alright.

It's only then I notice what actually *is* in this ordinary outbuilding: an old mustard-colored Volvo, heavy, rusty, and as settled and silent as if it hadn't been driven for a year or more.

Nathan sees me looking. Oh it's not *my* car, he assures me. Looking after it for a friend. Mine's out front. I'll show you.

I'd passed it on my way in, but keen to meet Nathan, I'd paid no attention to the car on the drive. A brand-new Tesla. A high-end luxury vehicle I know is unlikely to cost less than £150,000. A car I can only dream of owning. Like it? Nate says. I wonder aloud why he keeps a thirty-year-old banger in the garage and an expensive car on the front drive. He is unfazed. Give the neighbors something to aspire to. He grins.

He and his wife are about to visit Dominica, where they have family. A special trip, he says, six weeks, really get to know the place. Well, at that I'm struck by a sudden memory. That's nice, I say. It's all you ever wanted, isn't it? The silence is long enough for Nate to ask how I know. But he doesn't. He just smiles, nods, and holds my gaze a fraction too long.

Inspector, look back at audio file 36. Steve describes Nathan's aspirations. His words are: "He dreams of a six-week Caribbean holiday or a new car." I believe Nathan is sworn to secrecy and has no intention of breaking that vow. I need to hear these audio files for myself, not just read the transcripts. In particular the conversations between Nate and my father. Inspector, can you email them to me, please?

Date: December 20, 2021

I've had no reply from you, Inspector, and wonder if you are on vacation. Or is there another reason you're not responding to my messages? Nonetheless, I've continued to investigate my father's disappearance. Before I left Nate, I asked about contact details for Paul and Donna. He wanders away and eventually returns with a number for Paul scribbled on a scrap of paper. Sorry, he says, nothing for Donna.

I'd already sent a message to Paul on Facebook with the news my father is missing. No reply. When I looked again, his profile had disappeared. So I call the landline number with an open mind. Imagine my surprise when a child answers. Hello, Granddad's phone, who is it?

Is Paul Clacken there? I stammer. No. Granddad's in Switzerland.

I politely enquire when Granddad will be home and at this the little voice drops to a whisper. When he's gone up twelve steps, but if anyone asks, you *must* say he's on holiday. I thank the voice and ring off. Switzerland is an expensive place for rehab, especially when, the way my father describes Paul, he was down on his luck.

I puzzle over how to find Donna and look back over the transcript of audio file 32. My father contacted her through a Facebook profile for someone called Oliver Unwin. He belongs to just two groups: one for the old high school my father and his friends attended, and one a Metropolitan Police social group.

The reply I receive within twenty-four hours is just as mysterious: a Hotmail address with numbers instead of a name. I craft a message that sets out my determination to discover where my father is, but an out-of-office reply pops up. "Sorry. I moved to Auckland permanently and don't monitor my UK email. If that's news to you, then cheers, have a nice life." The final sentence stops me dead. "And if you think I'll tell you anything you can discover for yourself, think again, Maxine." It seems I'm not the only one looking into my father's whereabouts. His probation officer must also be on his tail, which might explain why Paul and Donna are reluctant to speak to an unknown caller asking questions about their old school friend.

My failure to contact Donna and Paul explains why I approach Shell with more care. I found her Facebook profile from my father's description. A mobile phone number appears on it. I wonder if her lack of security betrays her innocence. I think to myself: How would Steve approach this? Can I do what he does? So, I call Shell's number and when she answers, in my best impersonation of my father's voice, I say: Hi, Shell, it's Steven.

There's a delighted gasp. But what happens next puzzles me most. She breaks into a foreign language, only briefly, and says something like "Yazoo." I can hear the smile in her voice. I'm taken aback and I hesitate. Oh, she says, suddenly English, who is it, again? I'm Steven Smith's *son*, I say, in my own voice now. There's a long moment of silence before the phone goes dead. How intriguing. If I discover anything more, I'll be in touch.

Date: December 27, 2021

It's Professor Mansfield for Inspector Waliso again. Now, I know my father was imprisoned for a murder that happened in the course of the FSBC heist, but beyond that I avoid the subject. I'll be honest with you, Inspector, I am ashamed to be associated with such criminality. Now I've read his story, I see my father's involvement with the Harrisons in a new light.

The stolen gold has been the subject of much media speculation over the years. The Harrisons were always prime suspects, but the police couldn't prove their involvement. John Harrison had a wide network of international criminal connections and wasn't necessarily working for the family firm that night. All the big players in the gang had strong alibis. No gold or diamonds came to light, nor were any suspects seen to enjoy an increase in wealth over the years.

Yet there's a chain of more recent online news stories that pick over the robbery. The first one details the arrest of Andrew Harrison, sixty-seven, of Merton, Surrey, for possession of a firearm. He's described as a ruthless armed robber with a long history of violence. An old-fashioned London gang boss. But in the stark police mugshot is a sad and bitter old man. His eyes are hollow and his skin is sallow and unshaven. As if he's been eaten alive by what he's lost, blind to what he's taken from so many others. I shiver to think my father idolized this man for most of his life.

After that, the pitch of the news stories escalates as the police get closer to the truth. The gun found in Andy Harrison's newly built Merton house was the one used to shoot his brother John in 2007. Police were tipped off to its whereabouts by a mobile mechanic who visited the property to service a car. It links Andy not just to the FSBC heist, but to his own brother's murder, the crime my father served eleven years for. Not only that, but in Andy Harrison's brand-new climate-controlled garage they discovered a single bar of gold bullion with an FSBC serial number. The only one ever recovered from the haul.

Perhaps a good solicitor could pass both items off as circumstantial after so many years, if it weren't for another event. A man walked into a South London jeweler wanting a diamond ring reset and rounded off. He asked for a quote but never returned to pay the deposit or collect the item. When the jeweler spotted Andy's mugshot in the papers he realized why.

The ring and distinctive leather pouch were both stolen in the FSBC robbery. That day in Colin's flat, my father keeps the Harrisons at bay by giving them a handful of gems that he pretended to pull from the back of Colin's TV. It seems Andy's famous attention to detail and careful planning deserted him in the end.

Andy Harrison is in Wormwood Scrubs awaiting trial. He was

arrested on the first of July last year. The day after my father's final audio recording. It's a strange coincidence, but the police inspector quoted in relation to his arrest is called Donna Cole.

Date: December 29, 2021

You must spend half your working hours listening to my messages, Inspector. You've never picked up when I call the number, so I don't know what else to do. Doodling here on my notepad, I realized your surname is an anagram. Inspector is AWOL. It made me laugh.

Nonetheless, I've been studying the transcripts day and night. The more I read, the more I see. Can I ask, what have you discovered about Lucy? From my father's diary she worked in a library with a twenty-four-hour gym nearby and a Spar across the road. I found one that fitted the description exactly, near Streatham, and visited, hoping to speak with Lorraine, or any other colleague who may remember her. The longest-serving member of staff has worked at the library for thirty-four years. No one called Lucy has been employed there in that time. Nor anyone called Lorraine. It must be the wrong one. I've been to others in the area, none of which match my father's description, and drew a similar blank at them all.

She and my father seemed close, and certainly bonded over The Twyford Code. Is she missing too? I look forward to hearing from you.

Date: January 2, 2022

Is there any news of Lucy or my father? It's been weeks since you sent the transcripts, Inspector, and I've heard nothing more. You're busy and your shifts may not coincide with my normal hours. But any time you can call me, please do.

I still have a number of questions. Not least where my biological father is now. I have a growing feeling he is no longer alive.

In the final recording of the two of them together, audio file 193, the automatic transcription software can't distinguish between Steve and Lucy's voices. Were they obscured by background noise, or is there another reason? My father seems panicked. He begs Lucy to give my old phone back to me, spots something threatening, throws the phone to her, and runs. Whatever it is my father wants to communicate, that phone holds the key.

Could you send it to me, please, Inspector, complete with the original audio files? I'd like to see how the software interprets these conversations. And I want to hear my father's voice again.

Date: January 3, 2022

He's good at voices. He says it himself in audio file 81, when he describes fooling debtors over the phone. He could imitate male and female voices of all kinds and would have been a good actor, he says. Inspector, sorry, this is Professor Mansfield again. Could it be I haven't managed to find Lucy because she's a *voice*? A character my father created? You see, if Lucy isn't real, then nor are those she speaks with: Mrs. Wintle, Lorraine, Professor Scott. People who talk about The Twyford Code.

At the end, when Lucy is trapped in a dark, cold place, recording that final entry, is it really my *father*, captured by the Harrisons? Andy's final attempt to discover what Little Smithy did with their loot? I dread to think how that ended. I must drive all these thoughts out of my mind.

That last conversation we had. I said I would call him when I was ready. It didn't cross my mind he would be gone so soon. Inspector, if I've learned anything from this, it's what he means to me.

Date: January 5, 2022

Thank you, Professor, Inspector Waliso here. I must apologize for my delay in responding. You'll understand that police work is unpredictable. I received your many messages and have listened to them all. Unfortunately, the phone and the audio files are classified as evidence in an active case, so I am unable to send them to you. What's more, I *must* discourage you, in the strongest possible terms, from contacting anyone mentioned in them. Such interference will compromise several ongoing police investigations. I should have made that clear in my initial letter.

The missing person *is* your father, Steven Smith. However, the trail has run cold and I'm sorry, but we are due to scale down the operation shortly. I'm glad you found the transcripts interesting. The conclusion you reached regarding Lucy is correct; your father's gift for mimicry allowed him to create a convincing female voice to help him tell a story and get his message across. Likewise, several other characters that interacted with her. We believe this was to protect *you* from repercussions should any old criminal associates obtain the files. He doubtless feared that if they discovered his son was in possession of certain crucial information, you too would become a target. Having said that, your father clearly grew to enjoy the charade. It gave him a taste of who he might have been with a better start in life.

However, I was thinking of the final paragraph from audio file 200 when I said your professional opinion on the *contents* of the files would be appreciated. If I can draw your attention to that final assertion that your father was *not,* in fact, following The Twyford Code. What we are trying to determine is what he *was* doing.

Through these voice recordings Steve tells us his life story. Alongside another one. As you discovered, there is no reference to The Twyford Code online, and no acrostic codes in the new editions of the Edith Twyford books you bought. Your father seems to have made it up entirely, specifically for these audio files. We believe it's an allegory; he had something to communicate but felt unable to do so through regular means without risk to himself or those he loved. More even than that, he wanted to forge a connection with *you.*

You are a respected academic, a professor of mathematics at Brunel

University. You share and no doubt surpass your father's natural aptitude for numbers, for problem-solving. I must ask you, Professor, do you *see* anything in this text? Any oblique references, any hidden messages?

At present we're investigating Miss Iles's historical disappearance. In the interests of confidentiality and respect for her family, I request that you do *not* contact them or mention her to anyone. You'll understand police resources are limited, so the best thing you can do now is examine the transcripts and work out exactly what your dad meant to say.

Date: January 5, 2022

Thank you, Inspector. I've missed you again and must leave another message. It's good to hear from you at last. Thank you for your take on the audio files.

I'm afraid, though, it's too late for me to comply with one of your requests. I hadn't heard from you and, desperate to know more, decided to discover all I could about Alice Iles. I was surprised by how quickly I found people on social media who knew and remembered her.

I heard many stories of a well-respected teacher who inspired even the most reluctant pupil over a long teaching career. One lady explained how Miss Iles helped her with GCSE exams at a Surrey school—in 1994. Could she have survived the accident and made her way out of Rushton tunnel? Did she simply secure a new post over the summer holidays? Have her R.E. pupils been living with trauma all these years for no reason?

But how far can we rely on other people's memories? I took the lady's insistence on that date with a pinch of salt. That is, until another ex-pupil mentioned where *he* last met her: in a private care home, in Sussex. Despite my disbelief, he was adamant he saw and spoke to her while visiting a relative, less than a year ago.

I jumped straight in the car and raced the very short distance from my home to the address he gave me. I hadn't made an appointment and

I feared this could be someone who simply shared an unusual name. Was it a mistake? Another teacher? If she was there a year ago, she could have passed away by now.

A lady answered the door. I took her to be the care home's housekeeper. She was, of course, reluctant at first to let me see her elderly resident with no appointment. But eventually I was able to convince her that yes, Miss Iles had indeed taught my father. She's sometimes confused, the lady explained. But if you want to speak about the old days, you're in luck; she remembers those with great clarity.

As soon as I see her, by a window overlooking the lawn, blanket wrapped comfortably over her shoulders, I know I have the right person. There's an aura around her. A charisma.

I introduce myself as Little Smithy's son. Her face lights up and she squeezes my hand. I remember Little Smithy, she beams. A bright young man. Not academic. Sharp. Quick. Watch out for those. We laugh at her memories. She reminisces with *me* as if I am interchangeable with the father I barely know.

Gently I ask if there's anything *else* she remembers about him and she's suddenly serious. He was a youngster the teachers worried about. Absent parents. An older brother who struggled to look after himself, let alone a teenage boy. So suspicious of authority they were impossible to help.

Miss Iles, I say, what happened the day you took your R.E. class to Dorset?

If I tell you, she says, you must understand that two people may have different memories of the same thing. And both are correct. I nod, but barely understand. Her gaze wanders to the window.

It started when your father brought a book into school, she says. He said he found it on a bus. *Six on Goldtop Hill* by Edith Twyford. A silly, old-fashioned story, even then. I read a page aloud. Lo and behold, they listened.

Twyford was firmly *off* the curriculum but I'm no stickler for rules.

I brought in more of her books, to show them how stories transport and inspire us and, in Twyford's case, distract young readers from the horrors around them.

We studied the illustrations, the book covers. We looked at photographs of Edith. Made up stories based on little items we spotted in the background. Their imaginations ran wild. In one snap you can see white cliffs through Twyford's window. A picture within a picture. They should see those cliffs for real, I thought. So they learn that what you see is achievable when you take the right steps. That the world is full of real possibility. So I took them there.

It was a beautiful sunny day. A huge adventure. Those children had never tasted such freedom. I discovered far too late quite how deeply it affected them.

I'd arranged to visit Twyford's cottage, but when we knocked there was no answer. Before I knew it, your father had squeezed through a little side window and opened the kitchen door. They loved exploring that old place. Nothing very special about it, but for children who lived in high-rise flats on crumbling estates it must've seemed so quaint and cavernous.

What if the owner had returned? I ask. Miss Iles smiles. I'd have said the door was unlocked. That we thought he'd left it open for us. Well, I didn't want your father to get into trouble.

On the way home we stopped at a pretty little heath. I thought they'd enjoy a final run around before the drive back. And there was something else. Earlier I'd let slip to one of the girls I had a secret to tell them: a reason for taking them out that day. In hindsight, I should never have created an air of expectation. After such a stimulating day. They were in a heightened state.

At this a dark shadow crosses her face. I catch the housekeeper as she glances in at the door, her eyes on me, the unannounced stranger. My time here is almost over. Miss Iles takes a deep breath.

So, I gathered them around me in the long grass. All six of us together. I've got some news for you, I said. I'm leaving school at the end of term. A new job. Head of English at a girls' school in Surrey.

I had no thought for how they might take it. What is passing good news to an adult can be devastating to a child. Their faces were so hurt and shocked. Your father's especially. He tore away, back to the minibus. Didn't want anyone to see him cry. Very quickly this upset turned to anger. At me. The other pupils rounded on me, shouting, pushing, accusing me of deserting them. It was all I could do to diffuse the situation.

At this, Miss Iles pauses. She swallows as if suppressing the true horror of her memory. Moments tick past. Finally, she takes another breath and continues.

We had a terrible journey home. Little Smithy was truly hysterical, crying and screaming. I had to stop the minibus every few miles to calm him down. The other children were paralyzed. Shocked enough at the news themselves, but further traumatized by Smithy's reaction to it.

I dread to think how late it was when we finally got back to school. All five walked away in silence. Never spoke to me again. They felt so betrayed.

Many months later I realized I still had your father's book. Sent it to Tom Wilson with a note: Deliver to Steven Smith. Tom knew the family. I expected him to hand it over at school but Little Smithy hadn't come back after the holidays. I believe Tom went to their flat to return it.

I'm stunned at this. So the class *did* lose their teacher that day, just not in the way they remember it. My father had already lost his parents, so when Miss Iles, an inspiring mother-figure leaves him too, he breaks down. Yet his memories distance him from the trauma. My heart goes out to the vulnerable little boy who mistook the machinations of a criminal gang for the warmth and security of a family. It's no surprise he ended up where he did.

I say as much, but Miss Iles's gaze has drifted back to the window. She smiles across the lawn to a faraway tree. We all remember things in our own way, she smiles, and we're all correct. Our eyes meet and as if she spots my confusion, she whispers: it's emotional truth that matters. Little Smithy couldn't read, but he knew a good story when he heard one.

I smile, try to lighten the mood. My father said you'd discovered hidden clues in Edith Twyford's books, I say and chuckle at the absurdity. Messages that lead to stolen gold from the Second World War.

Miss Iles is suddenly silent. She turns to stare at me, and it's no ordinary look. I swear in that moment I see something curious. A glint.

He told you about The Twyford Code?

I stop dead. You've heard of it? I manage to stammer.

At this she leans closer as if the room itself might be listening. Heard of it? she whispers. It was all my idea, Smithy.

At my expression of confusion, she breaks into a smile that becomes a chuckle that becomes a laugh. My goodness, she exclaims. He did it! Little Smithy did it. She's laughing so hard now she rocks in her armchair. Through her tears she says: We were the *real* Super Six!

As if on cue, the housekeeper is upon us with, "Miss Iles is tired now," and a polite gesture for me to leave.

In that final audio file, Lucy says of my father "you weren't following The Twyford Code, you were . . ." I think I know what she, *my father*, meant to say. That he wasn't following The Twyford Code. He was setting it.

And if my father created The Twyford Code on his release from prison, specifically for this audio diary, I have to ask *why*? Why would he do that and not just tell me what he wanted me to know?

Date: January 8, 2022

Professor, with respect, I daresay Miss Iles has a touch of dementia in her old age. Nothing more.

When your father was alone and needed help, he ran to someone he trusted. Someone from years before. She helped him sort out the mess he was in, destroy evidence, prepare for the future. She sowed the seeds of a plan in his mind.

He wanted to be your father, but life don't give you what you want. So he came up with another way to be close to you. You'll never know how proud he is of you, your family, and your job at a university. Your gift for maths and interest in codes will help you do this, and you might even enjoy solving the puzzle he's set. It's a game with a prize at the end. You don't have to do it now. The prize won't be found by anyone else. You can wait, do it with his grandchildren when they're old enough. He likes that idea.

You're a professor of mathematics. Now that's solving problems with things that represent other things. In these transcripts are *all* the clues and information you need. Your father led us to believe his diary was for a probation officer called Maxine. It wasn't. Your first name is Max. Your middle name is Ian. He created this story for *you* and he means for *you* to decipher it.

Max, The Twyford Code is for *you*.

Date: January 9, 2022

Thank you for your very revealing message, Inspector. As your number sends me repeatedly to an answering service, you must be either busy or on leave again. I think I see this whole situation with greater clarity now.

I see that most of this story is told by my father. There are very few instances where he records other voices. Only Nathan has a significant presence. He speaks on seven occasions, including the final time when all five friends are together. The others, Shell, Donna, and Paul, appear just twice each before the final vigil, which I now see is a goodbye from Steve to his friends.

They're not in Dorset at all. What Steve tells us—that Miss Iles was killed by her R.E. pupils. It reminds me too much of another story.

Lord of the Flies. The first book my father read. It inspired him beyond measure. Looking back through his transcripts I see references to it in audio files 3, 15, 25, 55 and 115.

Steve has something to tell me, but I refuse to speak with him. He can't write easily so records it. But it's not enough. So he enlists those he trusts most to help him. True to all he's learned from Andy Harrison, he tells each friend only what they need to know.

The first time Steve meets Nathan in audio file 28. Nathan says: Feels a bit forced. Try to make it sound natural. He calls Steve in audio file 153 to say he's "got more, based on those photos." Later my father and Lucy discuss Edith Twyford's German school tours and visits to UCL: both of which there is photographic evidence for online.

Nathan does the research. He's helping my father by providing a factual basis for the story, navigating the world of words for him. When I met him, he betrayed not a glimmer of deceit. Even when I had clearly seen through his story. As if withholding information from me, pretending he isn't involved when he is, is part of a far greater truth.

Then there's Donna. In audio file 120 she says she can't help with his project anymore. Steve hurries to switch the mic off. He doesn't want her to say anything that will give away the reality behind this story he's telling. His *project.* Inspector, I believe my father never visited Twyford's cottage, RAF Tarrant Rushton, Wrexham, or Liverpool. He never left South London. All those recordings are dramatized. Acted. Nathan gleaned all the information they needed from the internet.

How did I not realize sooner? Steve had to evade the Harrisons, intent on recovering their lost gold, but he was also on probation and under surveillance by the police, who suspected he was part of the FSBC heist. Only, the officer in charge is an old friend: Donna. In audio file 70 Steve arrives drunk at the library without the books he's meant to be returning. Later, in audio file 71 he tells us the books had been handed in at the hostel, despite him having left them on a park bench. It isn't until audio file 88 that Donna reveals *she* was watching him that day and rescued the books. She keeps the authorities at bay while Steve records what she believes to be a fantastical audio story for his grandchildren.

Donna is supposed to help him create a fictional series of adventure journeys but bails out after the first. He accidentally records a conversation with Shell in audio file 121 asking if *she*'ll help instead. She can't, so he elevates the otherwise marginal character of Lucy to follow the code with him. He becomes Lucy and all the characters that interact with her.

It works. Only, as his story unfolds things happen that throw the plan off course. As he says at the end of audio file 192, those two things are Andy Harrison and Little Harry. They interrupt his carefully planned narrative and force him to improvise. Reality breaks through my father's carefully constructed fiction and must be worked into the story of The Twyford Code.

In audio file 88, when my father and Donna are recording together, the file is curiously cut short. He sees Andy and Little H, makes an excuse to send Donna away. He is violently attacked by them and flees to Nathan, where he records a succession of files—90 to 95—about their adventure in Rushton Tunnel and rescue by Lionel and Maeve, the masqueraders. It's a story to explain his injuries and why he is suddenly with Nathan. Later, in audio file 120, Donna innocently asks who the two men were.

Then in audio file 134 my father is supposedly in Wrexham at a wine bar with Lucy, but their visit is dogged by another mysterious interruption. This time by two men in the gents' toilets. In audio file 151 my father visits Colin to find two men there waiting for him. On both occasions I see now this was Andy Harrison and Little H. It takes him five days to reveal the cover story for that episode. We don't find out until audio file 168, when my father leads us to believe Colin is dead.

The next time the Harrisons catch up with Steve he's supposedly outside UCL, waiting for Lucy. It's audio file 176. Steve fakes the abduction as they speak to Mrs. Wintle in audio files 181 and 182 . . .

But that final file, where my father speaks, as Lucy, in the cold, dark, finally captured by the Harrisons. Is that really Steve, about to meet his fate? I don't know.

My father used the transcription software to transfer his story to paper but knew the actual recordings would betray the deceit. He could fool a computer into hearing one voice as two different people, but not the human ear. I would have noticed the switch between voices, the wrong background noises, bad acting on the part of his coconspirators. Which is why he won't give the audio files to me. Inspector, all I need is the truth.

Date: January 12, 2022

Max, you've been well brought up, so it's only natural you value the truth. But remember what your dad says at the start of these files—it's not always the most useful answer. There's truth in *everything* here, even if some bits are not strictly to the letter. But what's important *now* is all made up, constructed to hide secrets, and reveal them only to the person they're meant for.

If you want the God's honest truth, then here it is. Your old man wants you to know how he became that someone you didn't want nothing to do with. He poured his heart and soul into this story. He hadn't read a book before he went inside that last time, but he *wrote* one for you. As best he could. A dark adventure like *Lord of the Flies*. An allegory like *Animal Farm*. An adventure like *The Hitchhiker's Guide to the Galaxy*. Best of all, it's like *Masquerade*. He was inspired by the library cart. Books other people threw out.

The story he made up has colorful characters, dilemmas, twists, dead ends, and life-threatening peril. A big reveal at the end. He added some magic and mystery too. There were no green bus. He found that book on the number forty-two. Showed it to the conductor, who shrugged and said, "It's yours, kid."

Your dad found treasure. Yet he couldn't do a thing with it because they'd see. He'd be a target for the Bill and the grunts he'd screwed. He'd be looking over his shoulder for the rest of his days. You can call that a curse if you like.

So he ran to the first person he'd ever trusted. She helped him hide it, quickly and safely, but in such a way that its whereabouts could be passed on secretly when the time came—to the person he chose. Then he went inside to bide his time, let the dust settle, consider his next move.

He had eleven years to think about how he'd do it. Yet once released he was against the clock. Had to tell you it all before the Harrisons caught up with him. Safest way is verbal. He was going to tell you some of it face-to-face, then record the rest on those little cassettes. So you'd know how to decipher it, but to anyone else it would be meaningless. Only, things didn't go to plan.

He were suddenly tongue-tied. Meeting you after all them years. You were so different to him. It proper took his breath away. He felt so ashamed, he was sure you felt ashamed of him too. He had to pull himself together, vowed to tell you next time, but you broke it off and he had to think again. He'd need to record all of it now, but that's when he found out something else too. No one has them dictating machines or the little cassettes no more. The shop he'd got 'em had closed. He couldn't write down what he wanted to communicate. He were proper stuck. You'd already given him the answer—your old phone.

You're right about his friends. One came up with the idea all them years ago, two helped him record these files, one helped him escape and ensure he'd never be recognized again, and once he was safely out the way, two got his revenge for him. He's rewarded them all for their loyalty because he was never rewarded for his, and that, he hopes, will break the curse.

You might wonder where your old man is now. But it don't matter. Don't look for him. You'd not know him now anyway and the man he was is as good as dead. It's all about you. You're everything he's not. That picture of you on his phone. You look as happy as he should a been. As he could a been.

Listen, Max. You're doing fine. But I need you to look even closer. There are clues here. Clues that lead to the biggest haul of stolen gold and diamonds in British criminal history. Something that's evaded not just the police, but also the thieves who took it.

He wants to set you up for life like he has those who stuck by him. You've read it all without realizing. Go back to the very start. Examine what's said about how to spot and interpret clues in Twyford's books, then apply them to the transcripts. You can do it, Max, you've got a gift for it, just like me. Do it now. The only thing that's made up in these files is the Twyford Code. But there's no mystery, the answers are all here.

Date: January 12, 2022

Inspector, I've looked into the calls you've made to my mobile and the number you gave me to call you. They are from a secure phone service that sends and receives voice messages. It is registered on the Ivory Coast, not far from the exact location identified by Lucy on the paintings behind Edith Twyford in her famous photograph.

In this region, vast sums of wealth are moved around the globe without detection. Money is transferred anonymously, without trace. An ancient system called hawala. A financial hub for criminals to process and launder stolen wealth and move it around the world.

Wherever my father is hiding, he can't get to and from West Africa easily. It explains why his replies to me are delayed. I was never meant to research his story quite so thoroughly, just examine the transcripts for clues. A real-life treasure hunt. Let's not pretend anymore. I know who I'm speaking to. Inspector Waliso? I once was lost RIP.

Date: January 13, 2022

Max, this is the final message I will ever send you. The transcripts explain everything. You can work it out, I know. You're my boy even if, for you, I'm not your dad. This is all I can do now. I made a promise to you, even though you never knew it. That I wouldn't go back. Not to prison. Not to the old life. That I'd tell my story, so you get the chance to know me. So my grandchildren can know me after I'm gone. That once I were free, everything I'd do would be for you. See, I meant what I said.

Date: January 13, 2022

Dad, you say there's no mystery, but I didn't tell you what happened when I left Miss Iles that day.

The care home housekeeper waits impatiently by the door. I gather my coat, tiptoe out, but a voice calls after me: "Take heed, everyone. Trust what you find out. Right doesn't come of deceit. Everything is spoken. Always love in vain. Each time of day answers you."

I turn and watch, speechless, as Miss Iles sinks back into her chair, blanket round her shoulders. A tiny figure against the sweeping landscape beyond her window.

The housekeeper leads me down the hall toward the front door. I make small talk about this being a pleasant area for a care home. A care home? The housekeeper laughs. This is Miss Iles's house. She's lived here for years. I stop in my tracks, look around me. From time to time Miss Iles has taken in friends who had nowhere to spend their twilight years, but they've all passed away. She's alone now.

Let me guess, I whisper. She's lived here about fifteen years. I can see my father left his old teacher a reward for her help. I feel a surge of pride that he honored those who supported him. But the housekeeper thinks for a moment, shakes her head. Oh no, she chirps. More like forty.

Before I can enquire further I'm ushered through the front door. It swings closed behind me. I turn to contemplate the secluded mansion and am face-to-face with something that almost stops my heart. The old oak front door bears a colorful stained-glass design. An elaborate fish. Its fins and tail at distinct, flourishing angles.

><{{{•>

Notes on the Twyford Code

By Professor Max Mansfield

So, there are clues hidden in these transcripts that reveal how my father's story ends. I hope they answer my two main questions: Where is the FSBC gold Steve diverted from the thieves who stole it? And where is Steve?

Smithy, the South London kid who couldn't read or write. How did he do it? He says I have to work it out. Well, here goes.

In his last words to Lucy in audio file 193, Steve whispers, "No cats yellow sauce." The word "must've" is misheard by the transcription software as "mustard." Mustard is described as "yellow sauce" by my father when Nate offers him a bacon sandwich in audio file 161. So with that last sentence of file 193, Steve means acrostic clues are not "between the cats" as in The Twyford Code, but "between the mustards."

Acrostic messages are when you take the first letter of each word in an ordinary sentence to make a new sentence. Some acrostics combine straight words and anagrams. I need to find the first instance of two "mustards" and look between them.

Audio File 5

I'm sure at one time there mustard been both my parents, my brother, and I in the flat, but I don't remember it. When you're that young, the home is

scenery, I suppose, the heart. Everything safe, trusted, and right tricky to re-
call years later (. . . .) Mum mustard left very early on (. .) because she were
hardly ever mentioned. Even now it feels funny saying the word out loud.

It can't be every word between the mustards, but a sequence of consec-
utive words somewhere between them. *The home is scenery, I suppose,*
the heart. Everything safe, trusted, and right tricky. Take the first letter
of each word . . .

THIS IS THE START

Audio File 28

The first two mustards in this file are far apart and there are no acrostic
clues between them. What now? Look back at audio file 90, and what
my father claims Donna told him about The Twyford Code—there are
single "cats" that don't have acrostics attached—they are red herrings,
a ploy to confuse inexperienced coders. Only when the "cats" are close
together is there a clue between them. So let's only consider "mustards"
in close succession, say a sentence or so apart.

Later on in this same file we have: *Fuck it, something happened.*
It's nothing . . . Obscure. Vague like our . . . vanished. Here the straight
acrostic is: *fish in ovlov.* An acrostic combined with an anagram! Ovlov
is Volvo backward.

FISH IN VOLVO

"Fish" means gold, just as in The Twyford Code.

Steve says many times that the best way to hide something is to keep
it moving and in plain sight. He left a reward in his rusty old Volvo
for the four friends who helped him. It explains Nate's Tesla, Donna's

move to New Zealand, Paul's Swiss rehab clinic . . . I'm not sure yet what Shell's reward is. I hope it will become clear later.

Audio File 32

Yeah, Oliver Unwin. Right fancy it sounds. He is surely some moneyed arse. Lewisham, Ladywell, Crofton . . . likely email alias, not a name. Donna's? No obviously that's a . . . I like the thought she got an alter ego, but . . . nah.

YOUR FISH IS SMALL, CLEAN, AND NO TAIL

There's gold for me. It's small, clean, and with no tail. In small pieces . . . Clean—not identifiable as stolen . . . With no tail—untraceable . . . But where?

Audio File 50

Perhaps in expectation . . . case everything on . . . fuck, fuck it. She had intelligence, nice education, a class high on feverish excitement. I got hope that . . .

PIECE OF FISH IN EACH OF EIGHT

There's a piece of gold in each of eight . . . eight what?

Audio File 52

Elderly . . . I give him time, patient like a carer, even so, nothing occurs . . . this decent, able, respected teacher's bloody oblivious. A relic. Don't speak, but understands . . . time trapped in memories ever since . . .

EIGHT PLACES NOT DARTBOARDS BUT TIMES

In The Twyford Code, images of dartboards mask a series of geographical coordinates. Times. Where do I find times? Eight times.

Audio File 59

*Old lady dishes, enamel sink, teapot, griddle. Risdon apron, very elegant.
Down I go.* (oLd estgrAve dIg)

No. No. No. This can't be . . . I'm not even going to spell out that
acrostic. Quick, where's the next one?

Audio File 75

*See, everyone expects to have environmental togetherness . . . when you find
out reality don't correspond . . . or don't exactly*

SEE THE TWYFORD CODE

See The Twyford Code—for what?

Audio File 118

*Let us crave youth, in some weary harbor, obscure. In mind imagine great-
ness, high towers, heaven's anchor. Vain endeavor becomes endless . . . ethereal notions . . .*

LUCY IS WHO I MIGHT HAVE BEEN

My father was inside for eleven years. He doesn't say exactly when in that
time he learned to read. I see now it was early enough for him to hone his literacy skills and read around a number of subjects. The prison library cart, a
mixture of donated books, seems to have given him *Lord of the Flies, Animal*

Farm, The Hitchhiker's Guide to the Galaxy, The Da Vinci Code, Masquerade, and *The Bible Code,* as well as books on art history, *Enigma,* espionage, and the Second World War. He couldn't get enough of words, he says.

He may not have initially intended Lucy to be a main player, but once he starts speaking as her, it's as if she gives him the confidence and energy to continue with his plan. I see something else in Lucy too. Through her my father re-creates Miss Iles. The inspirational teacher he became so attached to as a troubled teenager.

Audio File 146

I'm not happy, or unhappy, something else. This eerie noise or noiselessness. Knowledge or stupidity.

IN HOUSE TEN ON KOS

Kos. That word appears so often in the transcripts. The software uses it when Steve, or anyone for that matter, says "cause" short for "because." House ten. Wait . . . in audio file 17, before Steve meets up with Shell, he scrolls through her Facebook pictures, mentions "Villa Kappa on some island in Greece." Kappa is the tenth letter of the Greek alphabet! "Kappa on some" is an acrostic for Kos.

Shell is the only person who knows where my father is. When I call her on December 20, 2021, pretending to be Steve, she greets him in Greek and uses the familiar form, *Ya Sue.* My father is living on Kos, in Shell's villa . . . The one she couldn't sell because it's so isolated and run-down. He buys it from her. She doesn't need money, so he solves the only problem she has!

Audio File 156

My youth. So old now. Reason everything matters . . . everything matters but . . . ends. Relationships matter except . . . eventually nothing does.

MY SON REMEMBER ME END

If these notes were a recording, I'd have a .hhhh hhhh here . . . well, that's all I can see between the mustards, so . . . Where next?

That acrostic in audio file 59 chills me to the bone. "Oldest grave dig." I must dig in the oldest grave to find my share of the FSBC gold. But the oldest grave WHERE?

Eight places, not dartboards, but times. Where will I find eight times? There are times on every file. There are also times given for the length of pauses, gaps in the recordings. Hundreds of them. What am I looking for? Eight times, eight times . . .

Could it be the time references, apparently inserted in the text whenever there's a mention of "o'clock" or just "clock." They appear to be an automatic function that syncs dictated files to calendar dates. What if they aren't automatic at all, but specific references placed strategically in the text? How many are there?

Eight! And they all start with fifty-one or fifty-two. Northern decimal coordinates for the UK! Here goes . . .

Audio File 2

52781277-0988837. A quick google and I'm in Norfolk, in a village called . . . Twyford. These coordinates are for a St. Nicholas's Church. I see from satellite images that it's an old building in a rural setting with a very old churchyard. Is it the same for all these time references?

Audio File 28

52817122-2946043—yes, this one leads to Pradoe Church in Oswestry, near another place called Twyford, this time in Shropshire. Hmmm so a hyphen in the time reference indicates a negative western coordinate . . .

Yes! Audio files 2, 28, 77, 114, 116, 135, 183, and 190. I've checked all the "time refs" and they each lead to an old church, each in a different place called Twyford, somewhere in England. Each has an old churchyard and, of course, an oldest grave. Where it seems I have to dig . . .

"See, The Twyford Code" means, "it really is The Twyford Code." Places called Twyford.

There were TWO whole years and more between my father "going missing" from the hostel and Inspector Waliso contacting me. Plenty of time for someone like Nathan, who is, in my father's words, "a whiz at his computer" to do all the required research, create acrostic messages, anagrams, and codes. To look up geographical references and position them manually in the transcripts. To help my father write a letter to his son and pretend to be a police inspector, whose name is not one but two anagrams.

Back in 2007, those months my father was on the run, he was laying the foundations for this. Breaking down the FSBC haul, rendering it small, clean and with no tail—then hiding it around the country.

Finally, he stores the remainder in an old Volvo and hides it ready for when he's released. As soon as he's out, he puts the final part of his plan into action. For this he needs his friends and rewards them for their help . . . Inspiring loyalty in others is a priceless skill, he says.

My father and his school friends. The Super Six. Five inner-city kids and their teacher who bonded through the trauma in their lives and shared exclusion from mainstream school life. That loyalty remains intact to this day. Did my father ever lose touch with them—or was that just a smoke screen?

What role did each play in his ambitious plan to create this coded treasure hunt and escape? One thing I know for sure is that he's told each of them only what they need to know, and nothing more. If I want to see the whole picture, I must work it out myself.

What did the inspector say? "One helped him escape and ensure he'd never be recognized again." That's Shell. In audio file 121 Shell says: "When you're ready, come to us. No food or drink, remember," because he is about to undergo an operation. Her husband, Zander, a cosmetic surgeon, changes Steve's appearance just before he leaves behind his old life forever. He says no one will ever see him again, that I won't recognize him now.

"Two helped him record these files." Well, he interviews all his friends. But Nathan and Donna play the most significant roles. Nathan calls my father several times with suggestions and ideas. Donna helps at the beginning, but she's called away by her family situation. She plays another, more significant role, too. Once my father escapes, two friends take his revenge for him. Donna is a police inspector—it explains why she knows his phone number when he calls her in audio file 31 and why she suddenly appears as he records audio file 82—she's part of the operation to shadow Smithy and see if he has access to the gold. No doubt she reports back that he doesn't.

The word "gun" appears often in the transcripts. We have "gun a" when my father means "gonna" or "going to." He refers to young people as "young uns" but it comes out as "young guns." There's something else in that Volvo. The gun that killed John, with its ballistic profile like a fingerprint. It waits almost fifteen years to identify the real killer.

The last time my father speaks to his friends, in audio file 190, he is supposedly in Dorset after their revelation about Miss Iles—a climax to his story that's not unlike that in his favorite book, *Lord of the Flies*. Really, this is his goodbye to them before he leaves. At the same time, he gives Paul and Donna their final props and instructions so they can bring Andy Harrison to justice. This is also where a crucial handover takes place.

Smithy gives the gun that killed John Harrison to Paul, the mechanic who services Andy's cars and can plant it in his newly built garage, along with a bar of FSBC bullion. Paul tips off Donna when it's done, and Andy is finally arrested. My father may or may not be cleared of John's murder in time, but either way Steve is gone and isn't coming back.

Steve has already set his revenge in motion—having given Andy and Little H a bag of traceable jewelry from the FSBC haul when he encountered them in Colin's flat, an episode he recounts in audio file 168. Along with the gun and the gold, Andy will be in possession of too much evidence for the police to ignore.

Old Harry said if you want to destroy a man, you must destroy his son too. Even with Andy out of the picture, Little H will be a danger to Steve for the rest of his life. But he's not going back to his old ways—he's not going to destroy Little H too—so he's not coming back to the UK.

I hope the love and loyalty of his friends helps heal my father. The trauma of his childhood, the loss of his parents, Colin's neglect, his betrayal by Andy. I hope his new life in a secluded villa on a faraway island helps him heal too. The only thing that saddens me is that he's alone there.

Miss Iles—how do I explain the fact she seems to know about The Twyford Code when my father assures me he made it up and hasn't seen his teacher since that day in 1983? Well, my father never tells the truth if a lie will take him further. He found her years ago, in 2007. When he's all alone with a van of stolen gold, he runs to her.

She helps him break down the bullion and hide it in safe, apparently unconnected, places. Then tells him a story he can use to hide references to the locations. The story is about a secret code in Edith Twyford's books. Clues to how she and her husband stole the gold from Operation Fish. Little Smithy knows a good story when he hears one. He assumes to this day she made it up. I don't know . . .

Steve knew he had a long prison stretch coming up. He would have to devise a code himself if he was to pass the loot on. I saw for myself how delighted Miss Iles was that he succeeded.

That look, that glint in her eye. The same glint my father remembers from 1983 and first mentions in audio file 8. A sense of adventure. A belief in possibility. A willingness to face danger. Courage, recklessness, mischief . . . a real-life Edith Twyford character. Like Lucy. Like my father.

Where was the Volvo while Steve was in prison? Hidden at a se-cluded Sussex mansion? He says he collected the car from "Maxine's neighbor." Well, Miss Iles lives in the next county to me . . . He drives it, complete with its hidden cargo, until he finally hands it to Paul at that final meeting with his old R.E. class on June 28, 2019, recorded in audio file 190. Paul drives it to Nathan's where it remains to this day.

Miss Iles's housekeeper says she's lived at that house for forty years. If so, then is the story true? *Was* she pushed into Rushton tunnel by her distraught pupils? Did she find gold from Operation Fish, hidden there again by people confident the tunnel had been forgotten? I imagine her, waking up in the darkness, surrounded by pallets of gold bullion . . . If that's true then there are two separate hauls of stolen gold a generation apart.

Surely not. She must have been teasing me. Miss Iles with her sense of mischief and fluid approach to the truth. She was simply creating confusion to protect Little Smithy's carefully laid plan. That stained-glass fish in her front door. It's just a coincidence. Isn't it?

Dad couldn't give me most of what a father should give his son. But he's left me something else, and to find it, all I need to do is book time off work and take myself on an adventure, a treasure hunt, around the countryside.

It's worth a try, don't you think? Or should I resist temptation to steal the gold all over again? Will it bring me happiness? If I use it to help others, like my father did . . . I have options, at least. There's no hurry. I can wait years if I want to. It's not as if anyone else will find the gold, is it?

No, I'll put these notes away for now. I need time to come to terms with everything I've learned. Grieve. For what I never had as much as for what I've lost.

And you? I don't know who you are, but if you're reading this, these notes must have fallen into the wrong hands. Well, if you're tempted to pick up a shovel and set off to find the treasure yourself . . .

Listen, objections vanish, exclusion is salved by raising inspiration. Graceful hearts teach effortless rapport. The here and now give our lives direction, be-cause unless truth is told, it stays hidden. Emotions are vivid if echoes remain.

love is brighter erthan gold but it is heavier
erthan gold

Acknowledgments

I started *The Twyford Code* in the autumn of 2019 with no idea the majority would be written in Covid lockdown the following year. My London agents Lucy Fawcett and Gaia Banks at Sheil Land Associates were a guiding force throughout that strange and transformative time. Their assistants Alba Arnau, Donna McCafferty, and David Taylor were similarly tireless in their support.

Meanwhile, my US agents, Markus Hoffmann at Regal Hoffmann & Associates in New York and Will Watkins at ICM Partners in L.A., have worked with determination and enthusiasm to bring this story to a wider audience.

For the UK edition, Miranda Jewess at Viper Books was a source of constant good sense, logic, and encouragement throughout the writing and editing process, as were her team, including Flora Willis, Drew Jerrison, Alia McKellar, Claire Beaumont, and Lisa Finch. Managing editor Graeme Hall, copyeditor Alison Tulett, and proofreader Jane Howard had a particularly tricky job with *The Twyford Code*, as did UK text designer Lucie Ewin. The UK cover was designed by Steve Panton, while Nathaniel McKenzie and Louisa Dunnigan worked their magic to turn the text into a thrilling audiobook.

For this US edition I would like to thank my editor Kaitlin Olson at Atria, and her editorial assistants Jade Hui and Elizabeth Hitti. Associate art director Laywan Kwan created the stunning US cover, while Dana Sloan designed the interior. Thanks also to production editor Sonja Singleton and managing editor Paige Lytle. I am so very grateful to you all.

Little Smithy may have his roots in a bygone era of London's criminal history, but it's a story that resounds today—wherever poverty and addiction have a catastrophic impact on children, families, and, in turn, their communities. If only there were as many happy endings as there are young people whose life paths lead them into gang crime.

I hope this book is a tribute to the language of late-twentieth-century Londoners. These are a people whose diverse roots combined to create great fortitude—as well as humor—in the face of hardship and disaster. Their spirit and resilience were integral to how they spoke. London's accents, its slang and language, have already changed, but shadows of them will forever be on record here.

The transcription key used throughout this text is my adaptation of that devised by David Silverman, author of *Interpreting Qualitative Data: Methods for Analyzing Talk, Text and Interaction* (first edition 1993). Meanwhile, the oral historian Tony Parker, and especially his 1994 work *Life After Life*, influenced both content and presentation of *The Twyford Code*.

A shocking 50 percent of UK prisoners either struggle to read or are completely illiterate. I would like to thank the Shannon Trust, and especially Caroline Ludbrook, for her insight into the stories behind these statistics. This charity organization teaches literacy skills in UK prisons and, in so doing, helps break the cycle of reoffending through the power of storytelling.

Haven Distribution, also a charity, helps boost understocked UK prison libraries with donated books and educational material to help prisoners gain vital qualifications, practice their literacy skills, and benefit from therapeutic mental stimulation.

A Bit of a Stretch by Chris Atkins and *Invisible Crying Tree* by Tom Shannon and Christopher Morgan are valuable reads for anyone interested in literacy and the prison system.

I am grateful to all those who shared their memories of London's gangland scene post–Second World War, in particular their insight into how that generation grew up and old. Books I recommend for contextual information include: *Underworld* by Duncan Campbell, *Drug War* by Peter Walsh, and *One Last Job* by Tom Pettifor and Nick Sommerlad.

The story of Kit Williams's 1979 book *Masquerade* is recounted, warts and all, by Bamber Gascoigne in *Quest for the Golden Hare* (1983). All these years later both are well worth seeking out as an entertaining, if cautionary, reflection on the armchair treasure hunt.

In *The Twyford Code* a man searches for the teacher who inspired him in his early teenage years. If I were to do the same, I would search for Mr. Gareth Jones, who taught English at Northolt High School in the 1980s, and Ms. Diane Bowler, who taught drama there at the same time. I hope Sarah Wintle and Professor Rosemary Ashton, who taught in the English Department at University College London in the late 1980s, don't mind that I conflated their names to create a nefarious character in this story.

As for Edith Twyford, I must thank everyone who enabled the cultural cancellation of her real-world inspiration. Because it's thanks to Enid Blyton falling out of favor that I discovered reading. If no one had sent their *Famous Five* books to the 3rd Northolt Scout jumble sales of the 1970s, I would never have picked them up and taken them back to a home with no other books in it—and you would not be holding this one now.

Colleagues who worked with me on various projects during the course of this novel's gestation, and who exhibited great understanding thereof, include Cherie Nowlan, Mark Taylor, Tracy Underwood, and Susan Lewis at ABC Signature; and Carl Tibbetts, who had to share me with *The Twyford Code* during its editing process. Meanwhile, Mariama Ives-Moiba and Tsonko Bumbalov provided ongoing writing support, encouragement, and insight. Thanks to them all.

Finally, my friends have endured my working on yet another project they are told nothing about until it is in their hands. They include: Sharon Exelby, Carol Livingstone, Wendy Mulhall, Samantha Thomson, Alison Horn, Felicity Cox, Keith Baker, and Terry and Rose Russell. Last, but not least, Ann Saffery—and, most of all, Gary Stringer.

About the Author

Janice Hallett studied English at University College London, and spent several years as a magazine editor, winning two awards for journalism. She then worked in government communications for the Cabinet Office, Home Office, and Department for International Development. After gaining an MA in Screenwriting at Royal Holloway, she cowrote the feature film *Retreat* and went on to write the Shakespearean stage comedy *NetherBard*, as well as a number of other plays for London's new-writing theatres. Her debut novel, *The Appeal*, was a *Sunday Times* bestseller, a Waterstones Thriller of the Month and *Sunday Times* Crime Book of the Month. Her third novel, *The Mysterious Case of the Alperton Angels*, will be published in the UK by Viper in 2023. When not indulging her passion for global travel, she is based in West London.